VIOLET
MADE OF
THORNS

GINA CHEN

DELACORTE PRESS

Text copyright © 2022 by Gina Chen
Jacket art copyright © 2022 by Sasha Vinogradova

All rights reserved. Published in the United States by Delacorte Press, an imprint of Random House Children's Books, a division of Penguin Random House LLC, New York.

Delacorte Press is a registered trademark and the colophon is a trademark of Penguin Random House LLC.

Visit us on the Web! GetUnderlined.com

Educators and librarians, for a variety of teaching tools, visit us at RHTeachersLibrarians.com

Library of Congress Cataloging-in-Publication Data is available upon request.
ISBN 978-0-593-42753-8 (hc) — ISBN 978-0-593-42755-2 (ebook) — ISBN 978-0-593-57256-6 (int'l edition)

The text of this book is set in 11.5-point Sabon MT Pro.
Interior design by Jen Valero

Printed in the United States of America
10 9 8 7 6 5 4 3 2 1
First Edition

For the readers who believed in me before I did

RIVER DISTRICT

PALACE DISTRICT

GARDEN DISTRICT

MARKET DISTRICT

1

TODAY, PRINCE CYRUS RETURNS TO THE CAPITAL with a bride, or else.

From the Seer's Tower, the tallest point in the Sun Capital, I can see a train of purple banners fluttering amid the fields outside the city—the royal caravan making the steep approach to the south gates. Cordoned-off crowds pack the streets, waiting to welcome their prince home. Six months have passed since Cyrus departed to tour the continent, since he set out to "seek from the land and its generous people all the wisdom" that he could not learn in a palace.

Or something like that. I stopped listening to his going-away speech midway through.

Mostly, his tour was to find a bride—a solution to his curse. Cyrus didn't mention that in his speech. I know this because his father, King Emilius, berated him afterward for the omission; then I had to mention it in *my* speech, a few days later, when I announced that I dreamed a new prophecy.

The best part about being Seer isn't the tower or the amenities or the access to the king. It's how easily everyone believes what you say.

"The capital was less lively without His Highness. I do miss those girls running amok, trying to save him," says the peach-faced woman sitting at my divining table. "I suppose that will change for good. He's chosen our next queen by now, hasn't he?"

If Cyrus listened to me, he would have. "He better," I mutter, turning from the window.

"Pardon?"

"I said, he *met her*." I flash an enigmatic smile at my lone patron. With the caravan's return, I didn't expect anyone to visit my tower today. This woman has the weathering of someone too practical to line up for a peek at a royal face: a brimmed-hat tan and calloused hands, turned upward on the divining table's marble surface. "If you speak of the prophecy I received before His Highness left, my dreams told me, 'Prince Cyrus will meet his bride before his journey's end.' No more than that, no less."

She nods. "I didn't recall the exact words you used—"

"The exact words are important." I paced this room for four nights to decide on those words, and I won't have them misremembered now when they finally matter. Picking up my robes, I take a seat across from her and push my heavy braid over my shoulder. The sooner this reading is over, the sooner this small talk can end, and I can leave for the palace and greet the prince myself. "What is it that you want me to see?"

The woman's brow twitches. My curtness offends her, though she won't say so. "My only concern is the harvest season, Sighted Mistress Violet. Anything regarding my farm's future. I pray the Fates be kind."

I don't like doing these fortune readings, but the king insists I interact with the populace regularly so they trust the girl behind their kingdom's prophecies. It was either this or matchmaking, and seeing buffoons in love makes me want to empty my stomach.

I lay my hands over hers, and the brush of my fingers against her skin sparks something sun-bright in my mind. I shut my eyes and focus on the grooves of her palm, the folds and scars, the blood that pumps underneath—any physical mark of her history that I can use to anchor my magic. In my mind's Sight, I find the threads that bind her soul to the turning of this world:

A hillside farm, golden with fayflowers.

Rides to the Sun Capital, part of her monthly routine.

A different farm in the borderlands. Family? A lover's home? The Fairywood looms on the horizon.

Long days of fieldwork stretching into nights . . .

And so they go.

The clearest threads are ones that have already happened—her memories. Future threads, on the other hand, look hazy and can even be contradictory. The Fates are fickle gods, and fortunes are always changing. If I can't see the future directly, I might feel the Fates' intentions instead: foreboding feels like the wet gust before a storm; opportunity, like a dip into warm honey. But much of the time, the Fates don't like showing their hands.

Not unless they mean to, anyway.

My patrons have to deal with what little I see. I'm the only Seer in the Kingdom of Auveny, the only choice they have. This is not a coincidence. There are nine known

Sighted in the world, every one of us in the employ of various courts—we're too useful to be left alone. I hear that one Seer in Yue, in addition to her prophecies, can predict storms from the ripple of a pond, and another in Verdant knows the date of every birth.

I'm the youngest Seer at eighteen, plucked from the Sun Capital's very own streets seven years ago. All I know how to do is dream, read threads, and lie.

"I don't think you need to worry," I murmur as my Sight peers into the fog of the woman's future. I embellish my vague visions with details from her memories. "Your fayflowers should grow fine this year. But stay diligent. Don't wander so much, maybe, and keep to your farm."

When I open my eyes, the woman withdraws her hands. "Kind Fates—that's very good to learn," she says. "Anything else?"

I ramble until she's finally satisfied. Thanking me, she throws silvers into the dry fountain basin that's become a vessel for offerings and departs my tower.

I peek over the fountain's scalloped rim and sigh. I don't rely on the coin, since the palace provides everything I need, but under the previous Seer, the fountain overflowed with offerings. Under my tenure, it's gotten . . . dusty.

And now that Cyrus has returned, my reputation will only get worse.

The din outside rises and falls with cheers. I barely need to glance at the window to know the royal caravan is inside the city. The court has been scheming over Cyrus's homecoming practically since he left. King Emilius has grown more sickly, and Cyrus is expected to ascend to the throne before the end of the year. The time to make an attempt for his favor is now.

My teeth grind. That goes for me, too.

⤜⤛

Seven years ago, Sighted Mistress Felicita—stars guide her soul—uttered her final prophecy:

"The land will bloom red with blood and roses and war. The prince—his heart will be damnation or salvation. His choice may save us all. His bride—it is up to her! A curse, a curse, accursed curse—gods, be wary—"

And that was all before she died. A maidservant who attended her sickbed claims the Seer's mouth was frozen wide, her fist clenched by her neck, as if she had been fighting against someone in order to speak. Even in death, they couldn't uncurl her body.

The kingdom plunged into paranoia. Was Felicita heralding the end of Auveny? The end of the world? Why was Prince Cyrus the catalyst? I became the new Seer after her death, but I was just a child then, a waif play-acting in silk, confused as everyone else. I never dreamed of what Felicita described.

My lack of answers didn't endear me to anyone.

We sought aid from Seers serving in neighboring lands and warned them in turn, but even they couldn't sense any coming omens. The grandmotherly Seer of Balica had us consider that perhaps—if Felicita wasn't simply fever-mad—it meant that whatever she saw was far in the future. We had time to prepare.

And so, with every new season, every gala, every visiting dignitary, the kingdom has held its breath, hoping for Cyrus to fall in love. Felicita's prophecy was clear enough here: the future rests in the prince's heart, his choice, his bride.

In seven years, Cyrus hasn't chosen anyone. A sinister prophecy on his shoulders and he's decided to be *picky*.

But he can only stall for so long.

I head to the palace to witness the results of his tour myself. It's a short walk, thanks to the bridge connecting my tower's entrance to the north end of the palace grounds. Without it, I'd have to trek down two hundred stairs to the tower's base, sitting far below on the banks of the river Julep. The Seer's Tower is a gnarled relic of the Fairywood that once covered the continent—grown, not built, so it was never crafted for practicality.

Tales say that one of the first Seers drew the walls out of the ground and raised them high so that she could live among the stars. Feats like that used to be common, supposedly, when the Fairywood was wide, nations were few, and the land seeped magic. I might not have believed it if I didn't sometimes dream of long-past threads—of times when trees were taller than mountains and canopies were lit with fairies and we humans weren't the cleverest creatures wandering the forests.

Today, the Seer's Tower is simply out of place. It juts into the sky like a fang, a trunk of petrified vines rising from the riverbanks, stark green against the developed city. A breeze tangles through my robes as I cross the bridge away from it. The views of the Sun Capital disappear behind the marble berth of the palace and its gold-tipped spires. I pass through a set of gates, and the gardens unfold before me: a patchwork of neat flowerbeds, carved fountains, and ornamental trees.

On the way, I receive a few greetings: a quick bow or curtsy, along with a murmur of "Sighted Mistress"—others know that I don't care for formalities. Stealing down a narrow caretaker's trail on tiptoes, between the hedge maze and a row of newly trimmed begonias, I arrive at one of the palace's back entrances with only a bit of dirt on my slippers.

Inside, every room and hallway is filled with chatter. A frown stitches itself across my face; I'm troubled by what I overhear. What I *don't* overhear.

I ascend the staircase to the royal living quarters and the conversations fade away. The guards outside Cyrus's rooms look uneasy as I approach, but they don't stop me.

I throw open the double doors to his bedroom.

"Do not let her in—Violet, leave."

My eyes land on Cyrus by his wardrobe. The prince is dressed, mostly. And—ugh—handsomer than before.

Cyrus Lidine of Auveny is cut from the cloth of storybook dreams: dashing, well-read, witty if he deigns to speak to you, and beautiful even without fairy glamours. He could make a sack look fashionable, and his smile is responsible for more fainting spells than the summer heat.

Now at the wane of his nineteenth year, he's filled out his height, muscle smoothing out the angles of his adolescence, his clothes no longer pinching at junctures, since he's done growing. Color has returned to his cheeks, once porcelain-pale after a bout of childhood illness. He's shed his boyishness with a fresh cut of his copper hair.

But some things never change, including the disdainful

gaze he levels at me as I do not leave. These months apart haven't tempered the loathing between us.

A lifetime apart wouldn't.

"You can't come barging in here—" Cyrus starts.

"And yet I just did," I murmur, glancing around the room. I'm the only other person here, which is a problem. The bed is unrumpled. His bath seems empty. I saw no retinue downstairs, no court ladies huddled around some latest addition to Sun Capital society. So it begs the question: "Where is she?"

Cyrus turns to the mirror and resumes buttoning his vest. "Who?"

"Her future Majesty. *The girl you're marrying.*"

"None of your business."

I march over, braid swinging. "Entirely"—I wedge myself between Cyrus and the mirror as he heaves a heavy sigh— "my business." If I wasn't underfed during my early childhood, I might have grown enough to be eye level with him. As it is, he's a hand taller, and I have to jut out my chin to glare at him. "I foretold that you would find a bride, and here you are, with no one in your arms. Do *not* make me a liar."

"Then you shouldn't have lied."

My eyes narrow. Cyrus ignores me, shrugging on a bird-patterned jacket.

It was just a small lie, something to smother talk. Last autumn, there were reports of Fairywood turning black near the borderlands, of bloodred rose petals blowing through villages at night. People were getting anxious, so King Emilius asked me to search the future for any clues or elaborations about Felicita's prophecy.

But my nights were fruitless, my dreams frustratingly empty.

So as Cyrus left on his tour, I made something up to calm the court:

Prince Cyrus will meet his bride before his journey's end.

A small lie goes down like overwatered wine. You hardly notice it, and if you do, it isn't a big enough problem to complain about. Cyrus needed to find a bride eventually. All I did was give him a timeline.

"Fine," I say, arms crossed. "I didn't really dream that you'd find your bride. I shouldn't have had to. You should have chosen someone by now." You could pave a footpath with the admirers swooning in the streets for him. How difficult can it be? "As long as Felicita's prophecy hangs over your neck, people will be afraid of it, and they'll fear for your reign, too. They call you *cursed*. Not to your face, clearly. I bought you time, Princey—time and optimism."

Checking his cuffs, Cyrus tweaks the lion's head–shaped buttons, continuing in his bored drone, "More concerned with appearances than the prophecy itself, I see."

I flash teeth. "I can be worried about two things at once."

"Of course: your precarious reputation, and my father's opinion of you."

"The latest patrol reports came back last week. They found rotting trees in the Fairywood."

"I'm aware. I saw it." He finally stops fussing with his clothes and lowers his gaze to mine; disquiet frames the green of his eyes, but I don't behold it for long before he glances away. "My father should have already sent troops to burn it."

"But the *root of the problem*—"

"—might be Felicita's last prophecy, yes, but I can't do anything. I don't get to decide when or with whom I fall in love."

Felicita's prophecy only mentioned a bride—love doesn't have to play a part in it—but Cyrus is a romantic; he thinks it matters. Otherwise, he'd be celebrating his third anniversary with an arranged Verdantese princess by now. "You're not even trying," I scoff.

Cyrus only shakes his head. "I'm not giving false hope the prophecy will be broken. That's all there is to it." He pivots toward the bedroom doors.

I follow on his heels, out of his quarters and into the hallway, where courtiers are milling about. They turn to the prince with lighted eyes and ready questions. Cyrus flaunts a dazzling smile before dropping it sharply as soon as he jogs down the stairs, avoiding them all. Two guards fence him off, but I slip through.

I lower my voice. "Do you at least have a plan for when you spark a panic amongst your people?"

"I'm not discussing this with *you*," he mutters.

"*Me?*" I mock in the same tone, fingers pressed to my chest.

"You, who took every chance to undermine me for years."

"Years you wouldn't have if I hadn't saved your life."

Cyrus glares. He hates when I bring up how we met. I love bringing up how we met.

As soon as he lands on the ground floor, he makes a sharp turn to avoid the crowds drifting toward us in the atrium. Carpet muffles the quickness of his steps as he tries to lose me and everyone else, but I keep pace, the blue silk of my robes fluttering behind me.

"This isn't just a matter of prophecy," I call after him. Many dukes are less than enthused about his ascension. They find Cyrus too *honest*. "The Council will use fear against you. Call you unsuitable for the throne. What part of *'You're cursed'* don't you understand?"

His mouth thins to a line. Cyrus knows I'm right. "The Council should focus on their own dominions, rather than a fevered prophet's last words that gave no details, no time-line. Tomorrow, we could be felled by a quake or flood or falling star, and no one's paranoid about that."

"That's very logical, but people are as allergic to logic as I am to fairy dust. Princey—"

He spins around without warning, and I nearly run into him. The edge of his cloak sweeps around my feet. "You don't even want me as your king. Why should I listen to your advice?"

I swallow a bitter lump in my throat. Because he *will* be king. No matter the panic. No matter what the Council thinks. Cyrus always gets what he wants in the end. "We either spend our energy fighting or learning to work together. We don't have to like each other in order to be smart about this."

"What if I don't want to work with you?"

"You'll have to, one day. I'm your Seer."

"I could change that."

I laugh out of habit, but the dip of his gaze has a cold edge. We've always argued like this, yet—no, Cyrus couldn't really let me go. He doesn't have the nerve to do something so unprecedented as removing a sitting Seer, not when there are so few in the world.

I lick my lips. "You need me more than you hate me." Arrogant, maybe, but that's the only way to call a bluff.

The edge of Cyrus's mouth curls upward, the only hint that he might have enjoyed any part of this conversation. "Is that so?"

He turns back around. I watch as he leaves down the hall toward the gilded doors of the Council Chamber. A footman opens them for him with a bow, and Cyrus disappears inside.

⁂

Most of the Council's fourteen dukes or their stewards arrived a week ago for their twice-annual session. There's plenty of pomp and very little progress as they squabble over taxes and Dragonsguard allocations for their respective dominions. Auveny is the largest and wealthiest of the three Sun Continent nations—outpacing the Republic of Balica to our south and the Kingdom of Verdant beyond the Fairywood and eastern mountains—a status that encourages a mix of ambition and complacency in our leadership. We also pride ourselves on being a model kingdom, with fair laws and opportunities for even the lowest subjects.

So there's a great deal of self-importance, too.

It's too much hot air to make eavesdropping worth it for me, but anything interesting will find its way around soon enough; secrets jump like fleas in the Sun Capital.

And if there's a matter that requires a Seer's attention, King Emilius will call me in himself.

After Cyrus enters the Council Chamber, I await the fallout in the upstairs library. I spend many afternoons among the curated tomes; dry as they might be, they're one way I put names to the unfamiliar things I've seen in my dreams. I've never been far outside the river-veined hills of the capital myself. My duties keep me here, and I try to be reliable in presence; I get enough criticism lobbied at me without *lazy* being added to that list.

I'm flipping through a travelogue of a famous Yuenen explorer from the Moon Continent when I hear doors slamming open, followed by a spill of shouts. It hasn't even been an hour. Setting the book down, I follow the racket along with a growing crowd to the main courtyard, where Lord Rasmuth of the Seventh and Lord Ignacio of the Thirteenth are quarreling.

The latter stamps his foot loudly enough to startle birds into the sky. "Efficiency be damned!" Ignacio bellows. "The prince is still cursed! I will not support him as king until he finds a queen—and, dare I say, even then!"

Even with my shorter height, I stand out among the crowd with my black rope of hair and shimmering, shifting robes. Nearby eyes begin turning toward me for answers— exactly the situation I wanted to avoid.

I sigh heavily as the shawled lady at my elbow does a triple take in my direction, as if drumming up the initiative to ask. She finally speaks up on the fourth gawk, after a short bow. "Sighted Mistress, will we not have a wedding soon? But you said—"

"That his Highness would find his true love before his *journey's* end," I finish with emphasis. "Not his *tour's* end. Clearly, his journey isn't over yet." This is why the exact words are important.

I excuse myself, feigning a headache. Pushing a path into the palace, I can see the fresh implications of my reply rippling through the throngs in shocked expressions and whispers. The news will bleed through the entire city before dark.

Cyrus's footsteps echo near, louder than everyone else's, sending the message that His Highness will *not* be answering questions right now. The tail of his jacket flaps past me as he heads toward the wing containing his father's offices.

I can't resist calling after him, "Hate to say I told you so, Princey—oh, wait, no I don't. *I told you so!*"

He doesn't even stop to glower.

Cyrus's attempt at rebellion inconveniences both of us, but more him than me. King Emilius knows his son's moods. Despite the diplomatic smiles they wear in public, Cyrus might argue with his father more than he argues with me—and Cyrus never wins. I know this because I've never in my life heard the king change his mind about anything.

I, on the other hand, have always been in the king's good graces, and Cyrus resents me for it. His father's respect is hard-earned, rare as a treasure plundered from the depths of a dragon's lair. That respect will protect me even when Cyrus ascends. King Emilius will likely keep one hand on Auveny's puppet strings even after passing on his crown; the Council of Dukes—all appointed by him—are loyal to Emilius, and that is where the true power lies.

Evening curtains the sky soon after I return to my tower.

I relish these hours, when it's too late for anyone to call for my services. Up in my bedroom, I light the hearth and draw a cold bath. I slip my robe from my shoulders, unbutton my skirt, pull my blouse and shift over my head.

Bracing myself, I plunge into the tub, then scrub down by firelight. Old scars have mostly faded from my soap-softened skin. My hair pools around me, dark as ink and heavy with perfumed water.

Seeing me today, you wouldn't guess that I was born a scraggly weed of the Moon District slums. Now I have my own tower with its own porcelain bath and a bed of silks. I can read and write, I eat as heartily as the royal family, and people bow to me.

Still, a title and a tower don't erase a fear of things people don't understand. When something as strange as magic lives in someone as strange to them as a foreign-faced girl, I will never stand a chance. I should remember that when I get arrogant with the prince, even if I am right.

After drying off, I yank on my nightgown and tumble into bed, exhausted.

When I shut my eyes, something clinks downstairs.

Then again, in repetition: *kak-kak-kak.*

Cabinets settling? I frown.

Kak-kak-kak-kak.

Snickering.

My heartbeat fills my ears. No reason I wouldn't be alone. Slipping out of bed, I grab the closest blunt object I can find in the dark—a long-handled brush by the tub. I hold my breath and pad downstairs, careful to not make the stairs creak.

In the pitch-black, I circle the room, feeling along the ridges of the walls, but the only sound is the scrape of my own feet against the floor.

There's no one here. But I ask the dark anyway, just to settle my skin: "Who's there?"

I hear a hiss like a tongue meeting hot steel. Swinging the brush in a wide arc, I strike something solid that clatters and skids across the floor.

A wooden tray and bowl. I exhale.

Laughter bubbles forth. *Hah-hah-hah.*

Vi-o-let.

I swing around again, stumbling. The echo of my name sticks to the back of my skull, here and nowhere all at once.

What a fitting
name
you have,
Vi-o-let.

Words layer upon each other—many voices, merging into one. My heart hammers; this is no earthly sound.

Vile.

Vi-o-let.

Violet of the Moon.

I've never heard these voices before, yet they're familiar as instinct, innate as a layer of my soul. "Who are you?" I ask, even though I know the answer.

Two dim lights flicker in the distant dark. My breath catches in my throat. Nothing makes that kind of glow in this room.

We grant you your power, wretch.

Brush held in front of me, I approach the lights with stuttered steps, toeing around the tray I knocked over. I recognize what I'm walking toward: the offering fountain, where my patrons toss in gifts and coins. And carved at the top of it is the faceless statuette they sometimes pray to.

Formerly faceless.

The blue-copper statuette has been worn smooth for as long as I've seen it, barely recognizable as a figure at all, let alone one of a Fate. It's only remarkable for an antique, said to be nearly as old as the first Seer.

But as I near, the grooves of the statuette form a woman, coldly serene, draped in a cloth that flows from her like a waterfall. Her eyes blaze blue fire. From her mouth spills a chorus:

Seven years gained,
one life owed.
You saved the crowned boy
who was ours to claim.
Diverted his death
so you could live in your tower.
It is time to pay it back.

Memories rise: the prince running through the Moon District marketplace. Me, pulling him away from the crush of a horse-cart. We were barely more than children then. Felicita was still alive. It was long ago. "I don't understand." Every vein in my body pulses, aware of a danger I can't place. "Is this a threat?"

There is always a price for defying destiny.
One life owed.

The boy must die
before summer's end,
or you will burn.

"Why? But I didn't—" My grip on the brush's wooden handle shakes, the only tether I have to anything solid. My feet have gone numb.

The boy must die
for all tales must END.

Wind rushes through the room—or did I imagine it? Is this how Felicita went mad? I can't really be talking to the gods. This is impossible.

The voices surge, deafening, solid enough to fill the dark:

IT IS TIME,
AT LAST, AT LAST,
BLOOD AND ROSES AND WAR.

I slam the end of the brush into the statuette. The top half of its body smashes to the ground. Black tendrils erupt from the marble stump, spiderwebbing down the fountain. A cackle bounces off the walls. I clutch my head, keening.

I'm going mad. This is mad. I scrabble around on the floor for anything to make the laughter stop, and I slice my hand on broken marble. I cry out at the bright pain. Lightning flashes. The room shudders, as if divinely struck.

YOU ARE NOT WORTHY OF ANY LOVE THAT WILL SAVE YOU.

I breathe in smoke.

The tower bursts into flames.

I wake gasping from a memory of ash, hands curled around my throat, legs twisted in the sheets. Fire sears my skin for a white-hot second. Another blink, and the night is dark and cold. Above me, the gems studded into the tower's ceiling wink, unburnt, as if they know what I saw.

Slowly, I unclench my hands from my neck.

Was it a prophecy or—? What else could it have been? A hallucination? It was so vivid.

It didn't feel like any prophecy I've had. None have spoken directly to me before.

None have *threatened* me before.

Kicking off my covers, I crawl out of bed and put on my robe with trembling hands. A chilled wind rushes up my knees as I push through the balcony doors and press myself against the railing. Dawn is brightening. The scaly rooftops of the Sun Capital glimmer below. Beyond the city walls, the land dips into shadowed valleys.

"What do you want?" I say to the sky.

Nothing speaks back. Maybe because I don't believe in the Fates' influence, not truly, and what do gods do all day besides find the barest reason to be insulted?

Fog curls from my breath like smoke. The reminder of Felicita's prophecy unsteadies me most: *blood and roses and war.* If the prophecy is true—if it's *here*—

Why would it be because I saved Cyrus seven years ago?

Why would the Fates have wanted him to die?

People think that because I have the Sight, that makes me some messenger of the gods. As if I understand these forces or how my magic works. I've dreamed across time and now I'm hearing voices—

But I never know why.

If the Fates control our future, I don't understand to what end. Here in Auveny, the belief is that the Fates judge us. That if we are generous, honest, not too chatty, placable, forgiving, they might twist our threads so we find love and earn our heart's weight in gold. Everyone has heard of the miller's kind daughter who marries richly, of the maid who coaxes the man out of a beast, of faithful girls in locked towers waiting for their knights.

But I don't believe in anything that supposes it knows me better than I know myself.

I am a better liar than I am a prophet. I don't believe there's reason to our destinies. I don't believe the world is just. I believe in wolves—in con men and crowned men who wear wickedness as if it were a talent. Who don't ask for judgment before devouring what's theirs. They know the future is no better than a roll of rigged dice, so they may as well do the rigging.

Kings and their dukes have been writing futures with nothing but lies and smiles. I understand *this* power more than any of some fleshless voice in the dark.

I shut my eyes and remember what the voice said: *The boy must die before summer's end, or you will burn.*

Or. If it isn't a threat, then it's a choice.

It means I can be saved, if he dies.

I brace myself against the railing, knuckles turning white. For now, they're only words. For now, it's only a nightmare.

No one needs to know about this.

With one last glance to the quiet sky, I turn back to the tower, shutting the balcony doors behind me.

2

WHEN I WAKE AGAIN, I FIND A SPOT OF BLOOD on my sheets. My cycle started earlier than expected—a bad surprise on an already terrible morning. I bundle the bedding and place it in a basket, where a chambermaid will pick it up.

Downstairs, the statuette on the offering fountain is whole and faceless and dull to the touch. It was a dream, then. That makes last night even more unnerving.

My dreams always come true.

I cover the statuette with a cloth.

I glance around the divining room. It looks just like it did yesterday. Not much of note: a table and chairs for my readings, a small carpeted sitting area, and a hearth. I did my best to clean up this place years ago. Centuries of Seers built up clutter, and people are too afraid of committing accidental blasphemy to throw anything away. I did the next best thing and stuffed everything I didn't need into the cabinets to never see light again.

Outside, a bell tolls. I blink, a memory jogged. I'm forgetting something.

Another toll. *Clang.*

Oh. My weekly meeting with the king—

Clang.

Shit. I stick my head out the window. There's another toll from the clock tower, which will be followed by eight more, judging by the sun's position overhead.

I *overslept.* I am *late.*

Stupid nightmare, stupid—whatever it was. Not to take a page from the prince's book, but I have more urgent worries than cryptic warnings, which do feel silly in the light of day. King Emilius might not threaten me with flames, but his gaze could wither every rose in his garden when he's disappointed.

I never disappoint him.

I pull a comb through my hair and pin it back, no time to braid it. I put on a clean dress and my robe, which currently shimmers a bright, cloudless blue. The Seer's robe is an Auvenese heirloom, cut from a piece of the heavens, according to legend. The fabric changes to match the skies overhead.

It also has very spacious sleeves. I grab two cold buns from the hearth, shove one in my mouth, and the other into one of my sleeves. Stars willing, I won't be shaking out crumbs at His Majesty's feet, but better that than a growling stomach.

I rush toward the palace. Halfway across the gardens, I realize I'm brushing shoulders with too many strangers on the tiled pathways. There are more guards patrolling too, though languidly, as if there is no real danger afoot.

Am I forgetting something else?

Following the flow of traffic, I circle around to the front

of the palace, where a raucous well-dressed crowd blocks the entrance. At the outer gates, guards are letting a spare amount of people in from the even larger mob outside.

My darting eyes land on a fidgety girl at the bottom of the entryway steps who looks young enough to intimidate. I clear my throat and lean toward her. "What are people waiting for?"

"O-oh! Sighted Mistress!" The girl drops into a curtsy. Her dress is plain, though well made, and I don't recognize her as any daughter of nobility. If the guards are allowing in commoners, there must be an open audience. "The prince is making an announcement about the ball."

"The *what*?"

"The ball. Did you see the flyers? They're all over the city."

She flashes a piece of paper and I snatch it. It bears the briefest of details:

ALL ARE INVITED TO THE

Masked Menagerie

On the eleventh of Annesol,
doors will open at the palace at 7 o'clock
to reveal a spectacle within.

Young ladies encouraged to attend.
Dress your best and impress. Mask mandatory.
Our prince will be present.

So this is what came out of Cyrus's talk with his father last night: an emergency ball.

"Thank you." Trying not to grin too widely, I hand the flyer back to the girl. That's one problem taken care of, at least.

I still have to get inside the palace, so I jostle my way through. I regret my decision to bring breakfast as I lose one of the buns in my sleeve to the floor and the other is squashed into a custard pancake. Around me, heads swivel and feet shuffle, and people part to make a path when they see who I am.

The audience room is packed closer than mortared bricks and itchingly hot, a sweaty thicket of feathered hats and the pastel ruffles of this season's fashion. Everyone's overdressed to impress. Some even brought their fairies, who aren't taking the heat well, all passed out on hat brims, their golden glows dim.

Fairies used to only bless kind, luckless paupers and were seldom seen outside of the Fairywood borders. Magical creatures are all hoarders of some sort, and these tiny, squeaking creatures are hoarders of the best humans, although phrasing it like that gets you dirty looks. Now fairies follow anyone born with a spoon of ambrosia in their mouth. Ambrosia is preciously distilled from the golden nectar of Fairywood fayflowers and is the only currency fairies take, because it's the only thing that gets them shit-faced drunk.

When King Emilius saw the demand in glamours, he encouraged Auvenese farmers to learn how to cultivate it, despite the plant's Fairywood origins. Its trade has since become our biggest industry. You can't walk through any of the upper districts of the Sun Capital without seeing fairies zipping overhead.

You can have a heart as toxic as a rotting pumpkin, but trade a few drops of ambrosia and a fairy will gladly enchant your hairs to stay put, your laughter to sound like music, and your dress to be so grand that you won't be able to fit through the ballroom doors. Only the wealthiest can afford to have one on daily retainer; I can tell which attendees have glamoured skin: their makeup isn't melting off their face.

Who needs kindness? That's for ugly, poor people.

King Emilius is seated at the edge of the stage, hands resting on his cane, looking healthier than I've seen him in weeks. Relief sags my shoulders when he inclines his head and smiles at me; he hasn't been waiting. I mirror the same motion and nearly knock into someone's voluminous flared sleeves.

Princess Camilla is at the front of the room as well, surrounded by her handmaidens. She's impossible to miss; as Cyrus's twin, she has the same arresting looks, with the added radiance of pale gold–dyed tresses. Taller than her brother by a thimble, she would be called a graceful beauty if not for the muscle she gained through sword-fighting and hunting.

She grins when she sees me escape the throngs. Taking my gloved hand, she crosses my arm with hers, so that we're close enough to have something of a private conversation. "A bride search for my baby brother. He truly is all grown-up." She's half an hour older. "Time goes by so fast."

I scan the room for the one other friendly face I might

find. "Dante's not here?" He should be even easier to spot than Camilla—there are few Balicans in court—but I don't see his gawky figure nor his mess of black curls.

"Thought he'd arrive with you."

I thought he'd be glued to Cyrus's side. With Cyrus's return, Dante will go back to being his friend instead of mine; yet another reason the prince should have been devoured by a dragon instead of coming back. Dante is the only person I might tell about what happened last night.

The crowd hushes. My attention turns back to the stage.

Cyrus has stepped up to the dais, dressed in a sleek purple coat with a sunburst print along the lapel. He doesn't even look like he's sweating. "Welcome," he says as he slips a charming smile on like it's mirror-nature.

All those young ladies gripping flyers surge forward, pressing against the velvet ropes that corral them, and the air in the room sucks in for a collective enamored sigh.

Gods, I hate how easy that is for him.

Cyrus begins his speech benignly enough, talking of his travels around the continent. He praises the development of the borderlands, credits the courts of Balica and Verdant for their warm welcomes, and laughs over an encounter with lost fairies traveling to the city.

"Now, as for the ball—"

"Your Highness," a gravelly voice interrupts from the balcony, "eager as we are to celebrate, we expected a wedding, not a ball. What happened?"

Peering up, I frown. I don't remember her name, but I know the speaker is Lord Ignacio's newest wife. Stirring trouble on the duke's behalf?

King Emilius flutters his wrinkled hand, urging Cyrus to move on, but the prince only broadens his winsome smile. "Nothing happened. I met many fine ladies, but I didn't find a queen. People were hopeful for something that wasn't certain. Perhaps you shouldn't believe everything the Seer says."

His gaze pierces across the room at me, a threat. Bemused murmurs tide through the audience, including an "Oh, Cyrus, *no*" from the princess.

My face heats. Toad-brained brat. "His Highness—"

But few pause their talk for me, and I'm drowned out.

Growling, I loosen my arm from Camilla's and push my way forward until I stand below the dais and its scornful prince. I've always struggled to be seen and heard on my terms. The court never stopped expecting me to be demure since I moved from the slums to the Seer's tower. As if my place in the court is charity, like it never completely belongs to me, when I belong here more than they do.

I only know how to be brazen. I refuse to earn respect any other way. So I begin again, louder. *"His Highness"*— chatter ceases—"will find his true love before his journey's end, as I foretold. He wants to blame me for his own dawdling. Perhaps his journey would go quicker if he stopped questioning my wisdom."

"Perhaps if you were a more accurate Seer, I wouldn't question it," Cyrus presses on amid the titters; our public scuffles are an all-too-familiar sight. "Can you even say *where* my so-called journey ends?"

"Not up your own ass, so maybe you should pull your head out."

Laughter bubbles through the crowd—Camilla practically guffaws—as color splotches Cyrus's face.

"*Witches and princes, like cats and dogs,*" someone snickers.

King Emilius drums his fingers on his armrest—a simple gesture without anger. "The point I believe both my son and my Seer are making is: we are not all blessed with an easy search when it comes to love. I consider myself lucky to have found it with my dear Merchella, in the time she was here with us. Stars guide her soul. It is good to remind ourselves of how true love will save us from the dark." His mouth closes in a solemn crease.

The room is subdued, and the prince and I glance in opposite directions. I can't imagine Cyrus taking his father's place before the year is over, armed to the teeth with charm yet commanding only a grain of the same reverence.

As the quiet yawns into a chasm, Camilla huffs and moves toward the dais. "Time to save Prince Charming," she mutters. She makes a flapping motion at her brother and shoos him away. Camilla Lidine is a wholly different kind of storm compared to Cyrus—one who understands and embraces the thunder of her steps.

Once Cyrus is shunted to the side, she spreads her arms wide to address the audience. "Let's get to the fun part, lovely people of Auveny. The ball. *The Masked Menagerie.*" Approving hums. "Splendid name, isn't it? I came up with it. Now, *what,* you might ask, are the strange creatures on display in this menagerie?" With a roll of her shoulders, a pair of wings seems to unfurl behind her—a shawl painted with a swan's likeness. "Us, of course."

The crowd oohs.

"Wear your best and most daring outfits, and the most brilliant mask you can conjure. Let's fill the palace with creatures from lands unseen. Impress me—but more importantly, impress my brother. If you catch his eye, who knows . . . ?" The crowd rumbles. "A kiss on the hand? On the cheek? Could you charm a *ring* out of him?" Squeals erupt. Cyrus breaks character briefly in an audible groan. "Very exciting, isn't it? Any questions?"

Every hand shoots up. Camilla is fueled by attention; she'll draw out this circus for as long as possible. Cyrus seems resigned to his current fate, his eyes just shy of glazed, his smile frozen stiff.

I'm also weary of the noise, and unlike Cyrus, I don't have to stay here. I slip toward the doors as easily as I'd come in, the crowd slobbering and eager to fill the space I left; etiquette is barely keeping the floors free of drool.

Once outside in the yard, I shield my eyes from the glare of the high sun and the marble walls of the palace, white as the day they were built. From afar, the palace looks like a gleaming crown atop the tile-roofed buildings that make up the Sun Capital's tiered districts.

At the gates, I find the face I didn't see in the crowd.

"Dante!" I call. "You missed the fun."

Upon first glance, one wouldn't expect someone as scruffy as Dante Esparsa to be the prince's best friend. He's dressed more casually than those around him, in his baggy shirt and the peacock-plumed hat Cyrus gifted him. Amethysts twinkle from his ears and a sash of the same jewel shade cinches his waist; like me, he doesn't care for the capital's pastel fashions, opting for richer hues that better complement the clay-brown of his skin. A satchel bulging with papers is slung over his shoulder—work, probably; he's been translating texts for the palace's library when he's not busy attending classes at the university.

His roots aren't truly so humble; as the adopted son of a former Balican leader, Dante would have a title if the Republic of Balica had notions of nobility, but he prefers to avoid courtly nonsense anyway. "If I wanted to be patronized all day, I'd have stayed at my nana's," he once said. He's lived between Balica and Auveny since his early teens, initially planning to become an ambassador, until politics gave him a headache. It's a shame: he's the type of person who could get along with anyone if he wanted to, but it turns out he usually doesn't want to.

He befriended me years ago when I was looking for a tutor, even though I don't make nice company. But maybe that's why we work: sometimes, you just want someone to complain with.

Dante jogs toward me, tucking his hat under his arm as we meet in the middle of the courtyard. "Consider this: if the announcement's over, then I'm right on time."

"Where were you?"

"My uncle's leaving today. Had to bribe him with lunch so I could drop off a few letters for family." A leisurely ride to the Balican border takes up to two weeks; his uncle won't be back anytime soon. "So, what'd I miss, hmm?" Dante claps his hands. "What horrors hath Camilla wrought this time?"

We stroll around to the emptier west gardens, following a path of mosaic sunbursts as I tell him about the announcement. Patches of dirt, prepared for new planting, are dusted with the tender green of shoots. A topiary sheared in the shape of a lion roars at us as we pass underneath its arching paws.

Dante taps a thoughtful thumb against his chin. "Cyrus mention anything else about his tour? Anything worrying?"

"Like what?"

"Patrols found rotting trees at the edge of the Fairywood."

"In the Eleventh Dominion. Old news. I heard they're burning it. Oh—it's close to Balica, isn't it? Can't imagine they're happy."

He grimaces. "They're not."

On record, Auveny and Balica have been peaceful for two centuries, but there's a history of territorial disputes between them, mostly regarding the Fairywood at the heart of the Sun Continent. It's the last parcel of sovereignless land: a tangled mass of gnarled trees and thorny undergrowth, inhospitable to all but the strangest creatures, like the fairies that give it its name.

Balica considers the Fairywood a sacred area. The Auvenese treat it like a clump of overgrown weeds that will curse us one day if we don't torch it first.

The rot isn't even the problem, though some worry about it tainting the groundwater; it's just a symptom of how unpredictable the Fairywood is. It doesn't behave like a forest. It doesn't change with seasons, and its plants grow at whim. Some say that it isn't a forest at all—that its trees are just magic that's taken the shape of them, and it can shift and create anything it may please. Along the border, you'll hear tales of phantoms that flicker in the woods' shadows, of charmed fruit that lures you toward death, of things that should not be, there and gone in a blink.

But it still burns like a forest. And Auveny is quick to use fire to curb it—or invade it, depending on who you ask. The four newest dominions are sitting on land that was Fairywood at the beginning of King Emilius's reign. Balica has warned against overstepping, but the king insists on the Fairywood's danger and eradication. He only acquiesced after those warnings escalated to a skirmish eight years ago. An isolated incident, but tensions have been fraught since.

"You think we shouldn't burn it?" I take the flattened custard bun from my sleeve, tear off a chunk, and offer the rest to Dante, but he declines.

"Just because it's strange doesn't mean it's dangerous, but . . . the problem is, it might *actually be dangerous,* more than we know. Cyrus passed the rotted area during the last leg of his tour. Went right up to the edge of the Fairywood—you can't see this from the road—and the ground there was covered in roses."

I choke on my next swallow.

Dante slaps my back hard. "All right?"

Blood and roses and war. I wheeze, hacking bits of bun. "Normal roses? *Prophetic roses?*"

"Here—first, don't die." He takes the flask from his belt and pushes it into my hand. "Was sort of hoping to see if you knew. Have you dreamed anything lately?"

I nearly choke again while drinking from the flask. I considered telling him about last night, but if there's some truth to those omens . . . It's one thing if I wanted Dante to convince me it was only a nightmare; it's another task entirely if I told him his best friend is truly doomed.

"No, but I'm still worried." I take my time wiping my mouth. "A . . . gut feeling. Big things tend to happen all at once. There's his ascension, this ball . . ."

"Cyrus thinks Lord Denning planted the roses intentionally to start rumors. They weren't live ones—just the buds and heads—but they were fresh, and I doubt anyone keeps a massive rose garden out there, so where did they come from? Cyrus paid off the patrols to keep quiet, but if something prophetic is emerging from the Fairywood . . ."

"Then he *knows* he shouldn't be stubborn about picking a bride."

Dante snorts. "He isn't without reason. But I agree." He stares past me toward the palace. "Hmm. Speaking of Cyrus."

I turn around. The prince in question is striding down the path toward us, purple cloak billowing, looking like one of the garden's statues come to life: perfectly carved body buttoned beneath perfectly tailored clothes, and—chiseled upon his face—a perfectly pissed-off glower.

I can already hear the long-suffering sigh in the back of Dante's throat. "Violet . . . you wouldn't happen to know why he looks like one of us force-fed him a lemon?"

A flush rises to my cheeks. "Earlier, I might have, um, said his head was up his ass. In front of everyone."

"For the love of—"

"You think so too!"

"Yes, *under my breath.*" Dante massages his wrinkled forehead. "We're not children anymore. He's going to be king soon, capital K *King.*"

"A capital T *Toad-brain* if he doesn't *listen*— Hello, Cyrus."

The prince's steps slow a few paces away as I meet his gaze, aimed at me like the tip of a knife when I utter his name. Was he this handsome before? The palace's fairies must have done something—accented his brow, tweaked his freckled nose, maybe. He doesn't look doomed. He otherwise looks exactly as he did yesterday: infuriating.

His attention flicks toward Dante. "Anyone can steal you away once I'm gone, is that it? She'll corrupt you, you know."

"I can corrupt myself just fine, thank you." Dante coasts above any apparent tension with a grin. "Besides, integrity only matters if people *care* about integrity. A good leader is better a clever liar than honorable and useless."

"Are you calling me useless?"

"And honorable."

The corner of Cyrus's mouth quirks upward. Dante goes forward to clap him on the shoulder, and they grip arms in greeting, knocking fists, snapping their fingers in a secret gesture too quick to see. Gods, I feel like I'm intruding.

Then the prince pivots to me. "After traveling to Balica and Verdant and seeing their perfectly mannered Seers, I have to wonder how I got stuck with you."

"Sorry, should I have been prostrating myself while you insulted me?" I scoff. "You started it."

"It was a warning. I could have said worse. I won't do it again. But if you'd like to remain Seer, you should start behaving accordingly."

I mock a curtsy. "Earn my respect and I'll treat you with respect."

In one swift step, Cyrus closes in on me with hardly an ear for Dante, who murmurs, *"I should go."* I rock forward as if in dance, heart racing. I've missed this—these arguments where we circle like fencers, trading beats and feints. He used to claim that dealing with me was a waste of time, but he could never resist trying to humble me.

"You're clever," Cyrus murmurs, "but arrogant. And you'll discover that people only listen to you because you have a king who supports you, which won't stay true for much longer." A single lock of his smoothed hair falls out of place as he dips his head, his gaze shadowed beneath long lashes. "You don't have a single selfless thought in that blessed mind of yours, and I will never oblige myself to someone like that. Be proud, because pride is all you have."

My blood hums. If he wants to put me in my place, I'll put him in his. I strip off my gloves and tuck them into my sleeve. "Maybe I should take a better look at your threads." He hasn't let me read them since my first year here. "If you're so confident you can make your way without me, I should see nothing but success in your future."

I reach for his fists, clenched at his side, and Cyrus flinches as my fingers brush the peaks of his knuckles. Was that fear—or shame? He knows I could reach for his memories; I wonder what he has to hide.

"Violet." Dante tugs me back by the shoulder. He steps between us, hazel eyes narrowing. He lets me go to press Cyrus back as well, who jerks away from him.

"Let her do it," Cyrus snaps.

"There are people in the gardens."

Cyrus exhales sharply between his teeth, as if suddenly

aware of the ugliness of our scene. There's no one close enough to eavesdrop, but the story is clear to anyone who may be watching: the prince is unable to control his Seer, who, not a half hour ago, gleefully humiliated him in front of his courtiers.

"You wouldn't be here without me," I say. "Never forget that, Princey."

With a shake of his head, Cyrus buries a hand in his hair as if wringing out the last of his frustration. "I've never forgotten." A dry chuckle cuts through his words like a garrote. He doesn't give me another glance before his back is turned. "I'll see you at a better time, Dante."

I watch until he's surrounded by his guards and his boots are clicking on the marble path.

Behind me, Dante grumbles, "Could you maybe not put me in that position?"

"I wouldn't be offended if you chose Cyrus over me. He clearly needs the support."

"There is no *choosing*, Violet. You're not fruit at the market. It doesn't work like that. I care for you both."

I shrug, biting my tongue. I can't glimpse into my own future, but I know I'll always be on the fringes, laughing from afar. I'm too strange to fit in the court, too ambitious to be happy among common folk. I'm glad to have this much of Dante's friendship already. Most people would tell me I should be grateful that I'm blessed with the Sight, grateful that I'm here at all—I'm never supposed to feel anything *but* grateful.

Dante understands, even if he doesn't like it. He knows how precarious it is being an outsider.

A decade ago, his mother, the Head of Hypsi, led the skirmish that would halt Auveny's progress into the Fairywood. As the Balican state adjacent to Auveny, Hypsi has long borne the brunt of dealing with border disputes. The Head believed that threats that wounded were the only kind that were heeded, and she wasn't wrong.

When news of the skirmish arrived in the capital, Auveny threatened to send more soldiers south. To avoid outright war, the Republic of Balica and King Emilius negotiated: unsanctioned burnings would stop, but the Head of Hypsi would be removed from her position. If Cyrus hadn't fought tooth and nail for Dante, who was staying in the Sun Capital at the time, he'd have been expelled from the Sun Capital, too.

The demand for my magic and my favor with King Emilius protects me, like Cyrus's favor protected Dante, but it will never be enough. Feelings can change, after all. Kings change. It's easy to lose everything you've built through no fault of your own, like lordly scuffles or princes with inflated heads taking offense. I don't have the luxury of being nice. The only people who are nice are those who have never had to claw for anything they've wanted.

There are *kind* people, like Dante, who know how unfair life is and somehow hold on to their compassion. I'm not kind either.

Kind people get eaten alive in this world.

Dante and I finish our turn about the gardens, talking about anything but Cyrus or the future, but the prince's sharp gaze when he confronted me lingers in my mind, too assured for my liking.

3

IN THE EVENINGS, I LIKE TO PERCH ON MY tower's balcony, legs swinging through the iron railings. My robe is shrugged from my shoulders, blushed with the purple-pink of sunset.

Here, I have the best view in all of Auveny.

The river fog is rolling through the emptying streets of the University and Arts Districts. In the lower portions of the city, red buildings mark the Moon District, where many lower-class immigrants from Yue settle in Auveny to live and work, including the mother I never knew. Those labyrinthine alleyways are where I spent the first eleven years of my life.

Back then, I could barely read the Yuenen signs that swung from the windows of offal restaurants and second-hand shops. I thought every treasure could be found at the marketplace, where a kind busker bought me honey sweets once. I thought the world ended where I met walls too tall to climb.

I'd seen stranger lands in my dreams, but my mind hadn't learned how to hold fast to the images yet. The mountain-sized forests, the endless horizons, the laughter and war cries of other eras—my days were so narrow and dusty in comparison. How could these glimpses be anything but a fantasy, some other-lived life?

When I was old enough to understand the gift I had, I knew I was destined for greatness, but I'd have to prove myself in order to get there. Being Sighted didn't hold any weight if I couldn't convince anyone of it.

Mad beggars were plenty. Prophets were not.

Who was I to claim that my mind was special? A coin-less orphan on coltish legs, tented in ragged castoffs, with a face that was more dirt than skin. People only know what they can see and only see what they believe, and I was just another matchstick child of the alleyways. Indistinguishable as vermin.

My chance to escape the streets arrived in a dream.

The buildings of the Moon District rose tall and too bright in my mind, as if some lens over the world had been lifted. A horse-drawn pearl of a carriage, white as the walls of the palace, rolled through the district's arches with horns trumpeting.

Doors swung open from the carriage's carved sides. Two children leaped out: a brother and sister, dressed in purple-and-gold finery. They had matching noses and dimples and hair that shined amber under the dazzling lights in the sky—a dreamed sky, filled with more stars than I'd ever seen.

The children escaped into a maze of shop stalls ahead of their guards. In a blink, the image blurred. A shattering, wet crunch silenced the marketplace.

The vision dragged me through the stalls, their piled

wares, the witnesses clustered in the street . . . to the rubble of a pottery cart where the boy's broken body lay, his skull crushed under the hooves of a draft horse.

The horse had torn free from its load, and its master reacted only a second too late to catch its reins before tragedy struck. The magnitude of the mistake hardly mattered; the boy was dead.

Would be dead.

I didn't know who he was, but I saw his clothes, the carriage, the horror. He was someone important.

He was exactly who I needed.

When I awoke, I went to the marketplace. Stood in the shade of a towering apartment, a few paces from a cart double-stacked with painted urns, and waited. I did this day after day, until one morning, when the air was sweet as ripened fruit and just as sticky, I heard the horns of the carriage.

The boy came skidding around the cart laughing. He saw me, with my feet planted in the dirt and my arms outstretched, and met my eyes like he knew I was there for him.

Before he could shape a question, I yanked him forward. The cart burst into a mist of wood and porcelain. A horse came crashing down on the spot where the boy had just stood.

When the boy's shock ebbed into a manageable trembling, I told him everything about my visions and how I knew to save him. He asked for my name, and I gave him the one I made up for myself: *Violet*. He asked for my family and I said I had none, so he called me *Violet Lune*, Violet of the Moon, after the district I called home.

He gave me his name in return: Cyrus Lidine.

I'd saved the crown prince.

In that moment, I saw my future clearer than ever; not through my Sight, but in the way he looked at me, as if I were a miracle. I could ask for anything and he would grant it.

I pointed to the tower at the center of the capital, the one that looked tall enough to pierce the sky. I asked about the witch who lived there and whether it was true that she saw the future like I did.

I asked, *Could I live there too?*

Cyrus brought me to the palace, where I knelt before the king and swore to serve him. Each day afterward was a whirlwind, removing me further from the life I knew, into a life I'd only ever imagined. Necessities were no longer questions of *if* but *what kind?* I learned I liked sweets, well-steeped tea, and pillows that weren't too soft, and I could have them brought to me at any hour. I grew my hair down to my waist and twirled in front of mirrors wearing dresses picked out by the princess, who was eager to have a new playmate in the palace. People saw me. They *sought* me. The world unfurled, and so did my ambitions.

The only setback was the passing of Sighted Mistress Felicita. She was already sick when I arrived, and later that month, she would die speaking the prophecy that still haunts us today, leaving me untrained in her traditions. Maybe it was the Fates themselves meddling; big things tend to happen all at once.

The aftermath of my robing as Seer was something I couldn't predict—my turbulent entry into the court, the years gaining respect, the decay of Cyrus's goodwill as his father favored me over him. I didn't notice the latter until Cyrus closed himself off entirely. He stopped smiling at me and only spoke to lecture me. If my memory were anything less than perfect, I would think the dazzling-eyed boy I saved in the Moon District never existed.

I remember that boy, if only for this: he kept his promise, made as he held my hand tightly that first startling day we met.

I will give you a home.

A knock interrupts my thoughts.

Sighing, I extract my limbs from the balcony railing and pad downstairs. I was getting too sentimental, anyway.

At the door, the king's footman greets me in yellow livery. "Good evening, Sighted Mistress." He bows. "His Majesty is in the rose garden."

Right—I haven't had my meeting with the king yet. Smoothing down my robe, I follow the footman outside and leave my past to the past.

Dusk has given way to the dark. When I cross the bridge to the palace, the gardens beyond the gates are no more than broad, murky strokes of hedges and treetops. Budding stars wink overhead and on my sleeves. A single lantern glows on the path to the roses, where a stout figure waits alone.

The rose garden is King Emilius's favorite corner of the grounds—or, more exactly, the late queen's favorite, and he took up the mantle fiercely after she died. Roses used to have as many meanings as there were colors of them, but they've only meant one thing since Felicita's prophecy: *curse*. No one grows them anymore, but they persist at the palace as a mark of boldness—a declaration that the crown doesn't fear the future, for the prophecy will resolve in their favor.

I approach the king, inclining my head forward in a small bow. "Your Majesty. You look well."

"Seer." He doesn't hunch—the most obvious sign of his health—though his hold on his lion-headed cane trembles. A blood disease runs in the Lidine men that weakens their bones and muscles late in life. It accelerated rapidly in the last year, and while it won't kill King Emilius, it's only a matter of time before he's permanently bedridden. "Any news from the stars?"

The boy must die before summer's end, or you will burn.

"None this week," I lie.

He nods, eyes shut in thought. "Then presently, we need to deal with the problem of Auveny's next queen. We've stretched our people's patience thin enough. There are more signs of the prophecy in the borderlands."

"The roses near the rot," I say, like a paragon of vigilance.

"Yes. There were also reports of fields turning into roses overnight in a village farther from the Fairywood. Fortunately, the farmer affected has a reputation with neighbors, and most believe it is a hoax to cover for his poor crop." His next breath draws out into a sigh, rasping with the anticipation of a cough. "Regardless, I have been preparing for the worst, if that damned prophecy is finally upon us—and I will require your assistance, Seer."

I tilt my head for a better glimpse of the king's expression, but it's too dark to see much more than his profile; still, I know that tone well.

It was King Emilius who first asked me to be deceptive about my prophecies. To make use of the fact that no one else in Auveny can deny what I see, for no one else here has the same magic that I do. When I was younger, I still had the mind to be shocked about it. Not because he asked me to lie or that it went against the virtuous reputation I had known him by, but because someone like him *had* to lie. That even the power of a king might rest on the whims of a street rat.

He told me that a lie is a tool, just as much as honesty is. Both are about choosing what words to say. Both can have consequences.

What you achieve in the end is what matters.

"There will be a girl attending the Masked Menagerie unlike all the others," he continues, turning toward me with the faintest smile. "She will make her entrance at eleven o'clock. Her mask will be a splendid green in the likeness of butterfly wings, adorned with a ransom's worth of dragon-scale, emerald, and jade, and her dress will be covered in golden fayflowers. She will be unmistakable. And she is to be Cyrus's true love. Do you understand?"

I don't, not for a long moment, because the only thing he could mean is . . . unless he *does mean* . . . "An arranged match?"

"Precisely. A fine Balican lady, set up by someone I sent along with Cyrus during his tour."

A halting chuckle escapes me. Cyrus has gone through all this arguing just to end up with an *arranged match*.

"That's perfect. That's what Cyrus should have done years ago." And it's one less thing I have to worry about, too.

The tips of his gray mustache lift upward. "I'm glad you agree. I hope Cyrus does as well. You must convince him that she's his true love."

"What do you mean?" I blink. "He doesn't know about her?"

"Stars, no." Tucking his cane under his arm, King Emilius folds his hands over the buckle of his belt, a gold-carved sun. "*We* may understand that a bride is merely a bride—a practical affair—but my son is unfortunately stubborn about falling in love. This arrangement will go down better if he believes this meeting to be fate. The ball will be a smokescreen." He raises two fingers; his tremors are more pronounced in the air. "First, it will draw attention away from the borderlands. Second, it'll be the perfect setting for the beginning of a love story, in full public view. And who is to say? Perhaps Cyrus *will* fall in love. She seems extraordinary in many ways."

An elegant plan—if *I* didn't have to be the one convincing Cyrus.

The king studies me. "You seem uncertain."

"Well—" I barely suppress a sputter. My mouth is agape. I snap it shut. "I can convince *the public* of this, but Cyrus doesn't exactly trust me."

"You will be his Seer soon. You will need to build this trust regardless."

"Over time, I hope so," I say slowly, trying to be diplomatic without hiding my distaste, "but you saw us during the announcement."

"Cyrus was angry that you were correct. He knows he is being obstinate. I think he will change his tune soon." King Emilius pauses, as if deliberating something, then says, "You're cleverer than my son, if I'm being fully honest. If he had your mind, I would worry less about the future of these lands."

I can't help but smile. I'd never imagine the king values me more than his own child, but we share a more similar worldview. We can discuss schemes in plain terms, and he's never reprimanded me for talking baldly of my opinions, even if they involve his court or his son's shortcomings. He is, foremost, looking out for the future of Auveny. Nothing is personal.

I'm more smug than confident, but that has to be enough for now. Ultimately, I can't refuse unless I have a better plan. "You don't have to worry."

"That's my Seer." His eyes crinkle, a pair of shadowed crescents. "Give the kingdom a love story for the ages, Violet. One fitting to bring down the terrible prophecy Felicita left us with."

I haven't disappointed him yet. "I will, Your Majesty."

4

SIX WEEKS TO THE BALL. THE SUN CAPITAL'S
storefronts transform overnight. Displays fill with purses,
fans, jewelry—anything a girl might need to catch a prince's
eye. Dressmakers strip their mannequins of seersucker summer wear in favor of silks and ballooning velvet skirts. Per-
fume sampling stations pop up across the city, next to mask
hawkers and haberdasheries.

And it becomes impossible to get within five feet of
Prince Cyrus Lidine.

Inside the palace, he's surrounded by court sycophants.
Once he steps out into the city, it's shrieking admirers.

His bachelorhood has attracted two kinds of Sun Capital menaces: those who think themselves delicate fayflowers
waiting to be plucked by some dreamed-up idea of Prince
Charming; and those more like the Fairywood brambles,
who climb—with teeth. Hungry for the things only a prince
could offer: the jewels, the white-horse carriages, the envious society surrounding them.

A prince without the fixings, after all, is just a boy.

When Cyrus holds a question-and-answer session about

himself in the University Square, I attend in hopes of cornering him afterward. I'll request a temporary truce for Dante's sake; surely this much we can agree on.

The audience is massive, stretching from the pillars of one hall of learning to another, and I scrunch my nose as I struggle to find a free spot on a building's steps. He may be His Handsome Highness and exceptionally eligible, but his pretty face is worth half this crowd at most.

He regales the crowd with inane details about his likes and dislikes, his exercise regimen, what he finds attractive in a partner—all peppered with frequent winks. I'm nodding off in the middle of some groanworthy flirting when an audience member faints. Cyrus leaps down the stage to catch her just in time, and at the sight of his heroism, five more girls come toppling down, hoping for the same treatment. People surge and swarm to get close to him, reaching for a snip of his hair, a fingernail, or even his spit—love potions are in high demand.

It becomes so chaotic that the Imperial Guard has to be brought in, and I leave without speaking to him. As much as I dread the prospect of gaining the prince's trust, I'm not intentionally avoiding reconciliation. I honestly can't get close enough to him to *try*.

I consider sending Cyrus an invitation to meet, but it feels too bold. He already assumes I'm constantly scheming—and, well, he isn't *wrong*. He's known me longer than anyone else, and the only thing that's come out of that is that it's impossible to lie to him.

I need to seed a little friendship. Wear my sweetest smile and hope I don't look like a jester. I could start agreeing with everything he says: *Yes, I do exist just to vex you, Princey, how astute of you.*

Practicing in front of my mirror, I can't get through a conversation with a straight face.

My tower opens for public readings again, and I shift my focus to building out the rest of Cyrus's epic love story. If there's one thing that every tale needs, it's *drama*. As the saying goes: every future is earned and no destiny is without blood.

Though the Masked Menagerie is a ruse of a ball, I have to pretend it's not. The attendees should feel like they have a chance with the prince. Our fated bride needs to compete for him, even if the battle is as insignificant as securing the last dance.

So, on top of the fervor already sweeping the Sun Capital, I prepare to make the obsession around our Crown Prince *worse*.

Stars help me.

I wake up already hearing the muffled noise of patrons beyond the divining room door. Even the sun hasn't been awake long enough to break the cold of the dustless floors. I drag out my morning tasks. I try on three different outfits, brush my hair until it shines, wipe down the divining table, and read through every newsletter dropped off by messenger bird.

Ever since Lady Gilda got hold of a printing press and started printing *Gilda's Gab,* all the court gossips decided to invest in one themselves. Lady Ziza Lace's *Lacy Things* is the most engrossing rag, thanks to her sordid descriptions of Cyrus that could double as an anatomy class. Today, the newsletters fight for readership by doing profiles covering everything from the prince's favorite foods to his birth constellation. He's a Swan born under a quarter moon, whatever that means.

I fold the newsletters into paper gliders and fling them off the balcony. The din in my antechamber has become background noise at this point, punctuated by the occasional shriek. I'll never be ready to face it, but I'll have to.

Finally, taking a deep breath, I open the door—

To sparkly, ruffly chaos.

The antechamber is packed—arm to arm, breast to breast, tighter than a goat cart heading to market—with every eligible lady in the Sun Capital. If the announcement was crowded, the sight before me is a *suffocation*.

I can make out some of the shouting:

"I EARNED MY FAIRIES, YOU NECTAR-SHILLING RATFACE!"

"—Prince Cyrus's favorite color? I need to go to the tailor later for a new shawl."

"—could grate a radish against those new muscles of his—"

"The Seer is *finally* here!"

A fatigued sigh scrapes from my throat. One nightmare after another. I should be thankful for being in demand, though. The public route up the Seer's tower involves two hundred stairs crawling with slippery vines and no railings. It's a hazard on a sunny day and a death sentence on a rainy one. The fact that these ladies marched up here in the foggy dawn just to hear what I have to say—well, in these tumultuous times of throne-changing, that's job security.

First in line is a gap-toothed girl, standing inches from where the door had been. She bows low and begins reciting the formal greeting: "I seek your wise words, Sighted Mistress. Your connection to the Fates is blessed and—"

I wave her in, already tired. "Yes, yes, let's get this over with."

She scurries across the threshold. "This is so exciting. My friends have all had fortune readings from you and they said it was the most interesting experience and you were such a strange delight—oh, strange in a good way, of course. . . ."

We settle in the center of the room, on opposite sides of a carved marble table hefted up by four serpentine dragons. A tea set and a stack of fortune cards are set aside, to be used upon request.

The girl—Sicene, she called herself at some point during her chatter—looks around the room wondrously. "It's so empty here—not that that's bad. It's clean, I mean. Simple living is healthy living, as my father used to—"

I clear my throat. "What would you like to see?"

"Oh, yes, um. I'd like to know what the future holds for me with regard to His Highness Prince Cyrus. If that's possible."

I hold out my ungloved hands, palms up. "Give me your hands, and we'll begin."

Sicene happily does, and I close my eyes. In my mind, unrooted to the earth and somewhere only the stars fathom, another pair of eyes opens.

Sicene, shopping in the Palace District with her sisters, their chattering effuse.

The royal caravan parading down a cobblestone street. Prince Cyrus's reflection fills the carriage window. He's the loveliest thing she's ever seen.

Gold—a flash of the palace ballroom? A tinkle of music echoes, muffled and distant.

I search a while longer but there isn't much else. The Fates are wholly unconcerned with this girl. It's about what I expect; we're not all princesses or plucky orphans or, stars forbid, plucky orphan princesses, with grand destinies to fulfill.

My tongue searches for something cryptic to offer her. "You might have an enlightening conversation with Prince Cyrus." Sicene's talkative, and if I mention this, she'll have the confidence to do it. "They might be the only words you ever exchange, but if you find the *right* words, he will treasure them forever. Don't lose hope."

Tiny gasp escaping her, she clutches my hands tightly. "I won't! Happy to even be in his *thoughts*."

I indulge her rambling about potential conversation topics for a while longer before shooing her off. She throws a generous offering in the fountain on her way out.

After Sicene, the pattern continues: patrons filter in, their hands falling expectantly into mine. Their hearts belong to the prince, but their hunger belongs to me. "Do you see love?" most ask, too shy or coy to utter anything more specific, even though everyone is here for the same reason.

As I traverse more threads, I build out a better scene of the ball: twirling gowns, outlandish masks, enough towering cakes to feed our army. A gent in a golden fox mask sticks out in particular—the subject of every attendee's attention—and I'm confident enough that he's Cyrus that I suggest to a few patrons to seek out this person. "For good luck," I say, to be enigmatic.

I get insufferable patrons, too, like Lady Mirabel, who doesn't like my outspokenness but still puts silvers in the offering fountain like the rest of them.

"You think you're being funny, witch," she says, "but the only thing you're showing off is your jealousy. You have to cause a *scene* to be noticed, while His Highness can enrapture a room with just his gaze! Oh, I bet deep down, you don't even *want* him to find his bride."

"*Ooh*, you caught me." I wave my fingers spookily, snickering as she shies away. But my spirits are doused as a bright glow zooms into my face and squeaks at me. Glittering dust tickles my nose; I sneeze. "No fairies in the divining room!"

Mirabel scowls but makes a gesture to shoo it away. When it doesn't leave, she takes a golden vial from her purse and drops a golden bead of ambrosia onto her thumb. The glowing fairy descends onto it and, in a blink, licks it clean before buzzing tipsily out the window.

I then take great pleasure in giving Mirabel a terse reading about how she'll drown herself in drink and embarrass herself. She flounces off after spitting in my face.

Next is a surprising patron: Lady Ziza Lace, niece of the Lord of the Fourth.

Before her newsletter, Ziza was best known for her many near-engagements, a list reputed to be longer than Auveny's tax records. Her reputation spans both sides of the sea; she often travels to Yue to visit her father's side of the family. I heard she planned to be a spinster after finding every suitor unworthy of her hand. Now in her thirties, with successful ventures of her own, I don't expect her to be interested in the prince.

Black ringlets frame her pearly, overpowdered face. She's squeezed into an ochre dress with a bodice tight enough to milk cows. Everything it's lifting bounces when she sits down. "Did you read today's *Lacy Things*? What'd you think of the constellation analysis?"

Ugh, birth constellations. If Cyrus really cared about false divinations, he'd outlaw *those*. "I don't really deal in—"

"As a quarter-moon Swan, Prince Cyrus is a naturally private person. He likes riddles and keeping tidy, and dislikes obnoxious people."

I open my mouth, then close it again. "Does anyone *like* obnoxious people?"

"I do. I'd be a hypocrite otherwise." Ziza cackles and leans over the divining table with a gleam in her eye. "So, Miss Lune. Tell me who it will be—the bride Prince Cyrus will choose."

My brows rise. She couldn't know of the king's plans.

She laughs again. "It won't be me! I'm ambitious, not delusional. Consider the odds: he's only going to marry one girl—one girl *at a time*. Not good odds at all. But the future queen can have as many friends as she likes."

So this is her aim—smart. Even better to befriend a queen before she's crowned, to make the connection seem more genuine. "If I knew the answer, we wouldn't be having this bride search in the first place," I say coolly, reaching for my pot of cold tea. Chatty patrons like Ziza parch me.

"Well, that's a pity." Ziza slumps in her chair. "My uncle thinks there's a chance Cyrus *doesn't* find his true love. I know Sighted Mistress Felicita might have been mad, but the Council seems very anxious about her prophecy still. I heard they're considering Lord Fidare of the Tenth again."

As I pour into my cup, it nearly overflows. "For the throne?"

Lord Fidare, lovingly nicknamed "Fifi" among impolite company, is older cousin to Cyrus and Camilla. The Council of Dukes made a considerable effort to get King Emilius to appoint him as heir instead when Cyrus fell gravely ill at fifteen and the fear of his curse reached a mania.

But I heard what they shouted behind closed doors, what they whispered to each other when they thought they were among friendly company—their push for Fidare wasn't born from fear. No, the dukes didn't like that the prince met so briefly with their sons and daughters and preferred the company of a Balican—Dante. Nor did they like that he was so stubbornly vocal against the Fairywood burnings and ambrosia fad that's made them rich.

Ultimately, Cyrus got better and King Emilius sent Fifi to the borderlands to preside over the Tenth Dominion instead, where he's been for the last four years. Haven't heard a peep about it since—until now.

Ziza flaps a hand. "Oh, but it's just noise. The Council can't push for anyone while Cyrus is alive. His Majesty would never replace his son! I do wonder if Lord Fidare will be at the ball, though."

I lift my cup to my lips. "Fifi— Lord Fidare is already engaged." To some Yuenen mercantile heiress, from what I recall.

"You say 'already engaged,' and I say 'not yet married,'"
she declares, and I nearly choke on my gulp. "Wouldn't *you*
prefer Fidare on the throne?"

I snort automatically. Fifi's a nice gent—too nice—but
he's about as sharp as a loaf of bread. There's no question
he'd end up the puppet of the other dukes if he ruled, and
the other dukes aren't interested in anything but multiplying
their own coin.

"You wouldn't?"

I look up and find Ziza appraising me as much as I am
appraising her. "What do you mean?"

She shrugs. "Forgive me if I speak too frankly, but the
animosity between you and Prince Cyrus is well-known. I
myself wondered if he would return from his tour with a
poached Seer and replace you. Verdant has two Seers, after
all, and he visited their court, did he not?"

A prickle of a threat runs down my spine. "Replacing a
sitting Seer is unprecedented in Auveny."

"Ah, but it's a king's job to set precedent. You are a
dangerous woman, Miss Lune, and I mean that in the best
sense." Ziza's fingers clink with a dragon's hoard's worth of
rings as she folds them together. Her smile could cut glass.
"Kings may rise and fall by the love of their people, but a
Seer demands nothing as fickle as love. It is *we* who demand
you. Your Fate-blessed words carry weight with or without
a formal title. Words that could prevent His Highness from
taking the throne, if you wanted to."

My eyes narrow. Treasonous. *But true.* I could foretell
any number of dreadful things about his reign and send
Cyrus's coronation plans spiraling; it'd have consequences,

like any knife to the back, but I *could* do it. Easy as a whisper, as long as people believed me.

But . . . I couldn't stomach giving the dukes an easy win. I dislike Cyrus, but he's right to demand integrity from them.

I don't receive as many patrons from the countryside, but I see enough in their threads to paint a picture of struggling villages. It doesn't match up with the wealth that floods in from their dominions. In the threads of lords, I see their safes full of coin and smudged ledgers, and I wonder what they've done to make the math favor them. Greed is more common than flies, but it still repulses me when I think too long about it; they already have so much.

I might admire the prince's idealism if he had practical plans attached to it. But he'd have a better time trying to squeeze integrity out of rocks.

No, I wouldn't choose the wolfish Council or Lord Fidare or some other untested scheme over Cyrus. But the possibility of my betrayal exists, like a weapon sheathed.

Without breaking my gaze, I swallow any hint of temptation. "I think you speak too frankly."

Lady Ziza bows her head, a tiny smile playing on her lips. "My apologies, Sighted Mistress."

The patrons who come in after Ziza are not nearly as interesting as her. For a brief while, I'm thankful, until the hours start feeling like days. Beyond divining love lives, I also give readings to a woman investigating a family secret, travelers from Yue seeking approval from the Fates for their crusade, a farmer who wants to know what his newly bought magic seeds will sprout into—my Sight doesn't work on inanimate objects, but my regular eyes could see they were dried peas.

When the bells strike seven, I turn away anyone still waiting and go upstairs and fall back onto my bed.

People exhaust me.

I shut my eyes—just for a rest. All the threads I traced today meld together into blurry snatches of the Sun Capital and masked revelers. Visions of the past imprint into my memory easily, but trying to remember threads of the future can be like cupping water with open hands.

I hear the clock tower again—eleven tolls this time. Night falls into further darkness and stars light up the sky, spinning and spinning, fluttering and twirling. . . .

No, not stars.

Fairies. A sky full of fairies.

I'm dreaming.

I open my eyes—and the fairies don't go away. They hover like golden ornaments, silent save for the hum of their wingbeats.

I am on my feet, standing on nothing. No matter how often it happens, this slipping between waking and dreaming never gets easier to distinguish. As I reach out, a trio of fairies land on my knuckles. Their tiny limbs tickle. At least with dreamed fairies, I don't sneeze.

It is time, voices in the wind rasp. *They will rise—beast and briar—at last, at last.*

A shiver runs through my body. The wind dies down.

One fairy crawls to the tip of my finger and tugs. It's

too small and bright for me to see what it's gesturing at, but it keeps pulling, hard as a pinch, like it wants to show me something.

I walk forward.

Another step, and the darkness seems to part. Craggy edges of underbrush take shape where nothing existed before. Under my toes, moss springs to life. When I breathe, a chill fills my lungs.

The rest of the fairies surge into the underbrush. I follow the path they light, elbowing through boughs and vines. Thorns tear tiny cuts into my skin. My grip is slippery as I clamber in deeper, but I maneuver with the grace of memory: I'm a little thief again, weaving among the clotheslined rooftops.

This place doesn't feel like a forest. There are no tree trunks, no ferns or stone, only ropes of leaves, twisting and twining, stretching toward some center. When I halt long enough for the rustling to fall silent, I hear a steady pounding, and the vines around me pulse to the same beat. Like a heart.

I shouldn't be in real danger, but I'm unsettled just the same. I quiet my breathing and check every footstep. The fairies get scarcer. A sliver of moon breaks through the growth to light a gap in the greenery. In the knot of bramble ahead, something is caught—

A body.

A boy.

Lashed upright, eyes shut, lips as red as fruit. So beautiful, even I want to kiss him once.

The prince.

His chest rises and falls, the only movement there is. He's sleeping, not dead, though he's pale as death. I'm shaking as I near. The shadows around his eyes are bruises; his mouth is split with a gash. It's easy to hate Cyrus during my waking hours, but here in my dreams, he's just a pawn of prophecy. He might die before the summer, if everything those voices told me is true.

A budding tendril threads through his hair and curls near his cheek. I can *see* it growing before my eyes, and it unnerves me enough that I lift a thumb to brush it away.

His eyes fly open. I recoil.

Thorny vines snake around his body, drawing pinpricks of blood that bloom into roses. As the leaves shift away, his ragged shirt comes into view, stained rust brown across his front.

The wind fills with whispers. I hear none of it. I can only focus on Cyrus's piercing stare, green as the tangle surrounding him.

"My curse," he utters like an accusation. "My ruin."

The growth swallows him.

5

THE KING TASKED ME WITH BUILDING OUT
Cyrus's future.

My dreams tell me that Cyrus might not *have* a future.

Dante says that everyone has dreams. But the way he's described them, they're very different from the kind I have. The last one he told me about, he was riding a frog into his hometown to meet his sister to congratulate her on her new carrot.

"You don't have a sister," I told him. "And why would you congratulate anyone for a carrot?"

"Exactly," he said. "That's just how dreams are."

I didn't understand. Everything I've ever dreamed has happened or will happen—or was *meant* to happen. And now, I'm getting cryptic messages directed toward me from gods and fairies and dream princes, when I've never had these kinds of omens before.

I can't warn Cyrus about this.

My ruin, his dream-self accused.

I believe it.

Maybe there's another way. It wouldn't be the first time I

changed destiny. That was how this trouble started: I pulled a prince out of danger when I wasn't supposed to. There must be other things the gods want besides the prince's life or mine. Can Cyrus even die before Felicita's prophecy comes to pass? Maybe it's all connected. Or maybe I'm going mad. . . .

I'm absolutely going mad.

Between the bedlam of the readings and my anxious nights, I lose track of time. A week passes and I have to meet with the king again. He requests an update on my progress, and I scrounge up meager excuses for why Cyrus doesn't know of his fated bride yet.

"It is important to be fastidious. If he suspects the falsehood, the idea will not plant," King Emilius says. "But the ball is approaching."

"I understand, Your Majesty."

He nods, concern tightening his gaze despite his smile. There is never an exact threat behind the king's words, but I can sense it in his habit of discarding advisors and dukes when they are no longer of use, in the grandness of his visions and his ability to achieve them. I've seen maps of Auveny from previous decades. This kingdom is now twice as big as it was when King Emilius's reign began—and it's still growing.

You can't accomplish something like that without being pragmatic to a fault.

Though the king has raised me like his own blood, I'm still disposable—unlike his own blood. If I can't pull this off, I don't know how eager he'll be to support me when

Cyrus finally ascends. I've ridiculed it, but I can imagine dozens of scenarios where Cyrus follows through on his threats to remove me. Even the court gossips see it as a possibility; with the accuracy they have, I might not be the only prophet here.

Better to be pleasantly surprised than vulnerable. I've clawed my way up to the very pinnacle of this kingdom, and it's a long fall down.

After the meeting, I head straight to the second floor of the palace to seek the prince in his quarters. This will be inelegant, but I can't hope for a perfect place and time.

I knock on his bedroom doors, which Cyrus has learned to lock, and I wait. Glancing around, I see his antechamber still hasn't changed much. It's furnished to make him look impressive: framed curios, ornate books, an astrolabe—all pristine and unused.

I knock again.

The door to an adjacent room opens. I shirk, startled.

Cyrus stares out from the shadows of his study, bags under his eyes and a red mark on his cheek as if he fell unconscious on the hilt of a paper knife—a monogrammed one, if the backward *CL* is any indication. I feel like I discovered him naked; he isn't wearing any glamour.

He rubs his eyes and quickly tugs at his wrinkled shirt. "What do you want?" he mutters, not quite low enough to hide a sleepy rasp.

An urge rises to smooth that mark from his cheek, like how I wanted to brush away that tendril in my dream. I always liked him better like this, not that he cares. Glamours make him look so predictable. But seeing him worn makes me wonder what he's been doing, when usually I don't think of him at all.

I stick out my hand. "A truce. For Dante's sanity, if nothing else."

Cyrus glances down, unfazed. "Did you think I wouldn't notice your hands aren't gloved?"

For the love of— "This isn't a *trick*, Princey. I just—"

"If you want to apologize to me, it should be before the entire court."

I bristle. I'd choke on my pride if I tried to swallow it. "Did I offer an apology? I offered a *truce*."

"Not interested." Cyrus grabs the doorknob.

I throw an arm out, pushing the door wide open. "You look awful, Princey, you must know that." I snort as he reflexively musses his hair; I can't believe he's actually self-conscious. "What are you losing sleep over? The ball? The Council? Heard they're bringing up Fifi again. Honestly, you *should* let me see your threads in a proper reading. I'm not interested in your boring memories; I was probably around for most of them, for stars' sake. But I can warn you of what's to come."

Ink scents the air as Cyrus sways closer, brow furrowed. "Did you talk to my father before coming here?"

"We had our meeting."

"What did he ask you to do?"

I resist flinching. His tone isn't accusing, but I sense another question lurking beneath. "Nothing. I only gave him updates. I had a lot of readings this week."

"You should know that my father may reward loyalty, but he has none himself."

Is that a threat or—he couldn't be trying to *warn* me? "He's the *king*. We *all* have to be loyal."

Cyrus doesn't answer immediately, his chest rising and falling behind his gauzy tunic. "Some are more loyal than others."

My lips pinch as he retreats into his study, the slouch of his body indicating he's done humoring my presence. No matter how often we genuinely try to make amends, it always comes back to this: a trade of trust that neither of us is willing to give first.

"Cyrus," I say, knowing it'll be futile.

He shuts the door.

⚬⚬⚬

My next few nights of sleep are less jarring, filled with the kinds of visions I've had my whole life. I dream of pastoral scenes—homes warm with supper, herders chatting in languages I don't understand, tusked beasts of burden roaming shrubby hills. This morning, I wake from a dream of a journey at sea that must have happened long ago, on the decks of a massive, shallow ship with a construction unlike any of our current vessels.

In more leisurely times, I might try to figure out exactly what era I saw, whether the ship had Auvenese or Yuenen origins or maybe even that of a collapsed culture that we only have relics of; there are rumors of a third continent on the other side of the world. I may not act humble before the courtly folk, but the breadth of my visions subdues me into a speck. We don't realize the scope of what we don't know. What lies on the deep-sea floor or in the ether between stars? Even the heart of the Fairywood, so close to us, remains uncharted.

Right now, I only have one dream I want to decipher. The dream I had about Cyrus wasn't like my usual visions, nor quite like the dreams that other people have. It felt *made* for me. The setting didn't seem real, but it might have been based on something real, like the Fairywood.

That's where I'll start searching for answers.

My tower has been open for over two straight weeks, and the patrons have finally winnowed enough for me to take a free day. I head into the palace library without the fuss of my robe and gloves, spinning in light summer wear: a creamy blouse with a wide lace neckline and a skirt striped with silver threads cinched high on my waist.

The stacks are dizzying in all directions, nearly as tall as the arched ceiling. I choose an aisle where I once spent an afternoon reading about Fairywood botany and prowl from ladder to ladder, peering at spines. There are mostly folktales and medicine books. A few thick tomes on cultivation of fayflowers are well-worn.

A leather book embellished with gold script catches my eye: *Traditions & Magics of the Wood*. I slide it out and flip it open. Thank gods—diagrams. Some of these books have tiny squashed text that may as well be pages of solid ink.

"Violet?"

Below, Dante is peering around the corner, looking neat in his vest and bow tie. An emerald teardrop dangles from his left ear and scruff feathers his chin, grown out for the ball. He thinks it makes him look roguish; I think he looks like an overworked student who forgot to shave.

"Need assistance?" he asks.

Where to begin that isn't *My dreams are threatening me* or *If either Cyrus or I had to die, who would you miss more? This isn't a rhetorical question.*

"No, I'm all right," I say. Tucking the book under my arm, I slide down the ladder.

"Traditions & Magics?" He points at it. "That's an old one—should still be helpful, though. The previous Balican archivist translated it, so they wouldn't have skipped over the best bits."

"The best bits?"

"You know, the commentary. The reasons why we do things the way we do." Ever the scholar. "Everything the head Auvenese archivist translates from Balica reads like a how-to manual, and it's a shame."

I follow Dante out of the stacks to the study tables, where a blackboard is scrawled with his messy handwriting.

"By the way, has Camilla been in?" he asks.

In addition to archivist work, he also tutors the princess twice a week—hypothetically, anyway. She usually skips. "Haven't seen her. Probably busy with her *Masked Menagerie.* Everyone is." Flopping into a chair, I dangle my arms over the sides, grousing, "It's ridiculous. I got a patron two days ago *literally* foaming. She drank these drafts some peddler claimed would make her more alluring, only they missed mentioning they'd make her alluring to *flies*."

Wiping down a side of the blackboard, Dante turns a history of borderland disputes into chalk dust. "You don't often get a chance to become queen. May as well give it your best shot, even if that chance is slim."

"*Knife*-slim. It's not worth the energy, let alone your pride. Don't get me started on the ones who are actually in love with Cyrus. They don't know what he's like at all." Toying with the fluffy end of a quill, I deflate farther into my seat. "He's still being a wart. Doesn't want my help unless I grovel. Couldn't you convince him to give me a chance?"

He glances over his shoulder, surveying the empty stacks and shut doors. "I don't approve of your, ah, less-substantiated prophecies either. If that's how you're planning to *help* him."

I scrunch my nose. "I bet if you had a crown on the line, you'd let me make one." I only glimpse the edge of a grin before Dante turns back around.

"It's not that dire."

"Are you sure? He just pretends everything's okay. Look: it's in Cyrus's interest to become king, it's in my interest to get Cyrus to trust me, and it's in your interest to have us get along. Win-win-win."

"It is in my interest to better this world, for the sake of us all living in it," Dante says lightly as he assembles a tall column of books. Before I can warn him about throwing out his back, he lifts the whole thing with relative ease; archivists moving library stacks are in better shape than our soldiers. "And my first course of action will be finding the princess, so that she can have a proper history lesson on Auvenese-Balican treaties."

Not wanting to be left alone, I join him in scouring the palace for Camilla. We check through the courtyards and training grounds she frequents. I go upstairs to her bedroom and wonder if I'll find her dead asleep, blinds drawn, sleep mask on, a girl in both arms. Even with the ladies, Camilla outmatches Cyrus—*pining for the Lidines* is a seasonal euphemism in the Sun Capital—but since she won't be sovereign, no one pays her any mind except gossips.

But she's not in her quarters either. My ankles are on the verge of giving up when, finally, Camilla's frustrated shout echoes from the ballroom:

"Bread, bread, bread, bread, I'm *sick* of bread!"

The behemoth space has been cleared out, chandeliers brought down for dusting, the floors waxed. White-coated servants bustle past with trays of desserts all bound for Camilla, the only occupant of a table that could entertain fifty. She has a breadstick in both hands and is gesturing wildly at what appears to be a replica of the palace done entirely in baked goods.

"If I see *another* bread sculpture, I'm going to strap it to the next passing toad-brain and lock them in an aviary. The Masked Menagerie is the event of the decade. We can at least have a fruit arrangement! An ice sculpture!"

"In summer, Your Highness?" Next to her, her lady-in-waiting jots rapidly in a journal.

"If we can have heat in winter, why can't we have ice

in summer? Forget the ice, then—a piece made of spun sugar? Chocolate?"

As I sidle up to Camilla, I'm careful to not trip over the princess's inky-blue cat, Catastrophe, who twines around my legs. She's apparently dessert-tasting as well, if the crumbs along her whiskers are any indication. "Have you considered bread?" I ask.

A breadstick smacks my cheek as Camilla swings around. "Not funny, Violet."

There's a joke among farmers that Auveny would turn into a sea of alcohol if the fields were left to rot, for all we sow besides fayflowers are grain and grapes. Most of our produce is imported from Balica, where the soil is richer and hasn't been exhausted by fayflower farming. Over-ground transport to the Sun Capital takes weeks, though, and sometimes you still end up opening the cold wagons to a bunch of spoiled fruit, which means spoiled celebrations.

"There you are," Dante pants as he catches up to me. He drops his stack of books on the table in front of Camilla, sending a bouquet of used skewers clinking over the silverware. "Is this where you've been all week, Princess? Eating?"

"*Planning.* I've taken on the task of deciding the Masked Menagerie's desserts. The first step is, obviously, sampling all of them." Camilla offers him a plate of caramel-doused cakes, each no bigger than a coin and with a stick poking out of it.

"You know, your lessons are for *your* benefit."

"And yet, I sense no benefit. I don't plan to dabble in politics."

"Anything that comes out of your mouth *is* politics," he

sputters, yanking his bow tie loose for breath. "Just because you aren't on the throne doesn't mean—"

Camilla yawns loudly, tipping herself out of the seat. She scoops up Catastrophe, who yowls. "I have a few errands in the city. If you want to keep arguing, you're welcome to come with. Company always makes the trip better."

Dante and Camilla squabble the whole way to the stables. I tag along, still hoping they can clear my head of other noise.

We take a white-horse carriage instead of opting for any discreet transport. As we ride out of the grounds, I glimpse Cyrus in the plaza—at least, I *think* it's him. His frame is barely visible amid the swarming ladies, many of whom I recognize from my readings. His guards stand nearby. Part of the royal twins' popularity is due to their approachability; when you can walk right up to them, it's easy to believe that anyone could grace their arms.

I bet Cyrus is preening like a peacock.

The plaza disappears from view. I lean against the glass windows to watch the Palace District roll past. The jewel of the city's seven districts, it's the oldest and best-kept part of the city, flaunting centuries of architectural styles. Stark white marble apartments nest between newer buildings painted in pastel. Lacy awnings and swirling iron fixtures outfit storefronts. Along the walkways, magnolia trees are blooming.

The carriage shakes as Dante and Camilla insist on gesticulating like an orchestra to make their points.

"As terrible as it sounds, what if something happened to Cyrus?" Dante's finished going through the logical arguments and has now moved on to emotional appeals. "You should be ready to take over."

"What if!" Camilla crows from the seat across from me. "What good is a 'what if'?"

More likely than you think. "It *should* be you on that throne," I say, playing with the tail end of my braid. Camilla is a firstborn, after all, if only by half an hour. "Even if Cyrus wasn't cursed."

Camilla smiles. We've discussed this before. "Power is nice, but responsibility is not, and I would not like to see this kingdom burning from dragonfire because I provoked someone. Which, stars know I will. Right now, I have no meetings to attend, no feet to kiss, I can ride through the countryside at my whim—why would I want to rule?"

I do understand. I just hate when someone else wields power over me, so I'd rather wield it myself. Camilla has never been afraid of losing her way of life. I have no family to fall back on.

The arguing finally stops when Dante steps out at the courier's to check for letters from home. Camilla and I take the carriage down another few streets, and we arrive at the tailor's to pick up her new suit for the ball. Her fairies will put glamours atop, but she still wants a fashionable base.

"I'm thinking of glamouring wings," she says, flexing at the panel of mirrors. The changing room in the back of the tailor's is bigger than apartments I've squatted in. "Too much?"

"Probably."

"Excellent. What are you wearing?"

"I'm not going to the ball."

She pulls off her shirt and tries another, this one deep crimson. "The palace's fairies will conjure up something nice for you."

I grit my teeth. "That isn't the problem."

"You're right. The *problem*, Violet Lune, is you've been cooped up in that tower. The Masked Menagerie is going to do double duty—getting Cyrus married and getting *you* out of your shell."

"I don't need to get out of my shell, other people need to *cram themselves back into theirs.*"

"You should figure out what dress you want, otherwise the fairies will decide on their own to drape you in enough taffeta and tassels to rival the ballroom curtains." She poses at the mirror, then after a *hmm* unfastens another shirt button for an even lower neckline. "And I know you're not allergic to their glamours, so you can't use that excuse this time."

"I'm still allergic to their dust!"

"So put a clothespin on your nose. Ooh, Lady Emmacine has a baby shower this afternoon. We should go. It'd be good practice for you to mingle."

Accepting invitations to parties is a surefire way to spend four hours playing divine matchmaker to frisky aristocrats who think drinking wine is a hobby. "I'd sooner go toad-kissing."

"See, that's exactly the kind of thing you shouldn't say to people," she tuts. "You are pretty and clever, but you're as charming as the backside of a mule, Violet, and that needs to change. It's bad enough that people look at you like some common witch."

I scowl. If it keeps these people away, maybe it's a good

thing. I am common, I am a witch—it's the truth. I want to be respected, not liked. I don't want to be trying to impress people at all if I can help it.

Shirt hanging loose, Camilla peers out of the changing room to call for the tailor's assistant, who rushes toward her red-faced, gesturing futilely at her to cover up. As Camilla sifts through fabrics for yet another outfit she wants commissioned, I tromp outside for fresh air.

The streets are busy; everyone's shopping for the ball that will happen in two weeks. Golden-winged fairies flit overhead like daytime stars; a drunk one splats into a freshly washed window.

The Lord of the Sixth strolls by with his family. "Back in my day, we didn't have such a wealth of ambrosia that everyone had a fairy on hand," I hear him tell his daughter. "We put on powder and arsenic like everyone else."

I consider buying a tartlet from a street vendor before remembering the mountains of dessert in the palace. I go sit on the carriage's steps instead. As I do, passersby slowly turn toward something up the street, and my own eyes follow.

What in the *stars*?

Dusty pastel blobs are rumbling toward us, taking the shapes of dresses and waving handkerchiefs. There's shrieking. One lone figure sprints ahead of the mob, the collar of his shirt blown open by the wind and his legs pumping as if his life depends on it. I nearly choke on spit when I see his face.

It's Cyrus.

Running from a stampede of his admirers.

His guards clang far behind, slowed down by the weight

of their armor. Bystanders are stumbling out of the way. A few *join in*. But why—

"A PRIVATE DATE FOR WHOEVER PLUCKS THE FLOWER FROM HIM!" someone hollers.

Ah—Cyrus is close enough now that I can see the pink bloom pinned to his breast, bobbing along as he flees. He probably tried to be playful and make a little competition, except it got out of hand.

"THROW US THE FLOWER!"

"THROW US *YOUR SHIRT*!"

To put it lightly.

As they barrel in my direction, I scramble inside the carriage. Mobs are like weather: part chemistry and part chance, a concoction of sticky emotions shaken with a furious hand. Anyone who gets in their way once they set their hearts on something may as well be mincemeat.

Poking my head out the window, I see a girl in what's probably her best gown tackle Cyrus to the ground half a street away. The swarm grabs him by the shirt—well, by the everything. A dozen hands claw for the flower, tearing it to pink shreds.

But the hysteria doesn't end. There's a scrabble for the petals, then for the prince's limbs, all akimbo and no longer in his control. The first of his guards has just descended, but they can't make any headway as the chaos swells and pulls in gaping onlookers. One girl with a shoe-shaped mark on her forehead tunnels out of the wall of skirts lugging him by the legs.

"Let's be *civilized*—" Cyrus gasps above the crowd, pretty cheeks bulging red.

Gods, he's about to be drawn and quartered.

The bottom half of his shirt's buttons burst apart and someone clinging on his hem trips backward, taking down an entire stack of people like bowling pins. Cyrus tears free, shirt open, every newly toned muscle in view.

Shrieks escalating, the chase resumes.

I press back into the plush of the carriage bench away from the window, hand over my mouth, stomach aching with laughter. He doesn't know I saw the whole thing.

The carriage rattles and the door yanks open. "Sorry, I have to—"

Cyrus stares inside. I stare back at him and his half-covered torso, both desperately in need of sanctuary. In that second, I swear I can hear the Fates laughing.

No, the Fates aren't laughing; it's just the hysteria behind him. Cyrus snaps out of it and tries to climb in. I'm on my feet in a blink, blocking his way with my whole body.

"Let me in!"

"*Absolutely* not!" I nearly yank the door closed onto his fingers, but he wedges it open.

"You're always right, I'm always wrong, now and forever—"

It's the panic, not his words, that convinces me. Because the longer we stay here, the more likely I'm going to be trampled in that mob too, and wasn't I supposed to get him to trust me or something? It's hard to think as the shrieks hit a frequency that could shatter glass. *"Fine."* I step back. "But that won't always work—"

Cyrus catapults himself inside. He shouts at the driver, "Go, go, go! *What are you waiting for?*"

The carriage jerks into motion and my head hits the ceiling. The door slams shut and I tumble into Cyrus in a mess of elbows, nearly toppling both of us onto the floor. He catches me around the waist before we do.

"A little warning would be nice!" My vision steadies and I'm dimly aware of the sweat dampening my side and the fact that I'm crushed into his bare chest. "Camilla's back there—"

"She can take another carriage! Do you see what's chasing me?" he says, groaning. "It's the damn glamour. I put on too much."

I squint at him. His perfect face doesn't seem any different, but what do I know? Clearly everyone's seeing something I can't. "Well, congratulations, Princey, you can't even control your own admirers!"

Cyrus glares at me and I offer him only a tiny, bitter smile back.

"You can let go now, by the way."

It takes a second for him to register that I am in his lap and that his arm is pinned around my middle. He was red from running, but his flush deepens into a scarlet just before he drops me on the carriage floor.

6

IT'S A BUMPY RIDE.

Cyrus buttons up what's left of his shirt. I slump onto the opposite bench, arms crossed. The carriage slows down as it enters the narrow streets of the Arts District. Sledges transporting marble and lumber hold up traffic ahead. I can't hear his horde of admirers anymore, but if they're determined, they can't be far behind, and the royal carriage sticks out like snow in summer. It's only a matter of time before we get caught.

A few signs outside flash Yuenen characters. Soon, we'll enter the Moon District, and the pedestrian traffic might bring us to a full stop. I know these streets still. I could probably guide Cyrus through it, out to a place where he can escape back to the palace unseen.

I could also shove him out of the carriage.

I know I need to swallow my pride and learn to play nicely with him. I don't need Dante and the king and everyone else reminding me that Cyrus will ascend soon. If the prince lives long enough to take the throne, I might have to bite my tongue until it bleeds to get through it.

I had to earn my place in Auveny. My mother was exiled from the Kingdom of Yue, according to the orphanage that took me in. Some whip-scarred concubine who stabbed an official through the throat, then hid on a ship bound for the Sun Continent a thousand miles away. She ended up in the Moon District like most working-class Yuenen overseas, but she didn't last long; when she withered to sickness, she had nothing to leave me, not even a name. I made up my own after dreaming of a field of flowers in a color I'd never seen in such abundance. Like twilight painted across the earth.

Violets, an herbalist told me when I pointed to a dried batch of the same flowers at her stall. Weedy, stubborn *violets.*

I couldn't have been older than eight or nine when I ran away from the orphanage. The streets were dangerous, but I needed to know: what else from my dreams was out there?

I learned how to speak Yuenen like a hawker, how to speak Auvenese like a liar, how to be clever and observant and better than everyone else.

I had to, if I was going to hold anything that I could call mine.

So I know—I know what the smart thing to do is, but forgive me if I want to throw Cyrus to the mob anyway. It might not be wise or even all that satisfying, but the boy sitting across from me just had to be *born* to have everything, and he will never do enough to deserve it.

The carriage slows to a crawl, nudging through crowds that won't stop, though we have the right of way. The tall red sign of the Sweet Celestial Inn rises above the apartment blocks to mark the border of the Moon District.

As I take a deep breath, my squabbling pride simmers

down, quieter and quieter until it's drowned out by the squeak of wheels turning over cobblestone. I open the carriage door and grab Cyrus's forearm, careful to not graze his hands with my own.

He flinches at my bare touch. "What are you—"

"They'll catch us if we stay here." I clutch the carriage frame and spin on him. "We can lose them on the streets. Let's go."

Cast in dappled shadow, the prince's features don't seem as severe. Or maybe I just caught him in a genuine moment of surprise. "I don't know this area."

"I do."

He doesn't move.

"Or I can leave you here. It's your choice."

A heartbeat. Cyrus steps out, eying me with more confusion than mistrust. He tells the driver, "Go back to the palace. Lead them away."

Then he follows me into the marketplace.

I don't *want* to be dragging the prince around, but there's a satisfaction nonetheless, to roaming a place where I'm more comfortable than he is. There's little here that I can't get at more upscale Yuenen establishments in other districts, but I miss this atmosphere. Food vendors fill this avenue of the Moon District. The air is thick with smoke and grease, and we can hardly move without elbowing into some skewer or hot stove. Everyone around us shoves us onward; they don't care about who we are, prince or Seer or not—they have their own destinations to get to. The court thinks this slice of the Sun Capital is nothing but clutter and chaos, but they don't see how it's like the rapids of a river: chaotic but flowing, efficient in its own way.

We weave our way to an emptier edge of the marketplace. I grab a straw hat and a costume banyan jacket off a woman selling wares from a blanket, tossing her more silvers than they're worth. Cyrus declines the hat and pulls the banyan on. It's tight around his shoulders and doesn't wrap him neatly, but it covers his pitiful shirt. Continuing on, feet light as a pickpocket's, I guide us out of the marketplace through a side alley.

A butcher and a medicine shop have taken up the shuttered spaces that used to be here. The walls are painted over with a wash of white. Cyrus stops, craning his head up, then around. He won't find the exact memory he's looking for, but he recognizes the place well enough.

The street where I saved his life, seven years ago.

"You remember," I say.

He's silent.

Only a few more blocks divide us from the river. From there, we can follow the shores north to the Palace District without attracting much attention. I haul my skirts up as the streets turn muddy. We walk single file down a sliver of sidewalk keeping us above sewer water.

"Watch out," he says.

Cyrus throws an arm around me, pressing me to the wall. A wide handcart hauling dirt scrapes past us.

When the cart is gone, he doesn't move.

I've felt his gaze bearing on me since we left the carriage, and I meet it at last. His eyes are green as emeralds and just as bright and heavy, the jewels of an already handsome face. Even in a banyan that was likely made from bedding scraps, Cyrus looks like the hero of a storybook. That's the most unfair thing about him of all.

"Why are you helping me?" he asks. The question is quiet and curious.

Because I need you to trust me. Because I need to feed you lies from your father. Because it might be the last nice thing I do for you before you die.

I can only offer him a different truth, in the place of the ones I can't give him: "Because you will always have everything, and I will always be the one to compromise."

The faintest surprise furrows his brow. He searches my expression, but I don't wonder what he's thinking until his eyes linger on my lips for a beat too long. Somewhere in him is the boy who gave me the other half of my name. *Lune. Violet Lune, Violet of the Moon.* Such a pretty thing to gift me, before he knew any better. After I became his father's liar, we did nothing but argue.

But feuding has its own kind of intimacy.

I glance away. "It's like I've said. We can spend the rest of our lives fighting, or we can help each other just enough so that we both get what we want. Then, we never have to speak to each other unless we need to."

"Swear your loyalty to me."

My gaze snaps back to him. "What?"

The edge of Cyrus's mouth curls up. "Swear your loyalty and I'll believe you. It's a small ask. You swore to my father."

"When I was a *child*." Because I had no other choice

if I wanted a place here, because I didn't yet grasp what kings did. "Couldn't I fake it? Cross my fingers behind my back?"

"Then fake it."

The words course up my throat, but my jaw refuses to move. I flush. "No."

"As I suspected—too prideful to truly compromise." His arm slackens, leaving a ghost of warmth where it'd been, and he walks past me toward the river path where the cobblestone turns into dirt.

"Wart," I mutter. I follow him, a little lightheaded. " '*Too prideful*' says the prince too prideful to accept anything less than a prostrating Seer."

"I have standards."

"Is that why you're entertaining any lady in the capital with a pair of lips?"

He doesn't turn fast enough to hide his smile. "I should be courteous to those who show me affection." Cyrus has a diplomatic response for everything.

The path widens as we arrive on the banks of the River Julep. The waves gleam like dragonscale, and a smattering of boats drift along its brackish waters. Idle fishermen play cards on a jetty. They look up at us briefly, pointing and chuckling, then resume their game. On the far shore, too distant for anyone to spot us, is the bustling boardwalk of the University District.

I kick up a flat rock to skip. "Aren't you curious about what I've learned from my readings? You're not the only one being hounded because of the ball. I've seen secret relationships, all sorts of courtiers you should be suspicious of . . ."

Cyrus stops walking long enough for me to fling the rock into the river, then graces me with the full distaste of his frown. "You shouldn't be rifling through your patrons' memories with your Sight."

"I can't help what I'm good at." I grin, having grown bold during our momentary cease-fire. "I found out a few fun things about the future, too. Girls you'll dance with. Council plans. You only have knowledge to gain, Princey—but you have to lose the moralizing."

He shakes his head. "Violet, do whatever you want. Just . . ." But he doesn't finish the sentence.

"Just what? Don't use what I see for my terrible, wicked ends? That's what you're always implying. I wouldn't lash out if you didn't single me out—it's that simple." I only meant to make small talk, but it's nice to say this aloud.

He still doesn't respond—probably because he has no good answer. I narrow the gap between us, unwinding my hands from behind my back to splay them before him, palms turned up.

I paced in my bedroom practicing this part: I offer to read Cyrus's threads. Tell him anything I truly see, of course—and then, pretend to see a vision of his true love. The one adorned in fayflowers and butterflies who will arrive at the stroke of eleven. The little lie gifted from his father.

But I didn't anticipate the question leaping to my tongue, now that he's here in the flesh: "What are you so afraid of when it comes to me?"

Something flickers in his eyes, as piercing as his earlier scrutiny—as if he knows something, like the Cyrus in my dreams knew. Lips chewed red, his coifed hair wilted and windswept, he isn't so far from the version of him wreathed in briars, ready for a darkness to swallow him.

My curse. My ruin.

A blink and measured breath later, the expression is gone. "You're imagining things," he says, stepping away, boots squelching and uncaring of the puddles on the path.

⚬⚯⚬

We make it back to the palace before anyone thinks we're dead. Camilla is tapping her feet at the entrance hall steps, not at all pleased. The replacement carriage that brought her and her enormous shopping haul home has driven away.

She doesn't let Cyrus pass inside until she gets an explanation for her missing carriage, and when Cyrus finally tells her what happened, Camilla bursts out laughing.

"I remember the first time I was chased down in the streets. You have to cultivate the attention like a garden," she tsks. "Set boundaries early, trim it back if you need to. An overloved plant drowns." She plucks at his raggedy sleeve. "So did you find anyone you like?"

Cyrus shakes his banyan off and leaves it pooled on the hall floor as he heads in. "Very much not."

"Oh, there *is* someone. Is she pretty?"

"I need a long bath."

"If you end up tossing her, send her along to me," she calls after him. She turns to me. "Is she pretty?"

"There's no one."

"Wonderful. We're all doomed."

I watch Cyrus go upstairs from the corner of my eye. Today was progress. But I only have two more weeks until the ball; progress isn't good enough. And he isn't my only problem.

Camilla has turned her attention to the bevy of servants bringing her shopping haul to her quarters. I spot a basket of clothes, a matching saber and pistol, a tower of hats, and three more unmarked boxes. "Ah—not those," she says, hustling after a boy leaving with a stack of books. "Take those back to the library."

They're the books Dante tried to give her—and the copy of *Traditions & Magics of the Wood* I left behind in the carriage. "Hold on, that's mine," I say, sliding it off the stack.

I bring the book and my weary bones back to my tower.

After climbing the excessive number of stairs to my bedroom, I go bathe off the day's sweat and dirt. Then I light a tray of candles and spend the evening reading by candlelight, legs dangling over the armrest of my writing chair.

The first third of *Traditions & Magics of the Wood* is devoted to medicine and poultices. I skim for descriptions of vines that grow quickly or anything related to roses, but the book talks of few true plants. Most plants, it claims, can't be relied upon to be the real thing in the mercurial woods, which can transform strange magic into tempting plants and berries.

The next section is about clearing the woods for habitation. All growth above the surface must be burned down, then a line of blood must be drawn on the ground as a border. Blood is the stuff of mortality, like oil to magic's water, and where blood stains the earth, no Fairywood grows.

Unlike common Auvenese sentiment, this text treats the Fairywood as something to be preserved. It goes on about things I never hear discussed: cleansing rituals, the proper disposal of the ashes, the importance of clearing no more than necessary because the destruction is permanent. The western side of the Sun Continent is a reminder of that: before the Lidines united the kingdom, centuries of bloody wars between feudal lords destroyed any Fairywood that once grew there. Even after two hundred years of peace, the Fairywood hasn't regrown on these lands.

As I'm yawning through blocky passages of text, one of Camilla's handmaidens comes by the tower with a basket of desserts from the earlier tasting. Only then do I realize I forgot to eat dinner and I'm starving. After she departs and I shut the door, I do a double take at the fountain at the entrance of my divining room.

I recently emptied the basin of coin, and the bottom is stained red—rust, I've always assumed. But having just read that chapter, I remember something I never thought much about:

The Fates are associated with blood.

That stuff of mortality, that tether to time, a thread un-raveling from ancestors to mother to us—blood rolls des-tiny's dice the moment we're born. The most devout say that our bodies are but Fates' vessels.

People used to offer blood, too. I've seen grandmothers keep bowls of goat's blood in their homes for luck, and if you explore certain copses outside the capital, you can still find altars where livestock was slaughtered in the name of the gods. I remember this past across my scattered dreams:

these practices faded when aristocrats started hiring fairies who refused to work in the presence of blood. Suddenly blood was a taint—it marred the beauty of glamours.

And those offerings? Unsightly and crude.

The statue at the fountain's center stares at me as I crouch down and draw a line along the bottom of the basin. Black dust speckles my finger.

This was once a vessel for blood.

How long has it gone unused?

I remember how the Fates spoke to me that night. They weren't indifferent beings. They were *spiteful*. Could the Fates be offended that we've stopped our worship—worse, that we've replaced them with earthly creatures? Some elders say fairy blessings are an insult to destiny, because they're now given to those who don't deserve them. Maybe there's truth to that.

Blood opposing magic, stars opposing earth.

What proof is there that gods have anyone else's best interests at heart?

When I return to my desk, I stare dully at the open book, rubbing my eyes. No amount of research will amend the fact that I don't know what the Fates really want. And I won't find the answer in some underpaid scholar's second-hand conjecture. Why am I pretending otherwise?

I bury my head in my arms. There's something here, if I only knew what I was looking for.

There you are.

The voice echoes in my ear, startling the breath from me as I sit up in my chair. I cough as I inhale something sweetly pungent—*roses?*—followed by a stink that makes my eyes water. Panic rises in my throat before my hands clamp down on my chair's wooden armrests, and I make sense of the pitch-dark.

I'm not in my tower at all. There is no desk or book or half-devoured dessert basket. This is the dark of emptiness.

I'm dreaming.

I've been looking for you, little star.

Toady hell, not the Fates again. When I hoped for answers, I didn't mean like this; this is why we use *gods* as a swear. *"What do you want?"* I shout. "I've had *enough*—"

You seek the prince's confidence.

I shut up.

I swear I can feel a presence smiling.

A *single* presence, I realize in a moment of calm. A single voice. Not the chorus of gods I encountered once before, who arrived with a gale of fragmented taunts.

Are you listening?

"Who are you? Are you a Fate?"

Answer my question, little star.

I stare into the dark, dimly aware of my insignificance and a gnawing, crunching fear. "I'm listening."

Good. Tell your prince these exact words.

If gods have throats, I just heard this one clear theirs.

The journey to love never runs smooth,
and yours, your father would not approve.

They will catch you by surprise, hidden in disguise,
but leave your grasp before midnight strikes.

"That's all?" I frown, scanning the empty dark for a figure, a face—anything. Those words sound like prophecy. "Why should I trust you?"

Do you trust anyone?

I scoff, but I don't reply. My tongue feels thick in my mouth. I should probably be more polite to a god; I could have worse allies.

I want to help you. The voice has a sultry quality, sly in the way Camilla can be. *I have seen your future, and I believe we have much to accomplish together.*

"Like what?"

I will tell you when the threads have finished playing out. They will betray you. They all will. Only then will you understand.

"Who? Understand *what*?" None of these is a real answer. I despise divine language.

That you are worthy of so much more, little star. That you should never again kneel for the scraps of kings.

7

TAPPING.

My head hurts. My cheek stings as if bitten, iron tang salting my tongue. I peel my face from the book page, damp with drool. How long have I been sleeping at my desk?

The light streaming through the window is thin, not enough to hurt my eyes. Draped behind me, my robe is silver-gray with fog.

More tapping.

My bones groan with regret as I uncurl from my sleeping position. Standing, I amble stiffly toward the noise. A shadow flutters at the windowsill. I expect to find one of the messenger pigeons that usually bring newsletters.

There's a snowy-white falcon instead.

I frown. A hunting bird has no business here.

Is Camilla on a hunt today? She'd be in the oak forests northeast of the Sun Capital, not near the tower. I unlatch the lock and swing open the window. The falcon hops in, chirping. A note is tied to its leg.

I remember now: Cyrus hand-raised a bird like this. He

took it on his tour, and I haven't seen it since. Its feathers used to be scraggly and dark.

I untie the paper. The falcon cocks its head to and fro until I give it a nibble of jerky and a short scratch under its beak, then it flies away.

The note only has two neatly penned lines:

I don't think I thanked you for yesterday, but I should have.

Thank you.

I snort, smiling. Leave it to Cyrus to be so completely aloof and to the point.

He went through the trouble of sending this, though, I guess. I crumple the note out of reflex but hesitate before flinging it into the fire grate.

Smoothing it out again, I fold it and slide it into the pages of *Traditions & Magics of the Wood* as a marker. A piece of sentiment, tucked away.

I have a prophecy to tell him today.

Navigating the maze of the palace courtyards and hallways takes delicate footwork if you're trying to get around quickly. One too-hasty step around the corner, and you'll be dragged into an undertow of scuttling servants or peering gossips.

I slip through conversation circles doing my usual round of half-hearted greetings, eavesdropping on talk of the Fairywood rot. News of it quietly spread over the last few weeks, downplayed as a nuisance that local patrols have already curbed.

But this latest round of whispers speaks of the Tenth Dominion instead of the Eleventh, where rot was first reported. Lord Fidare hasn't raised excessive alarm, as this new patch was easily burnt away, but clearly some advisors feel differently; they're concerned over the rot having jumped to a new location without warning or reason. I don't hear anyone speak of spontaneously spawning roses yet; the lack of a clear link to the prophecy might be all that's keeping these worries muted at the moment.

Outside of chatter, all else seems normal at lunch bell: no blood, no roses, no godly voices. Staring at the spread in the dining hall, I don't have an appetite, but I never deny a chance at food, so I tear off the soft parts from a loaf of bread and eat them with jam.

Cyrus usually has meetings with the Council around this time. I wander the halls looking for him as my thoughts bounce between *Maybe Sighted Mistress Felicita went mad from hearing gods, too,* and *If I had a better idea than listening to voices in my head, I'd be doing it.*

I peek into the grand ballroom, where the final preparations for the Masked Menagerie are underway. Wine barrels are stacked tall next to sculpture centerpieces. Ladders scale the walls and sparkling decorations drape from the ceiling. The palace probably employed half the artisans in the city, making this ball. The treasury is bursting at the moment; the Thirteenth's Dragonsguard raided a string of wealthy lairs during spring and the haul's caravan finally made it into the capital early this month.

Out of place and getting in the way of servants is a cluster of girls wandering the room. I recognize some from the group that chased down Cyrus. Their leader—I assume by how she walks ahead of the rest like a tour guide—is the Lord of the Thirteenth's quick-scheming daughter, Lady Mirabel.

"Remember this space. *Inhale* the space," she declares. "In a matter of days, this is to be your battleground, where you'll make your last stand to win the prince's heart, and all your hard work pays off. You'll need the whole package to survive: brains, beauty, and backstabbing." She must have spent all week coming up with that. "Keep insurance. Blackmail in your clutch. The wrong whisper around the room, and that's it—to the gutters you go!"

I try to keep a low profile as I cross the room, but one of the girls in the back starts waving frantically at me. "Seer!"

I cringe, recalling her bubbly face from a past reading. "Hello . . . Sicene, is it?" Reluctantly—it'd be more awkward if I don't—I move away from my hiding place by the coatracks.

"Yes! Have you any new foreshadowings about the ball?"

Mirabel scowls as attention turns away from her. "The Seer wouldn't know a frog from a prince if one kissed her! The unprofessional services I suffered—she'll tell you nasty things just because she's jealous!"

"Jealous of what?" I say coolly. "I'd take the frog over Cyrus. Unless the frog was you."

"Aha! A-*ha*!" She points vigorously at me, as if I've drawn a bull's-eye on myself. "She's proved it just now!"

"Mira." One of her frowning friends pulls her back before she throws herself at me.

"This court *tolerates* you, Seer. And that's generous!"

"I don't care," I say. "I would never exist just to be enjoyed." That's what porcelain plates are for, and sunrises and honey cakes and baby animals with heads too big for them to lift.

The girls sputter into gasps and giggles, and I'm puzzling out if what I said was really that funny when I hear footsteps behind me.

Followed by the silvery voice of the very person I was searching for: "What's going on?"

Wonderful—Cyrus caught me being petty for sport. He'll hold this over me for, oh, a decade.

I spin on my heel and spruce up a wide smile. "Princey. I was looking for you."

"Princey?" someone hisses behind me.

Cyrus dresses on the formal side for Council meeting days; his hair is slicked back and his shirt is buttoned to his neck, where a jabot frills. He fishes out a pocket watch and snaps it open and closed. "Looking for me for what?"

"We should discuss in private."

"If this is a waste of my time, I'm busy today."

"Why would you assume—" I grumble. Behind me, there's tittering. This is embarrassing. "I dreamed something, all right?"

He stares at me a little longer. Heaves a sigh. "Fine. Make it quick."

"Your Highness!" Mirabel shoulders past me to grip

Cyrus's arm. A few of his guards rustle with their weapons. "I know the Thirteenth Dominion is far away, but you're welcome to visit for as long as you like. My uncle hosts balls that are as splendid as this one will be."

Cyrus wears a new face suddenly, quick as the flip of a coin, his long lashes fluttering. "Thank you for the invitation, Lady Mirabel." Gods, his tone changes, too—sweet as honey. "I've already expressed my, ah, personal gratitude to your uncle for his contributions that are allowing such a lavish, even *overlavish,* Masked Menagerie."

"Anything for you. Do you think you might travel anytime soon?"

"I don't—"

"Not a big deal, if the answer is no. There are plenty of splendid things to do in the Sun Capital, too. . . ."

Mirabel begins rambling about the beauty of the riverfront and parks, and I can see Cyrus's smile cracking. His leg twitches like the reflex of prey, and I feel the hunger of the other girls encroaching at my back. Like decorative armor, the prince is polished and pretty, but unsuited for war, which is what this bride search is. Only this once, I'll offer him a reprieve, because *I* need to get on with my day, too.

I grab his other arm and start hauling him out of the room as Mirabel squawks. Cyrus stumbles before he finds his footing, rounding toward me with shock.

"You can't be rude but I can, so *let's go,*" I hiss to him, pulling hard enough on his cuff that the buttons snap apart. He finally falls in step with me.

An offended "Ugh!" from Mirabel echoes in our wake, and any further chatter is muffled by the sound of busy servants. Only laughter remains when I pull Cyrus into an empty vestibule.

His laughter.

It's bright and sudden and stops as soon as our eyes meet.

"Was that necessary?" Cyrus's smile curves into something sterner, just for me, and—gods—it makes me angry all over again.

"You're such a two-face," I snap before I remember I'm supposed to be establishing trust through our cease-fire, not dropping it like an expensive vase.

"Is the chronic liar telling me what to do?"

"You're a *hypocrite*."

"Our situations are different. The courtesy that I extend to my subjects—"

"Oh, for the love of stars, *shut up*." I could strangle him by the ruffled nonsense around his neck.

Cyrus leans against the patterned wall, arms crossed. "Fine, Violet, tell me about your dream. But I *am* busy." He's not taking me seriously at all. I *should* waste his time.

I exhale. Just get this over with. "I dreamed of you."

He stills, a curious look in his eye. *I've* only *been dreaming about you,* I'd say, if I told him the full truth.

"I saw you dancing with this one girl," I continue. "She arrives at the ball around eleven o'clock, wearing a butterfly mask made of jewels and dragonscale. Her dress is covered in butterflies, too—and fayflowers. She steals your breath away on sight. You kiss her and it looks like you just *know*. And I thought you should be aware that—well, you're finally going to find her."

"My true love?" he murmurs, oddly quiet.

"Good thing, because I think I'm dreaming signs of Felicita's prophecy."

He arches his brow.

"A bloody—body." *You.* "Covered in roses."

He studies me up and down. "You have a tell when you lie."

My face contorts. "No I don't," I say, and then in the same breath: "What is it?"

"What do I get in return?" His words carry a tang of mischief, better fitting flirtation. The slant of his smile drops as if he realizes it at the same time I do.

We don't belong treading in these waters, not when we're in such close proximity, breathy and hearts racing from our quick exit from the ballroom. I wouldn't mistake this for anything else, but—

"Violet." Cyrus clears his throat.

"The journey to love never runs smooth," I blurt at the same time.

He flinches.

Licking my lips, I dredge up the rest of the rhyme: *"And yours . . . your father would not approve. They will catch you by surprise, hidden in disguise, but leave your grasp before midnight strikes."*

"Where did you hear that?" He sounds a little awed. A little—afraid?

"I told you. In my dreams."

"The Balican Seer during my tour . . . she told me the same thing."

"The same exact words?" So it *was* a Fate who spoke to

me. Have they been speaking to Seers besides me? "But . . . your father told me you didn't get any foretellings about finding love."

He shrugs. "I lied. He wouldn't approve of her, right?"

The simplicity of his response jars me, and apparently it shows, because he scoffs. "Fine—I'm a hypocrite. Happy? I lied to Mirabel just now, too, if you care about that."

"What?"

"My *personal gratitude* toward her uncle involves stringing him up for bringing in stolen Balican treasure."

I'm still confused. We're always having conversations about two different things. "The Dragonsguard's haul?"

"The Thirteenth and the Fourteenth Dominions have been letting their dragons propagate on the cliffs near the border. The dragons fly southeast into Balica to raid and return to their lairs on the Auvenese side, pockets full of our neighbor's gold. Then the guard swoops in and eliminates them. Safe to say, we don't give everything back to who it belongs to. I've been dealing with this all morning."

No wonder such a large share of the Dragonsguard is sent to the borderlands. Dragons are pests in the less developed countryside, raiding villages for anything shiny and hissing fire when provoked. We'd be in dire trouble if they were still as large as their building-sized ancestors, but now it's mostly a battle against their rampant procreation and greedy claws.

And our dukes' greedy claws, it seems. I'm not surprised— Auveny may pretend that destiny is the fair judgment of the Fates and fortune falls to those who deserve it, but having sifted through the threads of my patrons, I know that truly good souls are one-in-a-thousand exceptions. The rest of us are just hoping not to get our sooty hands caught.

"You could have said something to me," I sputter, heart beating unsteadily.

"And what would you have done?" Cyrus looks unusually relaxed, hands shoved in pockets. Not even in a rush anymore.

"I don't know—I just heard about this! I could have . . . lured some advisors in for a reading . . . searched for secrets or discrepancies in their threads. I get it, Princey—you don't trust me, but you have to give me a chance."

"I am. I have been."

"And lower your damn standards, when you're here keeping secrets too." I narrow my eyes. "You should've told me about what the Seer said, at the very least. Everyone is in a panic about you finding love, and meanwhile, you *knew* you didn't have to worry."

"It's hard to believe until it happens. I've had prophecies follow me my entire life, every one of them vague." He admires the ceiling with great interest as a dozen thoughts seem to cross his face. "The ball still has to go on, I suppose. A dress of butterflies and fayflowers. That's something."

"What else have you heard? If I knew what other Seers said, I could interpret my dreams better."

"Do you know why we only keep one Seer in Auveny? Easier for a king to control." He drops his gaze to mine, words toneless. "My father's policy, early in his reign. He could have kept another Seer alongside Sighted Mistress Felicita, but trying to influence *two* Seers when he wanted a prophecy to be told a certain way—he didn't like the thought of that. He traded the other one to Verdant for some ridiculous price."

"I know that." I didn't know that. "You didn't answer my question."

He shakes his head. "The other Seers didn't tell me much. Have you dreamed anything else?"

A coldness has settled between us like a fog. I could warn Cyrus about the threats. The thorns.

The roses blooming from his blood-pricked skin.

His death, come summer's end—or mine, in his place.

But my task for the king is complete, and I am no longer feeling generous.

"No," I say, unblinking. "That's it."

I lay in my bed awake. I've kicked off my blankets; it's too hot. Every new worry I have presses into my skull like a pin.

"It worked," I say. "Cyrus believed me."

The balcony doors are cracked open, but it's a breeze-less night. I wonder if any gods can hear me. Maybe they're squabbling above.

One of them seems to want to help me. The rest wouldn't mind me dead. I don't know how to get a message to any of them.

"You spoke of betrayal in my future." I trace the patterns in the embroidery of my sheets, half hoping for a real re-sponse, even a mocking laugh. Even if that means everything they said was true. I just want an *answer*. "If betrayal is coming, I don't want to wait around. Tell me what's about to happen and I'll listen to whatever you have to say."

I shut my eyes, waiting for sleep.

The voice doesn't answer.

But, at last, I dream:

Wet, musky fur. A tangle of leaves. Iron scents the air.

A hungry growl, and a voice, barely human: "Help— help."

A monstrous creature rises from its crawl, spiral horns silver under moonlight. It is all wrong—man and beast and forest all at once.

It lumbers toward a lit window on a two-legged gait. Rose petals drift in its wake.

8

THE MASKED MENAGERIE FINALLY ARRIVES.

As the sun sets, carriages fill the grand plaza and revelers funnel through the palace gates. Before midnight, Cyrus will find his true love.

I think.

The rhyme plays through my head over the day. It must be a real prophecy, if that Fate told both me and another Seer, but the second line of it keeps drawing my attention:

Your father would not approve.

I let Cyrus believe that the girl I described and the one in the rhyme are the same person. But I know that his father set up the former, which means he'd approve of her; they couldn't be the same girl.

Will there be another who catches Cyrus's attention? Is there a double meaning that I'm not catching? I'm wary. Gods like toying with us.

And then there was that vision of—I don't know what it was. Some beast in silhouette. I wish I'd seen more.

At half past seven, Eina, the royal twins' former nurse

and a persistent old stump of a woman, knocks at my tower. "You're the last to get ready, come out now."

"I'm not going to the ball," I tell her through a crack in the door, but when I turn around, the three fairies in service of the palace have already found their way inside through an open window.

After a round of arguing, bargaining, and sneezing, Eina wrestles me in front of my mirror. She strips me to my chemise and snaps a clothespin on my nose to prevent me from inhaling fairy dust.

The fairies gives me a wide berth anyway. Eina watches them, then clucks at me, "On your monthly?"

"*Oh no,* is that a problem?" I intone. "Guess I can't go."

"They can handle a little blood. Just make sure it doesn't get on the dress." She makes a clicking sound at them.

"You can speak to them?"

"I pick things up."

The fairies chirp to each other rapidly as if quarreling over the details. Ribbons burst into existence and pop away with another flick. Ugh. I'll be satisfied as long as they don't make me look split in three; fairies have stubborn tastes.

A breeze swirls around my legs. When I look down, they've pulled petals of chiffon out of the air to cocoon me in—layers and layers of it, each one barely more than translucent. Gloves wrap my hands, shoes slip onto my feet, then the rest of the moon-gray fabric settles into the shape of a gown. As I step away from the mirror, the skirts trail like mist, drifting with the slightest movement. Tiny pearls on the low neckline glimmer like dew on a spider's web.

"Oh," I say in a stuffed voice, nose still pinched. "I look nice."

Eina nods, smugly satisfied. She undoes my braid and winds my hair up in some fancy knot. I lift up the mask the fairies conjured. A phoenix stares back at me, its silver wings spread, shining with a rainbow of color as they catch the light. The shoes are, thankfully, practical slippers, so I don't fall to my death when Eina finally shoos me out of the tower.

I guess I can *try* to enjoy the night.

The north end of the palace grounds is empty. No one witnesses me fail to juggle the purse, shawl, and fan also conjured up on my behalf. I end up abandoning all of them on a garden bench. I pass lions and dragons in the courtyard, each in their own splendorous outfits: gravity-challenging skirts, trains that change colors, embroidered scenes that would take a year to sew. One dress looks like a giant cage with birds fluttering inside.

All top-notch glamour. Fairies are indifferent to our mortal jockeying until *they* want to show off. On a regular day, I can tell who bought their fairy with ambrosia—those people's hands too soft, their shoes too clean, their attitude too coarse—but in costume, the rich are indistinguishable from real fairy wards. The true winners of the night are the ambrosia merchants.

I join the line to enter the grand ballroom as if I'm just another pretty face seeking my destiny. Once through the ballroom doors, I suck in a breath.

It's as if the stars have been brought down to the earth.

I'd seen the setup. I know there are mirrors on the wall creating the illusion of the ballroom stretching endlessly. The fog that skims the floor is a chemist's trick. Overhead, a thousand candles have been carefully placed to replicate the constellations of the night sky. Not real magic, but the palace has done a half-decent job of replicating it. When the clock strikes eleven, the girl arranged to be Cyrus's true love will walk through the doors—and for a moment, I forget it's a deception.

A servant guides me toward the central area, where the capital's population is dancing and dining. Snatches of conversation reach my ear: speculation over the prince's mask, his true love, and bawdier talk of how many will be debauched tonight and in which dark corners.

"Behind that aloofness, I can see that the prince has a kind soul and a profundity—"

"And he has the body of a god! Sorry, was that blasphemous?"

I've been to fancy events before. I can put on a smile. I do it every day. But for the first time in a long time, I feel out of place. Everyone's glad to be here, their heads thrown back in tipsy gaiety, while I . . .

I'd like to fill up a plate with food and leave.

I don't care to talk to anyone here. I don't *like* anyone here. The gossip bores me; I already know the surprise.

I've never been sociable. As a child, it was safer to be quiet, to be unmemorable as a shadow, and I couldn't speak of my Sight freely lest the wrong person take advantage. When I first arrived at the palace, I was admittedly shy until I learned my way around. Nobles are nice in ways I didn't trust. Many of them are related to the royal Lidines in some distant way, and they made me wonder if I was fortunate to have never had a family, so that they couldn't exploit my position.

The streets made me wary, but palace life frosted my heart in ice. A small part of me hoped that the Fates' judgment was true—that the best people lived the best lives—but as I settled into my duties, I accepted that no such hierarchy exists. People are cruel even when they have everything—more so, for fear of losing what they have. How petty my pickpocketing seemed compared to the crimes of the wealthy: merchants who flouted regulations, lords who struck deals that were rotten before the ink dried, a Council scheming behind closed doors.

Still, they came to me, unworried and unashamed, despite knowing what I could see in my threads. I learned at last what it took to make a kingdom prosperous, and it had nothing to do with goodness.

I've made my own bargains, my own allowances, but I can't laugh along in this company. Not without grimacing.

Sighing, I look for the largest crowd. That's where Camilla will be—with the wine.

It only takes a minute to locate the princess lounged atop a spare table like a throne, surrounded by no fewer than two dozen girls. A pair of iridescent wings sprout from her velvet blue suit. Her mask of peacock feathers is as wide as I am tall. She beckons toward me and, loath to ruin her ball, I melt the gloom from my face.

"Cyrus and I have a bet about who can woo more before the night is over," Camilla says, tipping a glass of wine onto the lips of a masked cat. Traditionally, girls kiss a trinket and give it to those they favor. The princess is sitting on a trove that would make a dragon envious.

"Is Cyrus even here yet?"

Camilla points up. On the second-floor landing of the ballroom, a gent in a golden fox mask leans over the railing. From the sound of the crowd's gasps, others have noticed, too. Cyrus's mask isn't much of a secret after I whispered about it in my readings. The goldsmith's apprentice blabbed about a special commission last week, too, and every newsletter had details by the next day.

But maybe Cyrus knows how to be clever after all—because another golden fox steps out from the shadows behind the first one.

Then two more behind them.

Then four more after that.

Eight identical golden foxes line up behind the balustrade and bow in synchrony. Seven imposters and only one prince.

They're swarmed as soon as they descend to the ground floor. A tune swells from the orchestra, luring them to the dance area, wide-eyed hopefuls in tow, mooning, clinging, tittering.

There's going to be at *least* three more hours of this.

I eye the exit.

"*Try* to stay until the next chime of the clock," Camilla says, as if she can see through the back of my head.

Grumbling, I head to the dessert table.

Nine bells toll. I conclude: the lights are too bright, the flirtations are horrendous, and one of the pastries I eat crumbles into the bodice of my dress, so if the Fates are watching, even *they* don't want me to be here.

I can't keep track of the fox-masked gents, but anytime I get too close to one, I'm dragged into a whirlpool of shoving and squealing, and I'm one breath away from screeching to all of them, *None of you toad-brains will marry Cyrus, you're all being duped!*

I flop onto a seat in the shadow of a swan ice sculpture that's melted into something better resembling a duck. There's so much food piled onto these tables, entire cakes are left untouched. On another table, there's a life-sized dragon made out of bread, its belly pouch stuffed with fruits and chocolate coins. I start cutting slices of my favorite cake—a triple-stacked blueberry and lemon monstrosity topped with meringue.

Camilla spots me as she's stealing an entire tray of drinks. "What are you doing?"

"Eating three slices of cake and five slices of regret, what does it look like I'm doing?"

After my second slice, I spot the only other person I don't want to kill. Wine flute in hand, his curly hair tied back in a ponytail, wearing a simple ivory mask and an outrageous lime feathered hat—Dante Esparsa, partner in misery.

He's with his own circle of friends from the university. "Esparsa, what are our chances?" I hear one of the gents say. "His Highness will certainly choose a bride, but there hasn't been enough discussion about his choice of lovers. I wouldn't mind these events if we had an opportunity."

"It's slim to none, I'm afraid," says Dante.

"You must admit to us lowly outsiders that it's unusual that you've been Cyrus's favorite for so long."

A grimace flashes across Dante's face. The implication is clear, even if his friends meant no ill: why else would the prince favor a foreign bastard over the rest of them, if he isn't sleeping with him? "Are you implying my conversation is so boring that I must be good in bed? I don't know if I should be insulted or flattered."

His friends guffaw. I touch his elbow, and Dante gladly tears away from the circle when he sees me. "Well, well, well—look what the fairies dragged in. Trying to give Camilla a run for her coin?"

Flushing, I cover my chest with a hand. "Shut up."

"You look nice."

"I don't feel like myself."

"I assure you that you can still be petty in petticoats." He glances over his shoulder. His friends have moved on to raiding the charcuterie without him. "*Thank* you. I would've gone mad if I didn't pass out drunk first. The gents aren't hooking and the ladies have Cyrus to find." Dante takes my gloved hand and leans down to whisper conspiratorially, "So you found Cyrus's true love, eh?"

"Hopefully." I flash a pale smile. I don't like lying to Dante.

"Patently unfair. You dream of kissing and it's a prophecy. *I* dream of kissing and it's, *Woke up wet, did you?*"

I waggle my brows. "Well, did you?"

He also waggles his brows.

The dance area is crowded with waltzing foxes and twirling gowns, like I'd seen in my patrons' threads. As the music quiets, a new set of dancers shuffles onto the floor.

Dante tugs me forward. "Shall we?"

I balk, a true nightmare flashing before my eyes. "I don't know how—"

His free arm curls around my waist, his hand warm at the small of my back. "Just relax."

I flail, mostly. Then, as Dante moves, my spine straightens and my feet unstick from the ground. I move in perfect tandem, almost like magic.

Exactly like magic, actually.

I look down at my feet. "These shoes are enchanted."

"Might've told Nurse Eina to give the fairies a request or two when they conjured your outfit. It's not every day Camilla successfully bullies you into attendance. You have *three* fairies at your disposal—may as well use them. Anyone in the court would murder to have *two*."

"So this cleavage—is *your* fault?"

"Oh, no, that was all Camilla. Please, I have some class." Dante winks. "But you do look lovely tonight."

My glower lasts all of a second before he twirls me around and the crescendo of the music carries my thoughts away. Dante can *dance;* he's the sort of tall, dark, and handsome that could make every lady and gent swoon if he weren't competing with a prince and if they didn't assume all Balicans were backwoods mystics obsessed with trees—which is their loss.

But even Dante can't take my mind off my worries completely, and it shows.

"What's wrong?" he asks.

"Thinking about some visions I had." I haven't *stopped* thinking about them. "Even if—*when*—Cyrus falls in love tonight, it doesn't mean Felicita's last prophecy is broken. Or that something else bad won't happen. Not that it will, but . . . It's these little pieces coming together."

"If something bad happens," Dante says, with his soft smile and a halo of star-candles overhead, "we'll do what we always do when everything seems hopeless."

I stare up at him.

"Hope."

"That's the worst answer. I need you to know that."

He laughs. The song ends and he guides me off the floor, my feet wobbly as I stop dancing and the enchantment fades.

"Do you believe in true love?" I ask. "Honestly?" Part of me wants to hear Dante say yes, just to have something to believe in.

"It's . . . complicated."

"That's what everyone says."

"No, I mean it involves a history lesson," he deadpans.

Snatching a full carafe of wine out of a server's hands, I jerk my head toward the exit with a fond, defeated sigh. "Well, anything's better than this."

⌘

Sometime after the clock strikes ten, Dante and I are tipsy and warm in a forgotten corner of the gardens, masks in our laps. Surrounded by fig trees and bodiless marble heads, we've apparently stumbled onto a graveyard for the palace's broken statues. They're already better company than anyone inside the ballroom—they don't talk.

Dante regales me with a yarn starring Emilius the First, namesake to our current king and Cyrus's great-great-grandfather. He had a love story for the ages, better known as the Prince and the Peasant.

For centuries, the territories that now make up Auveny had been small and divided, many lasting only the length of a single reign. When Emilius the First was a child, the lands were newly uniting under one banner. The farthest regions had no lords and were mostly homesteaders. The capital tried to place order upon them—and the taxes and laws that come with order—but they rebelled.

During this time, a witch of the rebels called on the Fates. She asked them to curse the prince to sing himself hoarse and dance until his feet fell off if the fighting did not end by his sixteenth birthday. The dukes laughed and said they would cease fighting when they won, but the seasons passed quickly, and when the prince turned sixteen, smoke still darkened the battlefields.

His feet started tapping. Song trilled from his throat at all hours.

The queen organized a special ball as a means to mask Emilius's condition. After fourteen days of dancing, a peasant girl by the name of Giraldine arrived. Giraldine wasn't even supposed to be at the palace—all things cruel and mortal rallied against her to keep her from it—but she was so pure of heart that the Fates intervened. They brought her in a crystalline carriage and had fairies spin her a dress so fine that a whisper could rustle it. She met the prince's eyes across the ballroom; he was so shocked by her loveliness that he froze in place and asked for her hand, though his voice had been long gone.

The curse was broken. The tales wrote themselves.

"Or," Dante says, lifting the carafe and taking another swig, "consider this: Giraldine was just a normal girl born in the cinders of a failed revolution. Old Emilius liked her enough; it doesn't really matter if he did when everyone else did. That was precisely why he chose her: because she was the kind of bright young beauty who men would go to war for—*had* gone to war for. He married her so those men would go to war for him instead of against him."

"You think Emilius the First's curse was faked to end the rebellions?"

After I take the next sip, Dante empties the last of the carafe onto his tongue. "It's not difficult to keep up the illusion of a dancing prince for a fortnight, and you can sing yourself hoarse after a night at the pub. Two hundred years later, who knows what the truth really was? So do I believe in true love? Do I believe in stories like this? The answer changes every day."

I shake my head. "I don't understand why the Fates would meddle with us."

"Balican stories give the Fates human qualities. They can be vindictive, impulsive, sympathetic. . . ."

"They sure are."

"You make it sound like you've talked to them directly."

"Maybe I have."

"Oho-*ho*, tell me your secrets, Sighted Mistress Violet."
His eyes are bright, his face flushed, as he leans in a little too
close, and I wonder what it'd be like to press my lips to his.

It's the wine. And a bit of curiosity that sparked when
we danced. I've never kissed anyone before. I haven't considered romance much at all. People don't think of the Seer in
that way, and, let's face it, I'm inviting as a stinging nettle.
Camilla may think I'm closed off and cynical and afraid of
taking chances, but I see endings clearer than beginnings,
and I don't have a heart that could be devoted to anyone.
Recognizing that is the most selfless thing I could do.

I believe in love as much as I believe in the scarcity of
it. I believe in tolerance and habit and codependence. And
that's enough, I hope. While Dante with his fine bones and
dimpled smile might tempt me for a diversion, I'd never bargain with his heart, not when he's half of all the friends I
have in the world.

Sitting up straight, I put my mask back on. "I'll tell you
secrets another night. I should head back to the tower."

He looks a little disappointed, but he's very tipsy too.
"It's nearly eleven. May as well stick around." Dim light
ripples over his cheeks like a tiger's eye and twinkles in the
black of his gaze.

"Already saw everything happen in my dream. Not exactly exciting." I rise, night air shivering down my arm. A
shortcut through the hedge maze is the best route to my
tower. It's dark, but I've run through it a hundred times during my first years here.

Unraveling a ribbon rose from my bodice, I kiss it and tie

the gray silk around Dante's wrist. "Thanks for making the night worth it. I'll see you when the city's sober."

✃

I get lost in the damn hedge maze.

I should have expected this, but the alcohol told me I'd be fine. I can *see* my tower over the hedge tops, I just can't reach it.

I turn a corner. The noise of the palace fades behind another wall of leaves. Dead end. I backtrack, take the other turn—

"Oh!"

A white-suited gent knocks me into the bushes. Branches scratch my shoulders. Wine splashes onto my arm.

"Miss—" Plucking me by the elbows, he brushes off twigs caught on my gown and wipes off the wine with his free hand while balancing a goblet in the other. I squirm away in case he reaches for my bodice. This ball really can't get worse. "I ardently apologize. Are you all right?"

The voice jerks something in my gut, familiar. My eyes fly up to his mask—and I nearly fall stumbling.

A beast's likeness looks down on me, all too similar to the one from my dream. The snout of his mask is pointed and furred, like a deer's. Delicate vines vein gold through his hair, and the deep russet locks are dusted with a shimmering powder. He seems born of summer's glow. Completing his transformation is a set of crystal horns curling from his head. Roses bloom along its spiral, red as blood.

"I apologize, I was—there was no excusing that, is there?" A keen gaze roves over me through the false face. Glamours never alter the eyes; they're too expressive, and magic dulls them to something strange and stiff.

They're Cyrus's eyes.

But he can't be here. If he's here, then the golden foxes everyone's been swarming around—

"Miss?"

"What are you doing here? Why are you dressed as—?" My shock hasn't diminished. What a coincidence—another one to add to the pile. Out of everyone I could have run into, I run into Cyrus, our cursed prince of the night.

The world seems to spin. I'm drunk. I'm seeing things. Turning away from him, I search the dark for a better landmark. Two steps later, I trip on my train and he catches me again. My mask goes askew.

"Violet?" The voice changes completely, now low and sharp. It *is* him.

"Congratulations," I mutter as a late spasm of embarrassment works its way through my body. I smooth back my mask's silver feathers. "I made it easy, didn't I? I don't exactly have decoys flirting around the ballroom to throw you off."

The corner of his mouth twitches, shaping into arrogance. I'm still half in his arms and the heat of his fingers bleeds through my dress. "Admit it: it's a brilliant trick. Commission eight fox masks, give them to glamoured entertainers, and no one pays attention to anything else."

"And you have to look like—*that*?"

He reaches up and nips off a tiny rosebud from the curling vines. "My true love wouldn't mind if I look like some beastie. The Balican Seer described a vision of my mask and I thought it was perfect. Provocative. Besides, everyone's having fun without me, and I can just wait for eleven o'clock . . . if your foretellings are to be trusted."

Bristling, I inhale deeply before my pride makes me say something foolish. I won't be ruining weeks of planning at the last minute. "Have fun. I'm heading back to my tower." I pick up my skirts, lest I trip on them again, and hope the path over my shoulder leads to the maze exit.

"No retort? You usually love having the last word."

I know Cyrus is baiting me, but he's too pleased with himself. "Looking for a fight?" I step into his space, wearing the smirk he so covets. "You always are, despite your act. What's a *trick* but a *lie* by a different name? The truth is, you like being a little devious, a little wolfish—a little like me."

"I'm nothing like you."

"You're right. *I* don't pretend to be better than I am." The difference in his behavior was never clearer than in those thirty seconds when he thought I was someone else.

He tilts his head. His crystal horns glitter. We circle each other in the smallest steps, the one dance we share.

"You hate me," Cyrus says.

"I don't hate you. It takes too much effort. But someone should."

"Resent, then."

I scoff. "If you want me to list all the reasons I resent you, grab another bottle of wine."

"Are you afraid of me?"

I only laugh.

His breath leaves the barest fog in the night. "You once asked what I'm afraid of when it comes to you. It would be the same reason you should be afraid of me. We could ruin each other, and we would not hesitate to do so."

"Is that a threat?"

Cyrus smiles. I can't decipher anything else with the rest of him hidden behind his beastly face.

"I am not afraid of you," I whisper, a distant thudding in my ears.

"We can't work together as king and Seer if we're not honest with each other."

I yank off my gloves. "If you really want to be honest—"

Cyrus tries to pull away, but I'm quicker. I snatch his hands, spilling his goblet, and his threads spool into my mind.

Taut at the forefront of his thoughts, a thread pulses with the anger of an old wound. A familiar scene blooms, one I remember through my own eyes.

He still thinks about that day, a lifetime ago. Only in his mind, the memory goes like this:

A girl comes from out of nowhere, pulling him away from certain death like a blessing from the Fates. A dirty, lovely thing. A miracle.

He brings the girl home to his hungry father and his hungry court. They place her in a tower, whisper promises that sate her own hunger.

He watches her become everything anathema to him.

He hates what she becomes, silver-tongued and sly.

He hates everyone else more for making her that way.

My lips part in question as Cyrus frees himself. I want

to laugh. "Don't tell me you're still wondering where the girl who saved you went." I mean to coat the whisper with venom, with a sneer, but I'm half-incredulous. "No one forced me to be like this. I was desperate to get off the streets. I used you to claim that tower—that's all it was."

Life in the palace made me cold, but I made that choice on my own.

His gaze is stormy. "So proud of being heartless."

"I know the consequences of being who I am. Do you?"

The ball, the city, and the stars have never felt so far away as the prince eyes me like I'm something dangerous. I'll cut to the heart of him.

"You think you aren't just as resentful?" I take a step closer. I relish this too much to ever pretend that I don't. "Every day that I walk beside you, I remind you I'm not the girl you thought I was. That I stole your father's affections and made a life here without you."

I take another step. In the heaving of our chests, our bodies brush. I can feel his heartbeat under his shirt. Or maybe it's my own. We're older now—not like the still-growing children we were years ago, who could shout and shove to our liking, so long as we ran away fast enough to avoid capture. Our worlds have grown large and dark, clouded by ambition.

By desire.

His lips are so close I might taste the wine. His hand collars the hollow of my throat, as if to stop my advance, or maybe—as his thumb traces up my throat—to tip me closer.

A bell tolls. The clock is striking eleven.

"Go meet your fate," I hiss.

Mouth curled in disgust, Cyrus lets me go.

9

I'VE CHANGED MY MIND. I WANT TO WITNESS the tale I've spun. I want to know whose arms I sent Cyrus into.

And I need to get out of this damn maze.

I follow Cyrus back to the palace. He ignores me all the way there. The noise in the ballroom has quieted. People are sleepy with drink. Even the flocks around the golden foxes have thinned.

Shocked gasps bubble through crowds as the prince moves through them. A beast is frightening, even in costume, even in a rose-covered mask as beautiful as the one he wears. He's tempting the Fates, but maybe he wants to.

I don't see the girl yet. I'm about to head to a higher vantage when a feeling in the back of my skull tugs my attention. I turn toward the ballroom entrance.

Under an arched statue of two Fates stands a figure alone in silhouette. I don't remember seeing her before.

The girl steps out of the shadow. Her face is half-hidden behind a butterfly mask, her visible features delicate as a dollmaker's finest work. The dress—it's the kind made of childhood dreams and grown-up envy. Green fabric swaths her as if she were something bloomed from the Fairywood, shedding petals and leaves that shift from spring-green to autumn-gold as they dissolve into glimmering vapor. A fortune of golden, fairy-coveted fayflowers drips from her skirts.

It should be gaudy. Even Camilla would call out this dress for being too much. But the girl looks beautiful, and I don't understand how. I can't describe her as anything less than a prince's destined match. *Someone's* destiny, at least.

It's her. It has to be her.

Heads begin to turn. A sweetness floods the air. When I spot the beast prince at the edge of the crowd, he's still as a stag, enraptured. They make a pair: rose-horned beast and fairy-blessed bride.

Camilla is waving at me from the corner of my eye, but I can't tear my gaze away yet. I have to see this tale to its end.

Eight gents in fox masks saunter up to the girl. No one protests; they're probably more jealous of the foxes than of her. They each extend a hand and chorus, "May I have the first dance?"

The girl considers them. A collective breath waits: will she choose the right one?

"I want to dance with him." She points past them, toward the beast.

A tide of murmurs. Those who are sober are slowly realizing the deception with the foxes. The real Prince Cyrus hesitantly takes her hand, as if awed that the girl exists—and exists for him, as far as he imagines. That at last, a future foretold for him came true.

The music resumes. The crowd quickly seals them off. I

lose sight of the couple except for the tips of Cyrus's crystal horns.

Someone grabs my wrist.

I stumble and whirl around. A terrifying peacock stares down at me with her hand raised. "Camilla?"

"Who's the most beautiful girl in the room?" she thunders. There's a sharp pin in her hand, ready to strike.

"What—"

"Answer me before I stab you!"

"Y-you!" I sputter, shrinking back. "What in toady hells, Camilla?"

Nostrils flaring, she lowers the pin. "That girl in the fayflower dress. She's more enchanted than a pumpkin carriage. I think she's a witch or—or—I don't know." Taking me by the arm, she hauls me toward the stairs that lead to the upper landing. Her own thumb is bloody, smearing a stain down my wrist and sizzling a hole on my sleeve.

"Careful! You're melting the glamour."

Camilla is barely listening, eyes trained below where her brother bows in front of the mystery girl. "I've never seen anything like this. I need to get that dress off her."

I bite my tongue before a lewd joke can escape. "Camilla, stop." May as well tell her the truth. She finds out everything soon enough. I lower my voice to the barest hiss. "Your father secretly arranged this. This girl—she was selected in advance. He told me to tell Cyrus that she was his true love."

She blinks in surprise. "Who is she?"

"I—I don't know."

"Then if the fairy magic on her is strong enough to do

that, who knows if this *complete stranger* enchanted Father into this as well?"

"Do *what*?"

"The charm. The—extra touch of glamour." Camilla gives me a funny look, as if *I'm* the strangest creature in this room. She shakes her head. "It barely affects you, doesn't it? That used to frustrate Cyrus."

I only have more questions. "I still don't—"

"Look at how that girl is drawing attention. It's the same way people look at me and my brother, but much, much stronger." Camilla snaps her fingers in front of a servant whose tray of glasses is slipping as he stares at the dancing couple, but it doesn't make a difference. "We aren't so desirable by accident. There's fairy magic on us all the time. It doesn't change how we look, but it adds a particular allure, charisma—call it what you like. You can't help but look at us. Be a little seduced."

The constant frenzy around Cyrus. How people *pay attention* whenever one of the twins enters the room. "That's why everyone's in love with you two."

"Well, I don't *need* it to be desirable," she adds quickly.

"Of course," I assure her.

"The glamours work best on those predisposed to us, which is why if someone likes Cyrus, they like him very, very much. It takes all three of the fairies in the palace to manage what my brother and I have. That girl is *dripping* with glamour. Thank the Fates I knew to prick myself as soon as I sensed it." She drums her fingers on the banister. "What to do, what to do . . . we have to get closer to them . . . Oh! Dance with me!"

Camilla shoves me back down the stairs and my arms

pinwheel to keep me balanced. Unlike Dante, the princess is a forceful partner. She presses me to her bosom before I can even answer. She drags my arm up in the air, yanking me into a flamboyant pose as I protest.

"Camilla—!"

"Hush! And *focus*!" She charges us forward, using our joined hands as a battering ram to part the crowd. Camilla's threads flicker through my mind.

The crowd applauding her at the Masked Menagerie's announcement.

A glass necklace with a drop of red liquid.

Parties upon parties filled with empty laughter, every gaze on the girl on her brother's arm.

In the present, if Cyrus and that girl weren't captivating every set of eyes in the audience, people might be wondering why a second pair of dancers suddenly joined the floor. Camilla and I spin our way toward them in a scramble of feet hardly better than a drunken jig. The candlelight above spin round and round, and I manage to kick my own shins; even my enchanted shoes can't save me.

"Just a little closer—how does she have everyone distracted? I've never seen anything so effective," Camilla mutters. "All right, don't be alarmed."

"I'm *already* alarmed!"

Camilla flips a blade out from her pocket. She slashes the soft pad of her thumb, wincing as it wells red. She grabs a jug of water from a servant at the edge of the crowd and shoves her hand inside.

Water and blood splash on me. I jerk away as my sleeves melt. "What—"

I stumble on the girl's train. She gasps. Cyrus sluggishly recognizes us.

Camilla runs forward and douses them.

"Urgh!"

The girl's mask shrivels and curls away. Her hands fly to her face as pinkish water drips from her chin. I can already see her dress thinning, the green fading.

Cyrus lunges at Camilla, yanking the jug from her hand and turning her bloody palm upward. "Are you out of your mind?"

She shoves back. "She's enchanting you—"

"Of course she is! She's my true love!"

"No, *literally,* you toad-brain!"

"She's getting away!" someone yells.

The ballroom doors rattle. The girl dashes through, her dress weeping magic behind her.

A wetness seeps onto my leg. I look down and my mask droops. I press it back to my face.

My glamours are falling apart, too.

Someone grabs me by my shoulder. I spin around and meet Cyrus's glare.

"It's always you, isn't it?" he snarls.

"I didn't—it was Camilla—" I twist away—easier than I thought, as some mix of enchantment and wine addles him. Diving into the crowd, I look for something to hide behind, but the crush of people propels me toward the exit as they give chase after the girl.

I need to get away.

So I run. Like a girl on the streets again, near-barefoot as one slipper melts.

My dress turns to rags, freeing my legs. I run even faster.

Clinging on to what's left of my mask, I burst out into the night. A sprinkling of raindrops catches on my lashes, blurring my vision. I can barely see more than the mystery girl's profile against the bright lights spinning beyond the palace gates behind her. Squinting, I make out the glowing shapes of fairies. One, two—three—

In rare instances, multiple fairies can favor the same ward, though having two fairies is often worse than having one—twice the magical firepower, but they'll bicker more than help. Having three fairies is the stuff of tales. The palace has three fairies, but those are bought with a hefty amount of ambrosia and shared among the royal family. According to rumor, it was a nightmare trying to find three fairies *willing* to work together. Nothing short of a miracle.

Any more than three is unheard of.

There are five fairies behind her.

The din of the crowd nears. I run behind the gatehouse, crouching in its shadow. When I look back, the girl is gone and Cyrus stands alone at the palace gates, looking out toward the quiet streets.

He calls for his guards and for horses. Minutes later, he rides into the city, Dante and guards beside him, and much of the crowd as well.

In the chaos, I scramble across the gardens, back to my tower. No one follows me. I strip off the sopping silk as soon as I enter my rooms, and climb into bed still damp.

Only then do I realize that I lost my other shoe.

10

SOMEONE IS POUNDING ON THE DOOR.

I roll over on my bed, waiting for it to stop. My shift is cold, sticking to me like a second skin. It's still dark out, barely sunrise.

The door downstairs rattles. And rattles. And rattles.

I curl my pillow around my head. Whisper a little swear-filled prayer to the Fates who blessed this tower before throwing the covers off. Pulling my robe on, I pinch the fabric tightly to hide my shift from view.

Last night is a blur I'm too happy to relegate to the threads of my past. I managed to piss off our future king by bragging that I used him. Then I pissed him off again by driving away the girl who he thought was his true love, which will also piss off our current king. Also, no one likes me in the first place.

But at this hour, I can't even bother to be nervous. "I'm up!" I shout, not that they can hear me through the sound-proofing enchantments. I pad down into the divining room with a candle. "The sun isn't up yet, but by the Fates, you made sure I'm up."

I yank open the door.

Cyrus is standing alone in the antechamber, eyes bloodshot.

He's still in the same clothes from the ball, his shirt untucked and collars askew, a far cry from the pristinely white-suited beast. He sways on his feet, smelling sweetly of wine and rain. In his hand is . . . *my shoe.* "Forgot this?"

Gaping, I take it from him. "Did you get in a bar fight with a troll?" is all I manage to say.

He pinches his nose, drawing out a long sigh. "Tell me the truth, Violet. Who was she? The girl who ran off?"

Her face winks into mind—her surprise and fear in that glow of five fairies. Surely Cyrus wasn't up all night looking for her. "I . . . barely caught a silhouette. Do you know what hour it is?"

"I'm tired."

"Because you haven't slept, probably. Princey, I don't think it's even *dawn* yet."

"I'm tired," he says again, "of everyone lying to me and thinking they can get away with it."

"Aren't you a cheerful drunk?"

"I know the girl is a setup."

Whatever words meant to leave my throat next come out as a cough. Cyrus looks up with a satisfied grimace as he clutches a fistful of his hair, flicking rainwater and the gold dust of his makeup. He's figured it all out and he looks like he wished he hadn't.

"So, can I come in?"

When I don't answer, he pushes past me into the divining room.

"Every lord I met between the Sun Capital and Verdant had a scheme up their sleeve. It doesn't surprise me to find out my father apparently hatched a plan, too," Cyrus says as I shut the door behind me. "I know you think I'm some honorable half-wit, and I appreciate that very much. I'll let you in on a little secret: I like it when my enemies under-estimate me."

Tread carefully. "I'm your enemy?"

"We'll see." He's jittery. Pacing. "Just now, Dante tracked down that girl who ran off and told me he knows who she is. Raya Solquezil. Raya of Lunesse, the Head of the largest region in Balica. The one with the most Fairywood jurisdic-tion, most clout. What a coincidence that she's my true love as well."

I set the candle down. I've built up enough goodwill with our current king; better to mend the trust of the future king. "Your father arranged it. I only knew what she was going to wear. That's it. I didn't know she was Raya. I barely know who that is." The Republic of Balica doesn't have a single monarch, but one leader for each of its four states: Lunesse, Gramina, Hypsi, and Solrook. I've only heard Raya's name in passing, spoken in terms of an ally to flatter.

"Father was desperate to see me married and useful. I was willing to give him and you the benefit of the doubt, but this match is clearly meant to turn our neighbors into our subjects."

Why does it come as such a surprise for Cyrus? Without the dangling threat of prophecy, kings never marry for love; they marry to make useful alliances and useful babies. "If you haven't found your true love by now, you can't think people would be fine if you just kept waiting. And I did dream that rhyme. . . ." How did it go? "What if this girl really is your true—"

"She's not." A sour cheer paints him as Cyrus swings around to face me. He draws a breath too quickly and I realize I'm standing in my shift. Flushing, I tighten the grip on my robe, refolding the starless silk around myself. He averts his eyes to the offering fountain, to the curtains, to the bare shelves—anywhere else.

My heart thuds a warning. Blood rings in my ears. "What are you doing here, Cyrus?"

"I needed answers. But for someone who claims she knows everything, you don't know much." Sobriety seems to have returned to him. His steps are sharp as he moves toward the door, but I block him.

"You burst into my tower at sunup, making it seem like *I'm* the one playing tricks, when you already figured out it's your father—"

"This is not about you," he says, clipped.

"It always comes back to me!" I jab a finger in his chest. "Whatever you're paranoid over, you'll blame me. It's always me, because everyone else thinks you're pristine and tragic, but I know better." Words loosen from my tongue faster than I can parse them; they'd always been there in the back of my mind, waiting to corner him. "As much as you loathe it, I'm the only one you don't have to pretend with, so here you are. I see the way you look at me." Those green eyes of his darken into twin chasms. "You don't hate me. If I didn't know any better, I'd say you're trying your hardest not to want me—"

Cyrus's mouth is on mine.

We slam back against the door, his knees against my thighs, the pommel of his sword digging into my hip. He's bruising. *Smothering.*

A surrender and an ambush—the truest thing he's ever done.

My shock is overwhelmed by the heat flooding through my veins, headier than any wine. This is not the bashful first kiss I imagined having, no small act to sate my curiosity; this is a taunt answered. Our feud turned physical. And I learn quickly—

I want him, too.

I don't know how to be soft. I barely believe in love. But I am the worst thing in Cyrus's life and nothing has tasted sweeter.

Gasping in his ragged breath, I search for something to hold and only find his shirt. His fingers sprawl on my chin, parting my lips, and he kisses me harder. His grip is too strong. I nearly bite his tongue off. We don't fit together without a fight. But body against body, we're like matches finally struck.

I want to twist his head back, fleck that gold makeup off his jaw. To have him delight in it.

I want so much more than I ever imagined.

Our next kiss snags teeth. Blood and ash mix on my tongue. Behind my eyes, roses bloom.

Two glowing blue lights flare and a cackle rings out: *You will burn.*

I break away, yanking my hands from Cyrus. They'd been entwined.

He notices. Grabs my hand again—but the vision is gone. A knot of futures remains, none that I can untangle in my current state. "What did you see?"

My head aches where it meets the door. He couldn't know—what does he *think* I saw? But a different desperation flickers in his expression, otherwise gentle as he lifts my chin.

"Violet, tell me."

"I didn't see anything."

"Liar." His swollen lips graze mine. "Do I have to convince you?"

I shrink from him, clarity returning with a vengeance. "You overestimate yourself."

But we always call bluffs. A laugh bubbles from his throat, and Cyrus kisses me anyway, deep and sweet like it was the most natural thing to do. "You talk so much, but what do you know? Only what you *see*."

His hands slide under my robe, roam down my body, under the curve of my leg, bunching the fabric of my chemise. I shiver as the cool air hits my thigh and his fingertips bite into flesh.

"Cyrus," I gasp.

I shove him.

He hits the ground hard, elbows scraping, blood dripping from his lips. A feeling skitters over my body, like I'm naked, and I hug my robe around me, skin burning underneath.

Cyrus rests where he fell, heaving with shuddering breaths. His head lolls back. "Well, I guess it isn't you."

"What?" I hate that the word comes out shaky. I don't think I can take a step without collapsing.

He mutters with a burst of miserable laughter, "What am I doing?" Flickering candlelight casts him in gold. He tilts his gaze to me, his mouth shaping soundless words that he doesn't have the courage to say.

The skittering feeling hasn't stopped, deepening into an ache everywhere he touched. What *are* we doing? "Cyrus—"

"You should leave Auveny," he says quietly.

I might collapse anyway. *"What?"*

"Make up some story about how the Fates are drawing you elsewhere." He swallows, gaze hardening. "Go to Yue, Balica, into the Fairywood, I don't care. Be anywhere but here."

As Cyrus gets up, I try to push him back down, but he wrenches me away, mouth twisted. Moments ago, he couldn't keep his hands off me; now he can't stand the thought of being in the same *kingdom*.

A chill spreads from my gut to my limbs. No, he could never stand it. It makes sense now—the disgust every time he sees me. He doesn't hate me for being a liar. He only hates that he can't control me and he can't control himself.

"Don't make this more difficult. I know you won't listen." The furrow of his brow smooths away, and Cyrus shifts into that benignly handsome Prince Charming the rest of the world knows: the honorable fool.

I should have bit off his tongue when I had the chance. "What makes you think I'm so easy to get rid of *now*?"

"I can tell people you tried to sabotage me at the ball. Dumped blood on my true love. They love a tale about a jealous witch." He fixes his hair and shirt, and edges past me to the door.

"Coward," I sneer.

Shutting his eyes, he breathes the word in.

I follow his exit into the shadowed antechamber, the buzz of my body a betrayal of everything I should feel.

Coward, coward, coward, *coward.*

I could set fire to this tower right now. Part of me wants to, just to scour the evidence of what occurred—just so that the worst thing I've done isn't kissing Cyrus.

Our steps clatter and echo down the stairwell. "You can't run from this," I say as I catch up to him.

Cyrus goes still, knuckles white on the banister.

"You—"

"Shh."

Is someone else here? "Let—" *Them hear,* I mean to say, but Cyrus claps his shaking hand over my mouth.

A bracing terror rims his pupils. He points below at the single entry point of the tower.

I hear it before I see it: a low, scratchy growl filling the silence of our held breaths.

Not some*one.* Some*thing.*

I don't know what to expect when I glance below. Nothing I know makes that sound, and now, heart pounding in my ears, I can't hear anything at all.

One enormous clawed limb grasps the archway. Leaves and rose petals blow in with the breeze. A hulking silhouette blocks the dim light of dawn.

Beast.

It maneuvers inside, one spiral horn after the other, too big to fit through all at once. It isn't like the finely wrought mask that Cyrus wore to the ball; no, this is the beast I saw in my dreams, a patchwork of shaggy fur and moss, no elegance to its shape. A shawl of jagged bramble wraps its torso, giving it the impression of a wolf caught in underbrush, except I've never seen a wolf lumber on its hind legs. It's a creature of storybooks—the terrible ones, told to deter children from wandering.

The beast peers up the stairwell with glowing green eyes, nostrils flaring, fangs bared. *It knew we were here,* some instinct alerts me. I can tell in the way it breathes us in, in the purposeful tilt of its head.

It charges.

"Shit!" I bolt up the steps, the prince at my heels. The whole structure shudders as the beast crashes up the stairwell. I trip and only barely catch myself on the banister. Cyrus, leaping two steps at a time, overtakes me and hauls me up.

Clumsy with terror, I lunge for the open door to my rooms, though I already know a slab of wood won't be enough to keep the beast at bay; I saw the glint of its claws, long as knives. We'll be trapped.

Something swipes my back, sharp and cold. I twist away, my hands finding a flower vase in the corner of the antechamber. I fling it at the mass behind me.

Porcelain shatters. The beast stumbles.

I grab the vase stand, made of sturdy wrought iron. Bracing myself, I shove the beast backward with it, trying to get some leverage before it comes to its senses again.

Steel flashes at the corner of my eye. The beast roars, pained, clutching its arm.

Cyrus, sword drawn, circles around to stand in between

it and me. Blood—I don't know whose—smears his cheek and stains his shoulder. "Go! Get help! I'll distract it." He brings down the sword again.

I'm nearly too shocked to move. A clear path to the stairs opens up, and I dart past the fighting. Bleeding and dizzy, I could faint, but if I don't make it down, we're dead. I know how to survive, and it's to never stop running.

Cold air rushes into my lungs as I burst out of the tower onto the petal-strewn landing, barefoot. The sounds of struggle grow more distant with each stride. There are guards across the bridge beyond the palace gates, if I can just reach them.

But.

My limbs slow.

But what if this is how Cyrus is supposed to die?

I could save myself, let him fall to the beast, and it would just be a horrible accident. It'd give the Fates what they want. He needs to die anyway before summer's end.

It's so easy, so tempting—the smart, cruel choice to make. The efficient, necessary choice, if I want what's best for myself. He wants me gone, and he said it himself: we would not hesitate to ruin each other.

But.

He protected me. Put himself between the beast and me. Let me escape, when he could have fled.

Isn't that truer than words?

Swallowing my spite for another day, I scream at the top of my lungs, *"Help! Guards! Anyone!"* I'm going to regret this.

I hear a grunt behind me, closer than I expect. I do the

foolish thing and turn around instead of running across the bridge to the palace.

A second beast, its horns in full bloom, shadows over me.

"No—"

It slams me down to the ground before I can scream again, claw pinning my chest. One sharp talon presses into the soft underside of my chin. My body flares with pain— there's too much weight. The scent of fresh soil fills my nostrils.

I scrabble at its claw and manage to get a hand underneath it, enough to block it from puncturing my throat as I writhe.

Images flash:

Curly-haired children running around a cottage on a hill, calling for their father.

A crowded Balican town gathering in a brick-built hall. They argue over mysterious attacks in the night.

Hatchets in hand, a group of men approaches a manor covered in vines.

I blink and there is only the glowing eyes of the beast and the maw of death before me.

Shouts of orders. A bone-crunching *thunk*.

The beast stiffens; the glow in its eyes vanishes. Blood drips from a crossbow bolt in the center of its forehead.

It collapses. Fur and rose petals smother me. Everything hurts too much for me to think. Distantly, I hear the clatter of metal and pounding of footsteps.

Someone frees me from the crushing weight. He repeats my name until he is the only sound I hear in the dark.

11

DAWN CREEPS STEADILY OVER THE MISTY LAND,
cresting over hills of gold and green, dipping into valleys
and through shuttered windows, up to the edge of the
Fairywood, where all light comes to a halt. Black clouds roll
through the sky, raining ashes. The woods are burning.

A nearby village is silent. Shriveled, torn-apart corpses
litter the streets. Brambles crawl, devouring body and brick
until the entire town is covered. Overhead, fairies flutter,
wink out, and dissolve into dust.

From the shadows rise beasts. Skin furred with moss,
fangs and claws dripping with crimson, two horns of
blooming roses jutting from their bulk. They lumber across
the countryside like heavy-footed soldiers, the rattling bones
of a hungry forest.

❧

I sneeze. My whole body seizes with pain.

"Eh—shoo!" Eina's voice is clear and sharp.

I crack open my eyes. The nurse swats at a trio of fairies like they're gnats. They fly out the door.

I recognize the gaudy decor: I'm in the palace, in one of its numerous guest rooms. This one is draped in too much crimson velvet, tinting the room in a bloody hue. A tray nearby steams with fish porridge and bread. My stomach pangs.

Eina glances over her shoulder at me, gray brows rising. "Ah, good. Drink some water. You've been out for a full day."

With great difficulty, I prop myself up on my elbows. The bed is far softer than what I'm used to and I only sink farther into the mattress. My muscles seem to be intact and functional; they're just stiff and complaining loudly about it. My head is strangely refreshed. That might have been the best sleep I've had in ages, even though I dreamed.

Did the fairies do something?

I can still taste fur in my mouth. I obey Eina's command and drink down the whole cup of water before asking my first question. "Where's Cyrus?"

"His Highness is preparing to announce his engagement."

"His *what*?" I sit straight up, wincing. My ribs feel like they're splitting apart.

"Lie back down, child. You didn't break anything, but you're still banged up," Eina chides. "How's your head? Follow my finger."

Biting my tongue, I oblige Eina with her tests. I'm dizzier than I ought to be. During a lull, I ask again, "Cyrus is engaged?"

"Lady Raya. Pretty thing. Came all the way from Balica."

Raya Solquezil of Lunesse. Cyrus had spat her name when he told me.

"It's a good thing he found her," Eina continues, "just as the beasts arrived."

"Yes," I agree half-heartedly. She doesn't know what else transpired last night. That among my bruises, the one I feel most is the one on my lips. "What happened to the beasts?"

"They took the bodies somewhere to be studied. But that is none of your concern. Only rest is." Eina smooths down the quilt, tucking me in, as if she senses my urge to return to my tower. "They left a mess of roses we're still cleaning up. It is . . . Felicita's last prophecy, then?"

"I don't know what else it could be."

She nods, concern melting across her wrinkled features. No one enjoys contemplating the unknown.

So much has changed in one night. The future is here, like I foretold, and it's nothing like I expected.

❧

With the royal twins grown and no little ones coming along from the widowed king, the nurse has time to spare for me. Eina thinks she's doing me a favor by keeping me company and finishing her mending here. It's not so bad while I'm eating, but she stays long after I lick my bowl clean of porridge.

I have people I need to see.

When she finally leaves to fetch a fresh pitcher of water and reading material I requested—the library is on the other side of the palace—I throw off the quilts and grab the spare set of clothes at the foot of the bed.

Then Camilla comes charging into the room with an armful of flowers and a plate of cake. "Thank the stars! Violet, you look half-dead!"

"I'm fine." I wriggle out of my nightgown. Lifting my arms still hurts.

"You were practically full-dead when you were brought in—"

"I didn't even break anything." The worst injury was a gash to my jaw that needed stitches.

"—and Cyrus wouldn't tell me *anything* about what happened. '*I'm tired, Camilla,*'" she mimics. "But not too tired to carry you into the palace himself—"

I pop my head out of the tangle of my clothes. "He did what?"

"—and I had to hear everything secondhand from Ziza Lace, but you know that woman is as trustworthy as a house made of candy." Camilla deposits the flowers into an empty vase, sets the cake on the table, and flops down next to me. "Have you heard? Cyrus is engaged. I tried to stop him. She is a *witch*, I stand by it."

"Lady Raya?" I can only recall her silhouette, dainty and shocked.

"It's just Raya, technically—Father calls her by that title so she can sound proper. They don't do nobility down in Balica. The Head of Lunesse would be a reasonable match if she'd ever bothered with diplomacy before. And if she didn't arrive in the capital with *five fairies*. One fairy, all right, you're cute. *Five* fairies? Five fairies, you're trouble!"

I pull on the linen blouse and work on buttoning a swishy yellow skirt around my waist. Camilla has a point, but Camilla is *also* more than a little irritated that she wasn't the most exciting thing at the masquerade, I'm sure. "*You* have three fairies that you use for the purposes of charming people. . . ."

"That's different!" She pouts and doesn't expound. Hypocrisy runs in the royal family. "The worst part is someone in the search party told Ziza about the fairies and she published the news in *Lacy Things* before I could tell her not to. Ziza's making Raya look good—says Raya deserved the fairies, for '*Who else but the prince's true love would be so special?*'" She makes a gagging sound.

"Ziza's eager to lick the next queen's boots."

"I need to see some prophecy-breaking before I let any crown grace Raya's head. I don't trust her one bit."

"Neither do I. But I'd like to meet her first." And hopefully read this strange girl's—woman's?—threads. Raya seemed hardly past my age from my glimpse of her, but I'm fairly sure she's been the Head of Lunesse for years.

I comb my hand through my hair and twist it over my shoulder to make it somewhat presentable, then lurch to my feet. "Can you butter up Eina when she finds out I ran off?" I ask.

Camilla waves a ringed hand. "Oh, you slip that crone a good bottle of plum wine and she'll forget how to speak entirely if that's what you want. Where are you going, though? I want to know what happened after the ball. What was my brother doing at your tower?"

Kissing me and then some, and I might not have stopped

143

him if my visions weren't acting up. But uttering whole truths aloud doesn't come to me as easily as it does for the princess. "We were discussing my future as Seer."

"Before dawn?"

Cyrus really should have chosen a better time to confront me, including the best time: never. "He was angry about the arrangement I made with his father. And probably drunk. He . . . threatened me." I grimace. "He wants me to leave my position."

"What! You can't." She cocks her head, frowning, as if waiting for me to react more.

I'm too busy thinking to worry. Worry only causes panic. Thinking at least lets me pretend I'm being productive. "Of course I won't leave! With the beasts here, Cyrus's priorities have changed. I'm not going to make hasty decisions because *he* does."

"Good. I'll speak to him. He isn't thinking straight, I know it. Fairy magic'll do that to you."

Or just me. I turn away to hide the rising blush. "Thanks. Could use some certainty in my life right now."

"The Seer wanting for certainty!" Camilla lets out a boisterous laugh. "We truly are in end times."

❧

In the palace halls, I find the chaos I expect: courtiers swarming like clicking-heeled beetles, asking after the prince's wedding plans and matters of prophecy. Weaving in and out of the throngs, I avoid them and their questions alike. I don't see Cyrus or Raya, but I do spot the purple feathers of the Imperial Guard helms.

I follow them. Next to the Imperial Guard will be the king.

"Your Majesty," I call after him. "Please excuse my appearance. May I have a moment?"

A smile stretches the wrinkles of King Emilius's face when he sees me. "Ah, Seer—you are up. Yes, join me. I'm pleased to see you're doing better."

We walk side by side exchanging pleasantries while we're still within earshot of others, airily discussing how the Fates blessed Prince Cyrus. The king is weaker today, needing both his cane and the help of one of his guards in order to walk. The pace suits me; I'm not at my best either.

Finally, we arrive at his study, a tidy, warm-paneled room nestled in the heart of the east wing. His private library takes up two walls, a fireplace sits in the third, and portraits cover the space behind his desk. If you told me it's against the law for a speck of dust to enter the room, I'd believe it.

King Emilius shuts the door behind us. With his guards outside, I guide him the rest of his way to his armchair. "The beasts—I dreamed there'll be more," I say now that we're alone. "Their numbers could overrun the kingdom." The vision of the empty village chilled me, but it was a future thread—one we can still prevent.

The king looks only slightly perturbed, as if he prepared for this. "From where do they come?"

"I might be able to pinpoint a location, but I don't think it will matter—they were roaming the whole countryside." I can't dull the nervous edge to my rambling; I need to be the perfect Seer, one who Cyrus could never dispose of without vicious backlash. I will be exact. I will be invaluable. "They kept close to the Fairywood. Whether they're emerging from there, however—"

"It's likely they are," he interrupts. "I brought in physicians from the university to dissect the beast corpses. The findings are strange. They are as much plant as they are flesh—sap in their veins, a woodiness to their skin beneath their fur. The growth on them is similar to that found in the Fairywood—turns black at the touch of blood."

"Did . . . did they seem human at all?" I'd seen memories when I grasped the beast's claw. And in my dreams, it had spoken like a man.

"A human, transformed?"

"Isn't that what the Fairywood does? Its magic can grow things. Change things." We never found an explanation for the black rot on the border, nor the roses that appeared. "If its magic can transform the land, maybe it can transform a human, too."

The king knots his gloved fingers below his chin, brows furrowed. "This is why we must tame those woods, as we've done the fairies that live there. Such free-flowing magic is unacceptably dangerous. If we cannot use it for ourselves, we leave it open for manipulation by darker forces—then who knows what is possible?" With a shake of his head, he leans back against his chair. "We will resume burning the Fairywood, no matter Balica's disapproval. We never should have stopped."

I remember the smoke rising in my last dream, how the

beasts marched anyway. "But if Felicita's prophecy is *already* here . . ."

"Then nothing we do may help, and Raya, as Cyrus's bride, may be our only means of salvation," King Emilius finishes. "I'm aware of that, too."

Salvation *or* damnation. But lingering on the worse outcome of Felicita's prophecy won't help. "I'm worried it's already too late. Cyrus barely knows her at this point."

He chuckles suddenly, and the sound tugs at a rare queasy feeling in my stomach. I'm being patronized. "I assume you do not believe in love at first sight, Seer? Fretting is unnecessary—he is already enraptured by her."

"Oh." Goose bumps prickle my arms. "Enraptured?"

"He's barely left her side. Follows her like a lovesick puppy. Frankly, it's undignified, but my son has always been an unfortunate sap."

My last memories of Cyrus flare alive at once, every muscle in my body seizing to will away the heat from my cheeks. *Actually, Your Majesty, I think your son is an accomplished actor,* I want to say.

"I see," is what I actually say. "How . . . blessed."

"I suspected Felicita's prophecy was unfurling. Intervention can be a catalyst for prophecy—I do not think it is coincidence that beasts began rising after the arrangement with Raya. We will attack this from all sides. A quick wedding to fulfill the requirements of the prophecy. Burn the Fairywood in the meantime as well."

"I should have a reading with her, too," I add quickly. "Her threads will be interesting."

He nods. "I'll arrange for you two to meet. I cannot force her to accept—we are not the first nation to use a Seer to pry—but in these extenuating circumstances, Raya must understand. She is the subject of prophecy, after all." One arm on the chair, he strokes his chin, eyes shut. "Learn as much as you can."

Pry, he means.

"Should I read your threads as well?" I offer out of politeness. "For your own foreknowledge."

His mouth twitches. King Emilius knows the extent of my magic, and he doesn't often allow me to see his threads. I'm not surprised when he answers, "No, I do not worry about my future. But perhaps you should divine my son's threads."

"Cyrus and I still aren't—that is to say—"

"Cyrus will be busy enough without starting feuds with his Seer. There is much I want to accomplish through his reign while I am well enough to guide him, so that the seeds I sowed for Auveny may continue to flourish. You have been and will continue to be key to that."

I bow my head, smiling genuinely for the first time today. I'm privy to his secret plans, more so than his own son is. I'm useful, and that's worth more than any love I could offer. "Happy to serve."

"Maintain the kingdom's morale as best you can. I pray the events of the prophecy pass soon. Then Auveny can, at last, focus on uniting the Sun Continent."

I'm barely prescient enough to not look surprised. *Uniting,* a clever word for *conquering.* King Emilius has brought up the subject of acquiring Balican land before, often while espousing the might of the Moon Continent across the sea, unified into the Kingdom of Yue. He has spoken hypothetically of annexing Verdant as well—though less enthusiastically, as the isolated kingdom across the mountains is not as valuable in his eyes. He has distant relatives among the Verdantese royal family who he would have to deal with, too.

But for all that the king has talked, he has never implied any plans for unification were in motion.

This arrangement with the Head of Lunesse is at least the start of some negotiation with Balica. Though with our Fairywood burnings and poor Dragonsguard practices, we haven't exactly been wooing our southern neighbors well. Maybe not *negotiation*, then. *Intimidation*. Auveny acts like it has a right over the entire Sun Continent already. After all, we named our capital the Sun Capital as if it stands for all three nations here.

But I don't ask further. I never reveal too much to the king, lest my opinions misalign with his, and I have enough on my plate to brood over without inviting his doubt.

King Emilius is famed for being just and magnanimous, as long as you aren't an enemy.

12

THE ROYAL ENGAGEMENT ANNOUNCEMENT should be noisy with equal parts barbs and fanfare, but no one knows how to act after prophetic beasts scarred their prince and Seer. Since the attack, I've had complete strangers apologize for what happened, celebrate my recovery, pour out their fears to me—a banquet of overfamiliar behavior that I don't want to respond to. Worse, people are actually being *nice* to me, which means *I* have to be nice in return.

It's exhausting.

I feel ready to keel over just standing here in the audience chamber, hand clenched around a near-empty ceremonial wineglass as I raise another tepid toast to our new couple.

Onstage, Auveny's future queen looks gawky as a stuffed stork—a far cry from her ethereal appearance at the ball— swallowed up by an enormous ruffled gown that, while fashionable by this season's standards, ill-fits her. Balican dress tends to be looser and more suited for temperate weather, but if Raya's seeking acceptance, then acclimating to the impractical local dress is one way of doing it. She wears

Auvenese purple well, her brown skin aglow against the rich color, and fayflowers sit prettily in her plaited hair. A veil of gauzy silk obscures her face.

She's been oddly reticent as Cyrus rambles through an introduction of her. "Raya is the rare combination of generous and shrewd," he says, taking her hand. "When I passed through Balica, we'd only seen each other in passing, but I felt that tug of destiny at once. She did too, clearly, traveling all the way here to meet me again." He smiles, leaning in close enough to—*nearly*—brush noses with her. How quickly he acclimated to nauseating lies. "Had she not come, I might have made a return trip myself."

Every time Raya fidgets, I hear another skeptical cough around me. Flowery speeches don't stop beasts. We all thought we'd have time to test her mettle and make our judgments, but the prophetic mantle is already upon her shoulders and now we're stuck with a bride who looks like *she's* the one stuck with *us*.

A shriek shrills through the room, followed by another. Chairs scrape.

Dragged out of my thoughts, I catch the end of the clamor—some girls trying to storm the stage, their arms viciously outstretched toward Raya, who hides behind Cyrus's cloak.

"She's a witch! *She's enchanting him!*" one screeches.

They're harmless society girls, not assassins; they wouldn't hurt a fly, because it'd be disgusting. Possessed by jealousy or some fairy magic in the air, their only target is Raya's reputation.

Somewhere in the crowd, I hear Camilla laughing.

Guards quickly restrain the girls and escort them out. Many in the audience sneak smiles amid the shocked titters; the princess isn't the only one who's suspicious of Raya.

I know Balican ambassadors have been busy behind the scenes as well. Rumor has it, they weren't informed of Raya's arrival, which is strange. Dante has been constantly at Cyrus's side, harried and conversing in a hushed voice; I wonder how much he knows of Cyrus's true feelings for his bride-to-be.

Presently, the prince has an arm draped around Raya and he's whispering something in her ear. Whatever it is, it seems to ease her. If you don't look too hard, you could believe they're in love.

If you didn't know the wide-pupil look the prince had for things he truly desired. If you never scraped off his veneer with your own fingernails as he pressed you against a wall.

No one would believe Cyrus would rather kiss me than her, even if the Fates shouted it themselves. People would sooner stop believing in the Fates.

When everyone is calm again, Cyrus at last announces the date of the wedding: the twenty-eighth of Hetasol. The day before the autumn equinox.

I finish off my wine. The Fates' deadline for Cyrus's death is the end of summer.

Few things are coincidence.

The fireworks begin in the gardens and the crowd sweeps away to celebrate the couple . . . or pretend to. I meet Cyrus's gaze for the barest of moments before he follows the others out. There is nothing in his expression: aloof brows, even mouth, starched shirt, like how he was the first day he came back from his tour and I was just a nuisance. Not yet crowned and he is already rewriting history.

I never expected otherwise. There are no love stories found upon the throne. Only secrets and schemes and spider-fingered kings.

Still, I wonder.

Was there ever a thread where things were different? Where we didn't end up resenting each other? Maybe even liked each other?

Was there one where I never saved him?

If I hadn't, would I have found my way to the palace through some other means? Would it be Camilla rising to take the crown? Or the Council puppeteering his cousin or some other choice of theirs in the dead prince's place? Would I be safe in my tower in those threads?

But I did save Cyrus that day in the marketplace. Wove that choice into the cloth of the world, severing the other threads. We kissed the morning after the ball, and I'll think about it every time I see him—the memory of it on my face, in my voice, in my judgment. There is no unraveling of what's been done.

Alongside my dreams, his touch haunts my sleep. That moonless night, I twist in my sheets, aching for things I never imagined before.

My tower is burning.

Black from char, black with rot, the vines around it continue to grow in their dying throes. Thorny like briar, curling and multiplying until the fire catches them, too.

I am burning.

His lips beg along my skin, trailing whispers from mouth to throat to hollows. His hands mold to me like they have always known me. I am the weakness in his heart made flesh.

Our bodies tangle, greed begetting greed.

A manor is burning.

Flames crackle like thunder, loud as the screams. On the balcony, a wide-hipped figure stands in stark silhouette, laughing.

The balcony collapses. The figure is gone.

A raven soars into the sky.

On the day that my tower reopens for readings, the king's footman arrives bearing a message for me. "Please set aside time later this evening, Sighted Mistress," he says. "Lady Raya will be visiting your tower."

The footman sidesteps the damaged areas of the antechamber while leaving. The carpet needs to be entirely replaced; claw marks go down to the woodwork. The maids cleaned up the blood the best they could, but the dark splotches are obvious. Sometimes I find scraps of fur caught behind furniture, musky as a fresh pelt.

Rain blusters against the woody walls of the tower as a summer storm drenches the capital and turns my robes dark gray. I receive a decent number of patrons despite the weather. A few seem optimistic about Lady Raya, but most are as doom-and-gloom as the weather.

Some ask how we'll know the prophecy is broken, and I tell them, "You'll know it when you see it," which isn't completely drivel. You can't call something a miracle if you can explain it before it happens.

I want answers, too. I'm receiving more omens, but I'm building a puzzle with no picture.

The rain clears early enough for a brilliant sunset, burnt orange darkening into deep blue as night engulfs the sky. Clock tower tolls grow in number.

Raya hasn't shown up.

I eat my supper by the hearth, a hearty meal of chicken and roasted vegetables, and light incense to mask the smell of it. Garlic is the only thing more stubborn than I am.

I wait some more, flicking off pillars of ash from the incense stubs. I could check for Raya at the palace—I heard she's staying there until the wedding—but I don't know if she's moved in yet.

Finally, just after the clock tower tolls seven times, a knock.

I leap to the door with a huff and open it. "Lady Raya, you are *la*—not Raya. Hi."

"Hi," says Cyrus. He's almost flawless in composure, except for a hitch in his breath when I'd spoken, giving him away.

His loose shirt barely covers a jagged new scar on his collarbone. Glimmering edges of glamour crisscross his face; he'd been scratched badly by the beast. I can imagine why he chose to hide the scars—because they're ugly and shocking, or they show that he was foolish, or they show that he was brave. But I wonder exactly which reason it was.

We stare at each other. We both sound witless, but at least I have an excuse: What do I say to a prince who kissed me, then told me to get the hell out of his kingdom, then protected me from a beast, before getting engaged overnight?

"What do you want?" I ask, clipped in tone. An implicit offer to go back to normalcy. To pretend like our kiss never happened.

"I've . . . thought long about the future." Cyrus clears his throat. Tweaks the gold buttons on his cuff. "My future and Auveny's future. I'm not optimistic that Raya is the one in the prophecy, but a bride is better than none. I'd like to try to fall in love with her."

"Good." I ignore a new feeling in my heart that feels like something is burrowing straight through it. It might be jealousy, but that'd be stupid. "Good that you finally listened to me."

He doesn't look happy about that. He's looks like he's holding something back. His gaze lowers to the gash along my jawline, and he frowns. Reaching up, his fingertips skim the stitches. I should be numb to this routine—his softness

156

is one of convenience—but a treacherous part of me pangs. I flinch away.

"You . . . remain a distraction." Cyrus sighs, retracting his hand. He makes it sound like it's *my* fault. "I won't make you leave Auveny, but you should leave the capital after you've finished your work here. We'll negotiate for the return of the Seer from Verdant."

So nothing's changed. Well, my answer to that hasn't changed either. "No."

"I'll tell you what I told Camilla: If you stay here, we'll always be at odds."

"*No.*"

"People get moved around all the time." His voice is placating, a dribble of honey over venom that sloughs over my ears. "Fidare was booted off to the borderlands when he was seventeen, just because Father disliked the favor he was currying. He loves governing the Tenth Dominion now. It isn't as dire as you think. I could handle your accommodations. Set you up in a furnished manor—"

"Alone, in some strange land. This isn't a *gift*." Fury curdles in the back of my throat: he's determined to talk about me like I'm a business transaction. "I'm not leaving for feelings *you're* ashamed of."

His eyes flutter shut. "For a Seer, you don't see the outcomes very clearly. What will happen when others find out there's something more between us?"

"Just because you used tongue doesn't make it commitment, Princey. It was *once*."

"I still have no place for a Seer who is an opportunist first."

"Like that ever mattered." I surge past the doorway, stabbing a finger into his chest; Cyrus sucks in a breath. It was just like this, how we kissed that night. "I've stayed out of your way, haven't I? I've been pretending—like you have—that the night of the ball never happened, letting you plan your little wedding—"

He grabs my wrist, and I am close enough to see the dull blue tint bruising his eyes. "And how long will that last? We fall into old habits."

I scoff, but the truth of it silences me. Already, my heart is pounding, my dream of him rising to mind. We can negotiate all we like, but the fact is, Cyrus is staring at my mouth like he wants to claim it again, and the part of me that falls asleep thinking of him wants him to.

"You can't make me—just because—" Only when the stuttered words tumble out of my lips do I realize they sound like a plead. *This isn't fair.*

"I'm sorry."

Reeling, I yank my arm from Cyrus's grasp, my flickering tenacity burning its wick fast. He doesn't get to do this gently. "I'm not leaving."

"I'm prepared to confess our kiss to my father, if that's what it takes," he continues, relentlessly calm. "He'll send you away himself. I might have to do it anyway, if we want the Seer from Verdant. For once, it's unfortunate that my father likes you so much, otherwise I wouldn't need an excuse."

I slap him—right across the glamour where I know he'd been injured. He staggers backward with a sharp hiss, red blooming across his cheeks.

"Fuck you," I spit.

Retreating into the divining room, I slam the door in his stunned face.

I'm shaking now that I allow myself to breathe. I use my throbbing hand to palm away nascent tears.

I know that as a last resort, I could beg Cyrus to change his mind. If I played damsel in distress and crumpled sobbing in his arms, he'd sponge up my tears, apologize, and think himself so charitable for doing so, while I'd be a sorry thing indebted to him.

I'd rather ship myself across the sea in a crate.

I fill my lungs, in and out, until the shaking subsides, then pace the cold shadows of the divining room. If he tells his father . . . gods, I'd be ruined. I'm too much of a liability, especially with his wedding imminent.

We're supposed to be an impossibility.

I can deny it. Cyrus kissed me; I don't have to admit I kissed him back. I can hope King Emilius takes my side.

Hope—the thought startles a laugh out of me. It's flimsy but it has to be enough.

And in the meantime, I will be irreplaceable. I had new visions of my tower and that menacing manor. Dark magic is afoot; I can figure out where it's coming from. And then I will tell the king how to stop it.

I just need to stay a few steps ahead.

At my desk, I crack open my borrowed edition of *Traditions & Magics of the Wood* again with twitchy hands. Cyrus's thank-you note slips out, and this time, I do fling it in the fire grate.

I reread the passages that talk about blood's effect on the

Fairywood. Blood can make the Fairywood rot, but could it turn it into something else? My twisted dreams and these chimeric beasts—they're like a corruption. More important, who or what could be behind it?

Humans with innate magic are rare as myth. I'm not sure if they've actually existed, except for Seers and our Sight. People have learned to extract magic from plants and haggle for magic from fairies, but I've never seen proof of anyone transforming that magic into something greater than its parts.

My thoughts slide toward the Fates themselves. What are *they* capable of? They don't walk our physical plane, but they must direct the threads of time *somehow*.

No one knows of the Fates' utter delight when they spoke of the curse. That night they threatened me, they laughed over my demise, my helplessness. They demanded Cyrus's life like it was nothing. Maybe they just wanted his life that was owed them, but I don't trust they have anyone's interest in mind except their own.

If the Fates *want* this prophecy of blood and war and rose-beasts to pass, what better way than to remove the prince at the heart of it?

I tip backward in my chair, juggling thoughts until my head hurts. All this guesswork to prove my worth when I shouldn't have to.

When it might not even matter, because a single scandal could ruin me.

A voice echoes in my mind: *You are worthy of so much more.*

That Fate who last spoke to me—*they* could help me, if

they ever came back to talk. They were the only useful god out of them all. If only I could call on them myself.

I drum my fingers against my wooden seat as I slowly set all four legs of my chair on the ground.

Maybe I could.

Gods are probably as self-serving as all of us. People call their offerings *tributes* and *gifts* . . . as if they aren't under at a least a little bit of duress when giving them. Bribes, more like it.

I am not above bribery.

And the Fates are probably starving with no one making sacrifices anymore.

Something in this tower must help me perform a ritual. I head back downstairs. Lady Raya clearly isn't visiting tonight; I'll do this instead.

I riffle through the cabinets along the walls, searching past ornate costumes, orbs that sparkle to the touch, charts and star gadgets that I never use. Finally, in a chest containing many smaller boxes, I find a set of knives.

I don't have a lot to work with regarding how to *do* a sacrifice—just scenes I've dreamed and the few mentions of them in the book upstairs, as it related to the Fairywood:

Perform blood rituals and other butchery with separate containers and knives to prevent contamination. Bloodblight can be lethal to Wood plants.

Of all types of blood, human blood is the most potent.

Drawing one knife from its jeweled sheath, I hold it up to the light. My distorted reflection frowns back from the blade. I knew, even as a child looking at reflections in windows, that I'd never look sweet, with my slash of brows, pinched lips, the blushed yellow of my skin like moth wings. But I looked ready to fight something twice my size, and that hasn't changed.

I test the knife's curved edge against a scrap of fabric. It's still sharp. This will do.

I light a candle and clean the blade's edge in the flame. Then I go to the entrance of my divining room, to the fountain that was once a vessel for blood and is now a vessel of coin from my patrons. I scrape out the day's offerings so it's empty, then kneel before it.

Grimacing, I press the knife tip into my finger until a dark red drop of blood wells up. I smear it in the bowl.

And wait.

The cut throbs faintly like a heartbeat. Soon, it stops bleeding. Nothing's happened.

So a *little bit* of blood won't trigger anything.

Biting my lip, I find a spare square of cloth folded away in my bedroom. I spread it out on the floor and place a jug of water and clean bandages nearby. I sit myself at the center with the fountain basin in front of me and turn the knife over in my palm.

This is stupid.

Maybe it's better if I don't do this.

Gods, I don't want to do this.

But I know if I don't do this now, I'll only end up doing it in the dead of night when I'm frustrated and can't sleep again.

The steel is cold against my skin but warming quickly. If I have a future coming for me, I want to know it. And if I want a plan, I'm out of options.

I squeeze the blade and slice my palm.

"Shit," I gasp, wincing. That felt . . . deep.

I drop the stained knife. Rising to my knees, I reach for the bandages, but between the sudden rush of blood to my head and the blood dripping from my hand, I can't get my bearings. I sway. Spots appear in my vision that I can't blink away.

"Shit." I think I'm going to faint.

And then I do.

13

HOW DESPERATE.

I open my eyes. My hand hurts. My *head* hurts.

With my good hand, I push myself up off the floor, woozy but fine. Blotches of dark red stain the front of my shirt. The candles have burned down, and the divining room is a little hazy, as if the edges to everything are trembling. Imagined.

I blink and rub my eyes. I must be dreaming again.

Or suffering from blood loss.

Awake at last.

The hairs on my neck rise. I look behind me out of reflex, but no one's there; it only sounds as if someone is whispering behind my ear. It's that same voice of that Fate who gave me that rhyme, who warned of betrayal—the Fate I need.

"Will you help me again?" I ask.

I am here, am I not?

I shiver at the ethereal timbre. "How can we stop the prophecy? Two beasts with rose-covered horns already attacked the capital—attacked *me*—and I dreamed of more in the countryside."

You speak true—the blood-soaked earth, the rose-horned beasts, the endless war—they are coming. They are inevitable. And they cannot be stopped.

"There must be different futures. The prophecy said the prince's heart will be salvation *or* damnation. He chose a bride—Raya Solquezil. The one described in your rhyme."

This is not an argument. I will say it again: They are inevitable.

Licking my lips, I rise to my feet. The room still wobbles. "I don't believe you. I think this is the easy way out." Gods must like simple obedience as much as any other authority. "If my visions are true destiny, then I wouldn't have been able to save Cyrus seven years ago. I changed that future."

And you are paying the cost of it now.

"But it was possible."

They pause, as if contemplating. *Answer this first: why do you wish to save this land?*

"I want—I mean—" I stumble over the starts of sentences, as none of them sounds exactly right. "It's my home. If it's in danger, then I'm in danger."

Then you only care to save yourself.

I flush. How often have I heard words like that from Cyrus? "If it comes to it, but I wouldn't—"

I am not scolding. I think it is wise. I think you do not do it enough. You are soft-hearted.

"Me? Soft-hearted?"

You could have let the beasts devour the prince, but you did not.

"He protected me." I swallow hard, doubting my choice. "In the moment . . . I couldn't."

But he must die anyway. It will be him or you. You know this.

I can't entirely reconcile the fact that the Fates *want* Cyrus to die. "You Fates really aren't what I expected."

Gods never are. There's a trill to their voice, as if they're delighted. It's such an earthly emotion, a jarring one. *Very well. I will give you a choice, if a choice is what you seek. Go to the outside of your tower, down to the new growth.*

Hope blooms in my chest despite myself. Half-conscious of the blood trailing in my wake, I stagger down the spiral staircase, out the claw-marked archway.

Outside, it's bright for what I know to be night. I can't see any guards across the bridge to the palace; usually two are posted by the gates. I don't hear anything but the wind.

Keeping close to the wall, I descend the tower's outside set of stairs. There are no handholds, and in shadow, the rain-slicked steps are difficult to see.

Halfway down, thin tendrils of green begin to vein over the woody walls of the tower. Another half-circle around and the walls disappear entirely behind thick, leafy vines, viridescent as the day they sprouted.

Touch the vines. Let your blood mingle.

The skin around my wound stretches as I lift my hand, the wind biting it dry. Pain induces a moment of clarity, and I let my hand hover. "Blood destroys Fairywood growth," I say.

Yours will do more than that, little star.

I shiver. Not because of the voice this time, but from the implication that there's a strangeness about myself I haven't discovered yet. My Sight may be boundless, but in the waking world, skin and bone anchor me like everyone else. The body I live in is of finite volume and countable parts, cold in the winter and fragile under a knife. There should be no mysteries here.

Yet when I press my bloody palm against the wall of green, the plant underneath quivers. It begins to shrivel, as I expect it to, but something is also growing, pushing out of the decay—

I pull away just as a thorn bursts forth.

Staggering backward, my heel meets empty air. I grab hold of the thorn and it breaks off with a snap. Barely managing my balance, I pitch myself forward against the wall.

I slide down to the steps, trembling. The thorn is nearly as long as my forearm and weighs too much for its thinness. The tip is a tempting apple red. *Poison,* I think suddenly at that color. On the broken end, the sap has crusted over into a hard amber, almost like a pommel.

Like a dagger.

My blood *made* this. "How?"

The Sight is but the surface of a Seer's magic. There is more to discover yet.

"You're being cryptic again." I have so many more questions: Who knows this is possible? What else can my blood do? Between the scarcity of Seers and our loyalties to different kingdoms, we hardly get a chance to share knowledge. I brush a thumb toward the thorn's sharp end. How easily it might sink into my flesh.

I ask the most important question: "What do I do with this?"

Stab it through the prince's heart.

"That's *murder,*" I say. And then I remember why I'm

here and what the voice said they'd give me: a choice. My limbs turn to ice. "I'm not going to *murder* Cyrus."

You would mourn the boy? A laugh. *As the Fates have said, he must die before summer's end or you will burn. Use the thorn and you will get away with it. When it strikes his heart, it will destroy his body.*

I frown, parsing the words again, a new chill spreading to the core of me. *As the Fates have said* . . . "You aren't a Fate?"

I am and I am not.

Half-god, half-mortal? Born of both? But the Fates don't walk this earth. . . . "Speak plainly." My hand throbs anew, a reminder of my earlier desperation. A warning to not let myself get carried away twice. I am bargaining with a stranger. "How are you in my head if you're not a Fate?"

Even a shade of my former power is vast. But I mistakenly placed my faith in mortals long ago, and now I am as much like the Fates as I am like you. That is why I wish to help you. The voice sounds nearly tender, even parental, like how the king sounds when he uses my first name instead of my title. *I see in you what I was: someone who clings to people who are destined to abandon you. They will never love you as you wish them to. Never see what you See.*

My throat is dry. "I don't know what you mean."

Do not deny it. This place does not deserve you. Neither does your prince. Kill him before his betrayals mount, if you have any sense left. Fulfill the Fates' wishes and you will be free to whatever life you seek.

A hateful part of me wants to believe everything they've said, because I certainly believe some of it. Cyrus would—*has*—cast me aside. And he doesn't deserve me.

But the better part of me knows this voice is guiding me down the bloody path on purpose. Whoever they are, they're intimately familiar with the prophecy and of what possibilities lie in the future. Familiar enough, maybe, to be behind the recent events themselves. They entered my dreams first, readied with information that would get Cyrus to trust me, so that I would trust *them*.

"If Cyrus dies, what happens to the beasts?" I ask carefully. Let them think I'm more tempted than I am. Let them tell me more. "The bloodshed and the war to come? How will they be stopped?"

It is not your concern.

"I've dreamed wars. I've seen how devastating they can be."

War will happen without you. This world is washed with blood and ash. Built by war.

Dimly, I think of King Emilius wanting to grow an empire; somewhere along his plans, he will surely use force to achieve his ends. History has proven we're cold and cruel enough without the aid of gods. The voice is right about this much: prophecy or not, blood and war will come.

You doubt me. I feel it.

I bare my teeth. "If you know me so well, you shouldn't be surprised this is a lot to consider. I still don't know who you really are. And I wouldn't like to snip off my ties to a king only to get tangled in new ones."

The threads will play out, little star, no matter your wishes. When you discover the depths of your powers, then you will truly See.

I can taste the poison in their words. I can feel the strings wrapping around my wrists. But their words are seductive, their promises new. Standing at the slippery edge of my tower, I've never felt more unmoored; a breeze could lure me to the earth below, so distant that I might have time to regret it. Kings and curses, girls and gods—these are the makings of tales. All I did was bleed and ask.

Could I bear killing Cyrus? I've always hated how people speak of destiny as if they had no part in it. How they stow their guilt in the stars instead of their hearts, blaming the Fates for their decisions. If I drove this into Cyrus's heart, I wouldn't blame it on anyone but myself.

Do not tarry. The threads must be woven.

I look at the star-filled sky, freshly desperate, searching for a source of the madness. "I want to know more."

Such greed. Ah, then, I will reveal to you one more treachery: the woman you know as Raya brought the beasts to you.

"What?"

At the same time a cry rings out, realer than anything that should exist in this world: "Violet!"

The new voice comes from up the stairs where a tall, shadowy figure of familiar frame stands. The figure runs toward me as the dream tears and an echo of laughter withdraws from my ears.

The tower is shorn in half, vines unravel, the sky a myriad

of unfathomable colors. Gasping, I stretch my hand toward the figure as they reach out with their own.

The ground beneath me gives way.

<hr />

Pain bridges me between dream and waking. When I open my eyes, the world is dully hued. I'm back where I fainted, the cold lacquered floors of the divining room beneath me. Firelight dances at the edge of my gaze. The frilly cushion from the footstool is stuffed underneath my throbbing head.

And I'm not alone.

Dante is crouched on the hearth, removing a steaming kettle. His curly hair is tied back, sleeves rolled up, coat laid aside as if he's been here for some time. When he turns around, he heaves a sigh of relief. "Thank the Fates."

"What are you doing here?"

"I *was* coming to tell you that Raya won't be able to make it." He pours out the kettle in a tub and tests the temperature with a finger. "Then I came to the tower, saw the doors left wide open, and when I checked outside, you're collapsed on the steps with blood all over you. I thought you were attacked by another beast."

"I . . . tried to induce a vision." Hazy memories return. "I thought slashing my hand . . ."

A groan. "What the hell were you thinking, Violet?"

"It *worked*."

He still shakes his head. "Hope it was worth it. I know

some tasty flavors of fungus that might do the same thing *without* the potentially fatal blood loss." Taking my left arm, he guides my hand over the tub and ladles warm water over the wound. I hiss as the gash on my palm stretches open.

"What do you know about Lady Raya?" I reach for the ladle myself, but he won't let me help.

"I've been helping her get situated in the city. She's . . . interesting."

"You're suspicious of her, too."

Dante sighs, tugging at his shirt's frilly jabot. "Relations between Auveny and Balica are fraught. I am trying to keep things down to a simmer. Have some understanding. The Head of Lunesse isn't what I expected. She's *supposedly* a very respected leader, yet . . . To put it delicately, I hope the standards in Lunesse aren't that low."

"That bad?" I frown. "Why couldn't she visit my tower today?"

He shrugs. "When I visited her apartment, she had some weird excuse—said her face broke out in hives. Something about a fear of heights? She was hysterical, so I dropped it. We've been trying to drag her out to discuss electing a new Head for Lunesse, too, if she is to remain here as queen, but some advisors think she ought to be *both,* which completely breaks precedent. . . ."

He trails off. There are hollows under his eyes; has he been handling her this entire time? Cyrus must be showing her around when he can, but at other times, I can imagine few others he would he trust his future bride with.

Dante's closeness to this situation puts me ill at ease.

But I have to tell *someone* about my vision. If Raya brought the beasts here, if she is the witch who Camilla and others suspect her to be, she has to be stopped.

"What are you going to be when Cyrus becomes king?" I ask.

Dante's muttered answer is distracted. "Gray-haired, at this rate."

"You're doing too much work for him."

"It's not just for Cyrus. Ambassador Pincorn needs a hand, especially lately. It's not as bad as I remembered—the paperwork and meetings."

"If you're going through that much trouble, they should make you an ambassador, too. Or Cyrus should appoint you as an adviser." Dante's lived in Auveny for so long, most people familiar with him in the Sun Capital consider him Auvenese. It's only that those who treat him like an outsider are louder.

"Not officially."

"Why not? A title will grant you respect."

A thought seems to hesitate on his tongue. "I . . . It might be easier to get certain things done without an official position."

The court sees Dante as a mere archivist who's bedding the prince; they don't think he's anyone special once removed from Cyrus. I always thought it was a pity—but maybe this is what Dante wants. Or it's the best he made of an irritating situation. I know the value of being underestimated.

With my wound cleaned, Dante applies a honey-soaked gauze and winds a bandage tightly around my hand. I'm careful not to let my fingers graze his palm in respect to his privacy. When he's done, I sag against his knee. I'm exhausted, the dizziness having become a headache.

I've missed his company. I've missed having someone to talk to who wasn't worrying about crowns and alliances and dutiful Seers. But I guess he can't be that anymore.

"My vision said that Raya brought the beasts here," I say without preamble.

For a long moment there's only the crackle of the fireplace as Dante goes very, very still. Eyes shutting heavily, he drags a hand down his face, the furrow in his brow deep enough to pinch a nail in place. If he were any more stressed, he'd just be one large wrinkle.

"Please tell me you're joking," he says.

"It's possible I'm caught in some divine machinations and a god—well, someone *like* a god—is manipulating me, in which case we have an entirely *different* problem on our hands." I take a deep breath, and Dante wilts further the more I keep talking. "But if they aren't, then the prophecy can't be stopped. And out of everything we *can* do, finding out if the lady about to live in our palace is lying seems like the easiest task to cross off, so . . . are you able to find out if this accusation is true?"

Dante looked so tired when I woke up. He looks five years older now. Nudging me off his knee, he slides his whole body down onto the rug, limbs splayed in limp defeat. "This room is soundproof?"

"Are you going to scream?"

"Should I do it into a pillow?"

"You can just go ahead."

174

He does. I wince through it.

"Tell me everything you know," he says, hoarse, "and then I need to check in on Raya so I can ensure we don't have an international incident."

"I've been dreaming about beasts overtaking the borderlands, corrupted forests—signs of the bad to come, but nothing about how to stop it." I move to sit beside him, pulling down a cushion from the sofa to use as a seat. "When I cut my hand, I called on a voice that spoke to me once before. I thought they were a Fate, but they seem to be working alone. I don't know their stake in Cyrus's curse, but they know things about the future. The first time we spoke, they told me the same rhyme that Cyrus heard from the Balican Seer. If this voice *is* telling the truth, they also elaborated on Felicita's prophecy. They added words. They said, *'The blood-soaked earth, the rose-horned beasts, the endless war.'*"

Dante sticks his hand in the air, counting off. "We have the beasts, and we can check off the other two in one go if Auveny thinks Raya was sent by Balica to kill us all." He flings his arms out. "I can see it already: His Majesty and his Council decry Balica's Fairywood protections—accuse them of protecting it all this time for some sinister reason instead of basic conservation. Balica is *already* mad King Emilius has ordered burnings again. They'll be indignant in the face of false accusations."

"What can Balica do? They're not equipped for war."

He hesitates. "At some point, you have to stand your ground, damn the consequences. If it were up to me, between a quick death through war or slow death from empire, I'd go down fighting."

Hearing that aloud, a lump grows in my throat.

"On the other hand, what a waste of this handsome face that'd be." Dante quirks his lips and I smile a little.

"Toady hell, what will I tell the king about Raya, though?"

"Nothing. Balica needs to be the one to collect her."

"So I should pretend everything's fine?"

"It'd buy some time." He sits up, hand scrubbing through his loosened hair. "We need evidence that what you've been told is true. And then we need to make sure that evidence gets in the right hands, without the Council or those zealous gossips twisting this for their ends."

"Bring her to me, if you can. I'll read her threads." Raya might be trying to avoid me, but we can drag her here if we have to.

"I don't want to involve you more than necessary."

I snort. "I'd say the same thing about you."

Dante remains decidedly sober, a grimace flexing his mouth. "Violet . . . I've kept information about this situation extremely close thus far. It's not personal, but as long as you obey King Emilius without hesitation, I will doubt your intentions. He could use Raya's betrayal to send armies marching south before the week is over, and I can't risk that."

My grin fades. Of course. I've loudly proclaimed I have my own interests at heart first. And Dante must know that I helped the king arrange Cyrus's match with Raya. "I do not just *obey* King Emilius," I still say, a paltry defense for myself. "He's the king. What am I supposed to do?"

"You'll obey Cyrus without question once *he* wears the crown?"

I press my lips together. "That's not the same. King Emilius's reign will end soon. I only have to endure a little longer." I spent my adolescence learning as much as I could, clawing for scraps of influence. No disagreement was worth stirring his wrath while I was trying to master my place in court. "King Emilius *expects* my obedience. I made sure that Cyrus *doesn't*."

"The first defiance is the hardest."

I nod. "I owe Emilius too much. He saw potential in me and taught me how to be shrewd in court. I suppose he's like what a parent would be—"

"It's easy," Dante interrupts, as gently as one can, "to confuse fear for respect."

I glance down, studying the bloom of red in the palm of my hand. I want to protest, say *I'm not afraid,* so confidently like I'd told Cyrus, but a cold feeling spreads through my gut, and it's all I can focus on. Dante sees the parts of me I don't recognize for my own sake, the worry and joy I shrug away, and he's known me long enough to be dangerous.

As much as Cyrus and I fight, a secret part of me looks forward to the prince's ascension as a fresh start. Or I felt that way before the ball happened, anyway.

"It's late. I should go," Dante says, gratefully breaking the silence. He gets to his feet, leaving my side empty. I hear him slide his coat on and his footsteps move toward the door. "Should we do anything about that new voice in your head?"

"I'll find out who they are if they come back." I whirl around to watch him leave. "We were only talking. . . . I don't think they can hurt me."

"Well, if anything changes . . ." He gestures vaguely at his weary self. "You should also visit a healer tomorrow to get your dressings changed—or I can stop by."

"You're busy enough. Just get some sleep."

He smiles crookedly. The door shuts behind him, and I'm alone again.

After a few minutes, when I'm certain Dante's gone, I take the remaining bandages and go outside the tower.

The lights of the Sun Capital twinkle below as I remember it. Tiled roofs cover the hillside like the scales of a sleeping dragon. For as long as I've lived here, I've kept my roots shallow, but it's home nonetheless. I know the servants and the quiet corners of the garden. I walk through the palace with my fingers drifting along the priceless art as if it were mine. I never thought that I might have to leave.

On the streets, getting too comfortable is begging for a knife in the gut. Up here, secrets cut just as deep.

I have so many secrets.

Halfway down the tower's outer set of stairs, I see a dark stain on the vines. In the same spot, there's fresh sap welling from something that's been broken off. I go all the way down to the bottom of the tower and circle around the base until I find it, nestled in a clump of grassy weeds: a shining, red-tipped thorn.

Wrapping it in a bandage, I tuck it into my sleeve.

14

WHATEVER DANTE IS DOING TO UNCOVER RAYA'S true intentions, he isn't doing it fast enough, and he certainly hasn't encouraged a healthy sense of self-preservation in the prince.

Cyrus and Raya begin going out on romantic dates, pretending they're in love. They shop for wedding jewelry. They share chaste kisses. They "flee" their guards to row a boat privately on the lake, all in view of Sun Capital denizens spying on them. A play in a theater couldn't be more staged. All that's missing is a string quartet hidden in the bushes.

I'm not jealous.

Fine, I'm a little jealous.

All the tales ever told speak of beautiful boys and girls falling in love simply because they're beautiful. But even the most beautiful witch is strange and wicked. Unhappy ever after, heart unmended, wishes unheeded, and alone, always alone.

Cyrus will get showered with rose petals on his wedding day.

I get thorns.

The thorn borne from my blood is hidden in a locked box in the back of a cabinet. I try to forget about it until one patron, a pock-cheeked farmhand, tells me, "Sighted Mistress, I am not sure if you have seen, but there is rot on your tower."

I follow him to check, pretending I have no idea what he means. The black scar of rotted growth is not only lingering where the thorn had broken off—it's spread.

Thanking the farmhand profusely, I send him on his way. Then I go back inside to retrieve a sharp knife to dig at the blackened parts. With my hand injured and little room to maneuver on the steps, it's tough work.

I can't tell anyone about this. The palace couldn't know about the thorn, couldn't know the reason this rot is here, but I'm paranoid just the same. Everyone's looking for more signs of Felicita's prophecy.

All the tale needs is the villain, and the line between revered and reviled is as thin as an accusation.

I don't plan on using the thorn. I don't trust that voice, and even if I did . . . Maybe to whoever is watching over me, killing Cyrus to save myself is an easy decision, but I'm no villain—just an opportunist, like everyone else.

Besides, what I really want is to look Cyrus in the eye when I best him. To strip away every trick and cunning smile of his until people see what I see.

I want Prince Charming to fall from grace.

Raya officially moves into the palace today. If she won't come to me, I will go to her.

I pull out a dress from the back of my wardrobe. The blue is a dark hue for summer, but I'm fond of the embroidery—sunflowers all along the bodice and hem. I shape my braid into a crown, tucking it in with pearly pins.

At the corner of my mirror, something glimmers.

I check my open window, where a golden choker rests on the sill. It's shaped like a wreath of leaves—a common design of conjured ornaments—and when I pick it up, it's featherlight, not the weight of real gold. I peer outside, but whatever fairy made this has gone.

Camilla must have sent it. It isn't my style at all and too glamorous for my outfit, but it's also too pretty to go unworn, so I slide it around my neck. It fits perfectly.

Raya's arrival is supposed to be informal, but people gather at the gates early and much of the court weasels their way into the halls one way or another. Cyrus and Raya's outings have fanned excitement, and those who think she's evil incarnate want front-row seats to observe her.

A small party is set up in one of the atria. Attendees fight for space among the plants and chairs and gifts, and lapdogs run amok underneath skirts. Fairies who arrived with their wards are overhead, drunk from their thimbles of ambrosia. The air tickles with their dust, tempting a sneeze.

I spot Camilla in the entrance hall, three rooms over. Her dress is a garish pink-and-gray checkerboard print; I could probably pick her out from the outskirts of the city if I tried. I go to her.

As soon as she sees me, she snaps her fan shut and loops her arm through mine. "Violet! Are you here for the party?"

I can't hold in my sigh. "Thought I should get out of my shell." Not entirely untrue. Doubt it'll help, but faced with imminent expulsion, it can't *hurt* to be friendly.

Camilla hums, nodding. "Whatever your ulterior motive is, I don't need to know. As long as you're here. You're just in time!"

All attention in the main courtyard is focused on a carriage stopped at the gates. Guards form two lines to part a path outside its doors. Raya steps out in an emerald gown with a skirt split down the middle, its two halves parted like petals. The lower portion of her face is covered by a veil and dark ringlets obscure the rest.

"She's always hiding her face," I murmur.

"Apparently, she's so beautiful that she does it for our own good." Camilla barely muffles an ugly snort. "Or what happened at the ball will happen again with everyone getting enchanted. *That*'s the story they're going with: her greatest flaw is she's *too pretty*."

"Prettier than you?" I bite into a custard bun I tucked away in a pocket.

"Let's not get carried away." She takes a second glance at my neck. "Oh! I like that."

I press my fingers to the choker. "I thought *you* sent this."

She shakes her head. "One of the fairies probably just decided to bless you."

"Me? It's a sad day if *I'm* kind enough to earn their favor."

"Maybe they needed a pet project. They're staying away from me right now because of this." Camilla taps at her own neck, where a tiny scent bottle hangs, filled with a dark red liquid. "A touch scandalous, like all the best things in the world."

During the ball, I'd seen this bottle in her threads, but I hadn't thought about it further. Up close, I immediately see what makes it startling. "Is that *blood* inside?"

She grins with all her teeth. "Clever, isn't it? I can't go around dumping blood on Raya every chance I get, but I *can* make wearing these a trend. It negates nearby fairy enchantments quite well—I tested it on the chambermaids. Fairies don't like them either, but that's all right. I don't need their glamour to be interesting. Can't say that about everyone else."

She throws a pointed look ahead, where Cyrus, sleek in a purple-plum coat, is escorting Raya the rest of the way across the grounds, hand in hand. Raya looks anxious. Not in a devious, secretly plotting way—mostly in an afraid-of-large-crowds way.

"Welcome, Lady Raya," Camilla says, when the couple arrive at the entrance hall. "So when does the curse-breaking start?"

Raya chuckles haltingly, glancing at Cyrus as if hoping for a cue. "I have, ah, learned a lot about the prophecy these past few days, Your Highness. I did not know there was this responsibility on my shoulders." A Southern accent inflects her words, drawing them out.

"Hopefully no more outbreaks of *hives,*" I say, recalling the excuse she used with Dante. Raya flinches. I don't expect Raya to be as exuberant as Camilla, but, well, I expect *something.* So far she's quick as a brick. "You know, as Seer,

I'm familiar with all kinds of prophecy. We should schedule another reading for this afternoon."

She chuckles again. "Oh, that sounds . . ."

"Like an excellent idea," Cyrus finishes.

I arch a brow. The prince wears his own false smile, the dimpled one he used to practice when his voice first changed and everyone thought he would marry quick. His face looks fully healed. I hope my slap stung for days.

He moves past us and guides Raya into the party. I want to talk to Raya, but so does everyone else. For now, I follow Camilla as she mingles among others.

But my attention splits. As I move from social circle to social circle, no matter what the conversation is like, I can't help but overhear Cyrus elsewhere, his laughter echoing across the atrium.

"If I could, I would have chosen every one of you to be my bride," I hear him say not far behind me. Even engaged, the prince has time to flirt.

If we were children still, I'd shove my head through the wall of lilacs dividing us and make a ghastly face to scare the party. For the longest time, I wanted to grow up and be taken seriously. But now that I *am* grown—all my height and teeth accounted for—I miss being reckless without care. It's not as if I want to be in these crowds fake-laughing at some lordling's terrible joke.

Though sometimes I wish I did. I *want* to want to be in this crowd. Everything would be simpler if I didn't know what I know, didn't think what I think, and I could just *be like everyone else.*

I'd hate that version of me.

Then again, if that were me, I wouldn't even know to hate myself.

That Violet would be grateful to have the Sight and grateful to have a place in the palace.

That Violet would be, well, *happy*.

The next circle Camilla drags me into is a mix of older ladies. Camilla flaunts her blood necklace, pulling empty ones from her purse to give to those who inquire. "Personally," the princess asserts, leaning in, "I think our use of fairies has gone too far. Consider: Lady Raya's fairies seemed to have skipped blessing her today, and the difference is utterly striking." The group titters. "I want nothing more than for my brother to find love, but to pin our hopes on a possible charlatan . . ."

Opposite us, a red-shawled woman cups her hand around her mouth. "I doubt anyone but Belina and I remember, but forty years ago, when I was a lass, fairies were considered a foe of the Fates. No one tells the tales like this anymore, but blood and fairy magic don't mix for good reason. Our blood is the Fates' dominion and they don't take kindly to magical meddling. It diverts destiny from its true course!"

Another who I recognize as the prim Lady Herina of the Fourth Dominion harrumphs. "We would do well to have some faith and hold our slander for when we have evidence."

"Slander?" Camilla barks a laugh. "Raya made a sudden trip across the continent, alone and without notice, wearing five fairies' worth of glamour. That's not slander. It's *strange*." For how temperamental she can be, the princess always chooses her words with care, knowing when to pin pleasantries and when to drive her points down like a fist.

"The *Fates* are strange, Your Highness. And they are hungry." Herina stabs a finger in the air. "There hasn't been a good tale in ages—odd curses and blessings, yes, but when was the last time real drama has swept the lands? His Highness's true love, a prophecy breaker, must be one of a kind. It only stands that she isn't like what we see every day. We have forgotten what strangeness truly is. Ah, Sighted Mistress—"

Herina steps toward me with open hands. I don't remember her being awful—she's always polite during readings and is reputed to have gained more wisdom than complacency over her management of the Fourth Dominion's financials—but I don't like the way she's looking at me, as if she found an answer. "We are living in times where destiny is in the making. Beasts walk among us. True love bespells us. What say you of Auveny's future?"

I'm used to acting as if I know less than I do, greeting patrons as if I haven't seen bits of their future in other readings, or making up excuses if my prophecies don't match reality. "I've dreamed conflicting accounts," I say judiciously. "We should temper our expectations about Lady Raya being any kind of savior. The future rests upon the decision of Prince Cyrus's heart, and he is *fickle*." I stress the word more than I mean to, but no one seems to catch it as they discuss among themselves.

"I admit, His Highness does not look like a man in love," someone says.

"Will it matter? Felicita's prophecy mentioned only a bride."

"No, no, the prophecy mentioned his heart, too, don't forget. . . ."

"Herina speaks true. As they say, there is no destiny without blood."

"Fairy enchantments bewitched him. Perhaps now he is regretting . . ."

"Why, he has looked this way more than he has looked at Lady Raya."

I glance up. Sure enough, Cyrus has turned his gaze in our direction—at me, if I want to be vain and precise. The blandest smile touches his lips, a polite acknowledgment of our group, but I feel the trace of his stare follow mine, lingering on my throat where the choker rests. My skin prickles, warm.

It's just the magic drawing his eye.

But the moment lends me a boldness. Enough tiptoeing around. "Why don't I perform a reading for Lady Raya right now?" I say. "I didn't get the chance to yet."

Camilla lets out a delighted whoop, clapping. "That's a brilliant idea. Raya!" She beckons with a frantic hand, drawing the attention of the entire room. "You must have a reading done by our Seer while she's free. She's been very in demand."

In a matter of seconds, the princess commands the servants to set up a table by the fountain, complete with decorative candles and a clean lace cloth on top. Raya, holding on to her veil, is hustled into a chair. Gaze darting around, she looks like a gopher that's popped out of the ground to find itself in a wolf's den.

I take a seat across from her. "I'll need your hands, Lady

Raya—er, just one." I extend my right hand. "Injured my other."

"Right. Of course," she answers in a tremulous voice. The first thing I notice, as her palm meets mine, is that her hand is calloused. Her bangles are cold as they slide against my fingertips.

And then I can only think of the images rushing through my Sight:

Sweltering, sleepless nights of travel. Three carriages cross the countryside. Two rattle with dangerous cargo locked shut in enchanted chests.

Fearful heartbeats to the quick tune of the orchestra. The palace glows in the distance, alive with revelry. Her carriages ignore the traffic at the gates.

Two chests tumble over the cliffside behind the palace. Wood splinters in the rushes of the river below.

From the water, hulking silhouettes emerge. The beasts growl.

My hand tightens. I bite my lip to keep calm. The voice was right.

The Sun Capital is behind her. She scales a rocky hill, fairies cupped in her hands. A whisper: "Just a little farther."

A set of crowns. A set of rings. A magnolia-lined hall in splendent white and gold.

The prince before her on the dais, frown carved in his expression.

My brows knit. Are those future threads?

Air thick with iron. Blood—too much blood.

Her terrified voice in a black-brambled ballroom. "Why are you doing this?"

A cackle and a crack of lightning and a burst of dark feathers.

"Seer." Cyrus's voice cleaves through my Sight. "You are crushing my lady's hand."

I open my eyes with a short gasp. Raya's long fingers are bunched in mine, sweaty and trembling. Everyone is staring.

"Oh." I let go, but there's no hiding the shock on my face: I saw something terrible. I can still smell the blood.

What do I say? Raya brought the beasts, but it doesn't add up. She seemed scared. There was—*will be*—a wedding, and then a disaster. But why?

What if it's because of me?

I barely hear the rest of what Cyrus says to the hushed crowd around us: "Would you pardon us? I nearly forgot— we have a meeting with my father today. It shouldn't take long. Let's go, Violet. Before we're late."

My chair scrapes against the tile as I stand up, movements automatic. It's a lousy excuse to extricate me, but I follow the prince without another word.

15

CYRUS DOESN'T HEAD TOWARD HIS FATHER'S study, but toward a less-trafficked hall in the east wing.

"What did you see?" he asks.

I'm still shaking, but we're far away from the party now. I don't have to follow him anymore. I spin on my heel.

"Violet!"

His steps clatter behind me. He grabs my arm. I whirl around on him, lips pinched. His grip is familiar in a way it wasn't a month ago. I remember it elsewhere on my body. The way he looks at me at this distance is intimate, no matter what we're doing.

"I don't need to tell you anything," I hiss.

With a muttered swear, the prince opens the door to the nearest room and unceremoniously shoves me in.

Hot, stuffy air greets me as I stumble into what appears to be a lesser-used armory. Polished plate mails and racks of enamel-handled swords gleam under a thin layer of dust. There isn't much space here for anything that isn't made of steel.

Cyrus shuts the door behind him. "You saw something."

I draw back against a suit of armor, riled as a cornered cat. "Maybe I did."

"Dante told me that you had a vision the other day. One that said Lady Raya brought the beasts here."

"Sounds familiar."

An exasperated grunt. "We're on the same side. I believe Raya's hiding something, but we need proof, and your cooperation could make all the difference." He acts as if *I'm* the addled one here, and I realize exactly what's going on in his head. "If you have *any* information—"

"Oh, sorry, *are we working together now?*" I bark a laugh. I want to think that I couldn't kill him, but he's tempting me. "Princey, you misunderstand the nature of our relationship. If you want my assistance, maybe you shouldn't *banish me!*"

Cyrus dares to look stricken. Shutting his eyes, he only chides, "As you said, we have more pressing dangers to focus on. We can discuss your future later, but right now, I am trying my best to contain a fraught situation—"

"You have some nerve sounding so damn tragic." I shove him square in the chest. He clutches my wrists, always careful not to touch my hands. We're too close again. The billow of his shirt brushes against me. "Coming here to beg my help before you throw me out. Traipsing around with Raya like she's your true love when we both know the night of the ball went *very differently.*"

In a flicker of his expression, I recognize the prince I knew growing up: unyielding but uncertain, shadowed by fate. "That night was a mistake."

"Was it?" I can almost pretend he was fevered—half-drunk and high on fairy dust—when he nearly broke down my tower's door and put his hands on me as if they'd been aching to for weeks. "Tell me something I'd believe at face value for once."

"I wish you were never in my life."

"Would've been a short life," I bark.

"Maybe," he says, wistful in a way that makes us both pause. "But you are. In my life."

His grip is still on my wrists, pinning them in the air. We breathe heavily in this scrap of privacy we found among the cobwebs. There's nothing between us except dust and lust.

"You still want to kiss me right now," I whisper with bitter satisfaction. "Isn't that why you're so angry?"

Cyrus sways closer. I know the collision is coming, but I don't draw away, my arrogance and my own body betraying me.

We meet—a brush of lips, then more, as we stagger into each other. He drinks me in like he's drowning. My eyes flutter shut at the pull. If I make a noise, he'd steal it with the tongue slipping between my teeth.

I forget our titles. I forget every prophetic warning. The world is as small as the taste of him, like liquored fruit. I hook my fingers in his collar. When we first kissed, I was too shocked to act on anything but instinct, but this time I am the one pulling him down, pulling him near. I learn fast—I've always had to—and surprising him is worth any fumbling on my part.

Maybe I won't ever stop him from wanting me gone, but I could unravel him like this.

I could burn like this.

We tumble into the shadows. Hands around my waist then buried in my hair, Cyrus pushes me into a space behind a rack of shields and a moth-bitten divider. I understand now how he wants me as much as he hates me: I'm the splinter in his heart, digging deeper with every attempt to remove me.

I understand now what inevitable means.

A distant thought reminds me, *This is dangerous.*

Rattling. A swinging creak.

The door.

"Shh." Cyrus slips a finger through my choker and tugs me toward him. He kisses me like nothing else matters, and I kiss him like I believe it.

My heartbeat is the loudest thing in the room. This is *stupid* and dangerous, but if we stop, we'll be arguing again. If we stop, I'll just have a memory haunting me. Tethered by touch, we're two mad lovers who know of nothing beyond this. I hardly know myself. I thought I was afraid of losing control.

I'm more afraid of how much I like it.

The door shuts. Clutter settles. We're alone again, and time resumes.

Wrenching him by the back of his head, I pull Cyrus off me, panting.

"Violet." His eyes are wide and dark. I remember his words from the labyrinth: *We could ruin each other, and we would not hesitate to do so.*

"Figure out what you want." I wipe my mouth with the back of my hand. "Figure it out, so I can ruin you properly."

I grab my hairpins scattered on the ground and storm out of the armory. If Cyrus calls out for me, I don't hear him past the pounding of my blood.

⤝⤞

It's a long way back to the tower.

In my room, I throw myself onto my bed face-first and bite down on my pillow, hoping it might cure me. My heart is still beating fast, and the heat of Cyrus's body smolders my skin.

Would I have stopped him at all if I wasn't worried about us being found? The dream I had of him taunts me, the one where I invite him to do things that have only lived in my imagination. I would have loved to pull apart the buttons on his shirt—the snap when they break, his groan on my lips.

A shudder passes through my body, all the way down to the soles of my feet. I dig my nails into my palm. In my mind, I list all the things I hate about the prince, starting with his slightly too-big ears and how he keeps his sword strapped to his waist everywhere he goes like he's compensating for something. How he can't stand to look at me for more than a few seconds without curling his lips. The way he speaks like he knows anything about me.

I roll over, staring at the jewels embedded in the ceiling.

I'd still rather think about Cyrus instead of those violent scenes in Raya's threads. I don't get it: if she wanted any of us dead, she's had every opportunity to make it so. In her past threads—even now—Raya seems frightened, not malicious. Like a puppet.

But if that's true, who is at the strings?

Someone knocks downstairs.

Ideally, I'd see zero people for the remainder of today—and this week, month, and year. I got out of my shell and all I have to show for it are traumatic visions. But I could find worse than Camilla swinging a basket of leftover cakes at my door.

She's changed outfits since the party; a bright red frock covers the clover-patterned blouse she picked up from the tailor, and her cat, Catastrophe, lounges on her neck like a feline stole. Glamours or not, Camilla always finds a way to make a statement.

"So," she says, inviting herself in. "That was bizarre."

I don't even know what she's referring to, but I agree. "Sorry. How was the rest of the party? Raya's moved in?"

"Into the worst room in the royal quarters! Last inhabited by a great-aunt who was obsessed with collecting stuffed bears. The furniture in there is *decades* out of date."

"That's not the kind of punishment you think it is."

"Let me have this victory." She twirls and flumps onto the sofa, setting the basket on the hearth. "What did you see in Raya's threads? Everyone's wondering."

Camilla is dear, but if you tell her something, you may as well be shouting it from your rooftop to the entire Sun Capital and then writing personalized letters to everyone out of earshot. "I saw . . . her wedding." I clear some plates off a velvet footrest, and Camilla stretches her legs onto it.

"That grim, hmm?"

A glamorous wedding with all the trappings, including a body count. "It was your brother's wedding too, before you get too excited."

"Those two make it all the way to the ceremony?"

"Maybe. The future isn't fixed."

"But it is very likely."

I grimace. "Especially because I don't know how to stop it."

Camilla's mouth pops open with an "*Oh.*" Catastrophe, the only creature more spoiled than the princess, climbs her way down onto her owner's lap and curls up there, as if that were the culmination of the cat's entire day's work. Camilla scratches behind her cat's twitching ear, humming a cheery tune. "You *want* to stop the wedding?"

"Don't you?" I slump onto the armrest next to her.

"We're not talking about me right now." She swings her blood vial necklace like a pendulum. I can't decipher her gaze, coy in one blink, a warning in the next, capricious as the shimmer and shadow that paint her eyelids. "I'm curious if you have *another* reason for stopping the wedding. Earlier, it was strange when you left with Cyrus . . ."

"He wanted to know about Raya's threads, too," I scoff. "Doesn't want anything to do with me until I'm useful." And he thinks he's so different from his father.

"Mmm, he *is* a brat. And how many pieces of clothing come off when you talk to Cyrus nowadays? Or stay on, if that's easier to count."

My cheeks heat to a temperature that could light a stove. "All our clothes stay *on.*"

Leaning on an elbow, the princess rests her chin on the curl of her hand, smug like she can read every dirty thought I had before she knocked on my door. Gods, maybe Cyrus is right. Maybe I *should* leave Auveny forever. "How long has this been going on?" she asks, singsong.

"There is no '*this*,' " I grit.

"Ah. No strings attached, I see."

"We're just—it's *not*—"

"*Oh*. This is *recent* for you both. Your first—no, your second encounter. And you're already stammering?" Camilla's pout scrunches to one side, contemplative, then to the other, disgusted. "So he's *that* kind of kisser. . . . I didn't need to know that about him, actually. I regret asking."

I can't feel my face anymore. I give up. "He's not that good—good *at all*—he's—"

"Runs in the family." She winks.

"*—a serious problem.*"

Camilla sighs at last. "*Alas.* You're probably right about that, what with, well, *everything* right now. Who else knows?"

"*No one*. I'm hoping it stays that way."

"Not even Dante? I bet he knows. He's just being polite about it."

"Ugh." I sink into the sofa. Catastrophe yowls and re-curls herself into a smaller circle as my weight bears onto her tail. I scratch her scruff in apology. "I mean it. Cyrus and I aren't anything. It was a one-time . . . two-time thing."

"And I bet you thought it was going to be a one-time thing before it became a two-time thing," she tsks. "Do you need a contraceptive draft?"

"No!" My blush reignites.

But the second I let my thoughts slip from the present, my body will convince me to want things I shouldn't want. Skirting its edges of intimacy has made me curious and hungry as if I left a half-devoured supper. I've never been shy around Cyrus, and that's maybe the entire problem.

"Are you sure about that?" Camilla grabs her basket of cakes and reaches into the middle of the stack, pulling out a pouch that smells strongly of herbs.

"You already brought—"

"Oh, I assumed. You've both been acting strange, and I saw you heading back here with your hair a *mess*. Which reminds me: be careful around the gossips. You know how chatter spreads. Even a single ember can be dangerous."

"I don't even *like* Cyrus," I mutter, one last protest.

"If that didn't stop either of you from throwing yourselves at each other before, why would that stop you now?" She bats her lashes, making too much sense. "We can't help what we want. People fall in love with us Lidines and—and it's *too* easy. We see into hearts like you see into futures. I know you're a big girl, but that doesn't mean you won't be silly, nor that you can't get hurt. Things can go too far. Fates, knowing you two, they definitely will."

I bury my face into the back of the couch. "Getting back to the matter of Raya—"

"Now that she's in the palace, I can keep a close eye on her. But *first,* I don't want a niece or nephew yet, Violet, cute as they would be." Camilla holds out the pouch. "Eina, ever-doting nurse, gave this to me, but I don't need them.

Brew two leaves to a cup, drink it every morning. Keep it for later if you don't use it now."

When I don't take it, she reaches over to stuff it in my pocket. I scowl, and she pats my cheek.

"Consider it a consolation gift for liking men."

❧

When Camilla is gone, I lock the door. I walk past the intricate cabinets in the front of the room, past the curtain behind the divining table, to a plain cabinet that sits alongside crates of unsorted instruments. I push aside bundles of cloth on the top shelf and reach around the back until my hands land on a box carved out of pure onyx, shining like the back of a raven's wing. I unlock it with the key I brought from my bedroom.

Lifting the lid, I find the thorn exactly as I left it.

Any normal thorn would have withered by now. The length of it is stiff as steel, and it remains as green as the new vines outside the tower. I grip it like a knife and swing it through the air, and it flies easier than any blade I've ever held, true as enchantment, as if it were made for me.

A sureness that would make me feel confident were I holding any other weapon, but this only makes me queasy.

Because if it's made for me, then I'm meant to use it.

I can't imagine piercing Cyrus's heart with this. When I push the tip against the wood of the shelf, it makes a deep mark. I don't dare test it against skin; the tip still shines with its unearthly red.

When it strikes his heart, it will destroy his body.

Though I'm furious at the thought of him, though I'm as vile as many in the Auvenese court, I'm no murderer.

Still . . . I took the thorn. I'm holding it now.

So maybe I'm wrong.

I could be goaded into doing it, couldn't I? I could do anything, if I was certain I could get away with it.

Is it only the fear of punishment that's stopping me?

Does killing, like lying, get easier after the first time?

I remember it was King Emilius who taught me how to prophesy for an audience. *You are not merely a receiver of prophecy, he told me, but a translator of it. The manner in which you describe what you see is as important as your gift itself.*

In my early years as Seer, my only audience was the king. I would tell him of interesting dreams I had and he would act accordingly: preparing aid if I saw a calamity, or seeking out a person if I saw an important destiny.

The first alteration I made to my foretellings was a small one: after I dreamed of dragons roaming the countryside, King Emilius had me announce to his court that dragons would wreak havoc specifically in the Thirteenth Dominion. That way, he could send more Dragonsguard to that area of the border.

Afterward, I waited for the lightning strike, for the accusation, for *any* consequence at all—and it never came. I changed the truth and the stars didn't fall. Later on, I'd realize the king wanted to send Dragonsguard there to intimidate the Balican side of the border. By then, so much time had passed, my guilt was stale as well.

My dreams didn't always show Auveny in the best light. I also glimpsed the threads of less savory work—bribes and double-dealings done in the very halls of this palace, the silencing of dissenters. For these, King Emilius told me to keep quiet. This was another way I could translate my prophecy, by saying nothing about them at all. By *not* interfering.

Even if these slights felt wrong, what would I gain through disobedience? No one's goodwill is as important as the king's, and my word couldn't outmatch his.

But there's a hidden cost to this thinking, too:

I will always be beholden to kings.

Once Cyrus is crowned, I will likely serve him for the rest of my life. If I stay. If he lives. We can't change our history and—as much as I resist the thought—I have doubts we can change our future. Every vision is worse than the last, and I see no end to our volatile dance.

The voice licks my ear, so close in memory, I'd swear they're standing in this room: *This place does not deserve you. Neither does your prince.*

I turn the thorn over and over in my hands. Did I grow too comfortable, settling for scraps of power? Nothing lasts in this world, least of all our lives. What is Cyrus's life really worth when his threads are placed against the endless weave of time? When the mourning is done, we will all move on, myself especially.

I know this is a dangerous path for my thoughts to stray along. I know everyone says it's wrong to think these things—but it's true. How much blood do kings shed in their wars? Conquerors write history and destroy histories in one triumphant swoop. How small is my evil in comparison, if I ended one prince's life for my own?

There are no rules to play by, there is no sympathy from the stars. Maybe any softness planted in my heart is the part that's wrong.

They will never love you as you wish them to.

Maybe cruel is the best thing I can be.

I put the thorn back in the box and lock the box in the cabinet, but my thoughts have spilled open.

When I lie back in bed, I dream of blooming briars crawling up my tower, red like blood, then turning black with rot.

16

COURIERS ARRIVE FROM THE BORDERLANDS.
The news is grim: beasts have begun their march.

King Emilius calls me into the smoky Council Chamber
to discuss the reports along with the lords; I'm one of the
few to know before the rest of the court. The palace has
been downplaying the scattered sightings of beasts for as
long as possible, at least until the wedding. But these recent
developments are on a different scale.

Nearly overnight, dozens of the rose-horned monsters
emerged from the Fairywood in the Eleventh, Thirteenth,
and Fourteenth Dominions at once, overwhelming the nearest villages. Some damage was curbed by the extra Dragonsguard units nearby, stationed after I warned the king of my
visions, but the reports included casualties. The paths of the
beasts seem to trend northward, toward the Sun Capital.

"We are dispatching more soldiers, of course, but we
must understand these beasts' origins," says King Emilius
at the head of the table. His eyes are dark with lack of sleep.
"A transport will be arriving soon with one caught alive. We

will redouble our efforts to eradicate the Fairywood in the meantime."

Alive. A sudden weakness bows my knees at the thought of a beast in the Sun Capital again. I straighten myself before anyone notices.

"What of Lady Raya Solquezil?" Lord Ignacio of the Thirteenth flicks his cigar. "Will she be our salvation or will she continue to shuffle from tea party to tea party until our hospitality finally thins?"

Outside of polite company, the words for the Head of Lunesse have become harsher. Encouraged by the princess's relentless distaste for her, the court has begun picking at everything about her—her fairies, her etiquette, her dress. *Our future Queen of Blunders,* Lady Ziza Lace writes in her newsletter. Camilla's scandalous blood necklaces have been making the rounds as well.

"Seer." Attention sweeps toward me upon the king's address. "You have investigated Raya's threads. Do you suggest a course of action?"

One doesn't need to be Sighted to see the downward trajectory of Raya's reputation. Though I'm uncertain if she's the mastermind of her place here, she's hiding *something* and we need it flushed out. Ever since I read her threads, she's either burrowed in her quarters or attached to Cyrus's side, and I haven't been able to do a second reading.

"Test her," I say, ready for the future, if only so I can be free from my fear of it. "I believe it's time for her to prove her worth."

"Hmm, I do agree," the king answers. "Now, more than ever, we need confidence she is to be our salvation and not

our damnation. The origin of these beasts is suspect. . . .
We have yet to rule out the possibility that Balica is weapon-
izing the Fairywood's magic and creating these beasts themselves."

Low murmurs rise like the lords have discussed this before. I frown. On paper, Raya and the location of the beasts
may be suspicious, but what motivation would Balica have
for such drastic escalation? They have never been aggressors, outside that skirmish when Dante's mother was Head
of Hypsi, and that had been a local border dispute.

"I would hate to think so ill of our neighbors," King
Emilius says, and I swear I glimpse the curve of a smile.

When the meeting is adjourned, the king requests I stay
behind. The last adviser to leave shuts the door behind him.
I rise from my seat at the other end of the mahogany table
to stand beside the king, hands clasped behind my back.

He waits until the footsteps have moved away, then says,
"What else have you seen in Raya's threads?"

*He could use Raya's betrayal to send armies marching
south before the week is over,* Dante said.

It's easy to confuse fear for respect.

I can do enough to not be the axe that begins a war. "I
saw her wedding with Cyrus."

"What about her past?"

"Nothing useful for Auveny's interests. I didn't get much
time with her."

"Is that so?" The king looks not so much frustrated as
perplexed. I've glimpsed him when he's truly angry. When
I wait to enter his study, sometimes he and Cyrus would be
quarreling, and through the jamb, I'd see him as red and

hissing as a kettle. The ugly kind of angry that can only exist behind closed doors.

No, this is a new displeased expression, just for me. "This is surprising, Violet," he continues. "I am used to more revelations from you, especially from such an important figure. I heard your reading caused quite a stir—at a recent party, was it not?"

I don't demur from his scrutiny, piercing as pinpricks. "It was because Cyrus interrupted me. He made it seem more dramatic than it was."

"I see." His expression does not change.

"But . . . I can meet with her again," I offer. Behind my lips, my teeth are clenched.

"Very well." King Emilius waves a trembling hand, as if my excuses are as fragile and transparent as glass. "But do not waste time. Hers or mine."

An enormous covered wagon escorted by more than a dozen soldiers slowly carts the captured beast into the Sun Capital. Even hidden, even muzzled, the beast's guttural growls strike enough fear on their own. The scratching, the rattling, the wet snap of its jaws—all it knows is hunger.

Watching from a safe distance inside a carriage, I thought I could stand it. But I find myself grasping at my neck as I recall the beast's jaws nearly closing over my head. The fumes of fresh blood.

Were I braver, I'd ask about finding a way to read the

beast's threads, but any attempt would reveal how shaken I still am from the night of the ball. It's silly—the beast that attacked me is dead; I'm safe now. Safer than ever, with the extra guards in the city. I've heard fear can linger from shock, but that's never happened to me before, and I loathe it in the way I loathe every feeling I can't control.

I return to my tower before the beast arrives at the palace, so I don't have to think about where they're housing it and all the ways it could escape. The nightmares I already have are enough.

I sleep uneasily that night, dreaming again of waves of green shifting into black, of golden fayflowers withering into charcoal. I can sense it, though I can't hear it: the silent, dying wail of the Fairywood as it's corrupted and burned.

The next morning, a messenger bird brings a flyer to my window. It reads:

ONCE-IN-A-LIFETIME EVENT TO ALL WHO WISH TO WITNESS
Lady Raya Solquezil of Lunesse

to perform a feat of prophecy breaking, today at noon.
The first of many miracles.

Raya has hardly spoken on her own stage since she arrived in the capital, and now she's bold enough to do a public demonstration? Already this seems like overcompensation, but maybe she's the kind of person who doesn't want to leave room for doubt. Especially if her failures mean Balica becomes Auveny's scapegoat.

I get dressed, not caring much for appearances, since I'll have to wear my robes and gloves. When I head down to the outer courtyard, an audience is already assembling around a generously roped-off space.

I join the royal family on the palace steps, behind a phalanx of the Imperial Guard, taking a place beside Camilla. The princess is eagerly tapping her fingertips together, craning her neck around the guards' feathered helms for a better glimpse. "Oh my," she murmurs. "*That* attacked you? How are you still in one piece?"

Only then do I noticed the barred cage being wheeled in from the stables, escorted by four guards with the thickest steel gauntlets I've ever seen. A green-eyed beast paces within, horns scraping against the steel bars. This one isn't as large as the two that were at my tower. It's starved and only about a hand taller than the tallest person in the yard, but it's just as monstrous: wolf-headed, human-gaited, a hulking body covered in fur and bark.

"What the hell?" I mutter, heart leaping into a run.

"Raya needs it for her demonstration. She claims she can cure it."

A hefty claim. The cage should hold; it's the type used for trapping dragons, which are of similar size and teeth-and-claw sharpness. The difference with dragons is, they're only after our glittering items—they don't look at us like we're *food*.

The beast hurls itself at the cage door and the audience gasps and shrieks. I physically recoil, even though it's more than twenty paces away.

The barest pressure squeezes my gloved fingers, then vanishes—a fleeting comfort.

I know that touch. I only notice now that at some point Camilla surreptitiously moved from my left side to my right, putting her brother and I next to each other.

I twine my hands behind my back and don't look at him.

A spectator at the front peers across the ropes. "What does the beast eat?" she asks.

"This one ignores the game meat we give it. It doesn't eat vegetation, either," says the handler, some captain from the Thirteenth's Dragonsguard. "We have even tried prepared foods—"

"I have heard they hunt people."

Fretful murmurs. The handler goes quiet.

"Yes," he says. "Yes, we have, ah, in fact seen disturbing scenes in the countryside that show that . . . may be true."

More questions erupt.

All falls quiet when King Emilius taps his cane against the marble steps, though the horror remains. "Lady Raya is prepared. Let us not waste any time."

The woman of the hour steps past the wall of guards, alone before a hungry audience and hungry beast. Her puffy yellow gown adds nothing to her beauty. I wonder if she should change into something more practical or at least roll back her sleeves. As Camilla says: "In dates or death, *go out in style.*"

Beneath the gauzy fabric of her veil, she lifts her chin with a certainty I haven't seen in her before, which both unnerves me and makes me like her a little more.

I glance sideways. Cyrus's mouth has thinned to a line, and his knuckles are white where he grips the pommel of his sword.

As Raya approaches the cage, she raises a shaking arm dangerously close to the beast's drooling maw. I am certain, like everyone else staring with bated breath, that in a matter of seconds, we're about to witness the Head of Lunesse lose a quarter of her limbs, and I flinch away from looking.

But the beast is frozen as a glow envelops her arm. Shoulder to fingers, brighter and brighter until it's a blinding flash.

I jerk backward—I can't see.

Shouts.

The beast roars, then chokes out a garbled, guttural groan.

A din rises:

"*Stars above.*"

"*She's the one!*"

"*It changed—*"

When the spots disappear from my eyes, I don't know what's more horrific: the creature it was before, or the pitiful thing I'm gaping at now, a naked, half-transformed man lying on the floor of the cage.

Though his skin is patched in fur, he is more human than beast. I can barely hear him beneath the clamor: "Thank you. The witch . . ." He collapses, moaning incoherent babble.

A tidal wave. People rushing forward, guards struggling

to hold the cordon, the row of us on the palace steps—even the usually stoic king—staring with our jaws dropped.

"She *did* it," Camilla blurts, crushing the fan in her hand. I can't tell if she's more angry or awed. Covering her mouth, a fresh horror startles her. "Oh no. Oh *no*. Does that mean that *all* the beasts are . . ."

"They are," I whisper. "When I was attacked, I thought I saw its threads—the memories seemed human—I—" What the *hell*? How is this possible? And how did Raya cure him?

Raya looks as shocked as the rest of us.

Surrounded by tumult, pinned by attention, she wobbles, her eyes rolling back. It's enough warning for Cyrus to leap down the steps. He catches her in his arms as she faints.

"Move aside!" Carrying her limp body, Cyrus strides into the palace. The cage is wheeled from the demonstration area as well, the man twitching on its floor.

As shock and excitement fly, King Emilius doesn't call for order. He only adds his own marveling to the shouts: "We have witnessed the making of history today, my friends! Let us pray for her quick recovery, so she may undo the dark magic plaguing this land. We are blessed to have Raya as our next queen."

The audience cheers.

❧

Raya has an impossible number of fairies, she brought the beasts here, and she did *something* to transform that beast back into a man.

It has to be another trick.

There's a prophetic air about her, but not in a good way. If there's one takeaway from these past months, it's that what the gods and their prophecies want aren't always things *we* should want. They want Cyrus's death, and if my glimpse of Raya's future is certain, they want a wedding drenched in blood.

After the demonstration, I go around the palace asking after the transformed man. I'm pointed toward multiple wrong places, and nowhere do I see his cage.

Finally, by one of the guardhouses, I find the captain who wheeled him out. He's midway through telling some boisterous tale to two younger officers, preening about how important the Dragonsguard is.

When I ask him about the cage, he says, with a jaunty wag of his finger, "We have our top people inspecting him. No need for your concern, Sighted Mistress."

"What hard work you do," I say, not believing him at all.

I offer to do a quick reading for him, since he's here, and he gladly offers his sweaty palms for me to examine. I snoop into his recent past and his threads snake through my Sight:

Shadows weaving in and out of the dungeons.

A growling, furred creature. A shaking cage. "Wh-why—"

One of the king's advisers frowns. "Hide him, quickly."

The man was turning back into a beast. Which means . . . whatever magic Raya has done has worn off already. These men must have been ordered to not jeopardize the engagement.

"The Fates smile upon you," I tell the captain. If I lie

outright, better to make them happy. "You might get a pro-motion soon, if you play your cards right."

"Hah!" He pumps a fist at the officers, who both wear celebratory looks fit for a funeral.

Leaving the men, I head up the staircase to the royal quarters, cursing myself. I've let this go too far; I should have confronted Raya sooner. Knowing the future doesn't mean I know when to act. It just means I regret it twice as much when I let something slip past me.

Earlier, Camilla told me that Cyrus carried Raya to her rooms and she hasn't come out all day. The king's personal healer attended to her briefly, and Raya requested that she recover before she meets with anyone.

Fortunately for me, courtesy has never been my strong point.

Raya's rooms are at the end of the hall. Portraits line the route there. To my left is a painting of Camilla and Cyrus as freckled children, followed by King Emilius in his prime. On my right is the largest frame of the hall—the late Queen Merchella sitting regally beside her hound. Camilla and Cyrus take after her more than they do their father. They have her cheekbones, her red-brown hair, even her elusive gaze, captured in vibrant paint.

People loved her. Auveny was in the tail end of her mourning period at the time I became Seer; every week, someone was building a shrine to some vegetable shaped like Her Dead Majesty's head. Many of my first patrons would ask after her spirit, as if my Sight allowed it. It doesn't. I learned quickly then how silly people get when they're clouded by hope.

The portraits grow sparser down the hall. Two of Cyrus's personal guards stand outside Raya's quarters. I smile in greeting. They're all too familiar with my snooping, which is good; they know it's less hassle to simply let me pass through, which they do.

In the antechamber, I knock on the bedroom door. I wait, then knock again.

I don't hear any movement.

I push open the door. The room is cavernous, themed in porcelain blue-and-whites and not nearly as ugly as Camilla suggested. Normally, I'd expect unpacked trunks strewn across the suite and the dressers to be full of traveling clothes, but Raya seems to have brought nearly nothing with her.

Also, she's not here.

A cool breeze meets my cheeks. The slatted balcony door is ajar. I peek through.

This side of the palace overlooks a gated garden. No one is ever there except caretakers in the early morning. Tall cypresses provide a middling amount of privacy for any shenanigans happening on the second floor.

Like, for example, a future queen jumping into the shrubbery below.

I peer over the balcony railing. A large indentation mars one of the bushes and stuffed behind it is a tangle of bedsheets that might have been used as a rope.

Shit.

Raya ran off.

Here is the occasional problem with lying: I'm stuck pretending I never knew about something. I could make up an excuse for why I didn't warn anyone about Raya, but I don't like stacking lies; they topple. As far as anyone except for Dante knows, I had mild suspicions of this hasty bride at most.

I doubt she's gone far. I remember a scene I'd seen in her threads: her, outside the capital, cupping her fairies, who aren't here right now either. She was on a rocky hill near a forest that looked like the hunting grounds to the northeast.

It's light out enough to make a trek there, though it'll be full dark by the time I get back. But that means *I* have to make the trek there.

I groan, glad that I wore boots. The next time I see her, I am making her answer *every single question I have.*

Leaving the palace grounds through the eastern gates, I take the steep path down the cliffs that overlook the river Julep. Everything in the city looks small and manicured from this distance: the rooftop signs, the tidy sprawl of parks, the odd-sized buildings where the city grew without plan, the river boats cresting out into the valley, and the trafficked thoroughfares lined with carriages.

At the bottom of the cliffs, I cross a wooden bridge to the other side of the river. The ground becomes jagged and rocky through the soles of my boots. A shortcut through a pasture and some stumbling around later, I'm at the top of the exact hill I'd seen in Raya's memories.

A laborer mentioned seeing some well-dressed lady heading down the same way, so my hunch seems solid. But I've underestimated the time it takes to get here—the sun is already setting. Scaling the hill would be the fastest way to the hunting grounds below. Being Seer means I never have to scamper anywhere myself anymore, but part of me itches to hike my skirts up and climb.

But I've also accumulated an impressive amount of injuries recently, so I start walking to a less steep area, accompanied by the sound of crickets and badger chitters.

I pass a lonesome cracked plinth that's stained dark upon the surface, a former altar to the Fates. Shards of pottery and cloth scraps litter the weeds nearby. There's conversation in the distance.

Grass rustles behind me. I frown. Or has the conversation been following me—?

"Violet?"

I jump. Something brushes my shoulder and I swing an elbow backwards, connecting into a body.

"*Oof.* Did you . . . aim," a familiar voice wheezes, "or am I just . . . unlucky?"

"*Dante?*" I whirl around. He's doubled over, eyes bulging as he processes the pain. "Toady hell, I'm sorry. What are you doing here?"

"I'm following Raya. What are"—he wheezes—"*you* doing here?"

"*Also* following Raya. She went missing, and earlier, I saw a thread where she . . . Are you sure you're okay?"

"Yeah, yeah," he says, face contorted. Mud stains his patterned trousers and heeled boots; he also doesn't look like he prepared for a trek down to the outskirts. "Been playing messenger boy for Ambassador Pincorn"—with one more wheeze, he manages to stand upright—"and *apparently,* news out of Lunesse is Raya's manor burned down, and that's not even the most shocking development. Gods, this is a mess."

"There was a woman," I say suddenly. "I dreamed of a woman at a burning manor."

"What was she doing?"

"Laughing . . . which seems like a bad sign."

"Not a fan of evil laughing, no." He grimaces. "That could be her. Who knows who Raya is, at this rate?" Taking a deep, reinvigorating breath, Dante gestures toward the hunting grounds. "But instead of speculating, we should actually *find* Raya. We mixed you two up in the distance at some point and lost her."

"We?" I hear the crunch of approaching footsteps.

A silhouetted Cyrus walks toward us, hands twined behind his head, gust-tousled hair nearly golden in the glow of sunset. He regards me with a sigh. I regard him with a scowl.

Dante pinches the bridge of his nose. "Is there something you two need to discuss in private first?"

"No," we both snap at the same time.

His gaze flattens. "I'm going to head down. In the meantime, whatever it is, work it out or *make out* or I swear . . ."

"You *know* about—" *Us?* I clamp my lips shut as I realize my mistake.

"Now I do." A smirk hooks Dante's mouth. Even in the fading light, I can see Cyrus turn a brilliant red while his friend clutches his chest in mock horror. "Cyrus, you harlot, here I thought you were a man of honor."

"I don't want to talk about this at this moment," Cyrus snarls, shoving Dante forward.

217

"Or ever, I assume? When I said you should tell her, I meant *before you got engaged.*" There is bite to his accusation.

"Tell me?" I glance between them, curiosity overtaking any embarrassment. "Tell me what?"

Now Dante looks flushed, and Cyrus is the one pinching his regal nose. Badger chitters fill the silence.

"Anyway," Dante says, as I continue sputtering. "We need to locate Raya before she slips away."

"Tell me what?" At this moment, more than any other moment today, I hate not knowing things.

"Quiet." Cyrus frowns. "Do you hear that?"

We all turn toward the forest's edge below us. Someone is loudly tromping through the underbrush and getting farther away.

The hill is still steep here, but I'll live even if I tumble. "To hell with it," I mutter. Getting to my knees, I start scaling the rocky outcropping, grabbing for any foothold.

"Be careful!" Dante clambers after me. With his longer limbs, he reaches the bottom faster than I do. The prince is last, slow in his stiff jacket.

All three of us land on the ground, then we fan out, taking different paths into the forest. The trails are narrow but clear, twisting and winding around large oaks.

Whoever was here has gone quiet. Hiding.

To hell with stealth. Raya must know we're looking for her. "Come out!" I shout, climbing over tree roots. The canopy overhead knits into solid darkness as I head off path through a trampled thicket. I might be able to flush her out; I remember in my vision, she seemed so worried about her fairies. "We can help you save your fairies!"

"Really?" comes the soft response. Her curls bounce into view beyond a berry bush.

Aha. I lunge at the movement, uncaring of whipping branches, and tackle Raya to the ground.

She yelps. Lights scatter around her, dim and blinking.

We're of similar build and height, and with the element of surprise, I easily overpower her, straddling her middle and pinning her arms into the dirt with my knees. Hovering over her, my hair frizzes from its braid. I pant with satisfaction. "I'm going to sit on you until you give us answers."

"S-Seer?" Raya seems to have only just registered who I am. Not every day someone gets thrown down by the kingdom's premier divine figure.

"Yes, hello. That's me." I squint at her face. She *is* Raya, right? I almost wonder if I'm remembering her incorrectly. Her jaw isn't the right shape, and her nose looks flatter, but she *sounds* like Raya, and her wide brown eyes are the same and so is her dark hair, tangled with leaves on the forest floor. "I don't care what magic it is you pulled today. I saw in your memories that you released the beasts, so don't even think about lying, or you'll be sent dancing through the Palace District in hot-iron shoes before the night's over!"

Shockingly, the first words out of her mouth aren't a denial, but instead, "You can see memories? Can you see a specific one?"

"What?" I hear Dante and Cyrus running toward us. "Usually I—I see the memories people think most often about, or one they're thinking of at the moment—"

"Let me go!" she gasps.

"No! Why would I—"

219

"Let me go and look into my memories. You have to look!" Wriggling and thrashing, she manages to get a whole arm free, which I attempt to smack down like an errant spider. She pulls off my glove and grabs my hand. "Please!"

Unfocused, my Sight catches a streak of images, blurry as a bird in flight. The sense in my mind settles, letting me pick out the threads bound to her soul. One is trembling with a need to be seen. It reaches for me as I reach for it.

The memory flares to life, vivid and frayed as if painted in terror:

A lady's bedroom and a storm raging through the open veranda. The furniture is askew and soaked. The style of the room is unlike any in Auveny: turquoise-tiled floors, linens dyed with the rich hues of summer blooms, a curving, generous shape to the furnishings.

It reeks of rot.

Two women struggling. The taller one wields a glowing orbed scepter, her callous smile brought into relief every time she swings it.

She moves with unnatural grace. Her face is wrongfully young, as if the years have been removed from it.

A witch.

She forces the other woman to her knees.

The other woman lifts her head. Raya, hair and blood sticky on her face, nearly unrecognizable. "Help," she mouths, voice weak.

The witch drags Raya across the tile floor. Raya claws and kicks and screams, but she's pinned down by that scepter, crackling with golden energy. It's not just a scepter: the orb is a cage, squeaking with fairies.

With her free hand, the witch brandishes a dagger from the inside of her cloak—

And plunges it into Raya's chest.

My hands jerk away.

"You died," I choke, staring at the Raya underneath me, alive and whole.

It's strange that those memories had such a distant vantage point. Usually, threads are through a person's eyes. Some can be more removed, but Raya's threads almost seem like they're from the perspective of a spectator.

Every angle of Raya's face ripples with tiny differences that unsettle my mind, and I can't really remember what she looks like. I focus on her gaze; glamours never alter the eyes. She doesn't look exactly like the person I saw in my vision, only a semblance of her.

But someone with five fairies in her arsenal could make her look close enough.

"Who are you?" I breathe. "You're not—you aren't—"

The girl beneath me shakes her head furiously. "I'm not my Mistress Raya. You saw it, didn't you? The real Raya is *dead*."

17

DANTE, CYRUS, AND I SURROUND NOT-RAYA IN A damp nook of forest. Not-Raya had the foresight to bring a lantern, and it provides the only light for us. We let her scoop up her fairies, which scattered when I surprised her. They barely have the strength to fly. Cyrus offers his jacket when she shivers in her muddied gown, and she takes it with quiet thanks.

"My name is Nadiya Santillion," she says, kneeling before the three of us, head bowed. "I was Raya's handmaiden when a witch emerged from the Fairywood and attacked her manor."

"Whatever you tell us, I will verify when I look into your threads again," I warn.

"I s-swear this is the truth." Her glamour has fully faded away. When she looks up, I see her real face for the first time. She looks much younger—closer to my age. Her features are less sharp and dainty. Freckles dot her nose and her ears stick out like a field mouse's. "She called herself the Witch of Nightmares. She killed my mistress and she made me impersonate her. She said if I didn't do it, she would kill the rest of the household. She told me to go to the Sun Capital and to take my mistress's place at the ball. And you are right, Sighted Mistress: I released the beasts, but I—I didn't know about them! The witch sent me along with two wooden chests and told me to toss them over the cliffs, into the capital's river. . . . I suppose I did know she locked something bad inside, but I—I was scared. I wasn't thinking. I just wanted it to be over!"

"Why would this witch ask you to do these things?" Dante asks.

"To start a war."

The three of us standing share glances.

Cyrus crouches to Nadiya's height. "How would you start a war?"

"That was all she said, Your Highness, and I don't ask a murderer for explanations." She chuckles in a squeaky, timid way—her nervous habit.

"Could just be the reasons we feared," Dante murmurs. "Make Auveny think Raya—stars guide her soul—caused the beast uprising or might be sabotaging your chances for real love. It'd be easy to call Nadiya a disguised assassin—there's plenty to make up if anyone *wanted* to blame Balica, like your father and the Council . . ."

"I know, I know." Cyrus groans.

Dante splays his fingers. "But what would the witch have to gain from this war?"

"She might not be working independently."

"Hired by someone who wants to weaken one or both countries?"

"But we would have heard *some* rumors about her. . . ."

As they lose themselves in guesswork, Nadiya furrows her bushy brows. "Blood. She wants blood to spill. She mentioned it makes her magic more powerful."

I suck in a breath. Everyone looks to me. Behind my back, I clench a fist around my injured palm. "Is it possible the Witch of Nightmares is a Seer?"

Nadiya frowns deeper. "I'm not sure, Sighted Mistress. She did say something about the Fates."

"If she's a Seer, that could explain why she set you on these tasks. She might have seen the path to a future she wants." I slowly piece out the possibility. From my glimpse of the witch, she looked too young to be Balica's and Verdant's known Seers, but maybe she never told anyone about her Sight. "Future threads can change or be contradictory . . . but maybe her Sight is stronger than what I'm familiar with. Or maybe the Fates are guiding her."

Cyrus rises to his feet. "The Fates? Why would the *Fates* help the witch?"

If he only knew that he's still alive due to my continued disobedience of their wishes. I deserve at least another thank-you note for that, but will I get one? Doubtful. "The Fates are the reason your cursed prophecy exists in the first place. Why *wouldn't* they help someone who's making it finally happen?" I scoff. "You've never spoken to the Fates. If you have, you wouldn't be surprised that they don't care about us. All they're after is blood. And what do beasts and wars do? Cause *bloodshed*."

Cyrus looks incredulous. "The Fates aren't *evil*."

"If you say so. They certainly aren't *just,* if that's what you think instead." If blood makes *my* magic more powerful, it's not such a stretch to wonder if they make the Fates more powerful too.

"Sighted Mistress, Your Highness . . . sorry, I don't mean to interrupt." Nadiya hesitantly gets to her feet and glances particularly at me, as if afraid I might tackle her again. "My fairies are very weak and I came here to help them."

In a blink, her doe eyes have distracted Cyrus, who turns away from me at a speed that's, frankly, offensive. "What happened?"

"Have some dignity, Princey," I mutter under my breath.

"My fairies drew the dark magic from the beast earlier— the one who changed back into a man. They were hiding in my sleeve the whole time. I didn't actually do anything." Nadiya raises her cupped hands. The glow inside quivers, and I can make out the shape of tiny, fluttering wings. "I wouldn't have risked them exhausting their magic, but the king was pressuring me to prove myself, and he was getting awfully close to finding out my ruse . . . so I agreed."

"That was my fault," Cyrus soothes. "I should have stopped him."

A faint hue rises to her cheeks. "You've done nothing wrong, Your Highness. I thought my fairies would be okay. They were near-dead when I first rescued them, but when we crossed through the Fairywood to enter Auveny, they recovered. So I thought, if I bring them to the Fairywood again . . ."

He glances around at the gnarled trees enveloping us, lush relative to our surroundings. "These are just the hunting grounds. There's no Fairywood for two days' ride from the capital."

"Oh." She bites her lip. She's definitely about to cry.

"Will they die? Do we need to make the trip?" Cyrus wraps his hands around hers, nauseatingly chivalrous. I roll my eyes; I guess it doesn't take much for him to trust *her*. "Will ambrosia help? Many fairies in the city subsist on ambrosia—"

"I tried. They need their home. They need the magic of the Wood."

"My tower—" I inhale sharply through gritted teeth. Now even *I'm* helping her. Unfortunately I do think she's innocent, and she's our best lead toward finding the witch. Besides, a poor girl caught in a callous court foreign to her? The similarities to my own beginnings aren't lost on me. She's lucky I still have heartstrings to tug. "If you need real, live Fairywood, my tower technically counts."

Her big, bashful doe eyes light up. "Can we go there, Sighted Mistress?"

"That's why I mentioned it," I drawl. "Let's go before your fairies turn to dust."

The trek to my tower is ironically less suspicious with us clustered in a group. It looks like Prince Cyrus and a few of his closest companions—and me—went for a quick hunting trip. Odd, but nothing that can't be explained by the presence of wine. Camilla once rode back into the palace drunk at midnight in nothing but mismatched underwear, a tale she still proudly tells at holidays.

Hand in hand with Nadiya, I check her memories as we walk. They open up to me, eager to be witnessed.

I learn the witch enchanted Nadiya to look like Raya, but the magic only lasted as long as the ball. Nadiya was always supposed to be discovered as a fraud, to cast doubt upon Balica. I don't think she was supposed to run from the ballroom that night. I feel her doubt in the moment her disguise unraveled—the desire to give up, just to escape the exhaustion of playing pretend—before a desperate compulsion to survive took over. I know that feeling well. However clumsily, Nadiya's been maintaining her ruse through veils and fairy charm.

I see how Nadiya came to have so many fairies: they were originally the ones trapped in the witch's scepter. Nadiya secretly stole the scepter and smashed it, releasing them just before she left for Auveny. The fairies have been loyal ever since—even risking their lives during the demonstration with the beast today.

The Witch of Nightmares herself . . . I wish I could see more about her. I wonder about my theory that she's another Seer. The magic she performed is beyond my imagination—but not so long ago, I wouldn't have imagined creating a thorn out of nothing but my blood and a bit of Fairywood. The witch had a scepter of fairies. If I only tried, could I manipulate magic the same way?

The thoughts shiver away as we near the base of my tower. The path here is narrow, with little space between the churning river swollen with recent rain and the cliffside beneath the palace grounds.

Nadiya stumbles eagerly ahead, releasing her fairies on a grassy corner by the tower's stairs. The fairies crawl up the wall. Before our eyes, they begin to brighten, their tiny wings fluttering as if a wind picked up, and the relief among us is palpable. Faint wispy ribbons of gold flow between the fairies and the vines, like something is being drawn out. The vines shrivel—

Blacken.

A stink of dead roses. It fills my nostrils so suddenly, I gag and pinch my nose.

When I look up again, rot has spread along the fairies' trail. The smudge spreads into a blotch like pungent ink, threading outward in black veins.

I'm dizzy as I shove Nadiya aside, pressing a hand against the wall, trying to stop it. "What the hell?" I hiss, feeling the jostle of the others behind me. I can chip at the dead parts with my fingers, but there's more rot underneath, continuing to expand. The blackened vines crumble off, petrified on the outside, oozing on the inside.

Like the corruption around the thorn I made.

Like the corruption in my dreams.

Whirling around, I grab Nadiya by her borrowed jacket's collar. "What did you do?"

"I—I didn't know this was going to happen, I swear!" she squeaks, hands raised. "I just know the Fairywood is where they recover. Please don't strike me down, Sighted Mistress!"

"The fairies must have been containing the dark magic from the beasts and needed a place to release it." A frowning Dante takes the lantern and inspects the vines himself, the hitch in his breath uneasy. The rot has stopped spreading, but the damage is already irreversibly enormous. "Their magic flows with the Fairywood, so they must be using it as a sponge."

The revived fairies take flight and zoom around me,

chirping as if in apology. All that makes me do is sneeze while I shake Nadiya roughly. "This would have been nice to know *before* they cursed my tower!"

"I-I'll fix it! I didn't mean to."

"Good intentions do not negate your mistakes. Do you know what I see when I look at you?" I narrow my eyes. "A liability." I let the girl go with a shove. I am never being charitable again.

Cyrus steps between us, glaring a warning. "Calm down. I'll have workmen dig out the rot tomorrow."

Easy for beloved Prince Charming to say. Never had to worry about an errant mark in his life. "*How* will you explain how it got here? Dark magic on my tower makes it look like *I* am the one who is corrupted."

"I'll figure it out."

As he reaches for my arm with the same gentleness he proffered Nadiya, I jerk away. I don't want his act. Something in his stare wavers, but he brushes past me before I can decipher it.

"It's fortunate we were able to save your fairies, Nadiya, but this is only the start of our problems." Cyrus paces the muddy ground. "I have to mobilize soldiers to find the witch, who could be anywhere. She might be behind *all* the beasts, and she clearly has confidence in her power and a plan under her belt. Ah, also"—he presses a hand to his chest—"I don't think it comes as a surprise that I wasn't in love with Raya, but my apologies if I've led you to believe otherwise. We'll have to figure out a way to reveal the truth of your identity."

"Not *this* soon," Dante protests.

"Why not?"

"If we're choosing between headaches, marrying a fake Raya might be the lesser of them." He wipes his hands on his trousers, leaving black handprints. "The people have faith in her. To break that trust *now?* That damage will be worse for both of you. It wasn't that long ago when your ascension was at risk because you hadn't found a bride yet, Cyrus."

The prince grimaces.

"And honestly, Nadiya, Violet is right. You *are* a liability. There will never be a good time to reveal your identity, but while beasts are rising from the land, this is *definitely* a bad time to do it."

Nadiya wrings a fistful of her dress. "I have to keep pretending?"

"I don't like the thought of extending this charade," says Cyrus.

Dante shrugs. "I'm only presenting an opinion."

"There's the wedding to consider—"

"Worst-case scenario, you two get married. It's not as if you were planning to marry someone else."

The prince tips his head back and sighs, battered by his friend's reasonable tone. "No, you are right."

"I'm always right."

With the lantern on Cyrus, I can see him shift into his most charming, dimpled self. "If you can do me the favor of continuing to be Lady Raya, Nadiya, it would help me greatly. I promise we will find the witch and bring her to justice."

I roll my eyes so hard that my whole head turns. "Any

promise he makes isn't worth the air he breathes," I tell her. I can't stand that syrupy tone of his any longer.

"Violet, not the time—"

"Cyrus will do what's best for Auveny. He has to," I say to Nadiya, ignoring him. Let me at least give this girl the truth if she's to flounder in our court; I won't have another soul fawning over the prince for his supposed charity. "You will be surrounded by people who want to use you and blackmail you. If you stand between him and the throne, I wouldn't bet on the prince staying true. Speaking as someone he would gladly banish for being *inconvenient*."

Cyrus glowers at me, while Dante raises a brow at him.

"We'll discuss later," Cyrus whispers, sighing, before returning to Nadiya with a fresh smile. "Violet's situation is different. That wouldn't have crossed my mind if I didn't think she could take care of herself. She'd be fine anywhere she'd go—"

"Exactly the kind of compliment a girl wants to hear," I mutter. *"Strong enough for exile."*

"—and it doesn't matter because I promise"—he places a hand on Nadiya's arm—"I will not do anything that harms you."

Not worth the air he breathes, I mouth at her.

If we argue any longer, Nadiya might wring a hole right through her gown. She looks terrified of *both* of us. "D-do I have to decide now?"

"No, no, of course not—" Cyrus starts.

"No, you don't," I say over him. "Go sleep on it and then go with the prince's plan—technically Dante's plan, which is how you know it's decent. I won't haunt you for it."

In the background, Dante sighs. "*I* would like to go home and sleep. Look, let's meet again. As in, *tomorrow*. I need to go through old correspondence, now that I know Raya's manor is compromised."

This ends up being our awkward parting. Cyrus and Dante exchange some private words, then Dante salutes his farewell, leaving for his apartment in the University District.

Cyrus leads Nadiya up the circling stairs around my tower. The north gate that I use every day is the closest entry to the palace. I march up after them feeling like a straggler.

When we reach the landing at my tower's midpoint, Cyrus urges Nadiya to cross the bridge to the palace first. The lights of her lantern and fairies grow distant on the bridge, then it's just me and the prince in the starlit dark. I hover by my tower's entryway, hackles raised for his reproach.

Fiddling with his cuffs, he doesn't quite meet my eyes. "Thank you," he says, with the mildness he reserves for Rayas and Nadiyas and people who are not me. "I am . . . grateful for your help today. Even in the manner you chose to provide it."

"When you run out of bigger problems, you'll come after me again," I scoff.

"You still are the biggest problem." His tone is unkindly, but when he glances up, his gaze is unmarked by the caution I'm accustomed to. Lingering and rueful.

"Don't look at me like that."

"Like what?"

"Like I matter to you."

The space between his brows twitches into a furrow.

232

Something like understanding filters through his expression. "Would that be so bad? You asked me to figure out what I want. What if what I want is you after all?"

A shiver passes through me, one that I can't blame on the evening chill. "I wouldn't believe you."

"Of course not. You aren't some easy mark. You care for no one but yourself, so you can never be played for a fool."

I open my mouth to protest, but actually . . . "That's right."

"Ever so clever." Cyrus smiles like he's won something, and I bristle.

We're more dangerous like this, bantering like we're playing a game, open and forgetful of the damage we could do. As if Cyrus hasn't spent all this time trying to be rid of me. As if I haven't been tempted to skewer his heart more than once. As if we don't shape the world with our very presence.

"Good night, Violet," he says, looking at me in the way I told him not to.

I bid no farewell before I leave to my rooms.

Wind rushes through the open balcony doors, carrying a chorus of laughing voices:

Vi-o-let

Vile witch

Stupid dirt-born.

I sit up in bed at once, sweaty and cold, bracing for the

headache. Fog is thick outside, and the sky feels closer than ever. Across my room, the moon seems to ripple in the full-length mirror.

The Fates are here again.

I pinch my nails into my palm, but their whispers don't go away. Hasn't enough happened today? Slipping out of bed, I walk across the blue-dark stretch of my room toward my mirror until I'm close enough to press a hand against my reflection, crowned with moonlight.

Somewhere in the back of my mind, I sense threads in the future that I can't grasp.

One life owed, the voices chant.

You will burn for him.

You will burn to ashes.

"I won't start a war for you. That's what you want, isn't it?" I'm finally seeing the bigger picture—the scheming of gods. Their taste for blood. Their taste for power. "You are helping that witch, too, aren't you?"

She chose, she chose,

blood and roses and war.

A pawn, a puppet, a player:

which will you be?

So it's true. "Is it a choice if you give me none besides murder or death? If you've been watching me, then you know there's nothing I hate more than being told what to do."

We will not mourn

when they betray you.

You are no one, nothing—

A shade, unwhole.

"Or being told who I am."

In the mirror, my face is weary and fraught behind my loose hair, all color drawn away in the dim light. My nightgown is rumpled from fitful sleep. My hand holds the thorn, though when I look down at my real hand, I don't see it.

You deny your destiny.

He poisons your heart.

"Better him than you all."

The thorn bursts into life, vines coursing up my arm, my neck, my body. I stumble back, reaching for something to smash the mirror, but the dull throb of my injured hand reminds me: I don't know whether I'm asleep or awake.

The writhing growth covers the whole of my reflection until I'm nothing but a speck of the eye. The voices coalesce, singing as if celebrating:

Something rotten lies in your earth.

It will unearth, it will unearth.

"Shut up, shut up, *shut up*!" I shout all the way back to my bed. The voices only laugh.

Something rotten lies in your heart.

Something rotten lies.

18

THE FATES DON'T WALK THIS EARTH—BEASTS AND witches do. No matter how much the gods know, no matter what they threaten, they aren't *here*. It will take soldiers and strategy, but we can corral the beasts until they can be transformed. We can find the Witch of Nightmares and stop her.

I will survive destiny by my own means.

King Emilius is less startled by the discoveries behind the dark magic than the sight of me and Cyrus in his study speaking in civil tones.

"The Fairywood isn't creating beasts," I say, a little breathless after Cyrus and I careened in, pretending we had only just discovered this news. "A witch is behind it. I think she's drawing upon the Fairywood for power and causing the rot, too."

I can't tell the king about Nadiya nor that the real Raya is dead, so I claim I saw the witch by reading Lady Raya's and Cyrus's futures. I warn of her unpredictable powers and of the awful scene that will unfold at Cyrus's wedding. Cyrus, playing his part of smitten husband-to-be, insists on

236

overseeing the plans of attack personally for drawing the witch out.

"Look for a raven, if you can," I say, remembering my glimpse of the witch's transformation.

The rot on my tower spread overnight, and the entire base has to be roped off so the outer vines can be carved away. I blame it on the witch as well—a sign of her approach. No one knows any better to believe otherwise. At least, that's what I tell myself.

On the upside, that means my tower is closed for readings, so no fussy patrons. I have time for clandestine strategy meetings in Nadiya's quarters, which I don't mind as much as I expected I would. I like pacing around the maps and letters that Dante brings, hearing about the movements that Balica has been making in dealing with the beasts themselves. Since they lack a strong military, they've focused on evacuating infested areas and moving refugees into better-protected cities. The patches of Fairywood spread throughout Balica seems to have slowed the beasts' advance as well; they are rarely seen crossing them.

I maintain a wide distance from the prince in the room, which means I join Nadiya on the edge of her bed. Though naive, she isn't insufferable, mostly because she doesn't try to strike up conversation when things fall silent. I take the opportunity to search her future better, withdrawing only when the scenes of her wedding prove too much.

"Screaming and chaos. Brambles covering the ballroom," I mutter, hiding a shiver. "Nothing illuminating, though." I can't help but feel something is missing from my Sight—as if threads are being pulled away from my grasp.

Nadiya has been opening up since she no longer has to pretend among us. "Could . . . we spring a trap on the witch?" she haltingly suggests, fingers twisting around her charm bracelet.

Sprawled on the chaise, Dante makes a middling grunt. "If we haven't caught her by then, I don't know if we can catch her *there* either, but that's an idea."

"And we'll guard the wedding as best we can," says Cyrus.

I don't ask, *What if it's not enough?* Or, *What if it backfires?* Because then I'd be admitting that no matter what I learn of the future, I won't be able to stop it.

Dante informs us of further grim findings about Raya's manor: For weeks, an enchantment had kept people away from investigating the manor. As soon as anyone touched the outer walls or gates, they would forget why they were there. The enchantment finally broke when the manor was set aflame. Afterward, locals found the burnt husk of the building littered with bodies of beasts.

"The other handmaidens ran off early, right as the witch attacked," Nadiya recounts of her last day in Lunesse. "My friend Lili was guiding the household out through the back. I was the only one upstairs trying to get to our mistress. I thought I was keeping them safe by doing as the witch asked, but I realized too late that she could have killed everyone anyway, whether or not I followed her orders. Or worse, she turned them into beasts. . . ."

"You didn't know. You couldn't have known," Cyrus assures, and I notice that he's been holding her hand this entire time, caressing it with a thumb.

Nadiya doesn't react to his touch—because it means nothing or because they're used to it? "I just wish their families knew the truth of what happened to them."

"Soon, I hope. After all this curse business is over," says Dante.

Each day, though, it seems less likely Nadiya's deception can *ever* end, but none of us speaks of that.

We move on to lighter topics, like outfits for the wedding and whether Camilla ought to be in charge of food for a party ever again, lest the palace have cake to spare for a year afterward.

Nadiya lets slip that she doesn't know how to dance. "I think everyone was too bespelled at the masquerade to notice."

"Fairies can conjure shoes so you don't even have to learn," I say proudly, as if it were an achievement on my part.

"But it's good to learn." Cyrus—ever graceful, ever gracious to all but me—pulls her to her feet. "It's easy, too. I'll show you."

They go round and round the room, Nadiya tripping half the time, a pretty blush painting her cheeks. A prince and a peasant, like the tales, delighting in each other's company. The sight should be a brightness in the gloom, not a bitter stew in my gut.

I lean toward Dante, ready to grumble about how Cyrus is never so gracious with me, how it's tasteless to lead Nadiya on, but I wonder: maybe the change in Cyrus's behavior has nothing to do with me. Maybe it has everything to do with her.

I whisper a different thought aloud. "The prophecy still fits."

Dante, sitting below me, turns from his reading. "Hmm?"

"The one that voice told me before the ball and the one he got from the Balican Seer. Did Cyrus ever tell you the exact words? *'The journey to love never runs smooth, and yours, your father would not approve.'* That one." It makes sense now. I thought I was missing something, because his father arranged Cyrus to marry Raya, so how could what I heard be true? But since she's actually *Nadiya* . . . "His father *wouldn't* approve of him marrying Nadiya, so maybe she really is his true love."

A funny look crosses his face, as if he had a thought ready but discarded it. "It's possible."

"It can only be a good thing, right?" Five fairies and a ruse that has lasted longer than it should have, and now the attention of the prince. Nadiya *is* special—something hopeful at last, regarding this prophecy.

My heart remains contrary, beating like an off-rhythm drum.

I rub my head. It's been pounding too with the constant interruptions to my sleep. I haven't rested well in a long time, and it's hard to muse further.

My thoughts get interrupted anyway as Camilla barges through the bedroom doors, huffy, a blaze of golden curls bouncing with each step.

"So this is where you are!" She waves a vial of blood around with the urgency of a cat swatting a moth, glaring daggers at Nadiya, who curls into Cyrus. "You are all *aw-*

fully cozy with Raya." She thrust the vial under my nose like it's a bottle of smelling salts and snaps her fingers.

I lower her arm. "I'm not enchanted." I sneak another glimpse at Nadiya, who stumbles apart from the prince.

"That's exactly what an enchanted person would say."

Unsurprisingly, Camilla refuses to leave or take any excuse we throw at her. Our furtive whispers only agitate her more, and eventually the four of us sit her down in a too-plush armchair and explain.

Camila, subdued, takes in the truth with quiet shock. "So, I was right about Raya—or Nadiya, is it?—this whole time? She *is* deceiving everyone."

"Yes." Cyrus sighs.

"But I have to pretend I'm *not* right?"

"Please, yes."

"Gods, you owe me."

Nadiya bows her head down to her knees. "I'm so sorry for the messes I've caused, Your Highness," she says, and Camilla only harrumphs.

"Compliment her," I hiss behind Nadiya.

"Oh—ah, especially because you . . . are the most beautiful woman in the Sun Capital," the girl adds hastily, "and it must have been very frustrating to see me steal attention because of my fairy glamours."

The princess immediately relaxes, her frown twisting into a placated pout. "Well. As long as you know *that*." Getting to her feet, she steps over the scattered papers on the floor to loom over Nadiya. The poor girl squeaks as Camilla digs her bright pink nails into her chin. "You have good bone structure. No wonder you could pull off pretending to be your mistress. You're quite pretty on your own."

"Th-thank you, Your Highness."

Camilla turns Nadiya this way and that, by the chin, by the shoulders, then lifting her arms. She makes a face as she takes in the rest of her—her bowed frame, her wrung hands, her modest blue gown, unadorned by glamour. "If you're sticking around, you'll need to learn to act important. And if you're sticking around *me,* you'll need to be at least half as fashionable as I am."

"Th-thank you, Your Highness?" Nadiya stutters again, expression caught somewhere between awed and afraid.

"You do love pet projects," I tell Camilla.

Camilla grumbles. "I *do.*"

Nadiya being taken under Camilla's wing will be a good thing, both for her social standing and her disguise. I'm more weary and stubborn than optimistic about what's to come, but I won't be a choosy beggar.

As much as I've rallied against the Fates, their warnings echo in the back of my mind, persistent as my headache. I glance around the room: would anyone here betray me? Cyrus would be the easy answer, but he doesn't have reason to anymore now that we've finally learned to compromise. I've only known Nadiya for a little while, but I know her threads—past and future—better than anyone else does, and she doesn't seem like a possibility.

The game board's changed, and I can't figure out where I stand, exactly. It's hard to imagine, but if—*when*—we emerge on the other side of this prophecy, Auveny will have a new king and queen.

Whatever happens, I'll ideally remain in the Sun Capital without much fuss—less obedient to the next king, but otherwise no different than who I was before.

Alone in my tower, seeing all and holding on to nothing.

‸❦‹

Slowly, I stop visiting Nadiya's quarters for these discussions.

Not like they need me anyway. Not when Dante is usually two steps ahead analyzing the latest numbers and movements, and Cyrus and Nadiya are busy flirting through their fated romance. Soldiers have already been dispatched to the borderlands to combat the tide of beasts and seek out the witch. The court is aflutter over Lady Raya's absence; we're hoping Nadiya can maintain a sickly ruse until the wedding.

I didn't think anyone would notice my own absence until a note arrives at my windowsill carried by Cyrus's falcon that says: *Meet today? New sightings in the Fifth Dominion.*

I toss it in the fireplace. I'll meet them if I feel like it.

I decide quickly that I don't feel like it.

I go the Moon District instead, in plainclothes, with a scoop of the coins I earned from my readings. Chatter about the beasts and the wedding exist here too, but to a lesser degree, and it's nearly peace. I buy trinkets from the marketplace—ceramic figurines, candy bracelets, a nutshell that cracks open to reveal a birth-constellation fortune—silly things I could never buy when I was a child. I sit at the fancy teahouse near the Arts District that every visiting dignitary raves about, and while it's excellent, it's also too fussy. I fill the rest of my stomach with skewers of fried street food and lick my fingers clean.

When I'm done with my trip, I take a carriage back to the palace, and the prince returns to mind with the swiftness of a weed.

I want to crumple his note and throw it into the fire again.

Cyrus and I have settled into some pattern of functional interaction, with an unspoken agreement to keep things unspoken. When he discusses plans, he includes me in them, as if there isn't a future where I'm not Seer here. We're all bound by mutual deception now, with Nadiya as our unlikely link.

Still, I trace his gaze from across the room. Sometimes I want to kiss him and sometimes I want to ruin him, but most of the time, I want those actions to be one and the same.

The ball was not long ago, and the wedding is not far in the future. Everything is happening breathlessly fast this summer, but it will get better soon. These feelings will go away, along with all this prophecy.

As I ascend my tower, I fish out the key to the divining room. When I approach the door, I find it already unlocked.

A thief? No one's been so bold in years.

I rush inside and find no one rummaging.

Instead, leaning against the divining table, is Cyrus, waiting.

His arms are crossed and his legs are outstretched. No fine royal attire adorns him, just the loose shirt and riding breeches he wears when he has a rare day to himself—not that he has those anymore.

"You didn't respond," he says.

Take a hint, I think of snapping, but my mouth is dry. He's claimed the one spot that best frames his features in the honeyed light of late afternoon. The tug of his collar is a little lower than it should be and a sweep of hair frays over his brow in an uncommon display of dishevelment. It's appealing.

A little too appealing. I narrow my eyes. "How long have you been posed like that?"

Cyrus pushes himself off the table. "I heard you come up the stairs."

"Half an hour?"

"Ten minutes." Which means twenty.

Everything about Cyrus screams premeditated seduction—he is here for a reason, and he didn't earn his title of Prince Charming from nothing. But if I don't move, he'll think I'm scared, so I force my legs forward. "What do you want?"

"You've been avoiding me."

"I don't *need* to be around you."

"You don't need to do a lot of things that you do." His gaze is hooded. "Have you been jealous of how I treat Nadiya?"

I bark a laugh.

"I only want to make her feel comfortable."

"I really don't care. What do you want?" I ask again. That question—the real, underlying question—remains unanswered between us no matter how many times it comes up.

Cyrus hesitates. In the space of that held breath, I imagine every thread that might unravel from this moment; so many are at his disposal to choose. The boy who was born with everything meets my gaze.

"You," he utters, no deflection, no adornment.

I swallow, overconscious of the sound it makes. I'm being too obvious when I turn away from Cyrus, moving toward the hearth in the hope of finding something to occupy my hands. Borrowed tomes and dirty dishes litter the table under the open window. I've cleaned up little in the past weeks; the dress I wore to the ball is still bunched in a corner, faded of magic and melted into kitchen rags.

"Violet."

"I don't forgive you for trying to push me out," I snap, staring through him.

"I know."

"Whatever you're doing here—it's an act."

"If that's what you believe."

A shiver runs through my bones as Cyrus nears. He isn't fighting back and it throws me off-balance, my tongue tripping over retorts I don't have the opportunity to say. He smells faintly of the river; he used to like to spend his afternoons swimming, and I'm close enough to see the damp under his collar.

My hands curl into his shirt. "You can't seduce me."

"I think I already have."

Cyrus lowers his head past my lips and presses his mouth to my neck, dipping down into the valley of my collarbone. Any hold I have on him is useless. If I could breathe, I would curse; it shouldn't be so easy for him, I shouldn't *make* it so easy for him—

"You're getting married," I manage to say before I lose all thought.

"So?"

"*So? What about the prophecy? What about—Cyrus.*"

"I have a bride." His lips move below my ear. "But I want you."

I grip him by his hair and think to pull him off but something roughens in his throat that makes me want to keep him there. "I am *Seer*. I will not be your *mistress*."

"Do you expect to be queen?"

An inane laugh bubbles out. I don't expect this to *continue*. I can't follow who Cyrus is anymore—the resentful boy I once knew, or the sly brat who has me in his arms.

As I'm about to retort, my stomach lurches: I'm crushed to him as he lifts me off the floor. Next thing I know, he's carrying me to the sofa.

He pulls me astride, my skirts rucked over my knees, the velvet cushions sinking beneath us. Doesn't push for more— yet. Even that's probably premeditated. He only kisses me lightly, like a question. A little condescendingly, if I'm being honest, overtly aware that he's done this more than I have and I'm at every disadvantage.

So I make him clumsy. Wriggling from his touch as his hands test where they should be, dodging his mouth until I catch his chin and kiss him myself. I feel him smile— impossible not to with my bottom lip in his possession.

Cyrus turns to kiss my injured palm, lingering on that still-gleaming slice of a scar, deliberate in its depth and angle. "Was this from the beast, too?"

The thorn borne from my blood is hidden in a cabinet not ten paces away. In a different thread, I'd be driving it into his heart this instant. It'd be so easy with him pinned down, distracted by the rest of me. He'd never see it coming.

I swallow. "I was careless with a knife" is the half-truth I offer him.

He doesn't notice my lie. Instead, his fingers slink behind my neck, the small intimacy treacherous in more ways than I understand right now, the kind that unspools new threads in the future.

Every rational thought shouts at me to stop. Princes don't dabble with witches on the side. What will happen when someone finds out? Bedroom mistakes are always the fastest to rear their ugly, wart-chinned heads. I read the papers; *Lacy Things* gets delivered to my window every other morning with a whole column of scandals next to the birth-constellation analyses. Cyrus and I wouldn't just be a headline. We'd be the cautionary tale in history books.

But when he pulls me in and I meet him with a kiss that steals the gasp from his throat, I can't resist having this power over him.

I shove him down on the sofa with a knee, and he sprawls upon the cushions at my mercy, a slyness crooking his lips. He plays with the tail end of my braid dangling between us—and yanks it so I topple onto him. "No promises," he says.

My heart is racing, my body hot. Our feelings can't be removed from the roles we have in the palace, which is why on any day, he'd rather see me humbled than kiss me good-night. But I don't need his trust or devotion. Our attraction is simple: we both think we're one step ahead and we have to prove the other wrong. I want him *because* I don't trust him.

Love is a fickle thing traded by fools, but lust is exactly that—no promises. It's as hungry as any starving creature but honest in what it wants.

And I want him.

"No promises," I answer and I kiss his open mouth.

Underneath me, Cyrus shudders, hands flexing at my waist, loosening the blouse from my skirt band. I could climb off, leave him cold, but what would be the point? We'd get back here eventually.

One kiss after the ball is a mistake. Two is a challenge. Any more is habit.

Freeing my braid, he buries his fingers in the twists, making a mess of it. "Violet," he rasps, no humor left. I like the sound of my name on his lips too much.

He undoes the buttons and strings of my clothes with ease as I fumble with those on his—how many times has he done this before? I pull his shirt over his head, and he's so fit underneath it makes me angry. He gets impatient with my chemise and starts pushing it over my hips, the seams stretching from his carelessness.

Camilla's bedded plenty of girls; she's told me about some of it and I know generally how it escalates. How it happens faster than you think the first time, how you have to be more careful with boys. I know what we're doing is stupid, reckless, a reckoning waiting to happen. But I want to know—

His hands slide under my chemise. I should stop him now. We're going too far, and I won't stop him later even if I want to. I curse my pride. I curse my shaking knees as I move into his touch, biting back gasps. I curse him most of all.

"Want more?" The question comes out a breathy plead as Cyrus shifts, rolling me over so I'm between him and cushions.

Yes, I mouth, head flung back. *Yes. Yes. Yes.*

A knock on the door, just as his fingers find the spot that makes me crumple to him. I'm never more thankful the room is soundproof.

A second knock. It seems so far away that it can't be real. My bare legs wrap around him. My body is at the edge of breaking.

Then comes Dante's voice like a drench of ice water: "Violet? You there?"

"Oh, toady *hell,*" I gasp, sitting up. Cyrus tumbles off me, tangled in his trousers.

There's a third and fourth and fifth knock in quick succession—the polite but pointedly impatient warnings of someone about to check inside. I pull my chemise down and search for my blouse among the toppled cushions, a thunderous heartbeat in my ears. Cyrus stares at the doorway, panting and flushed. Most of his blood probably isn't in his head right now, but that doesn't soften my pitch as I hurl his shirt in his face.

"Hurry up," I hiss. "I didn't lock the door. He's going to open it if I don't answer."

"Why wouldn't you lock—"

"You distracted me!" Hauling my skirts up, I pinch them

250

around my waist; I don't have time to do the buttons. "You could plan to pose for an hour waiting to seduce me but you couldn't plan for this?"

Legs wobbly, I stomp over to the entryway as Cyrus mutters, "It was *twenty minutes*."

The door cracks open as I grab the knob.

"Vi—?"

I stop the door from opening farther. I jut my face out, the rest of my body hidden. "Hi. I was about to take a bath." *And I'm breathless because I had to run downstairs, not because I was underneath your best friend,* I don't say.

Dante looks away, flustered. His arms are full of notebooks and loose papers. "Ah, sorry, there are a few wedding-day precautions we need your opinion on, but . . . Later is fine. Sorry! I'll come back."

"I can meet you in the gardens or the library in a little while instead?" I suggest. Unless Cyrus wants to sneak out via defenestration.

There's a scuffle of movement behind me, too soft to be heard outside I think, until Dante frowns and turns slowly toward me. "Er, is someone there?"

I stiffen. "No."

"Did you know that when you lie, you have a tell?"

"What?" I make a face. I have to stop doing that. "No, I—"

"Having someone over is nothing to be ashamed about," he says with a short laugh. His expression freezes, a thought blooming. "Unless it's—"

"There's no one!"

"I couldn't find him earlier, please tell me it isn't—"

"Yes, it's me," drones the voice inside the room.

Dante drags a hand down his face, and the crush of papers in his arms drop to the floor. "For the love of—"

Cyrus grabs the door from me, and I yelp, clutching my clothes so they don't fall. He's fully dressed, if disheveled.

Dante rolls his eyes as he reaches over and flattens Cyrus's hair and shoves his shirt into his trousers. "I don't want to know—actually—no, no, I do. Your crown and a kingdom-threatening prophecy potentially rest on your upcoming marriage and your pants aren't fully buttoned, so this better be damn worth it."

"It was until you interrupted." Cyrus scowls.

"It was a one-time thing," I say over him, mortified.

Dante picks up his dropped papers. "I am going to give you two a moment to sort . . . *whatever this is* . . . out." He backs away toward the stairwell, pointing a vehement finger at Cyrus. "Won't care if you're naked, if you aren't outside this tower in five minutes, I will haul you out of here."

I shut the door and slide against it, hand clutching my forehead. I peek through my fingers to find the prince nursing a smirk. "Don't look so smug."

I finish buttoning my skirts properly. Then Cyrus's hands find my waist, and he pulls me flush against him.

Jolting, I look up. "What are you *doing?*"

"I believe we have five minutes." His smile is easy and lethal.

"You seriously want to—"

"I already went through all this trouble. He can haul me out of here naked."

My sensations have dulled since our earlier thrill, but

something else in me flutters at his idle flirting, if only for how unexpected it is. Cyrus said he wants me, but even after all we've done, I don't believe it until now.

His fingers weave with mine and my mind fills with his threads as he kisses me once more:

A clock striking eleven. In the hedge maze, a masked girl in a dress like mist grins.

The gnarled Seer of Balica taking his palm between hers and speaking a prophecy in rhyme.

Grit and vines and splintering thorns enveloping his bloody body. "Violet," he utters with gasping terror.

I let go of Cyrus.

"Violet?" My name is a soft question on his lips, but I still hear the terrified echo from the future.

"You—" I nearly tell him the truth. That I dreamed a scene of his bloody body before. But this time, in his threads, I saw the setting.

A room in the palace.

I saw not an imaginary version of him but *him*.

"What did you see?"

Cyrus wants to fix whatever startled me. He wants to fix it because he wants me, and the thought seems more ridiculous the longer it lives in my mind. A question burns in my throat—a stupid one I'd never ask. But if I asked it, I'd tack it onto the end of some blithe statement like it's rhetorical: *I'm the best thing that's ever happened to you, but I'm still not worth this effort and we don't even like each other, so—*

Why me?

But I can only think of so many answers, and I can't bear to hear any of them aloud. "It doesn't matter," I say, pulling farther away with each word. "There's no future for us. I'm not—" A laugh bubbles out of me despite myself. "You're going to be *king*. And I'm going to be your Seer."

And that's that. We had our respite in this divine room, away from the world and our duties, as the gods sneered above. Now we move on, because we have to.

When Cyrus doesn't budge, I open the door to force the decision upon him. He looks neither stricken nor exasperated when he finally leaves, just resigned, aloofness settling upon him like a well-worn mask.

19

THE COUNCIL OF DUKES ISN'T HAVING A MEET-
ing so much as a shouting match.

When fourteen dominions are contending for weapons
and supplies and soldiers during the most anxious of prophetic times, every scrap of information opens a new avenue
of negotiation. A real pack of wolves would fight over a car-
cass in a more orderly fashion than the scene in the Council
Chamber.

While new reports of beasts have slowed down, dominions are struggling with containing the ones that are still
roaming. Now that we know these creatures were once
human, we're hopeful they may have a chance to be human
again. Old forts have been repurposed rapidly as makeshift
corrals, but it's difficult, dangerous work.

I enter the Council Chamber a quarter after the hour—
when the quarrels have warmed up and insults begin flying.
The first thing I hear is Lord Ignacio calling Lord Oronnel
"boil-brained" and, in retaliation, Oronnel calling Ignacio's
dyed wig an "aborted squirrel."

I find a seat perpendicular to the king, against the wall.

King Emilius didn't request my services for this meeting, but he wanted me to be aware of present plans.

Across the room, Cyrus is on his feet, fist driven onto the table. The golden whorls of his coat shine under the hazy lighting. He's tearing into Lord Denning's argument with a daggered look he would never wear in public. "We have no intelligence that says burning Fairywood is preventing more beasts. In fact, Raya believes that the Fairywood may be our greatest asset in removing the dark magic from these cursed men."

"Her demonstration doesn't fool me." Lord Denning has been dealing with the beasts for the longest, along with Lord Ignacio and Lord Arus. He recently returned from the Eleventh Dominion, where at least two villages suffered casualties. "She credits her magic to fairy blessings, but the man transformed back in a matter of hours. My wife has it on good authority that she is a charlatan. I make no apology for this, Your Highness, but your bride is in league with that Witch of Nightmares, if not a witch herself."

"How *dare* you." The prince plays his lovelorn part with zeal, no one the wiser of what he and I have done. "The rumors have been recanted—"

"No such thing—"

The noise escalates to a din. While the king and I have proclaimed the witch is to blame for the beasts, my lack of information about her has created a ripe environment for rumors to grow, and I don't know enough about the witch myself to lie in order to soothe people. Many in court remain suspicious of Raya.

Eventually, King Emilius drums the table. "Peace," comes

his low voice, barely audible, but it's enough to cascade a hush down the table. "We will have no slander against Lady Raya. Cooperation with our neighbors is the top priority. Lady Raya is our prophesied salvation—and I would gauge further, a sign that the Fates mean for Auveny and Balica to unite one day. The Fates must have reason for tainting our land with dark magic. Consider: is it so that we may defeat it with the joining of an Auvenese prince and a Balican leader? Seer, your thoughts?"

I lift my eyes. King Emilius usually gives forewarning if he'd like me to speak, but I hadn't prepared anything. He looks the picture of patience as he awaits my response, but his gaze is heavy with expectation and I know this is a test of my loyalties.

I err toward aiding Raya's reputation. "Lady Raya is chosen by both fairies and the Fates. Though some may doubt her now, what we remember in a decade will be that a spirited outsider attended the ball at the Fates' will, entranced us all, and brought hope in darkness. The first step of Auveny's new era." Pretty words that say just enough without overindulging.

Cyrus is thin-lipped. This isn't the response he wanted. But his fight isn't with me; he glowers at his father. "We shouldn't be thinking about widening our borders regardless. Beasts are walking the earth. Let's focus on our own issues first."

"I would argue it's the best time to think of it," Lord Ignacio muses down the table. "Balica is distracted. Weak. They beg our aid. We should demand something in return for the soldiers we sent to them."

"Speaking of aid, we're sending *too many* soldiers to Lunesse. Raya requested a small battalion to help secure the capital, not so many to occupy the state. I was supposed to coordinate these deployments with the general, but someone else spoke to him first. Who was it?"

"The orders came directly from me," King Emilius says crisply. "The extra soldiers were to guarantee her land's safety."

"The *safety*—" Cyrus scoffs. His eyes meet mine, as if these words are truly for me. "It's an invasion in kinder terms and one that will not be seen kindly by Balicans once Lunesse recovers."

Biting the inside of my cheek, I remain quiet in my seat. I won't pretend to enjoy these plans, but I won't pretend I didn't see this coming.

Shouting rises to headache levels again until the meeting is adjourned. Lords and advisers leave the room jesting and squabbling, continuing their conversations outside.

"Seer," the king says as I rise. "A moment in my study, if you have the time."

"Of course, Your Majesty." I wait for him by the arched doorway.

Cyrus brushes past me without acknowledgment. The back of his hand grazes mine, a jolt of a moment that feels more treacherous than it is, even with my hands gloved. King Emilius follows close behind him, and I force a smile to my lips just in time.

The king doesn't need the aid of another to walk today, but I offer my arm out of politeness, which he takes. Stress, more than anything, seems to be aggravating him. His hair has grown a shade grayer since the start of summer.

We make small talk about the wedding preparations. The main rooms have been redecorated in whites and golds. You can smell the kitchens cooking sweets at every hour.

I edge into more serious conversation as we turn down the hallway to his study. "I do think there is merit to what Cyrus is saying," I say, careful to seem neutral. "I'm afraid we tempt war with Balica—and Felicita's prophecy warned of war."

The noise in the king's throat is dismissive. "Balica has a minuscule military. We would crush them if events led to that."

But it's not about the victory, I want to say. *War is war, war is blood, war is death.*

I used to dream of wars as a child. It isn't the same as reading about them in books. I see the things that aren't recorded: the tears, the cowardice, the confessions given upon a dying breath. Forgotten threads that touch upon times long ago or, maybe, times that never were. It's all the same now; a history unremembered may as well have never existed.

The people and lands beyond our borders are mere numbers to King Emilius. Pins and flags on a map, valuable only in how they can help us. He doesn't care.

He unlocks his study and takes a seat at his desk. "I will say Cyrus has true passion for raising this kingdom up," he muses. "Some of his ideas are *ill-advised,* but he will grow out of them. I'm glad you're getting along better. I understand that you are working with him closely regarding Lady Raya's needs."

"Yes."

"Excellent, excellent. But do not overcorrect and become too soft on him. He is still rash, idealistic, overly influenced by his travels and his friends." *His friends.* He means Dante. "My son thinks we should walk away from fruit ripe for the picking. He resists bringing new lands under our fold, because he fears the responsibility. You would never do so— you grab every opportunity that gleams. That is the mark of true ambition."

I smile, even as his flattery suddenly grates me.

The king spreads his hands at the map of the Sun Continent on his wall. If I look closely, I can see where Auveny's borders have been drawn and redrawn again where the Fairywood was cleared to make way for new dominions. Balica seems so tiny in comparison in the south, a third of the size.

He coughs into a handkerchief, then folds it back into his pocket. "Auveny is a strong kingdom. You know this much. We are kind and generous—no wars waged since my grandfather's time. Cyrus will be a good king, despite our disagreements, and if we are a great kingdom with a good king, how could Balica or any others complain? They will be thankful."

Of course Auveny *must* be a great kingdom; the alternative is unacceptable. Because if we weren't, we would be brutes. Aggressors.

"When is his ascension?" I ask.

"For the time being, I'm well enough to continue ruling. Perhaps even for another year or more . . . depending on how long it takes for my son to shed his foolish views."

"Oh." Up until now, the king had implied that he would

abdicate after Cyrus married at the end of summer; did he only recently change his mind?

King Emilius doesn't seem to notice my confusion, smoothing into a new topic as he taps a finger against his bearded jaw. "I have a small ask."

"Yes, my king?"

"During the wedding, I'd like you to speak on Cyrus and Raya's union. Make the Fates' blessing official. Divine words will help curb naysayers. Prophecy maintains order where good sense will not do, as you know, and it will plant the first seed of unification."

"Of course. I'll prepare something."

"Excellent." He smiles. "I can always rely on you."

Bowing, I take my leave.

Outside in the hall, I can finally breathe again. I am sick of the futures I see in my dreams and in the plans that the king has laid out.

The voice in my head said war is inevitable. And isn't that what I believe, too? The world is built for wolves and their wars. It is built for taking. Each century brings new kings and new squabbles, but there will be the same short-sightedness, the same greed.

To be remembered as someone good, you have to *do* good.

To be remembered as someone great, you have to get elbow-deep in bullshit and come out looking spotless.

King Emilius will be remembered as someone great.

King Emilius grew Auveny from eight dominions to fourteen. He burnt down swathes of Fairywood, which we all know is dangerous and uninhabitable to unmagical creatures. I've always wondered how much of that belief traces back to the king.

He's an expert at making his actions sound wise and necessary. How interesting that with every acre of Fairy-wood torched, Auveny also gained an acre of land. It was a means of widening our borders, and I didn't even realize until Dante pointed it out one day.

After botanists learned how to distill ambrosia, King Emilius turned that knowledge into treasury wealth. All that newly scorched land turned into golden fields of fayflower to make ambrosia. Fairy glamour became a trend, a mark of virtue that could be bought. Old fables of fairies resurfaced, sweetened for the new generation to sell happily-ever-afters. Urging on the fantasy was Sighted Mistress Felicita, who often played matchmaker for the Sun Capital populace during her time as Seer.

These details taken separately mean little. Coincidences, scattered across time and anecdotes. But all together? Maybe the clever gleam in the king's aged eye shines a little too brightly.

Auveny's success isn't might or land or fairy glamour. It's the tales spun about our greatness. They tell us that what we achieve is fate, that we deserve everything in this world and more.

When truth is relative, you make yourself the axis.

In the dining hall, I find my only bright spot of the day—well, bright as a hunched, puffy-eyed, wrinkled-clothed scholar-turned-unofficial-adviser can be. Dante is also eating lunch, so this misery can have company.

I plunk down next to him and use a discarded copy of today's *Lacy Things* as a place mat for my bowl of soup. Below my food, a headline reads HIGH-HEELED TURN: CAMILLA ENCHANTED. The article details the sightings of the princess and Lady Raya around the city. Ziza Lace, as ever, leans heavy on the speculation:

They have shopped and dined in each district. Keen-eyed witnesses say they are even sharing fashions, leaving us to ask: is this friendship or something more? When wedding bells ring in two weeks, we might just see Her Highness challenging her brother at the altar for his bride. Stars know, our princess always gets what she wants.

I'd howl with delight if that happens, but Nadiya is too mousy to be Camilla's type. Although, maybe not after the princess is done transforming her. Ziza is usually at least half-right.

I'm midway through hate-reading the article when the steward to Lord Denning walks by with a plate of whitefish. Casting an eye at the newsletter, then at Dante, he says loudly, "I should've done more traveling. Clearly, our royals have a taste for the exotic."

I have to hold on to Dante's cuff as his mild manners evaporate in a blink. I can imagine his retort, unspent in the back of his throat: *Clearly, you have a taste for getting clobbered in the face.* But Dante hasn't lasted so long in the

Auvenese court without knowing how to restrain himself, even when others don't deserve it.

When the steward departs, Dante mutters, "Wart. I should've punched him." He picks up the bread crusts I discarded and reaches for a slather of butter to finish them with.

"And have a duel thrust on you?" I chide. "The Council meeting was rough. The king wants to spread the idea of unity with Balica, but I think he's creating more contrarians from it."

"The frustrating thing is, if Balica *could* trust Auveny, we would work together to find the witch." He sighs. "People think we only work together in one way, if you know what I mean. My visits to the royal wing haven't gone unnoticed. As if all I have to offer the crown is my *very* fit body!"

"Well, it is *very fit*," I say dryly. "They'll respect you when you're a king's adviser."

He waves a spoon around, vehement. "*If that happens,* they will think I *slept my way there.* The worst part—the absolute worst part—is that, frankly, I *am* a fantastic lay—"

A little bit of the soup I'm drinking goes down the wrong way.

"—and I wouldn't be opposed to certain arrangements if circumstances were different. I'd want Cyrus to have high standards."

"How generous of you?"

"Thank you." Dante gives me a sidelong glance. "Could be to your benefit, too."

"*Shut up.*"

When we finish with our meal, we walk out into the

gardens. I can sense Dante weaseling toward the topic every time Cyrus comes up, but anything we might discuss wouldn't be safe to mention in public.

As he can read my thoughts, he asks, "Want to go outside the city?"

"Aren't you busy?"

"I am *very* busy. But if I have to decipher another page of the Head of Gramina's handwriting, I will lose all literacy." He unholsters the pistol at his waist and spins it around his finger. "Didn't you want to learn how to shoot once?"

"No, Camilla just wanted to teach me." Last winter was nothing but constant rain and sleet, and she went stir-crazy indoors. A Yuenen princess had gifted her a set of pistols with grips carved in the shape of twin serpents, but the ground was too marshy to hunt anywhere interesting. The palace emerged from that season bearing a number of new bullet holes and short two sets of dinner plates. Camilla let me try them out, but I was a terrible shot and she was a terrible teacher.

"Could show you how to spar," Dante offers. "Never know when you face a beast again these days."

I've seen him spar with Camilla, but I thought he was humoring her; I didn't know he liked it. "They taught you this at the university?"

"Too many bored aristocrats sent there with father's coin." He grins. "I pick things up fast, is all. Come on, I need a distraction."

We head out near the hunting grounds again, where there's a wide-open space just for shooting and archery practice. The rippling grass is thick and golden-green;

wading through it is as satisfying as combing through a groomed horse's mane. I stretch my arms in the air to catch the breeze.

Dante ties his curly hair back with a string, and then we get started. He shows me a few weak spots, a stance where I can use my body as a lever, and how to best swing my limbs depending on what parts of me are trapped. I knot my skirt for better motion; I can match his moves well enough, just not with his speed. I knew he was strong, but he surprises me still.

While practicing a jab, I forget to give warning and nearly smash his nose with the heel of my palm.

Dante lowers my hand from where it had been, an inch in front of his face. "So. About your thing with Cyrus."

"Do we really have to talk about it?" I try to kick at him, but he sidesteps.

"I was just wondering," he says, shrugging with exaggerated flippancy, "are you . . . in *love* with Cyrus?"

"I'm not dignifying that with a response," I hiss.

"I wouldn't make judgments if you were."

"I am judging you for even thinking that!"

He easily ducks from my swipe. "His jawline alone has broken hearts—"

"Your taste in men is terrible. Don't drag me down with you."

"—and it's obvious he's gotten under your skin."

I take in a sharp breath.

He snickers despite his solemnity, like he *wishes* he could be more amused about this. "You don't need me to tell you that getting involved with Cyrus is dangerous."

"He started it, you know. He was the one who came to my tower. Found his bride to break the prophecy with, now he wants to make a mistress out of his Seer," I grumble. "But it's true, we shouldn't be risking the wedding and—"

"I mean, dangerous for *you*."

Dante moves so fast, I don't even register he's hooked me behind the legs until I'm in the air, stomach flipping. He catches me, one arm behind my back, the other behind my head, close enough to the ground that my elbows scrape the dirt.

He hovers over me, the sky brilliant blue behind him. "Do you know why some people like keeping the Seer in the tallest tower in the kingdom?" Sweat gleams from his brow, and his ponytail droops over his shoulder as it comes loose. "If things go sideways, it gives everyone someone to point at."

My breath returns to my lungs. "I know that."

"Do you?" The twinkle in his eye is as curious as a secret—it reminds me of Cyrus for a startling moment. They've shared mannerisms over the years, like the way they bury their hands in their hair or tilt their heads after hearing something absurd that they can't comment on. I wonder if there's a timeline where I kissed Dante instead of Cyrus at the ball, and whether that version of me is living with less regret. "You have a habit of convincing yourself that you're invulnerable."

I scowl. "I survive because I'm good at it. I'm *here* because I'm good at it."

"It isn't a mark against your successes, Violet. But the higher you fly, the more fatal the fall." Dante pulls me up by my wrists.

When he lets go, my fingers just brush his palm.

A countryside ride. The sun peeking over the ragged horizon. "I promise," says Cyrus.

The memory is so clear and sharp—recent. Instinctively, I reach to see more, pressing my palm flat against his. The scene unfurls in full:

"I promise," says Cyrus, "to keep Auveny out of Balica's borders. Both now and when I am king."

"And if you can't?" asks Dante.

"I promise I'll be a just king to them. More than just."

He shakes his head. "If you can't, there'll be war."

"Balica has no military—"

"I'm not saying resisting wouldn't be utter suicide. But I am saying that we won't be peaceful."

The image snaps out of mind as Dante yanks away.

"Sorry!" I blurt. "I didn't mean to—"

"Really?" He pins me with a glare, his anger more potent by its rarity, shadowed by the backlit sun. "Were you prying?"

"I only saw a conversation when you were out on a ride with Cyrus." Dante has every right to doubt me, but though I might pull these tricks with others, I'd never breach his privacy like this.

His frown lingers, and he rubs his hands as if that would erase what I saw.

"I thought Balica was trying to avoid war," I say quietly. "You can't let one start. That's exactly what the witch wants. Exactly what the prophecy warned about."

A strained breath deflates him. "Then maybe it means it's inevitable."

"Don't say that." I've heard that word enough in my head.

"This witch sowing distrust between kingdoms—it's a headache, but it's aggravating issues that already existed. Even if we find her and get rid of her beasts, even if Cyrus and 'Lady Raya' get married, that won't automatically solve Auveny's overreaching. It's easy to blame everything happening on prophecy, but the core of the problem is . . . *here.* This kingdom's greed."

I don't tell Dante about how the king asked me to speak at the wedding in support of unification. It's a guilt I'll bear in secret, like the thorn in my cabinet. *I will make that decision when I get to it,* I tell myself, even though I know sympathy has no place in survival.

Better to run among wolves than be devoured by them.

"What can we do?" I still ask.

"I *hope* that relations will be different under Cyrus and tensions will ease as a result. That is yet another reason why we need this marriage soon. He has dukes in agreement with him, but they are quiet at the moment, biding their time until he wears a crown."

"But King Emilius might not abdicate yet."

His brow dips. "I thought after the wedding . . ."

"He's been healthier." I kick at the dirt. "I suppose with Cyrus acting out, he wants to rule a little longer until Cyrus sheds his, ah, idealistic impulses."

Dante drags a hand down his face, smearing a line of sweat along his cheek. "Gods, this outing was supposed to be relaxing. It's like nothing we plan makes a difference."

Above, a thumbprint of a day-moon rises. I find little

comfort in the drifting clouds and darkening sky—the sign of cooler, shorter days as summer ends. A stray fairy blinks a trail overhead as it flies toward the capital.

The light is oddly familiar in its pattern, and as I stare at it, I think of a few of the dreams I've had lately without the Fates speaking to me, the ones where fairies seem to have slipped inside. Fairies lit the sky when I dreamed of beasts in the countryside, and even earlier than that, they guided me to a cursed Cyrus who was consumed by briars. It was like they were trying to warn me beyond what my innate Sight could show me.

My lips purse into a frown.

Including the vision I had seven years ago that allowed me to save Cyrus.

I remember it as clearly as the night I dreamed it: the sky above the marketplace had been filled with an impossible number of lights as the prince died below them. But I know better now than I did back then—those lights were fairies.

Were they warning me then, too?

A long-held thought turns and shapes itself anew.

"It *will* make a difference," I murmur. "That's what the Fates are afraid of."

Dante looks up. "What will?"

"Cyrus becoming king." The threads drifting in my mind coalesce into a clear picture. "I think he's cursed because the Fates don't want him to reign—because that future must be the only one where we avoid bloodshed." The Fates want blood, so they want war, so they want a king who will allow that to happen. "That's why they intended him to die seven years ago. That's why I wasn't supposed to save him."

The world shifts into sharp focus as I leave my thoughts. It's just a theory, but there's a rightness to it in every layer of my mind. A gasp of hope I can offer Dante—that maybe all of his trouble won't be for naught as long as Cyrus survives to take the throne.

But my present dreams are still barbed with threats and thorns, and there is so much I can't admit to him. I still can't answer the most important question of all.

Where will I be standing after this prophecy has passed?

⋘⋙

Blood returns between my legs at night. In my dreams, the Fate who is not a Fate sighs. They lurk in the starless shadows of my mind, that place my Sight finds unfathomable, though it knows something is there.

The boy yet lives.

Their condescension rankles even as I expected it. "What are you doing here?"

I have come to remind you of the prince's betrayal. And to laugh at you for your foolishness.

I narrow my eyes. "If you want me to kill Cyrus so badly, tell me exactly how he will betray me." I'm through with the vague phrases of prophecy.

What will happen when he bores of you? When you cross him? Use your imagination. Such is the veracity of kings.

"That isn't proof." It took a problem bigger than either of us could handle on our own, but working with Cyrus hasn't been so impossible. Even if our private activities are unwise. This voice in my mind gave me that thorn at my lowest of lows, and they'd known it. Now they're desperate to push me down again.

But when things get desperate is when true selves are revealed. "You say you're not a Fate, but you're working with them, I know you are," I say with particular smugness, "and you all want this prophecy to pass in the worst way. You're helping that other witch, aren't you? She's a Seer. And now you're trying to recruit me. Give me an answer, or you're just stalling."

You say you want answers, until there is a truth you cannot face. Their words quicken and sharpen. *You are his plaything. The truth is, you hate yourself for wanting him. Why do you let that hatred fester?*

A flush rises. Some conscious part of me claws my fingers into my bed. "I don't—"

Shameless, shameless Violet of the Moon—there is shame at the heart of you, all the greater for its smallness, hiding in the deep dark where even you wouldn't pry.

I lick my lips; I can still taste that tang of blood when I kissed Cyrus too roughly. "You're trying to worm under my skin—to manipulate me."

Manipulation is the common language of mortals. That is what love is, what hope is.

As their fervor escalates, I hear that human quality in their voice again, and I go still. "Who are you, really?"

Oh, little star. You seek the wrong answers.

I squint into the darkness, and I swear I can feel their presence near, someone on the other side of the echoes. Dragging my tongue along my teeth, I suck the last of that iron taste. Blood makes a Seer's magic more powerful . . . but what are the limits? Could they become powerful enough to invade someone else's mind?

A Fate who is not a Fate.

"No," I whisper. "*You're* a Seer."

Ah, wrong again. And now I tire of you.

I *feel* our connection snap this time. I hold on to the dream, willing myself to not wake yet as the darkness retreats—

I bite down hard on my tongue.

Pain sears. My mouth fills with blood. I gag it all down, thick and bitter, but I feel a fresh power rising in me, tethering me to this shadow world as it dissolves. Laughter responds, delirious and maniacal and closer than ever before. I remember this sound, echoing from a burning balcony and from a vision of triumph over Raya's dead body. In the bright space before waking, I glimpse a pair of black eyes closing, her face obscured by raven feathers.

The Witch of Nightmares.

20

I BURN THE THORN.

I watch it blacken and shrivel until it's nothing but ashes in my hearth.

How much have I helped the witch unwittingly? How much has she spied in my mind? She didn't call herself a Seer, but she has the Sight—she must, if she knows of the future. She talks about the Fates like she's spoken to them.

Villain she may be, I wonder after seeing her feats: what *am* I capable of, if I tried?

Your Sight is but the surface of your magic.

Just because she's wicked doesn't mean she's wrong.

But I suppose that's exactly what she wants me to think.

We are a mere two weeks away from the wedding. Two weeks from destiny. The answers will come, whether I want them to or not, and I'm buzzing with an anticipation that isn't entirely fear.

Meanwhile, the prince is preoccupied with everything but his bride. The three fairies of the palace follow Cyrus constantly, topping up his charm enchantments as he fumes from hall to hall, too furious at his father's plans regarding Balica for any pretense of poise. If only such enchantments worked on the Council, he'd have a great deal more allies.

In the next Council Chamber meeting, the general reports that patrols managed to track an unusually large raven circling the skies, but they haven't been able to shoot it down. It escapes into the Fairywood every time. It was last seen near the Third Dominion—closest to the Sun Capital it's ever been.

I consider telling someone—King Emilius or Cyrus or Dante or even Camilla—of my conversations with the witch. Confess what she asked of me, so they know exactly how dangerous and otherworldly she is. But there's too much to admit, too much to explain, and my tongue is knotted from all the truths I've omitted up until now. If I told them how she asked me to kill Cyrus, they'll know that I was tempted.

If they knew about the thorn, they might even be afraid of *me*.

The return of my mundane responsibilities is unexpectedly welcome as a distraction. My tower is free of rot, so I can resume receiving patrons. The sight at the base of my tower is eerie on the climb up; with all the blackened parts carved away, new tendrils are grasping upward to fill the gap. They grow so fast that if you focus, you can see it happen before your eyes.

Less pleasingly, I've been getting more headaches. "Out with the tower rot, in with the mental rot," I grumble as I open my divining room door.

I force myself through three readings, mumbling futures

that are half-nonsense. People are transparent enough; it's not hard to figure out what they want to hear, even while my head is pounding. Insecurities hide in their speech, hopes are locked away in a laugh.

A mother arrives at my tower with her two daughters. One is around my age and the other is too young to do anything but sigh and kick the table. The elder daughter had been preparing to move to the Sixth Dominion to be a nurse for her wealthy cousins, but travel remains dangerous, as beasts sporadically get past the army's cordon.

My hands are sweaty when I do the reading. I see a little of her arrival in her threads, but not much more.

The mother stops me midway, asking, "Sighted Mistress, forgive me if I'm out of place, but are you sick?"

I clap my hand over my forehead. It's burning hot.

Fatigue slams into me midday. I try to stay in bed, but going to sleep is terrifying. I dream and wake, dream and wake. I only remember snatches of what I hear and see; what stays is a neck-sticking dread of being watched in some other part of my mind.

The witch taunts from the deepest shadows:

How our fortunes have changed because I dare claim power. I was defiant like you once, when I didn't know better. You choose the hard way. But you will learn.

The edges of my thoughts fray, turning into the fanged, gaping maw of a beast.

The beasts are hungry. He will die and war will rise. You will be his damnation.

The darkness shatters into blinding light. I sit up in bed and sunlight strikes me in the eyes. Cursing, I pull the covers over my head and fall back into my pillow, restful-ness drained.

⁂

I receive worried visits from Camilla and Dante over the next few days, but I do feel better after bedrest. After my fever broke, no more voices disturbed my sleep.

Several groggy mornings have passed when a familiar falcon taps at my windowpane.

Its beady eyes stare me down as I unlatch the window. Tied to its leg is a cream-colored note with Cyrus's seal. Figures—kiss the prince a few times, and suddenly he won't stop sending me letters.

The message is as simple as his others: *Hear you're feeling better. Can you meet in my study?*

Sometimes, when sunlight falls across my divining table, I think of Cyrus leaning against it. Of the brush of his lips against my neck, sly as a secret. I should crumple this note, like I do his others. I should keep ignoring him, because his wedding is nearly here, and it seems imprudent to ruffle things now that we've settled into another calm.

Or I could give him a taste of his own medicine.

Craving for a scrap of joy, I can hardly resist. I tie my braid neater. Rummaging in the back of my wardrobe, I pick out a dress with a heart-shaped neckline Camilla would whistle at. It's a flattering dark rouge, embroidered with silver-threaded dragonflies, and sashed around the waist. A little more delicate and shapely compared to my usual outfits, but not obviously alluring, like I'm going out of my way to tempt him.

Which, maybe I am.

On top, I throw on my robe. This is an official visit, after all.

As I cross the bridge to the palace grounds, I lay out conversations in my head for every reason why Cyrus might call on me. If he asks about his father's plans for the wedding, I'll pretend I know only bare details. If he needs a favor, I'll request some light blackmail. In lieu of trust, that's the only currency that matters.

Then there are less innocent scenarios. I swallow as I remember the burn of his mouth. The sleeves of my dress only just cling to my shoulders; how easily he might slip it off if that was all he wanted to do.

I pinch myself.

Weaving through less populated paths, I enter the outer courtyard through a side entrance. Most of the creamy flowers have dropped from the magnolia trees and I can't find an unblemished one to pluck. The flutter of a purple cloak catches my eye in the opposite archway, followed by the glint of gold-tipped boots heading in the direction of my tower.

"Cyrus?"

The boots double back. It *is* him. "Good morn—ing." Something seems to stick in his throat when I walk toward him and the folds of my robe drift apart to reveal my dress underneath.

"I thought you said to meet you in your study."

"I thought you would ignore my letters again." Cyrus gives me a once-over as my attention turns up toward the sound of wing beats and he thinks I'm not looking. His falcon has settled on a sagging branch overhead. "You'll catch a cold like that," he says.

"Not if you keep staring. What do you want this time?"

He pauses, as if seeing me like this has made him reevaluate his request. "My blushing bride has prewedding jitters, and it would be helpful if the Seer could resolve them."

So we don't end up going to his study. We don't even go to Nadiya's quarters. We go to Camilla's quarters, where Nadiya apparently has been staying half the time.

The walk is mostly silent; neither of us is interested in feigning small talk, and anything more important can't be discussed in the open, though I do ask him quietly, "How are things with your father?"

"He hasn't disowned me yet" is his optimistic response.

In the royal wing, I sneeze before I see the fairies floating beside us. I try to shoo them, but they simply drift out of reach. One of them spins and a flower blooms into existence in midair—a perfect magnolia, I realize. It drifts down into my palm.

"Thank you?" I tuck it behind my ear. The fairies buzz away.

Though Cyrus is facing forward, I can see a smile stretch his cheeks. "They like you."

"Why?"

"Could ask myself the same question." Is it flirting if he makes it sound like an insult? "Some people think fairies are drawn toward hope."

"Sounds like some people are *wrong*."

The entry room to Camilla's quarters is a lounge area.

Above, a mirrored ceiling reflects my face in kaleidoscopic shards. A low-hanging chandelier drips sapphires.

As soon as Cyrus shuts the outer doors, his shoulder slacken, relieved, as if the public trek here was the worst part. He scrubs a hand through his hair, still not quite looking directly at me. "Camilla's been growing Nadiya's confidence with their short trips out, but she's still . . . skittish," he explains. "She gets nervous as soon as you talk to her about the wedding, which doesn't bode well for the *actual* wedding. She's afraid about what you saw in her future—about the witch showing up. Which, fair enough, but the palace will be locked down, and we need this wedding to happen. She'd be reassured if you gave her a more uplifting reading."

"I don't *decide* what I see in the future," I say, as if it were obvious. "The future is the future."

"So then . . . do what you do best."

I cock my head, confusion clearing, a bubble of delight rising in its place. "Princey. Are you asking me to *lie* to her?"

"I am asking you to do what you do best." He clears his throat as he knocks on the bedroom doors, and everything about his posture straightens at once. "It's Cyrus," he calls. "I've brought Violet."

The doors swing open and a cloud of yellow petals explodes in my face. I hear Camilla exclaim somewhere beyond the floral assault, "Violet—you look well! Thank the stars."

Racks of dresses in every color make a maze out of the princess's room—zigzags of brocade, shiny silk, and wrinkled taffeta. Enormous bouquets and tea tables stacked with snacks fill the gaps. There's enough stuff for ten weddings in here.

Camilla, for once, is the least-decorated thing in the room, dressed in only a towel and a gooey face mask. Behind her, the bathroom steams with a fruity fragrance. Cyrus tips his head backward with a grumble, eyes skyward, and she sticks out her tongue, sauntering back into the steam. "Don't mind me. Nadiya's on the sofa!"

I can't *see* the sofa. But I hear a rustling, and the girl's dainty face pops through a crush of petticoats. "Hello, Sighted Mistress! Sorry for making you come here."

When I wind my way around the racks, I find Camilla's cramped sitting area walled-in by fabric swatches and a sewing station piled high with spools of ribbon. Nadiya hastily brings over a tray of coffee, neatly stepping over Catastrophe, who is lounging in a sunspot. Cyrus takes a cup, I decline, and she returns the tray to the sideboard.

"I'd go to your tower, but every time I step out, it's like the whole city knows," she says, chattering fast. "I swear, there are nobles waiting behind potted ferns ready to ask me some question about Balica and my intentions and whether I'm some *witch*. How are you? You look lovely today, Sighted Mistress. Oh—and you, too, Your Highness."

"Just 'Cyrus' works fine," the prince reminds, for what seems to be the umpteenth time.

"I'm sure you're working especially hard, Your Highness," she answers, missing his meaning.

I take a biscuit from a second tray she brings over, just so she stops running back and forth. "You're talkative today."

"Her Highness thinks having an air of mystery is

overrated, so I'm trying to be conversational." Nadiya chuckles breathlessly. "She says you have to act like you have something important to say, and it projects confidence."

"Preparing that confidence for the wedding?"

"Oh. I—" She sits down. Folds her hands in her lap over her eggshell-blue skirts. "His Highness probably told you about my worries."

"Scared of the witch?"

"It's more than that." Her lips twist this way and that in an attempt to find an appropriate expression. "I-it's going to be such a long day, Sighted Mistress. One long party after another, an entire banquet. I don't know if my fairies' glamours can last that long. There will be Balican dignitaries, people who knew my mistress personally. Thankfully not many, due to the difficulty of travel—oh, I don't mean that I'm thankful that the beasts are making it difficult." Her voice becomes squeaky and tinny. "I have received letters from her sister, who is intent on making the trip, and I—I just know she will see I am a fraud. I'm afraid—"

"I understand," I interrupt before she hyperventilates. "It's not ideal. But you'd be surprised at what people believe because they want to—and many people want you to be Raya. They want her to be alive, to be a hopeful beacon. I can look in your future, if that will soothe you. Maybe we've changed the future."

"That would be nice. I wish I didn't have to go through it at all." With a frantic wave, she adds, "No offense, Your Highness, I am certain people would line up to marry you."

Cyrus smiles into his cup. "Nothing so orderly."

"I was . . . forgive me, but I was looking forward to fall-ing in love one day."

"Well, that's not out of the picture yet, hmm?" I say curtly, holding out my hands. "Come on, let me see."

Nadiya lays her hands over mine. Knowing what I saw last time, I steel myself for the grisly scenes that will appear. Shutting my eyes, I plunge into darkness. Distantly, threads of the past call to me, but I ignore them. In the future . . .

In the future, I see nothing. Not even the blur of threads being coy.

There is only emptiness. A void. A lack of what should be here.

My lips are pursing into a pout, but then I remember I'm supposed to be reassuring Nadiya. "Hmm," I murmur encouragingly, while my mental self would like to screech aloud. This has never happened before.

But my past few nights have been oddly dreamless. The last time my Sight stirred on its own was during that fitful fever earlier this week, when the witch taunted me. . . .

I open my eyes and meet Nadiya's gaze without blink-ing. "The wedding will go smoothly," I lie. "Keep your chin up, don't drink too much, and stick by the prince's side. I recommend some glamour, but not enough to enchant peo-ple with. Not enough to look suspicious if the glamour *does* wear off."

"Oh—oh, okay." She sits back hesitantly, smile more po-lite than genuine.

I grip her hand a second longer to add, "Highborn folk are all talk, no spine—take it from someone born penniless.

You might not know how to bargain with a king, but you can stand your ground and be better than one. You've come this far, Nadiya Santillion. The future isn't always kind, but you haven't let that get in your way."

A brighter smile lights her face. "Thank you, Sighted Mistress. I'll try my best."

Maybe the confidence boost will change the future in a small way. It's all I can hope for. My thoughts wander back to the void of my magic, and dread slicks my stomach. What is happening to me?

Camilla's humming and the sound of running water echo from the bathroom. The clink of the porcelain cup is particularly loud beside me when I know its owner is Cyrus. "I should get going," I say, as the cheerful decorations become claustrophobic.

Cyrus stands up after me. "I'll walk you back."

I shoot him a look. "I know how to get back to my tower, Princey."

He presses a hand to his heart, all innocence. Gods, his charm really is ridiculous when he uses it on me. "You're still recovering. What if you faint?"

"Then may the arms of a rosebush catch me."

As I leave, I hear him say his goodbye to Nadiya behind me.

The two of us walk out of Camilla's rooms in step. As soon as no one is around, Cyrus asks, "Did you lie to her?"

"Of course. You owe me, hypocrite."

"Times may be too desperate to rely on the truth," he relents, hands skimming down the gold trim of his coat. "We have Felicita's prophecy of ruin, a hapless girl in disguise for my betrothed, the dukes *and* my father to corral—and then there's you."

Me. The one he wants. The one he wishes was never in his life.

"But when have you ever been anything but a problem?" Cyrus sighs. A few noiseless strides later, he pivots in front of me, fingers tugging at his collar. "Violet—"

"Don't get the wrong idea," I say, before the sweetness can seep into his voice. "I'm making sure some prophecy doesn't kill us all. That's it." And I'm not even doing a very good job of it.

He smirks. "Is that why you dressed up for me?"

"It's arrogant to presume."

"Will you come to my study?" His question is a proposition—there's no mistaking it.

I open my mouth to refuse when Cyrus adds, more softly, "Just this once?"

A last time before the wedding, he means. The flutter I feel seems more absurd while I'm in this dress that I very much wore for him, as if my heart is exposed in that bare dip of my chest. If anyone were spying now, they'd say there's little reason for the prince and Seer to be observing each other so closely and there's nothing innocent in the way he's looking at me.

But there is no one.

So I follow him to his study.

21

TWO STEPS INTO HIS STUDY AND A CLICK OF the lock later, my back is against the wall and Cyrus's mouth is on mine.

They don't tell you this part in the storybooks. They go on and on about true love, even though no one can explain what it is. They don't tell you where your hands go when Prince Charming just wants to fool around. They don't tell you that his red, wet, wanting mouth is the ruby fruit, nor whether it's poison or bliss—or both. You have to nibble to find out.

And I'm not supposed to be in his arms at all. I'm the wrong girl, the witch, the one he should never give in to—

Yet I'm the only one he wants.

I force Cyrus backward, nearly tripping over the fur rug in the center of the room. He fumbles for the sash around my waist. My mind is racing, but if we don't go too fast, we'll stop, and I don't want to stop. We have no promises. No future I can fathom. Once I leave his study, none of this will have happened.

My dress slips from one shoulder as he kisses along its

neckline. Try as I might to stay impassive, I laugh. "You're so easy to read." I let my robe fall and pool at my feet.

"Then enlighten me"—Cyrus nudges me onto his desk, hands sliding up my legs—"as to what it is I want to do."

I don't trust anyone in this world, least of all him, but I know bargains, and this touch is a trade. There's a time for softer emotions, but not when the challenge licked upon his grin makes me want him to inconvenience me as much as possible. Nosed against me, he wears not the charming mask that I scorn, but something more roguish and secret. I like this side of him. I like that it's *mine*.

Pushing him onto his knees, I give him an order as much as an answer. "Humble me."

Throned on his desk, I learn what compromise means: a prince kneeling before me with a mouth free to roam. He pushes my skirts up to my waist, gaze turned upward like a question and smile crooked against my thigh, a smile that's also mine. I flush at that look, at how little I can hide, at how he delights in that very revelation.

When his lips finally press against me, I grip his hair gasping, the reaction so immediate I turn away. He kisses me until my legs shake, until I no longer care how I'm reacting at all.

I grope at the lump of fabric where his shirt has ridden up, pushing it over his head. Cyrus rakes off my dress. We tumble onto the floor.

I've been drinking draughts made from the herbs Camilla gave me, but I'm suddenly worried it won't be enough; I've had time since our previous encounter to worry about all the stupid things we almost did. When his body settles over me, I lurch upward.

"I don't—we shouldn't risk it," I gasp.

"Okay," Cyrus pants, salt on his tongue, his next kiss gentle. "Okay." And only in this reprieve do I realize I might even be afraid of how we always go too fast, too far when it comes to each other.

But boundaries can be fun, too; we've always skirted them. He slides a thumb, then his mouth, over the blushing parts of my body, and my knuckles turn white grasping the rug. It doesn't matter what he's doing; it's *him* I want—him wanting me. Both of us choosing the same carelessness. The tales are a lie: destiny isn't anything but the volatile beat of a prince's heart, and it's pounding out of his chest against mine.

When he looks too smug, I twist my hips and roll Cyrus over. He taunts me with his lip between his teeth, but I'm better at playing wicked, and I think I'll like it more, too. If there's any kind of trust in a feud as long as ours, it's the assurance that neither of us will hold back.

One hand around his throat, the other around the part of him that aches for me, I relish my victory as he utters my name in delirious prayer.

If I don't already haunt his dreams, I will now.

❧

We lie sprawled on the rug, half-dressed, gazing up at the starburst-patterned ceiling of his study. Our bare arms radiate heat, not quite touching.

"This is a bad idea," Cyrus murmurs.

"Was," I say. This *was* a bad idea. It all already happened, which is also the only reason we're clearheaded now. The gnawing under my skin has abated and I no longer think about his lips every time he so much as inhales. Bad ideas are either repulsive or very tempting; the pendulum had swung far to the latter side, but now it's swinging back.

Lolling my head toward him, I find him looking at me. People trample each other just to touch that face. He has more freckles than I remember. I think about his lips anyway, buried in the crook of my neck not ten minutes ago.

Even I have to laugh—so I do.

"What's so funny?" Cyrus asks.

Us. Everything. "This." I splay my hands in the air. "Prince Charming fooling around with the local witch. We're a diplomatic nightmare."

"That's not funny."

"It's a little funny."

The fate of an era rests upon our lips. I speak prophecies that could crown kings, and his kiss could decide empires when bestowed on the right person, whom I am not. The stakes are so big, they're absurd. If circumstances were different—well, it's useless to wonder.

I've seen my patrons stumble through life making poor decisions despite what I advise them. But things somehow tip in their favor, and by a narrow window, they avoid heartbreak. They grow old in bliss, because they don't realize the threads that could have been. They don't know any better.

The problem is, I always know better.

I can't see my own threads, but I can imagine them. I

know I shouldn't taunt Cyrus. I should bite my tongue and pretend, flatter him and address him by his proper title instead of a childish nickname. I shouldn't kiss him back. Our entanglement wasn't inevitable in the way of the stars, but in the way you can only toss so many lit matches at a powder keg before one catches—and I should have stopped tossing matches.

But it's quiet now. A sliver of curtained light skims the planes of Cyrus's needlessly fine body, his hair is tousled just so, and he gazes at me like he can see something I can't, like there's meaning to this moment.

"I told you not to look at me that way," I say.

Cyrus lets out a bright laugh and my heart stutters in its beating. He swallows the sound down with an apologetic smile, like he hadn't meant to let it free, and an impossible wish slices through me, the stupidest, most naive thing—

I wish that what we're doing were real.

That laugh was real. But Cyrus knows, like I know, that we have our parts to play, and we've broken our promises to each other too many times before to take any chances. How different we'd be if we hadn't been feuding when it mattered most . . . We might even find safety in our familiarity with each other, instead of suspicion.

I don't regret the lies I've told, nor following his father's orders, nor keeping that thorn tucked away for so long before I burned it. But I regret *this* moment, stolen from a different thread of us where we're oblivious and happy.

I should've never heard him laugh like that.

"Do you remember that prophecy you told me? That rhyme?" Cyrus murmurs.

The journey to love never runs smooth,
and yours, your father would not approve.

"It fits Nadiya." I swallow the feeling in my throat. "The prophecy didn't used to, when she was Raya, but now it makes sense."

"I guess it does fit Nadiya." He blinks at me, then at the ceiling. "It also fits you."

They will catch you by surprise, hidden in disguise,
but leave your grasp before midnight strikes.

I surprised him in the maze. I ran from the ball.

And most importantly, his father would be incandescent if he discovered us right now.

My mouth is dry. "What are you saying?"

He doesn't answer.

I sit up, blood rushing to my head. "Cyrus."

"It doesn't matter." He shuts his eyes as he echoes my own words from our last entanglement. "I will be king, and you will be my Seer."

"You could have anyone. Why do you want me? Why, after all these years—"

He only laughs, weary and strained. "It wasn't *after*. It was always."

Always.

Always.

He's *always* wanted—

"I knew, when I first saw you, that you were different. You spoke like you'd seen so much more than you possibly could have, living in the Moon District the entire time," Cyrus says quietly. "You were smart and quick and you never followed a rule you didn't like, and you have to understand

291

how startling that was for a young prince. And I thought you would become so much more." He turns to me. "I am angry at my father for many things, but for making you his liar most of all. What a boon for him when I discovered you. An orphan Seer. My father wagered you'd be malleable—"

The hairs on my neck rise. "No one made me like this."

"—and in turn, you've helped him a thousandfold more. But you're grown now," he continues without pause. "We both are. I thought you would break free of his influence. You've seen the world beyond, you know he is heartless. He would marry his son off and ask you to announce a future that leads to war."

"Your father is playing by the rules of this world—and he's only ever been fair to me. I am not throwing away seven years of goodwill just because you've been sweet-talking me for half a summer."

"Do it for the future you want. Dante told me your theory that my ascension will make a difference, which is a nice parcel of hope, but what if it depended on *you*?" His gaze is green and piercing. "What if *you* made certain my father abdicates, with a prophecy you conjure up? What if you weren't afraid to—"

"I'm not afraid of him!"

Beneath my glare, Cyrus props himself up on an elbow. His shirt hangs off of him—again, *just so,* infuriating for all its effortless perfection. "You hold your stare when you lie. When you're saying something true that you're terrified about, you look away. That's your tell."

My breathing has turned labored, my quickening pulse

betraying me. "And who will protect me when I defy him?" I whisper.

He cups the back of my hand. "I will."

"You wouldn't hesitate to ruin me." His own words.

He kisses my fingertips. "Not if you did this for me."

"Do you promise?"

Even with all his practiced charm, he hesitates before saying, "Yes."

"I don't believe you." I clamber to my feet.

We've chosen our paths: I will do what's best for myself, and the prince will do what's best for his kingdom. All we can ask of each other is to stay out of the other's way.

As I bend down to pick up my robe, Cyrus rises to his knees. Cups my face, tries to make me look at him. "You don't know how brilliant you could be if you had any courage."

I pull away, the aftertaste of his sugared words now bitter. "Just because you tack on a pleasant name for *foolishness* doesn't make it something worth reaching for." I pull my dress in place and tug the bodice a little higher than it was before. I run a hand down my braid. It's a little frayed, but neat enough to not raise eyebrows if I leave like this. "Have your *courage*. Don't wait for me."

"I don't want to end up on opposing sides again. I was reckless when I tried to force you to leave, but I did have reason. I need to see my own vision of Auveny through, and it'll mean making enemies of my father, the Council—and you, if I have to."

My blood turns cold. The threat comes out at last.

Such is the veracity of kings, said the witch.

Breath shallow, Cyrus licks his lips, chapped from our kissing. The white flecks frosted along the edges fade into skin. "I know my father asked you to speak at my wedding. Instead of listening to him, force his abdication. Say that my reign must begin for the curse to end—"

"Even now, you only wish I'd obey you." Unable to summon my usual vitriol, the words drop dully from my mouth. I am tired and everything hurts, from my head to my heart. "You might be a better king than your father, but you'll still be a *king.*"

"I promise I won't be my father. I won't—"

"No promises, remember?" I don't mean for the words to come out like an apology, and I tell myself, *Better to fight a fool than partner with one.* I feel myself trembling and I know I need to leave.

His thumb presses into my wrist to hold me here. He leans in as if to kiss me again, but I move away before he can. Before the image of him pleading can imprint into memory.

22

NO MORE DREAMS OR LETTERS INTERRUPT THE final days of summer, and all too quietly, Cyrus and Nadiya's wedding day arrives.

I ignore the muted revels on the streets. Anything celebratory is certainly planted by the palace to lift spirits. A parade of Balican dancers and musicians funnels through the Palace District in Raya's honor. Temporary stalls sell white tea cakes and paper masks to eager children.

Above, the sun is bloodred. The Fairywood burns beyond the Sun Capital and the smoke drifts over our skies. I've heard more stories of beasts killed against the cries of those who have had loved ones go missing in recent weeks. I pity them; they've heard the tales of Lady Raya's demonstration and have placed their hopes in a parlor trick.

In the privacy of my tower, I twirl and twirl in my chemise, my braid whipping behind me. The emptiness in my mind is unsettling—no longer a reprieve, but the theft of an intimate side of me.

I want my Sight back.

I want this all to be over.

I don't know what I want.

Somehow all of these things are true.

At twilight, I will stand before the wedding and utter the words that King Emilius asked of me. *The Fates bless this union between Cyrus Lidine and Raya Solquezil. They are destined, as is the union between Auveny and Balica.* I will think of a few more pretty words between now and then. It's not ideal, but life rarely is.

I could try to come up with a foretelling that will please everyone. Say something that sounds like I'm supporting King Emilius's ambitions, while allowing Cyrus to twist my words again in the future, when Emilius is no longer on the throne.

Would the king see through it? The thought flits through my mind automatically.

It doesn't matter if he does, I tell myself, *because I'm not afraid of him.*

I'm not one of the king's pawns. I see his deceptions. Cyrus says that I'm old enough for courage; well, I say I'm old enough to know goodness in this world is worth less than cold porridge. At least I can eat porridge.

I shut my eyes. I think of Cyrus smiling. I think of that stupid rhyme.

I think of him pleading.

The prince imagines a version of me who doesn't exist. I know how the tale that he wants goes: I loathe what his father and his court are doing, so I rebel and ruin their plans and unquestionably support Cyrus's quick ascension. And maybe I can be the domino that changes everything.

Or I can just be a drop in a pond.

Shifting alliances at such a precarious moment, when I've had nothing but omens in my future, means stretching my own neck across the chopping block and trusting Cyrus to stop the axe. I don't have Cyrus's starry-eyed faith. I've seen the memories of average people and the legacies of extraordinary ones, and instead of making me believe in storybooks and happily-ever-afters, it's done the exact opposite.

But I wish—

A sigh tears from my throat.

I wish his feelings were enough to change my own.

I wish they mattered at all.

I never used to long for that.

A glimmer catches my eye. A second later, I sneeze. The palace's three fairies land on my divining table, balancing on my tea set's cups and spoons. Somewhere upstairs, I must have left a window open.

Heart emptied and sore, I scowl. "What now?"

A ribbon of fabric pops in the air between them, dropping to my feet in a puddle. Camilla wheeled in a whole rack of gowns for me yesterday, but I haven't picked one to wear yet, and they all look more suited for a bride, anyway.

With a sigh, I lift my arms and submit myself to the fairies' whims. "All right, get it over with."

❧

The decorated ballroom is dull compared to the breathless magic of the Masked Menagerie. The room is still immaculate—archways spill with white magnolias and golden fayflowers, the drapery is profuse, and every accent is polished to a shine—but no gimmicks lie in wait. Current events have made anything excessive seem vulgar, so for the royal wedding of the century, we will have neither a candlelit night sky nor ill-planned ice sculptures melting amid thirty flavors of cake.

Chatter is loud among the spread of tipsy sycophants and courtiers milling about the rows of chairs and the center aisle where the bride will walk. A disquiet taints the air— the collective hope that this wedding will bring better things in the future and the complete loss if it doesn't. Everyone attending had to be inspected by guards and tested for glamour as a precaution, which preemptively soured the mood; no one enjoys having blood smeared on their nose, regardless of the complimentary handkerchief to wipe it off, but it's the best way to make sure we aren't accidentally inviting the Witch of Nightmares in.

I pick at the lace of my sleeves as I weave my way through the crowds. The fairies spun me a pale-green gown that wraps in front. Pearly flowers and gold leaves nestle in the pleats of its skirt and bodice. It's elegant without being distracting, a good choice for someone who isn't tonight's main event.

Camilla is helping Nadiya get ready and will be among the last to arrive. I think I spot Dante in the far back, but it turns out to be someone else with a similar jawline and love of floppy hats. I suppose he's with Cyrus, who I also don't see in the room yet.

I hate being alone at events. An isolated Seer is begging to be accosted.

"Miss Lune!"

I cringe. I never hear myself addressed that way. It's either someone trying to be patronizing or someone bold enough to not care for titles.

Turns out it's someone who fits both descriptions: professional gossip Lady Ziza Lace heads straight toward me with two glasses of wine. Her black hair is in a gravity-defying updo and she is flushed from cheek to chest, where her dress flirts with the edge of modesty. "Hello, hello, have you had a drink yet? I have extra, here." She foists a glass into my hand. "There won't be any after the ceremony starts, so drink up now!"

If I try to walk away, she'll follow me and be tenfold more persistent, so I humor her with a smile and cautious sip. "Thank you."

"Of course! Always thrilled when I'm not the only Yuenen lady in the room. Could you have predicted this, Miss Lune?" A splay of her fingers shows off her candy-colored rings. "Such a rushed wedding. Shame if this is all we'll have—I am hoping we get a more extravagant one after these beastly affairs are over—if Cyrus and Raya stay together that long, that is."

She pauses, as if to allow me space for an opinion. I have none.

"You're an astute girl who knows more than she lets on," she continues, tapping my glass with hers. "What do you say of the success of this couple? I think they don't quite have that . . . that *spark,* but that's just me."

"If they seem nervous, it's probably the evil witch out to get them," I deadpan, drawing deeply from my glass. Ziza ought to know: she's been publishing lengthy articles about the Witch of Nightmares—speculating over the witch's origins, goals, even her birth constellation—in order to compare her to Raya and to question whether Raya's love will be enough to save us. "All that pressure dampens the romance a little."

"True, true. Or *heightens* it, depending on who you ask, oho! You *are* young—cherish these times, before you wrinkle like I have." Her skin is flawless. "I hear the most *interesting* things about Our Highness, and I wonder if his reputation is true. That he may be Prince Charming on the streets, but he's a conqueror between the sheets—"

I choke on my wine. Toady hell, I have to stop drinking things during conversations.

"—lustful and demanding of the things he wants. Girls nowadays do love a bad boy. Perhaps it's all fantasy, but a little bird told me that you might know."

"Me?" I don't like where this is going.

"In my observation, feelings as passionate as hatred and ardor are two sides of the same coin. One bleeds into the other remarkably quickly, given the correct circumstances. More sparks fly from friction than cooperation, after all. Sometimes you hate someone so much, you fall in love."

And maybe if I start a hot enough fire, it'll start shitting ice cubes. "You've had too much to drink, Lady Ziza." I start walking away.

"I'm perfectly sober. . . . Ah, well, a little tipsy, perhaps." She totters forward after me, then leans in close enough for her lips to graze my ear. "Better to tell me the truth your-self," she hisses, "instead of having me dig it up in the worst way possible. You and the prince have been spotted close together—behind closed doors, even."

My heart hammers. "If you're not drunk, then you're delusional." I keep my stare level, even as a flush warms my cheeks, worsened by the alcohol. "Leave me before I have you thrown out of here for harassing the Seer."

"We don't have to get messy, Miss Lune. I am merely offering you a chance to divulge details on your own terms. Successful ladies such as we ought to support each other. But perhaps we can discuss this again at a more private time." Ziza's smile only grows, and it isn't until I turn around that I see why.

Cyrus has emerged from the side doors of the ballroom. He's dressed in swan white, his suit sweeping along the lines of his body, swirls of beads and embroidery unfurling from the hems. A single loose curl droops across his forehead, making him even more handsome, and below that are his envy-green eyes—looking straight at me.

Were looking. I barely meet his stare before his attention shifts elsewhere.

Toady *hell,* we *are* that obvious.

Around the room, people are shuffling to their seats. The harp swells with a romantic tune. Meanwhile, Lady Ziza awaits my answer with plucked, arched brows.

"Excuse me," I say with my most acrid glower. "I have to be on the stage."

Dropping my wineglass on the platter of a passing server, I stalk away from the gossip and her drunken guffawing.

As soon as I get closer to the stage, I realize why this

side of the room is so empty—it's so heavily secured, the Imperial Guard may as well be the wallpaper. No one wants twenty pairs of eyes on them as they knock back wine.

It's a sign that we don't really have a plan for if the witch arrives. What do they expect to do—snatch a raven out of the air if she appears? What *can* we do in the face of dark magic that this land has never seen?

Still, she doesn't know me as well as she thinks. She's studied future threads and I've managed to surprise her anyway. I refused her help. The kingdom is closing in on her. *She's* the desperate one.

I climb the carpeted steps to bow before King Emilius on his throne. His gray hair is newly dyed and trimmed, and his gold mantle is piled around him, gleaming under the lights. The smile he gives is as genial as a father's, but I don't find comfort in that today.

"You will speak after me and before the officiant," he says. "I trust your words will be very wise."

Nodding, I take my place on the side of the stage.

And the traitorous thoughts begin again.

What if I don't follow the king's orders and instead say that after this wedding, Cyrus should ascend? Would King Emilius deny my words, or will the damage already be done? Surely I could trust Cyrus enough to shield me against his father's wrath. Or do I just *want* to trust him, which almost feels the same?

I am antsy as the ceremony creeps closer by the minute, and after confronting Ziza Lace, I want to do something reckless just to prove I can.

The crowd hasn't quieted yet. I don't see Camilla or

Dante still. Nadiya better not have gotten cold feet at the last minute.

I hear a breath that isn't my own and feel a new presence beside me. I don't look at him.

"What were you discussing with Lady Ziza?" comes Cyrus's low murmur.

My flush had finally cooled away, and now it's back. "Your lack of discretion."

"Mine or ours?"

"Ninety-nine percent yours. You *moon* at me."

"Have pity, I'm lovesick."

"You are not."

There is thankfully no one around us, and the audience's idle chatter is just enough to cloak our conversation. I sneak a glance at the king. He's preoccupied with a member of the Imperial Guard, who is whispering something in his ear.

"Do we have to talk now?" I mutter. "People can see, and then *they* will talk."

"People always talk. This is the last time we can speak before I go through with a ceremony I might regret. I'll risk it." I hear the prince shift on his feet. "What if I wished the bride who will walk through those double doors was you?"

Now I look at Cyrus. His smile is like a hook. The way he says it—half-joke, half-not—sounds like truth as much as it does fiction. Or maybe it's half-love, half-not, two halves at odds. A dare as much as a confession and just enough of an act to deny things later.

I shouldn't humor him. But I want to know, so I ask barely above a breath, so quietly that I might not have spoken aloud: "Are you in love with me?"

A word seems to waver on his tongue, and the answer seems to change as my glare hardens.

"Stop trying to guess what I want to hear. It's a yes or no. *Are you in love with me?*"

"I don't know," he whispers, somehow choosing the most agonizing answer of all.

The orchestral music crescendos. It's time for Cyrus to take his place in front of the throne and await his bride, but still, he stays beside me to rush through these last words:

"You think it's foolish if I love you. If anyone loved you." Each sentence is a quick, hushed cut, sharp as his gaze. "Because you wouldn't be so foolish in kind. Your heart is stone. But the truth is, you never had to be so cold and cruel and mercenary to come this far. You only believe these things so that you don't feel guilty for being this way."

I'm trembling as he sweeps away. He's wrong, so completely wrong. Reacting to him is instinct at this point, and the anger builds up in my throat, wanting to snap something back. If only we weren't at his wedding.

As I force it down, another part of me rouses, the part that is weary of this world that doesn't change:

You are proud, but you still aren't happy.

Across the ballroom, the audience is seated and quiet. The space between me and Cyrus has never been vaster or colder. I focus elsewhere, hiding my fists in the flowers and folds of my skirts.

Finally, the double doors open. I nearly don't notice; I thought someone would announce the beginning of the ceremony first. A strange clamor erupts from the back of the audience.

The crowd rises. Even the king gets to his feet.

The officiant at the dais booms, "What in the stars—" Which is not the kind of introduction anyone ever wants to receive.

But that's what heralds the two women who barrel into the ballroom screaming. Their white dresses are torn, their coiffed hair frizzed, and their teeth are bared. When they look up, their doe-eyed fury is the same.

Exactly the same.

Attacking each other in the entryway are two Lady Rayas.

23

FOR ONCE, I'M AS CONFUSED AS THE CROWD. I scramble to the edge of the stage. Cyrus is already striding down the aisle, pushing through the throngs that divide us from the scene.

Imperial Guards surround the Rayas. As attendees shove to get a view and Cyrus and the guards try to maintain order, the Raya on the left lifts an accusing finger at her duplicate, her voice ringing clear above the din. "*This* girl—"

"I'm the real Raya Solquezil!" the Raya on the right interjects. She's red-faced and looks ready to swing a punch, if it weren't for a guard swooping in to hold her back.

"—has been masquerading as me."

"Don't listen to her!"

The Raya on the left flings a hand up, smile apologetic as she tucks one of her many wayward curls of dark hair behind her ear. "This fraud was one of my handmaidens. She stole my fairies and my identity."

"She tried to kill me!" the other Raya screeches. "But I fought back. *She's* the one who's dangerous!"

"If everyone could just *calm down!*" Cyrus yells, as if anyone ever calmed down from the words *calm down.* "We can settle this matter in private—"

"We will handle this *here,* with everyone as witness, so that I may have a fair trial," the left Raya harrumphs. She spreads her arms wide. "Test me for glamour. Drench us in blood if you must. I have nothing to hide, unlike *some people.*"

As I make my way closer, her dark eyes turn—to *me.* Not to the other Raya, but to me, and my heart beats louder and louder, as if it knows to fear something I've yet to comprehend. Her words thread through my mind again, and the sinister note in her voice hooks a memory, sending shivers down the back of my neck. . . .

The Witch of Nightmares.

As if she senses my recognition, a smirk slices across her face before it disappears with a bat of her lashes. I suffocate suddenly, veins throbbing ice as all sense escapes me.

"She's—" I snap my mouth shut as soon as I open it. No. There is too much that can't be explained in front of a crowd. Because the other Raya must be Nadiya; Nadiya can't act like anyone else if she tried. But if Nadiya's true face is revealed, she'll be marked as guilty immediately, when the truly dangerous one is standing next to her.

"Let me look into their threads," I say, moving past the guards. "No blood has to be spilled today. I can figure out who the real Raya is."

The witch narrows her gaze. "Why do you get to decide?"

"I'm the Seer."

"Seers can lie." She tosses her hair. "What do you have to lose if they test us both for glamour? Unless, perhaps, you were working with the fraud this entire time?"

"We can do both tests," I grit, peeling off my gloves. "It's not up to *the accused* to decide how we handle this. I think His Highness would agree, right, Cyrus?" I hope he can see which one is clearly Nadiya and which one isn't. He doesn't know that the other one is the same person who's been invading my head, suggesting I *stab him*.

When I glance at the prince, he's frowning at me, brow furrowed, as if conflicted.

"What's wrong?"

He looks at the waiting crowd, to the Rayas, and rolls a tongue around his cheek. "The only person . . . who verified that Nadiya was telling the truth . . . was you."

He says this as quietly as he can, but with all attention on us, we can't avoid being overheard. Murmurs of *"Who's Nadiya?"* blister through the crowd.

I shake my head. "So? I read her past threads. They're memories, not predictions. There's no guessing involved. What I saw was the truth."

But Cyrus only keeps staring at me, and I realize that's not what he means.

He doesn't trust *me*.

I gape. "You can't be doubting that I saw—I swear that's what I saw. I saw Raya d—" But I have to stop myself. I can't say that I saw her die, not in front of everyone else. That would require another explanation. "You don't believe me, do you?"

He inhales sharply and doesn't answer me. Only mutters

to himself, "I can't believe I didn't check. We've been relying on only your testimony, going on a wild raven chase. . . ."

"Enough of this," the witch scowls. "The only fraud is this former handmaiden of mine, and—from this looks of this—your Seer. She has clearly been prophesying lies to slander me. She has been trying to seduce the prince for herself, and it seems like she's succeeded."

I throw a guilty look at Cyrus too quickly, who only stares at me, frozen, and I wonder what's taking him so long to take control of this situation. With a disgusted grunt, I snarl, "This is ridiculous. Cyrus and I hate each other—"

"You're right." The prince finally speaks, but it's a second too late when I realize he isn't speaking to me. "Violet tried to seduce me."

The lurch in my stomach is so violent, I think it could drag me down to my knees. The gasps tiding through the room could be a roar. I whip around to face him. *What*—

Then I look beyond him, toward the crowd. If you weren't looking for foul play, you wouldn't see it, subtle in the too-wide eyes and open mouths on everyone's faces, like their minds are not entirely their own. They're enchanted. The witch is enchanting them, like how Nadiya enchanted everyone at the ball.

"The Seer told me I didn't have a chance with His Highness."

"I knew I shouldn't have listened."

". . . lied about other prophecies before . . ."

"Her mother was a prince's whore, too."

Every hair stands on end like a late warning. I can't feel the floor beneath me as Cyrus continues, stone-faced.

"Violet was jealous of Raya. I knew she wanted me for herself, but I pitied her and forgave her."

"You're enchanted—she's cast a charm over everyone—" But I speak too hastily, too desperately. I know it as soon as the sputter leaves my lips. That helpless fury builds in me again, the knowledge that I am powerless when doubted. Something that Cyrus has never had to fear.

I spring forward, grab his arms while a strong grip yanks mine—guards reaching for me. "Snap him out of it! Bring blood!" I'm already being pulled away. "*Stop!*" My protests sound pathetic as soon as they leave my lips, the mewls of a girl crying wolf. My heart's given up even as I scrounge for words.

Would it even matter if everyone were enchanted or not? I've told too many lies, and everyone in this city never did fully trust me. Always doubted me in the backs of their minds, and only soaked up my fabrications when it suited them.

And who wouldn't believe Cyrus over me? Who doesn't want a prince? It's me who's being ridiculous.

The murmurs grow worse:

"Did you see the rot on her tower?"

". . . heard she was sneaking around . . ."

"What if the witch was in front of us all along?"

". . . brought the beasts . . . even planned her own attack."

No—these accusations will get me killed. But they sound plausible even to me. I have known too much and said too little all this time. How easy it is to paint a picture from lies.

Nadiya has shrunk in on herself. She's tenuously trying

to reach out to Cyrus with an asking hand. "Your Highness, please—you must believe me. We're in grave danger."

"We will see where the real danger is," Cyrus says, ignoring her and me. "Guards, would you arrest both Lady Rayas? Have the fairies oversee them as well. Take care—they may know how to wield magic, but this may also be a simple case of an imposter."

"What about the Seer, Your Highness?" the closest guard asks. "Is she . . ."

"She's not behind the beasts, but she may be a pawn. Take her—" His throat bobs when he meets my furious glare. "Take her to a spare room and keep an eye on her. I'll deal with her later."

As a guard grabs my arm, I force down the heat in my cheeks lest it burn up my wisp of a reputation. Every retort I can think of will only make matters worse; this isn't a battle I can win by snapping back.

I hear that familiar laugh behind me. That laugh I know from my dreams, a cackle like a howl of wind.

I told you so.

"You enchanted him," I snarl, twisting around.

The witch's expression doesn't change, a perfect actor as she invades my mind: *I spelled everyone in the crowd— except him. He did this on his own.*

I spin to him, and Cyrus stares at me, looking neither charmed, nor angry, nor doubtful. Only determined. "This is for your own good," he murmurs, and it's like a slap across the face.

I'd been too focused on the two Rayas. That was my

mistake: forgetting that although Cyrus and I have common enemies, I was his first one, the one who has haunted his heart and mind since the day we met. He would be rid of me already if I were any less stubborn.

We could ruin each other, and we would not hesitate to do so.

He'd distracted me with his pretty smiles and pretty words and they lulled me to forget this truth, but I can think of nothing else now. A dark thought dredges up, an over-flowing poison: the witch was right. I should have stabbed him when I had the chance.

I'm almost resolved to my fate of being a laughingstock. Stared at and whispered about by slack-jawed courtiers until my tired feet drag me elsewhere. Like a rabbit in a snare, I can't do anything but struggle.

But I never learned how to fall gracefully.

"Cyrus tried to seduce *me*," I seethe, rooting myself to the ballroom's marble floor, so that the guard has to yank me in order to shuffle me out.

Laughter bubbles forth, but I don't care. Cyrus doesn't dare glance back.

"He wanted to use me. He convinced me that he cared and wanted me to be *courageous,* but he lies between his pearly white teeth." Tonight has been a reminder of how different I am. Beyond my Sight, beyond my dark hair and eyes, beyond the scowl etched in my face, I clawed for my place here. I have nothing unless I take it.

The crowd delights in this dressing down, because they'll take any entertainment they get. They don't look charmed anymore; no, this is merely what people are like—frivolous and wolfish and uncaring of truths. They just want something worth talking about.

"He just pretends to be Prince Charming, but you all know better. You've heard the rumors of how he's a scoundrel. Well, he wanted me first." I don't care if anyone believes me, but I will get this last word, just for the spite of it. I don't care what the witch will do to them afterward. They can all burn. They can all rot. "He kissed me in my tower and then some, then tried to force me out of the kingdom because of it, because he knows I'm a threat to his reign. And maybe you don't care. Maybe you think I deserved it. But know that whatever I'm guilty of, he's guilty, too!"

As I take another breath, an order from King Emilius emerges from the din, heavy with a sigh.

"Remove her from my sight, quickly."

24

I'M LOCKED IN A SPARE GUEST ROOM. A COM-
fortable prison, but a prison just the same.

I pace around on the rug, carving a path in the spotted fur. I can't calm down and I won't calm down. The
future, the past, all my mistakes, all that's left to come,
they fill my mind like bramble, leaving no space for
thought.

It's not even difficult to sneak out. The room is on the
first floor with wide windows I could squeeze through. But
what could I do if I escaped? Go back to my tower, sulk
there instead? Guards are swarming, and running away will
only make the accusations worse. Make people think I truly
have something to hide.

I'm trapped by what they think of me. That's the bullshit
part about this.

The guards outside my door—ones I recognize from
Cyrus's personal unit—gave me a carafe of wine and a tray
of food meant for the banquet. I've laid them out on the
bed and I pick at the crackers, thinking of what one of the
guards said when they dropped it off.

"His Highness is soft. This is more than you deserve. Witch or not, you are shameless."

Not too long ago, being driven out of the only home I've known sounded like the worst fate I could meet, but I was terribly unimaginative. Having Cyrus humiliate me in front of the entire court and make people suspect *I've* been behind the witch's schemes—that's much worse. That'll haunt me for another lifetime.

A sharp rap at the door. Cyrus barges in, his eyes darting until they find me.

I set down the food and march over to him.

"Violet. I—"

He brought no guards inside, so I can do whatever I like, and I start by shoving him as hard as I can. *"Fuck you."*

He grabs my wrists before I can rip the collar right off his shirt. He dares to look *distraught*. "My father's coming soon—"

The door opens and slams shut again. King Emilius is the only one of us who still looks meticulous in his attire, like he ought to be at a wedding banquet and not reprimanding misbehaving children. He folds both hands over his lion-headed cane, which he settles on the spot between his feet.

The king has never been outwardly angry toward me, but I can see the seams of it now—the flexed, jerked movements of his chin, the fury under his breath. The trembling is not his disease, but his anger. "I don't know who I'm more disappointed in. What were you thinking, Cyrus? Do you understand the consequences—"

"I do." Cyrus frees himself from me and meets his father

in the middle of the room, shoulders square. "Now you can't use her either."

I choke out a laugh. So this is his chivalry. Ruin me so I can never work as a Seer again, no matter which king I serve under. Gods—he thinks he's done me a favor.

Cyrus blocks his father's expression, but I can see the clench of the king's fist, mottled with red and white as skin tightens over knuckle. I expect shouting; I brace for it.

He strikes Cyrus across the face.

The rings on the king's fingers cut a line across Cyrus's cheek, blotched from the hit. In his next motion, with startling strength, the king swings his cane and strikes Cyrus in the ribs. It happens so fast—a crack, then Cyrus crumpling to the floor, face bloody—that instinct propels my body backward before I know to react. I clutch the nearby vanity for an anchor, throat too dry with shock to cry out.

"You rely too much on your good looks." The king nudges a groaning Cyrus with his cane. "You should learn other tricks."

Blood flecks the rug as Cyrus coughs.

King Emilius lifts his eyes—cold, pale green—toward me, and I flinch. "Is it true? Are you involved with my son?"

"Does it matter?" I realize I'm shaking.

"Hmph. You are right. It does not matter. How do you plan to fix this?"

"I—um." I sound small. Stupid. Scared. I can't stop it. "The—the easiest way is if Cyrus recants."

"Unfortunately, I will not make my son a liar before I make you one." The king stares at me a second longer. Frowns. "Or perhaps, better to cut off the whole arm before this poison spreads. There are two Seers present in Verdant. We will negotiate for one. You may retire."

I sag against the vanity, suppressing a laugh—horrified or relieved, I'm not sure. That could have gone worse. Cyrus still gets what he's wanted all this time: to get rid of me. And he only had to get a few ribs broken as consequence. Compromise, right?

Cyrus has pushed himself onto his knees, swaying and clutching his middle. Now that the initial disbelief has worn off, part of me relishes that hurt. He'll heal, but at least he suffers. "I know you set up Lady Raya," he says, gazing up at his father. "I've known since before the Masked Menagerie that you had Violet lie to me—"

"And so?" the king scoffs. "Raya is a better match than you could have come up with. Though I see you've squandered it—and what for? There is only one love that matters, Cyrus, and that is the love of your people."

"And an empire will make them happy? Our people don't want to be sent outside the kingdom. Our people wouldn't want stolen land if you didn't tell them to want it. You can't feed or protect people with *glory*. These choices only serve the worst of our dukes—"

"Who will support you. Who have no reason to support you otherwise. If you want to do anything, you need to keep your head first." He sweeps his cane toward me, then back to Cyrus with a jab. "You are both clever and prideful. Too much for your own good. Let today be the only taste of shame you need. I don't relish pushing the blade deeper. Although I will find some satisfaction in ejecting Dante Esparsa from the capital in disgrace."

317

Cyrus inhales sharply and I look up too quickly.

"Just to punish us?" I blurt.

"He's a spy. Earlier tonight, we seized correspondence that proves it. He has been sending coded secrets back to Balica."

"A *spy*? No. That's impossible." When would Dante have had time to be a *spy*—

My mouth drops open.

Unless that's exactly *why* he *never* had time.

And why he never let me read his threads.

Why he knows how to fight.

Is that why I haven't seen him tonight?

"He is the only reason we aren't at war," Cyrus spits. He doesn't look surprised at all. "He is no spy—he's committed to helping both countries. I gave him knowledge to barter and he maintained peace, in exchange for promises that I would fulfill during my reign. Balica would not have tolerated our treatment of them otherwise."

"You don't know who your real allies are," King Emilius sneers, "but I suppose they were played for a fool after all. You will have no reign." He takes his timepiece from his pocket and checks it idly before putting it away again. "Clean yourselves up. Then we will clean up this mess."

He leaves. When the door shuts behind him, the chamber falls into deafening silence. Cyrus gingerly lowers himself onto the floor. I am numb with shock and shaking with wrath.

"I hate you," I whisper. I'll be honest: I just want to kick Cyrus while he's down.

"I don't regret it," he says, wincing. "I would do it all over again."

"Don't you dare say this was for my own good. Don't you put up that act—" I surge forward and crash down on Cyrus on all fours. Push him flat against the floor, my hands at his neck. "Don't put up that *princely act* like everything you do is so *damn honorable*. You wanted to get rid of me, admit it."

"It'll always be one of us at the strings and the other one clawing at them." He shuts his eyes, letting his head loll. Smiles ruefully with those pearly white teeth, stained red. "I was never rash when I wanted to get rid of you, Violet. Only waited too long to do it. I knew we would never be able to work together. We'll never trust each other enough, and my feelings for you don't change that."

My thumbs press harder at the hollow of his throat and, limp in my grip, he lets it happen. I'm a mess in and out, skirts bunched at my bruised knees, hands still shaking. The only joy I have is in how labored Cyrus's breathing is and his hiss as my elbow digs into his chest. "I didn't lie about Nadiya. Not that you care," I say. "That Witch of Nightmares is going to kill everyone, and I don't even care if she does. It's going to be your fault, and I hope you witness it."

Blearily transfixed, Cyrus shakes his head. "The general and his men have them," he says. "One wrong move and he won't hesitate to slit her throat. After all this deception, we're going to do our damn diligence for once and ensure we have the right culprit before executing her."

"Weren't you paying attention? That witch is capable of

enchanting people. She's been invading my dreams, she's been—" I laugh bitterly. Trying to convince me to join her. I should have. "You're lucky I didn't listen."

"What are you talking about?"

"I've been dreaming for weeks until recently. The last time I had a full night's sleep was—gods, it must have been before the ball. I thought I was doing good by not listening. The Fates say they're owed a life because I was never supposed to save you, and now I can see why."

If I killed Cyrus when the witch told me to, I would have had the temporary satisfaction of doing it. I would've gone down a villain, but at least it would have been violently triumphant in its own way. Better than being some lovesick fool who has to be replaced and forgotten.

She warned me. Even the Fates warned me. *He will betray you. They all will.*

Cyrus stares as if I were mad—and hearing it all aloud, maybe I am. His rotten heart—*damnation or salvation,* Felicita's prophecy had said. Well, it's been the former. I should have done it. I should have stabbed him.

Like an answer, something shimmers at the edge of my vision.

It lures my eyes; magic is hard to look away from when it knows you want something. On the far side of the room, wedged in between a curio cabinet and a reading chair, is a potted plant. The leaves are a vibrant green—too green for the shadows, almost as if it were glowing—and trimmed in a bushy manner for ornamentation. The stem is thick and vined, leading up to a single golden flower, unfurled like a star. A fayflower.

Like the kind of growth found in the Fairywood. Or on the outside of my tower.

The scar on my palm itches.

I could do it, couldn't I?

Yes, yes, answers a distant voice that is all too familiar.

I don't even know if it'll work, but my blood is buzzing. In the back of my mind, I know it will.

He deserves it. They all do. Be cruel and you may live.

As I let Cyrus go and stand, I'm dizzy—half instinct, all anger, hopelessness scouring every space I've hollowed out inside.

"Violet?"

You hate yourself for wanting him.

I claw at the wound in my hand, digging past the scab with my nails. There's nothing left in me. What do my ambitions matter when the world is built on deception? I've built nothing real, and neither has anyone else. Auveny's empire will be born from false hope and a false love, because lies are the currency of this world. Lies, grand and small, the keystones of dreams.

You hate yourself.

My fingers come away bloody. The gash is ragged and red and fierce with fresh pain. What do my feelings matter when they are all fear in different masks?

"Violet." I hear Cyrus groan and shift onto his side. "What are you doing?"

Making certain that I will never lose control to him again, whether as king and Seer or as clashing lovers. He's claimed too much of me.

I grab the trunk of the plant and smear it with my blood.

Like a nightmare, a red-tipped thorn sprouts under my hand.

Use the thorn and you will get away with it. When it strikes his heart, it will destroy his body.

I break it off. It fits in my grip perfectly.

I was always meant to wield this.

Cyrus tries to get to his feet, but I cross the room quicker and push a knee down on his injured chest. I've pinned him like this before. I wrap my other hand around his neck and he gasps—whimpers, really, for a breath. I don't know if the Fates are giving me strength or he's just that weak, but he barely fights.

"This is what our gods want." I redouble my grip; the thorn is slippery with blood. "I was wrong to defy them. They've been right about everything else."

A sound comes out of his throat. I think he's laughing. "Do it, if you're so convinced."

I imagine that Cyrus is deliriously reacting to imminent death, but he grabs my wrist and doesn't push me away. He points the thorn's tip at his chest with all the strength I didn't think he had.

"Do it."

I dig the thorn into his flesh through the gap in his shirt, but with my pulse constricted under his fingers, I realize that I haven't stopped shaking.

"The worst mistake I ever made," Cyrus says, stained lips cracked and swollen, "was letting Camilla convince me we should sneak out to the Moon District that day."

I finish the thought for him. "Because you met me?"

"Because I fell in love."

Liar. Charmer. Liar.

"You're saying that to save yourself," I whisper.

"My curse, my ruin, my Violet—my heart is yours. It was always yours. Take it." Cyrus reaches up, thumb brushing my cheek. I flinch at the wet press of skin—my own tears.

I hate him. I hate him *so much* for making me feel this way. "Shut up."

"Make me." He has the audacity to smile.

I raise the thorn high. Enough of our games. Free him from my life. Free me from our destiny.

"Go ahead." His gaze is as sure as any challenge he's given before, tracing over my face with the marvel of a lover. So sure, *too* sure. "At least I'm not a coward."

"You don't know anything about me," I snarl.

And I drive the thorn into his chest.

Iron and earth flood the air. The spark of triumph burns fast as Cyrus's lips, too late, part in shock.

He never thought I'd actually do it.

Blood seeps between my fingers. My hand smears with it in its shaking. It's too late for regret, but nausea travels up my gut anyway, and I can't look at him a second longer—

The wound explodes with a spray of leaves.

Vines snake out in a starburst, running over his body and my knees and the rug and the floorboards. I scramble backward, tripping over the growth, and it tangles around my ankles eagerly with a cool touch of magic.

His body jerks as if under the control of something worming in his veins and—alive and horrified—he clutches the hole in his chest. "What did you—what's happening to me?"

But I can only gape at him, because I don't know. The nightmare floods my memories, vibrant: Cyrus in a bed of green, his lips red as blood. Red *with* blood. The wound is already closed up, a brown welt of a slash with ribbons of plants rooted in it. The caked gore falls away like dirt. No evidence of the thorn is left.

The door swings wide open. I try to yank my feet away and scramble back, as if the extra distance would make me look less guilty.

But it isn't the king or anyone from the palace who comes in. The two guards who had been at my door are slumped on the floor.

Standing in the doorway is a ghastly figure that one might call Lady Raya if not for the fact that half of her face seems to be melting away. A glimmering blink later and the remaining disguise fades to reveal the Witch of Nightmares I once saw in Nadiya's memories.

"Took you long enough," she trills.

25

DIZZINESS NEARLY TIPS ME OVER AS I PUSH
myself to my feet. The urge to run or fight dulls under my
hunger for answers. "You've been invading my head," I say,
low and seething.

"*Invading* is an ugly word. I was merely trying to help."
She sweeps in, wrapped in a cloak of night so dark that
no light pierces it. She's neither crone nor maiden, but in
between—eyes grooved and sage on a wrongfully young
face, framed in silky, black ringlets. She might have been a
queen, had she a kingdom.

"Who are you?" I brace myself for a scuffle, and I'm suddenly aware of how I look in turn: my glamoured dress is
tattered where Cyrus's blood has stained it and my chemise
peeks through. The pretty updo I pinned myself has become
mostly undone. I look more like a hag than she does.

"I never gave myself a name, unlike you," she answers
simply. "As I crossed this land, I have been called a Witch of
Nightmares, a Witch of Dark Fires, a Witch of Wanting. But
you, little star, may simply call me a sister."

"You—you can't be—"

"Come, little star, you feel it. We share a kinship, if not in blood then in soul. We are of the same kind." She paces leisurely around Cyrus and the explosion of undergrowth that's sprung up, clucking, "He is a pretty one. Fairy-tainted, but pretty."

He's still breathing; the sound is ragged and wet. His skin is ashen as birch bark. I swallow the lump in my throat and scramble farther into the room, eying vases and trays I could smash over the witch's head. "What did the thorn do to him?"

"Did you want to simply kill him? He will die in time, worry not. He is rose-cursed, like the other beasties." She bends over him, one eye on me as she curls a finger under Cyrus's chin. His gaze is glassy, his limbs limp. Something glints from his head.

The stubs of horns.

I should scream at the sight. This isn't possible. But the horns are protruding more the longer I stare, and I hear the awful sounds of transformation—the grunts of pain, the popping of joints and realigning bone as Cyrus twitches. What would I shout, if I called for help? *I gave him this fate worse than death.*

"If he does not feed, he will turn into a full beast," says the witch. "And then he will hunt or be hunted. A marvelous game of blood."

"Why?" I gasp. "Why would you—"

"The chaos they create pleases the Fates, and the beasts' strength gives me strength. You may feel it too, now that your thorn has taken the prince's heart: his life will give you life. How lucky you are to have claimed the heart of one

326

who loves you—perhaps worth the hearts of an entire village. You might even overcome the block I put on your mind to ensure you didn't see me coming."

My dreamless nights. My darkened Sight. She's capable of magic I have never heard of.

But just now, I transformed the prince from a thorn of my own blood. It's magic that has been hiding within me this whole time, too. "*What* are you? If you're not a Fate yourself, are you just a Seer?"

"*Seer* is a title for Sighted who lower themselves to serve mortals. Do not insult me so." Still, her lips curve into a smile. She narrows the distance between us in one gliding step, robes rippling as if her feet barely brush the floor. "I am Sighted—this is true. It is how I can speak to you through the mind. And why I wish to help you. Little star, we were closer to the gods once—all of us Sighted. That is what makes us special, from our tether to the weave, to the very blood that runs through our bodies. We are only here because we made the mistake of falling so long ago. Some long-ago incarnation of our kind stupid enough to choose mortality and live among creatures no better than beasts."

I stare down at my shaking hands. They are flesh enough—but as she points out this origin, she's given me a means to explain why some layer of me is never satisfied walking this earth. As if the stitching between my skin and blood and bone and the threads I can't see is older than I am. I came into this world wary of hope like I've already lived through too many eras.

"We are not like them. You feel it."

I've always been different. What's one more thing?

The witch extends an open palm—an offer of a future, tempting as a candied apple. "I have seen the threads. Together, we are destined for greatness. We will serve the Fates in the manner they are meant to be worshipped until the day we can join them again. Let us give them the blood they crave. The fairies are weak and their wood is burning; nothing can stop us now. Together, we might take back every shard of power we ought to have."

"I don't even know you."

"Liars never trust anyone." She sighs as if she expected as much, and I wonder how much of the future she's seen. She continues, as blithely as I do when I give a reading, "Think of what is happening right now, little star. Raya is a fraud. No marriage with the prince will go through. And when his court sees his transformation, along with the events of tonight, they will blame it on you and foreign witchery. There are many who think the beasts are coming from Balica. The army is already out there—you sent them along weeks ago. War is coming, as prophesied; your one life debt will be paid ten thousand times over."

Her words ring earnest, despite their obvious lure. Over and over, she warned me of what would happen if I didn't kill Cyrus. She may have carved a barbarous path, brought blood and roses and war to our doorstep—but she hasn't been a liar yet.

Even if this is a trick, what choice do I have? It's only a matter of time until someone finds us. I have nowhere to run, no sanctuary even if I *do* run.

Maybe there is no path out alive except hers. One single thread, no matter how much I hate it. And that's the only reason I hesitate—because I hate the idea of being bound to it.

From kings to storybooks, we make up rules for why the world works the way it does, wanting good to beget good and wickedness to face justice. But life isn't fair and it doesn't care if I'm stubborn.

I lift my own injured hand to grasp hers.

With the return of my Sight, I see my future for the first time:

Me, unbound by body, shifting between human and light, blazing with the knowledge of a fallen god.

A smear of my blood upon the earth. Shadows and thorns rise.

The seas turn crimson. Beasts tear apart beasts.

My bloody arms stretch toward the night. The moon crowns me.

Cold laughter peals from my lips and it sounds like a song.

I look otherworldly. Untouchable. If power is the only truth, maybe the perfect reaction is delight. Maybe the horror is all that is alive.

"Don't listen to her," comes a hoarse croak.

Behind the witch's dark robes, the growth is spreading and shifting, leaves rustling, vines snapping. Green-veined limbs emerge and I can't make sense of it—because what I'm seeing can't possibly be Cyrus.

The witch swings around and laughs. "You would protect her? After she tried to kill you?"

Cyrus lurches to his feet. Sweat glistens like dew over his transforming muscles, and moss creeps over his skin. His upper body strains against the confines of his shirt, already torn from our earlier struggle. Tangled through his hair is a crown of briars and rosebuds—he is a prince even as a beast. Terrifying as he is beautiful.

His mouth opens, revealing jutting fangs. "Violet. The prophecy—"

His heart will be damnation or salvation.

"—you can still save us."

Cyrus looks at me, eyes greener than green, like he did all those times before, like I'm a star he's wished upon. He was enamored with a girl he imagined, one with a heart of gold, not ice. One with courage, not artifice. The hole in his chest should be evidence that I will never be who he wants.

But he loves me anyway. That's his true curse.

That burgeoning regret catches up to my senses. *What have I done to him?* The very worst possible. It's too late. He is more beast than prince. I am more monster than girl.

There is no future for us.

"Violet," he pleads as his body is destroyed. He knows what my name on his lips does to me, and uttered now, it's like a chisel between my ribs.

I can't look away. I want to reach out—take his hand like a miracle as if I could save him again.

He is still mine. Mine through the loathing, the lies, and the truths.

Mine to ruin. Mine to love.

I hate him.

But don't I love him, too?

The only thing that is inevitable is us.

"It really does make fools of you all," the witch tsks. She

watches us with rounded dark eyes. "I will tell you now: humans are built to bleed. Hope was an afterthought. You are gobblers, leeches, burnt scrapings from the bottom of a pot. Nothing but a *scourge*. Love will not save you."

In one swift motion, she brandishes a dagger from inside her robe and hurls it at Cyrus.

He blocks against a lethal strike before I can find breath to scream. The dagger embeds itself in his upper arm instead of his chest, and milky sap runs down the length of his arm, alongside rivulets of blood.

My body makes its choice for me. I fling the nearest tea tray at the witch, hitting her in the thigh and only causing a scowl, but it's enough to distract her as I throw myself at her too.

Glass shatters as we knock into the curio cabinet. I fall with her, snagging scrapes and cuts on the way. I'm wrenched away midair—Cyrus catches me before I hit the ground.

His weight lurches; he holds on to me as much as I hold on to him. "Take the dagger," he gasps.

As I grab for it, the vines at my feet crawl up my ankles, constricting them and making me trip.

The witch rises, face bloody. She draws out a glowing ball from her pocket; within it, five lights blink. Nadiya's fairies. She holds it out, fingers sinking into the orb as she absorbs its power. "So you choose him still. Then suffer like him."

The rest of the growth surges upward to separate me from Cyrus. The vines crawl higher and thorns dig into my leg. I cry out.

The witch crunches through the broken glass toward us.

Maybe I would've always gone down this way—fighting, hurting, foaming mad.

I don't want to die like this.

I don't want to die.

Cyrus loves me. His heart is worth more than all the ones she claimed. If she can do this magic, so can I.

I shut my eyes and reach for my Sight. A caustic energy bleeds through my mind, a shadowy antithesis to the golden threads of time. Touching upon it, I sense the vines coiling up my legs. I see them beyond their physical form, as magic that I can twist and dissolve for my own means.

The vines seize and snap apart. I stagger forward, freed. Cyrus groans sharply.

"Ah, a quick learner." The witch raises new bramble as the fairies inside her orb squeal and squeak. I tear each vine apart by the stem before it can latch on. "But did you know that when you call upon your power, you drain his? His cursed heart fuels your magic, but it is mortal yet. Will you kill him to rid me?"

"Yes," I pant. My fingers just brush the dagger's handle in Cyrus's arm. I grip it fully and tear it free. He howls. I lunge and slice a ragged tear through the witch's robe, gouging flesh.

She hisses and recoils. I slash again and she backs away farther. I go for the orb in her grip. The fairies squeal and sputter as I latch on. Two have already turned to dust. The other three are dim.

"I'm sorry," I whisper, with no idea whether these fairies can hear or understand. "Your kind was only ever trying to warn me."

I sink my fingers into the strange glass, and fresh energy floods through my veins. The last few fairies sputter. If I must be a villain, I will be one of my own making, but tonight I will use this power to drive her out.

Tugging and tugging at the shadows in my mind, I turn her corruption against her, forcing the growth at our feet to reach for her instead. It isn't much, but I only need a distraction. She yanks me free of the orb, but I don't need it anymore.

My other arm swings upward and I thrust the dagger into her chest.

Shock lances her dark eyes.

Still, the witch laughs, sputtering blood with each cough. "You have wrought your own hell," she spits. "It remains your destiny."

Her body warps, shrinking with each staggering step. I reach out to grab the end of her robe, but it shifts along with her, melding to her like skin. Blue-black feathers spray from her arms, spreading into wings. Then there's no woman left—only a raven flapping unsteadily out the window into the moonless night. Bloody feather tufts drift from my grip.

My head splits in an ache as the wind blows in, chilling my fevered body. I remember to breathe and it comes out a sob.

I hear her laughter in my mind. *I will see you again—if not in flesh, then in dream.*

26

I CRAWL OVER TO CYRUS, WHO LIES CRUMPLED and weakened from the magic I drew. His limbs and fingers have elongated and he stretches across the entire length of the rug. His veins pump more sap than blood, spilled sticky over his tattered formalwear. What remains of his human skin is pallid; the rest of him is bark or fur or tender shoots growing before my eyes. Curving behind each ear is a horn grown to the size of a ram's, dotted with rosebuds.

Had I killed him, I might have simply carved him from my mind. But I had too much heart to play villain and not enough to be savior, so instead I've cursed him twice: once with a thorn and once with his love for me.

He's no longer the untouchable prince I hated. He's something else entirely now.

My heaves grow short and shallow, regret threatening to fracture me in its magnitude. I have a little bit of fight in me left, and I spend it all on holding myself together.

I take the fallen dagger. My vision is blurry and I'm weak from my own injuries, but I manage to slice off a strip of fabric from the bedsheets. Pinning Cyrus down in case he thrashes while transforming, I search for the gash on his arm. I would have caused more damage as I wrenched the dagger out, and I'm surprised he didn't pass out entirely.

But when I wipe away the milky sap, I find the wound mostly crusted over. Scabbed with brownish fibers and golden amber like the wound over his heart.

He's healing himself.

Cyrus jerks suddenly as his horns curl another inch outward and the roses on them begin to bloom. "Violet . . ." His voice is deeper, as if scraped from a tree hollow. I slide a hand over the rough skin of his cheek.

I don't know how long he has until he turns completely.

If he does not feed, he will turn into a full beast, the witch said.

Beasts feed on people, but I haven't heard of any cases where their curse was broken this way. But maybe my blood, tainted with the magic that turned him into this, has the power to change him back.

I thrust my still-bleeding palm toward his mouth. "Drink."

Cyrus lurches forward, as if the scent of iron agitated some primal instinct, then hesitates. Disgust warps his expression, and I realize the human part of him doesn't want to.

"You have to." I push my hand against his lips.

Instinct takes over and he bares his fangs; the pierce of his teeth is hot as a brand. If I wasn't prepared and already hurt all over, I might not be withstanding it, but as it is, I dig my nails into his bark-crusted side and clench through the pain.

He grips my arm tightly to hold me up, and he drinks, eager and deep, teeth slicing new veins open. I cry out, skirting consciousness. He clutches my slack body against him.

His horns stop growing. The roses wilt and brown. His body trembles with each swallow. When he drags his tongue over the wound, gaping from his messy eating, it seals itself closed, leaving a ragged red scar.

His limbs finally begin to arrange themselves in their proper places. He licks my smaller wounds, the thorn punctures on my legs, the scratches along my shoulders. The last of his bark-skin crumbles, and he gazes up at me, once again the Cyrus I know, crimson smeared over his lips and chin. If not for the horrors we just endured, it might pass for the smudged lipstick of a paramour.

But— "Your eyes," I whisper. Or is the color shift just a trick of the light? His eyes have always been green, but not like this—vibrant as new fairy growth. Almost glowing, like a pair of enchanted jewels.

Cyrus turns toward the vanity's mirror. He's visibly pained as he clambers to his feet; while his cuts don't bleed, there are many of them. The remaining bits of his clothes cling on like a mockery of modesty.

He stares into the mirror for a long minute, fingers paring over his face and pressing against the scar on his chest. The rest of him looks human enough. Does he feel human?

What do I say to him? *I'm sorry I tried to kill you?* It's so easy to take a life—just the single swing of a blade, done in anger. Flesh gives way so effortlessly. It should be more difficult to do something so monumental.

"I understand why you wish you never met me," I finally say, as close to an apology as I'll get.

The candles are low; they've been burning since before I got here. It's a wonder that we haven't been discovered yet. How will Cyrus explain what transpired? No one will believe any story I put forth. I won't be forgiven for this, and I don't suppose I should be.

Cyrus finally turns from the mirror with a weary stagger. "Let's go."

So forward we go, trudging into the future we've chosen.

Cyrus scavenges a bathrobe from the claw-foot wardrobe before we head out the door together. He leans on me for support. His right ankle doesn't look like it shifted back correctly, now that I see it in better lighting, or maybe it's just twisted and swollen.

I peer out into the hall. We're somewhere in the west wing of the palace, far from the audience chamber. At my feet are two guards who died choking on roses, their bodies punctured by thorns. A breath shudders beside me.

We trudge past them.

The palace is eerily quiet. When we arrive at one of the side ballroom doors, the crack of light shines upon a slick red floor. I don't want to look further. I know what I'll see.

When we glance in, I clasp a hand over my nose and mouth to cover the stink and to hold in my retching. Bodies strewn everywhere—and not all human. Petrified and rotting vines spiderweb from floor to ceiling, their roots feeding off the death at our feet. Leaves and stems crackle as they spread, unheeding of any horror.

The sight imprints upon my mind like a brand until I think I might bow from the pain of it. Cyrus slumps against the door with a shaky, wet breath, fist pressed against his temple.

A noise, like shambling, behind us. We jolt.

"We should . . ." Cyrus mumbles as he glances at the hallway's alcoves and shut doors.

Then, around the corner, a hulking, horned shadow.

We both stumble backward, hands and arms pulling each other in different directions. A rose-horned beast comes barreling at us on thick-trunked legs.

This beast is farther along than Cyrus ever was, but their gait is human enough, some remnant of panic hurtling them forward.

We haul each other down the hall we came from, certain that at least that space was safe when we'd left it, but the distance between us and the beast is narrowing fast.

I dart to the closest room but find the door locked. I lurch to the one across the hall, but that one's locked, too. Cyrus bangs his shoulder against it.

The floor rattles with the beast's steps. Shit, shit, shit.

I tear a pin from my hair, but my hands aren't steady enough to jam it in the lock, let alone try to pick it.

"*Help!*" Cyrus bellows. He coughs fitfully.

As if in echo, the beast moans, "Help . . ."

Blood will transform them back. But this beast's bared teeth are snapping without much restraint and I'd lose a whole hand to them.

I push the pin through the lock. A claw yanks me by the

sleeve of my chemise, spinning me around, and I scream inches away from the face of a fanged monster.

Their next words come out garbled, and in my open-mouthed shock, I'm too numb to shove it away. The beast rises stiffly, slanting to one side as green sap flows down their neck.

Another flash of a blade, and they fall, headless, victim to Camilla behind them.

She is panting and stricken, grime splattering up her trousers and bare arms, sword heavy at her side. She nudges the body over so it looks less grotesque, staring at it as if she's unsure of how to mourn. They were human not long ago, after all.

"Are you all right?" she asks hastily.

Cyrus looks about one breeze from fainting. "No."

"What's happened out here?" I ask.

She drags her arm across her forehead, wiping sweat. "That Lady Raya—that *bitch*—she killed the Captain of the Guard. She killed all of his men—no, she transformed them. And then the rest of us had to kill them." She swallows. "Most of the beasts are probably them. We had no choice when they attacked the ballroom. But it could have been a lot worse—probably half the attendees are cloistered in the east wing right now, safe. I came out here to find you."

We are all barely holding it together. "Are *you* okay?"

"That witch nearly killed me when she ambushed me and Nadiya in my quarters before the wedding, but it'll take more than some vines to strangle me." She grins shakily.

"I haven't seen Nadiya since, though—she *is* just Nadiya, right? I heard about the two Lady Rayas."

"Yes." Cyrus's eyes flutter shut, accepting his error far too late for it to matter. "She's just Nadiya. Have you seen Dante?"

"He was with me earlier, but I lost him during a scuffle. I'm sure he's fine—he has to be. He's never reckless." Then, as if realizing she's staring at the two *most* reckless people in her life, she adds, "Why don't I get you two upstairs? It should be safe there. You both look *rough*. You'll be more of a hindrance than a help down here."

Camilla takes over carrying Cyrus and we plod over claw-scraped carpets and broken glass toward the main staircase. I tell her the witch got away, though I got a good stab in. She cheers at that, because I don't tell her about anything else that happened in that room, nor does Cyrus.

I'm winded by the time we arrive in the royal wing. I could collapse and fall comfortably asleep on the carpet. Close to Cyrus's quarters, an open door farther down the wing catches my eye. I might not think twice about it on a different night, but there's never been a night like tonight.

"Are those your father's quarters?" I ask, lifting an elbow in its direction.

The three of us are suspicious enough of the eerie quiet to creep closer, trepidation jolting my tired muscles to life. Camilla peeks in and flinches away with a sob.

The guards inside are dead—one stabbed in the eye, the other scuffed up as if he put up a fight, but ultimately died with a knife in his neck.

Cyrus pushes past both of us, stumbling toward the shut doors of the king's bedroom.

"It could be dangerous!" Camilla hisses, readying her sword.

But he doesn't heed her at all. He pushes the bedroom doors open without any finesse, panting and desperate to discover what's inside, as if he already knew what he'd find.

When I draw up beside him, I follow his frozen gaze along the trail of shattered porcelain and the dropped lion-headed cane to the winged armchair by the fireplace. Where Dante, dressed in all black, has a dagger to King Emilius's throat.

A spy.

An assassin.

"No, no—you can't—" But at Cyrus's approach, Dante presses the dagger deeper until a red line appears on the king's pallid skin; the king groans, barely conscious. Cyrus halts, empty hands up. "No one has to know. Don't—"

"Did you think I would be here if this weren't my last resort?" Dante says, low and calm. There is still warmth in his eyes. *Pity.* "The Seer of Balica told me of many futures. This is the final one that might save us."

"Please—"

With a flick of his wrist, Dante slashes the dagger across the king's neck.

Emilius slumps fish-eyed in his shining mantle, red spilling from his cut throat.

Camilla screams. Cyrus staggers forward like the world has tilted. I am the only one who never looks away from

Dante, all at once horrified and understanding of what he'd done.

He saw his destiny. He chose without hesitation.

Dante paces backward to the open window behind him and climbs onto the sill in a single lithe leap. He pauses, framed by the night and the fluttering curtains, his mouth shaping things he seems to want to say.

All that finally comes out is, "I'm sorry, Your Majesty."

And without another word, he tips backward out the window.

27

THE SUN CAPITAL MOURNS AMID CHAOS. CELE-
bration banners are taken down. Regalia is exchanged for
somber black. Whispers are louder than ever.

I don't mourn King Emilius, but he was like a father,
even if he was an awful one. Close to everything in my life.
Once the most powerful man on this continent, and now
he's just gone. I can't be anything but shaken by that.

No official culprit has been named for his murder,
mostly because Cyrus refuses to do it. Camilla is silent but
furious about it. She won't out Dante directly—more sentiment lives in her heart than she will ever let on—but she was
attached enough to her father to want a taste of vengeance
as well, or at least an answer.

When I ask Cyrus about Dante, he only says, "He made
certain I would have the throne by any means necessary."

I wonder when Dante planned it. Whether it was spur
of the moment or whether he'd been waiting to strike at the
doomed wedding all along. Over and over, I replay that day
we sparred outside the city, so innocuous back then, when
I gave him hope that Cyrus's ascension might make all the

difference. And what had he learned from his own country's Seer?

Mostly, as the shock fades away . . . I miss him. Or, I miss who he was. Who we all were, before the bloodbath at the wedding.

I slip between the cracks at the palace. I'm lucky that the gossip surrounding a disgraced Seer pales in comparison to a massacre and an assassination. There were enough witnesses to the witch transforming people into beasts that people no longer think that I am responsible, but some wonder if I aided her. I watch my back closely whenever I leave my tower, newly aware of the suddenness of death and the target on me. No one believes what I say anymore, and goodwill is crumbling around Cyrus as well. He's probably glad I can be a scapegoat for our affair, as his hands are full with clamors for war.

At the first open assembly, everyone is shouting and no one is listening.

"Our king cannot continue putting his heart before Auveny—or justice!" Lord Ignacio proclaims from his seat. He lost a foot during the witch's attack. Nearly salvageable until it turned gangrenous. "All evidence points to Balica's involvement in Emilius's death."

Upon the throne, Cyrus states calmly, "The witch was the one masquerading as Lady Raya and responsible for the beasts. She's likely my father's murderer, too."

"Who's to say Balica didn't send the witch themselves? Who's to say they weren't colluding? Whose face is still missing among this crowd? Where is your dear friend, Your Majesty?"

"Dante Esparsa is a *scholar*. He isn't capable of killing someone."

"Where *is he*, Your Majesty?"

Cyrus scrapes a hand through his hair, lingering on a spot where a horn once grew. Sometimes I see him pinching at the lacings of his shirt, as if to further hide the scar I put on his chest. He never named me guilty of anything, soft-hearted fool. "I hope somewhere safe. I am not ready to mourn another. But we also haven't identified all the bodies of the beasts, and it's highly possible he was among them. One thing is for certain, however: we will not jump to conclusions in order to start a war."

The assembly becomes a complete wash, descending into insults and *how-dare-you*s from attendees. There are, as always, too many questions and not enough answers.

King Emilius is dead and Dante is gone. Nadiya is missing as well. I fear she may have been a true casualty of the witch; no one has seen her.

In the eyes of the public, two Rayas showed up, then disappeared the same night their king was murdered and beasts roamed the palace. One Raya was a failed savior—if she was ever a savior. The other was a witch who nearly killed them all.

Cyrus sent his condolences to Lunesse regarding Raya, continuing what remains of his ruse, but it isn't enough. A bride and a spy and a witch who all came from Balica. Strangeness after strangeness after strangeness from our southern neighbor.

War will happen. It is written across the lords' faces, and it is the Fates' will. No one has hope of avoiding the last piece of the prophecy any longer. Cyrus should give in to the demands to invade. Give the dukes their taste for whatever support he can get.

Otherwise, we might be looking at a coup.

$$\sim\!\!\times\!\!\sim$$

The only good news is the land has begun to heal. With the witch in hiding, there've been no new beasts nor bramble—except upon my tower.

I notice it too late. What might have been a few patches of rot turn nearly half my tower black. The whole place stinks like a corpse. Based on the rate of the rot's spread, I suspect the witch spilled her blood on my tower the night of the wedding. Maybe it was her source of magical thorns to make beasts, or an attempt to make me look guilty.

I visit Cyrus in his study to discuss what to do and where I might stay instead. The room is mostly as I last remembered it. A few things have been taken from his father's study, including the large map of the continent. Last time I was in here, I was in Cyrus's arms as he pleaded with me to listen to my heart.

Look at where that's gotten us.

Behind his desk, Cyrus barely looks up. The circles around his eyes are surprisingly dark; the hollows are usually hidden with glamour. "Your tower—" he begins, straight to business, because it's the easiest kind of interaction we have.

"The witch probably corrupted it. It's probably too much to salvage," I say simply.

He sighs into the pocket of his folded hands. "I'm afraid of it spreading, too. We have to burn it all as soon as possible. Move out anything you need."

It might just be the flicker of candlelight, but I swear something glints in the muss of his hair. Cyrus waves me away, but I keep staring at the top of his head. Catching my gaze, he sits straighter so I can't see. His eyes are still too green.

"Are you okay?" The words feel strange in my mouth, not exactly gentle but an attempt at it. It's a stupid question, anyway. Of course he's not okay.

But of course he says, "I'm fine."

"Have you heard from him?"

Cyrus hesitates, glancing at the pile of unread letters stacked in a basket on his desk. "No."

Every topic is dangerous between us: his father, his crown, Dante, his scars. In this new Auveny, with war brewing and old magic crawling out of the ground, I've tasted regret. There are things I almost want to say to him, but none are worth the price of broaching. If he still wanted me, if he wanted a moment to forget the world in the tangle of my body, he would seek it. He was never shy about it before.

But there is a kingdom to manage and a scar upon his heart, so I leave him to his work and head back to my tower under the wary watch of soldiers.

Most of the ceremonial items have been removed from the tower already, and I only pack up my clothes and saved coin. I have knickknacks from street festivals and patrons over the years, but nothing I would keep. No letters to remember anyone by, no gifts I like except a small journal Dante gave me. I only wrote on the first page of it. I slip it in between my folded blouses and skirts. I'm almost embarrassed at how unfilled the trunk is when I hand it off to a servant.

I take one last look from the balcony and remember the sight of the Sun Capital from what is—for the last time—the tallest point in the city.

Maybe I'll see it again in a dream.

The bramble continues climbing up, around and around my tower. By nightfall, it's covered all the way to the top, and curling, spiked briars spill through the palace's north gate. The smell of it carries downwind, stinking like rain mixed with gutter water, like dying roses.

I observe the burning from the gardens, close enough to see everything happening but not too close to catch suspicious glares. Soldiers are hacking off the thickest vines, piling dry fuel, and building up a bonfire. I can only see the shape of my tower's corruption as a shadow against the stars, and soon the silhouette is completely obscured by the smoke.

The boy must die before summer's end, or you will burn, the Fates told me. But Cyrus is alive and so am I. Was it my defiance of the witch that saved us, or was it what nearly doomed us? How close was that other future?

And is this one really any better?

Everything I worked for wasn't worth much in the end. I would curse out the stars and the gods who live among them if I thought it mattered.

I understand why others put such faith in the Fates: Don't we all wish—beyond any gold or fame—to be right? To have some authority tell us with certainty that we've done the best we could with the life we have? So we idly listen to kings and gods who tell us what to do, even when we have no idea what their true intentions are. Even if all they want is blood.

It's easier than figuring it out for ourselves. Easier than carrying the regret when we don't make the choices we should. For once, I'd happily let someone else make my decisions for me, just so I can blame my mistakes on them. Just so I don't feel like every choice I've ever made was a mistake.

I watch my tower go up in flames as it once did in my dreams.

And I finally cry.

28

I DECIDE ON MY OWN TO LEAVE.

Every night, I wonder where the witch is. Every night, I dread sleeping, fearing her voice in my dreams. In that future I saw when I grasped her hand, I was happy but not myself.

She said she saw greatness in our destiny. I doubt she lied—that was the only reason she spared me. Why she gave me a chance to join her. She just didn't expect to end up in the thread where I turned her down.

Honestly, neither did I.

Wherever my future is, it's no longer in Auveny. I'm a wandering shadow here, haunted by memories, vexed with helplessness.

Prepping for my departure from the Sun Capital doesn't take long. My trunk of things from the tower is already packed; I only need to scavenge for daily supplies. I haven't publicized that I'm leaving, to avoid making an issue of it. I'll miss Camilla, but we can still correspond. She has other friends, besides.

I don't have a destination in mind, but I also don't have

many choices. The borderlands are burning. Crossing through to Balica isn't an option, and it's difficult to find northern passage to Verdant. That only leaves the Moon Continent across the sea, where hopefully they've heard little of me.

In the palace's guest room where I've been staying, I wash up for the night and get ready for bed. I start unraveling my braid when someone raps at the door.

When I look outside, I nearly slam the door shut again. A hooded figure stands in the hall. But I recognize the hitch of his breath and the shape of the body becomes familiar. "Cyrus?"

Cyrus peels back his hood. The tips of crystal horns glint on the top of his head.

Gaping, I let him in quickly.

He sits himself on the bed, removing his robe. His face is roughening into something bark-like. Rolling up his sleeves, he reveals his arms matted in moss and broken stems where he's nipped off new growth.

Just like that, I'm shaking again. Of course the blood cure was just temporary, just like how Nadiya's fairies could only absorb some dark magic away. The curse lives in his heart, constantly pumping through his veins.

I cross the room and dig through the knapsack I packed for a knife. "How long?" I ask, as I pull out a roll of bandages too.

"Skin's been changing on and off for days. I thought it would go away. But then the horns—"

"*How* did you think it would just go *away*, Princey?" I whirl around to him, biting my tongue too late; Cyrus is a king now. "I know you're dealing with a million tasks, but don't you think changing back into a beast should be addressed immediately?"

With the knife, I open an edge of the wound on my palm. Outside of urgent danger, cutting flesh hurts more than I remember, and my eyes prickle with tears. Sitting next to him, I give him my hand and he takes my wrist gently. His mouth shapes into a grimace, even though I can hear the lick of his tongue behind his teeth.

He's disgusted with himself, I realize.

Finally, his mouth closes over the wound and he drinks. It's a smaller cut and the blood doesn't flow as freely compared to last time; it takes longer for the horns to shrink and for the plants to wither away. We don't speak, or even really look at each other, but sometimes I feel his grip tighten and my pulse races under his thumb.

When the changed parts of him have faded, Cyrus falls back onto the bed, heaving with relief. I start bandaging my hand, careful not to let any blood stain the white of my nightgown.

After a minute he sits up again, looks around the room at my neatly folded items and my traveling gear, and frowns.

"Are you—?" he begins to ask.

"I'm finally getting out of your hair."

"You can't leave," Cyrus says with such certainty as he stares at my bandaging.

I realize what he means and I laugh haltingly. "Because you need my blood? You have it the wrong way around. *You* clearly need to leave, too. Give the throne to Camilla or something. Look at yourself. You can't rule like this."

"If I give the throne to my sister, I may as well set the kingdom on fire myself. I'll get the same results faster. She would do it grudgingly, but . . . No, I need to rule. Otherwise what Dante did would . . . It would have meant nothing."

I remember who I'm dealing with—the once-prince tainted by the disease he calls courage—so I laugh louder in his face until he understands. "What's done is done. Your father is dead; who cares why? To hell with the good of this kingdom! The dukes were ready to keep you from your throne based on a prophecy that hadn't even happened yet. Now it's happening. Now you're turning into a *beast*. They will have your *head*."

But Cyrus is ever quick to mistake survival for selfishness. I can see in the dullness of his gaze that he doesn't get it. That none of this is ridiculous at all. "They don't need to see me like this. Which is why you have to stay. You and I can meet like this once a week, and it should be enough—"

"No." I stand, and he surges to his feet after me.

"This is *your* fault!" There it is—all the bite that he's held back until now. It *is* all my fault. And I'm running away from it, I know I am.

"You're going to get both of us killed." I glance away.

"Do I need to threaten you?"

"I have nothing to lose."

When Cyrus tilts my chin toward him, he only stares at me in desperate silence, until he asks, "What do you want in return for staying?"

"Nothing you can give me."

"I can make you queen."

Blood roars in my ears.

I know that look on his face. I've seen him hopeful, weary, monstrous, always handsome no matter the form, cheeks blushed with shadow in a way that invites mystery, and still freckled like the boy I grew up with. There's no deceit or compulsion in that look. Not even much in the way of disgust.

His thumb strokes my jaw wonderingly. "I've always known that the queen beside me would be better made of ice than flesh," he murmurs. "That it would be cruel to love anyone less resilient. But I didn't expect to find myself so willing."

I clench fistfuls of my gown, no longer caring of the blood seeping through my palm. Haven't I done enough to him? I remember when he said, under duress, that I would be the one to decide Felicita's prophecy. He couldn't still believe that. The prophecy has passed. Damnation has fallen.

But the witch is still out there, and war has not yet come. And *I* could still be his bride. . . .

I am dizzy with victory in a game I'm not supposed to be playing. "People would—they would never accept me. Besides, what good is tethering myself to a doomed king?"

"People accept anything if they're entertained enough. You know that more than anyone else. And, well, where do you plan to go otherwise?" Cyrus gestures at my few belongings. "You don't know a life outside this city. I can make your travels difficult enough that you'll want to come back."

Now it's my turn to glare. "I'll manage. You need me more than I need you."

"Then we both still need each other."

All this time, my mind has been working fast. The thing is, with Cyrus's help, I *could* craft a tale worth remembering. One that might absolve me of all I've done, even if I still seem like a pining damsel. It has to be that way; little lies go down easier. It'll be a love story like fate that'll make the world forget everything else.

My heart is racing—from thrill, not fear.

A grin spreads across his face, the first show of joy to grace him since before his near-wedding. "You already figured out a plan, haven't you? Tell me how, Violet. Spin me gold."

It'll involve some risky theater; he'd never agree. The playing field has changed. His father is out of the picture. His popularity is unstable. His dukes are practically in revolt. But given the choice to run or to trick them all—to sit myself on a throne that everyone else has coveted—

"It has to be convincing," I say, offering him my hand. "Nothing short of a miracle."

Cyrus lowers his lips to my bandaged palm. "Then we will give them one."

THE BRIAR KING'S BRIDE

ONCE, A GIRL SAVED A PRINCE WHO WAS MEANT to die.

You will hear many versions of this story and none will be exactly true, but this is the one inked in history: They grew up together. Their paths diverged. It was in their nature to loathe each other, for a palace-raised prince and a girl plucked from the streets are two very different creatures.

But on a night when the prince was fated to meet his true love, they saw each other anew, masked in a moonlit maze.

They found that they were not so different after all.

That same night, a wicked witch sought the prince for herself. She changed her appearance and called herself a lady of a neighboring land. With her enchantments, she lured the prince to fall in love with her instead. She made the prince spurn the girl and betray her.

Brokenhearted, the girl wept and raged.

The witch spread her dark influence from the safe vantage of the capital. Across the land, beasts emerged from briars with curling horns and bodies of moss. As her wedding with the prince neared, she grew bored with him; she had so many other playthings now.

So she slipped the spurned girl a dagger. She whispered in her ear, "Kill him for his capriciousness."

But the girl could not, for she loved him.

She plunged the dagger into the witch instead.

In her shocked, dying breath, the witch unleashed the rest of her dark magic, seeping it into the land to curse the kingdom for decades to come. She cursed the prince as well: he would suffer the fate of a beast.

The prince, now a king, transformed slowly. He hid his condition until he could no more, until one morning when a maid found a beast rooted grotesquely to the king's bed, limbs like branches and head covered in roses.

The palace flew into a frenzy. The girl, disgraced and forgotten, fought her way through the horrified onlookers. She threw herself over the beast and kissed him until her lips bled.

When she finally withdrew, the king was human in her arms, and he remembered he loved her.

There was a prophecy that the king's heart would be damnation and salvation. That the land would fall dark before it found dawn. The girl was the axis on which these words spun—for the king's heart was hers. It had been, since he was a prince.

Thrice she saved him. She would save them all again. There were greater forces at work here, but we are merely the Fates' playing pieces; they aren't for us to fathom.

This was all that mattered: the land was blooming with blood and roses, and war was coming.

He asked her to be his queen and she said yes.

ACKNOWLEDGMENTS

Eleven years ago, I started writing a story about a heroine who saw the world too clearly. She was brash, cynical, and unexpectedly personal. Little did I know her story would become the inspiration for my debut book. So many people helped make this journey possible.

First, to my editor Hannah Hill: we felt that destined energy radiating from each other from the start. You're wise and sharp and I feel like you know my characters better than I do. It's an utter joy to work with you to make my stories shine. Thank you to the incredibly savvy team at Delacorte Press, including Beverly Horowitz, Barbara Marcus, Wendy Loggia, Dominique Cimina, John Adamo, Tamar Schwartz, Colleen Fellingham, Alison Kolani, Casey Moses, and Jen Valero. This book would not be on shelves without you.

To my agent, Elana: I couldn't ask for a better partner in this industry. You saw the story my manuscript could be and made sure I got there.

To my friends: thank you for holding my hand, despite all the chaos that comes with that. Zeba, where would I be without you? What a wild eleven years and we're just getting started. If you were my only reader, it would be enough. Haley, the world may be small but I'm glad you're in it, and not just because you always ask the right questions. Diya, this book is your long con; brag as much as you want about that. Em, my handshake-emoji partner-in-crime, no taxonomy can ever quantify the scope of my affection for you. Farah, there's no one I'd rather share a dumpster with, and that's true love. June and Andrea, thanks for letting me pretend to be cool by standing next to you two. Hannah and Allison, you're my favorite eggs. Wendy, we'll lead the hatemance charge ourselves. Jade, you and your oasis of cool gamers are a balm.

To my oldest writing group: not all of us are writing anymore, but what great memories we made. I'm ridiculously pleased that I'm not the first of us to get published, and I already won't be the last. Annie, Julia, Sarah—you're the reason I'm ever funny.

To Lena: I'm ridiculously pleased that I *am* the first of us to get published, but you knew that. Thanks for yelling really loudly when I got the news.

To William and Sally: thanks for putting up with me so others don't have to.

Thank you, bloggers and booksellers and early readers, for the cheerleading. It means everything that so many people are excited for my prickly heroine.

And to the readers around the world who have followed me over the years: I hold all your all-caps comments in my heart. You watched me grow as a writer, you were the first ones to tell me my words meant something, and you made the biggest plot twist of my life possible. Thank you for your endless support and patience. I promise: update coming soon! ♥

ABOUT THE AUTHOR

GINA CHEN writes stories about fantastic worlds featuring heroines, antiheroines, and the kind of cleverness that brings trouble in its wake. A self-taught artist with a degree in computer science, she generates creative nonsense in all forms of media and always has a project stewing. She lives in Southern California, where the sunshine is as plentiful as the tea shops.

actualgina.com